To Cheryl Gibson, Charonne Boulton and Mary Portas

RUSSIA
N
W
E
S
Yenitelu
Perekop
Gulf of Perekop
Sea of Azov
CRIMEA
Eupatoria
Kertch
Arabat
Kaffa
Kalamita Bay
Simpheropol
Alma
Sebastopol
Aloushta
Yalta

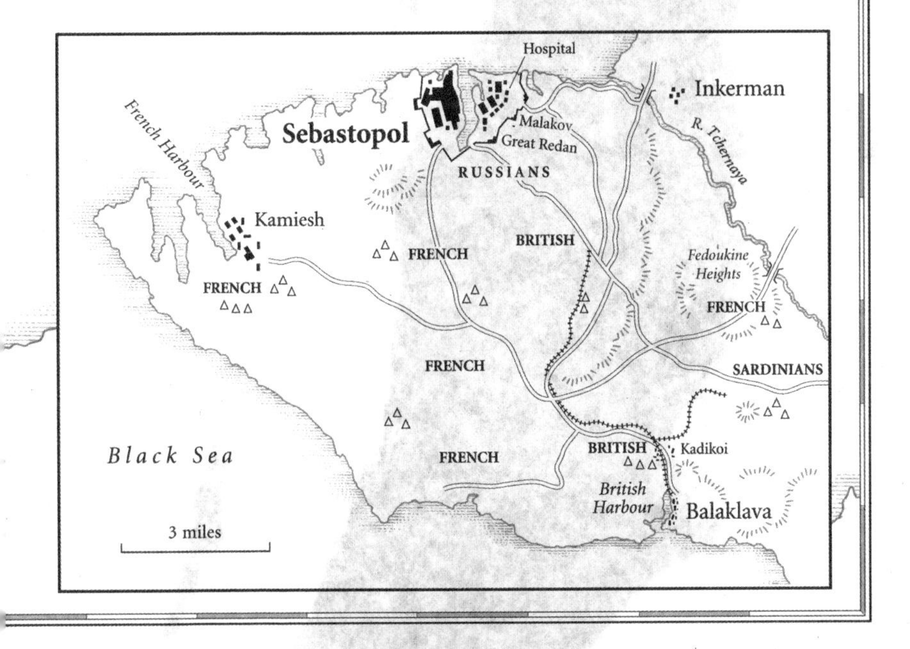
Hospital
Inkerman
French Harbour
Sebastopol
Malakov
Great Redan
R. Tchernaya
RUSSIANS
Kamiesh
BRITISH
FRENCH
Fedoukine Heights
FRENCH
FRENCH
FRENCH
SARDINIANS
Black Sea
BRITISH
Kadikoi
FRENCH
British Harbour
Balaklava
3 miles

PART ONE

Chapter One

Italy, 1855

We arrived in Narni late on a Sunday evening. Although the door to the Hotel Fina was locked the driver roused a servant who stumbled out with creased shirt tails, brought in our luggage and showed us to a bedroom that smelled of unwashed feet. Nora took away my cloak and bonnet, then I snuffed the candles and lay down. A man was shouting in the distance, perhaps the worse for drink. Instead of sleeping I rode through the night as if still in a carriage jolting over badly made roads across the plains of Italy. Eventually I heard a clock strike five and the rumble of a cart in the square outside and I fell asleep to the sound of women's raised voices and the clash of a pail against stone.

I woke to a blade of sunlight sliced between the shutters – it was nearly mid-morning. Nora was standing over me with a breakfast tray and a letter from Mother which I didn't read. None of the clothes in my portmanteau was fit to wear, being too crushed, so I put on my travelling dress again and said we would go out at once. In the lobby I struggled to make myself understood by the proprietress, who was dressed in black and whose mouth was pulled down at the ends, as if from despair, but when I showed her Henry's address she drew us a rough map.

Narni was an ancient town built near the top of a hill and the Hotel Fina was at its centre, in a little square. What with the bunch of women round a fountain and the confusion of streets and shopfronts there was no telling which direction was the right one so we set off at random up a flight of steps and under an arch. The sun was very hot, the street oppressively narrow and our travelling clothes too heavy so we stopped under a shady porch while I consulted the map.

A cluster of children formed around us, I asked one of them for 'Via del Monte, Signora Critelli?', and he set off back the way we'd come. We followed him, recrossed the little square, and this time plunged down a steep street with the houses built so close on either side I could almost touch them. Washing of the most intimate nature hung from balconies or was suspended like dingy carnival flags from wall to wall. I was surprised to find Henry lodging in such a poor quarter.

Eventually the child paused in front of an open doorway where there was a smell of wet stone and flowers because someone had just watered a pot of narcissi. I hovered at the entrance, my resolve gone, wishing that I had never left England or that at the very least had sent Henry a note to let him know I was on my way. Now that I was here I wondered whether he would think it appropriate. I was also afraid of seeing him ill. What if he didn't recognise me, or I him? Unlike Rosa, I never knew what to do in the face of sickness. I glanced at Nora but she raised an eyebrow as if to say: You got us into this; don't expect any encouragement from me.

In the end I crept along the passage to a kitchen where a woman stood with her arms immersed in a wash bowl. She squinted at me through the droplets of water that trickled into her eyes.

'Dr Henry Thewell?' I asked.

She gaped, dried her face first on a towel then on her skirt, leaned her hand on the door frame and let fly a torrent of Italian which ended at last in a question.

I shook my head. '*Non capisco. Inglese. Mi chiamo* Mariella Lingwood. Ma-ri-ella. I am engaged to be married to Dr Thewell. *Dov'e* Henry Thewell?'

I had learned from watching my father that it is better, in moments of crisis, to speak quietly rather than to shout. Certainly Signora Critelli calmed down; she went on talking but less rapidly, wiped her hands again, gestured that I should get out of the way and led me up a narrow flight of stairs to the first floor where she knocked sharply on a door, flung it wide and announced me with the words: '*Signorina Inglese*.'

I took a step further, and another.

The room was in semi-darkness because, though one shutter was half open, a drab blue curtain covered the window. Through the gloom I saw that the room was small and contained a narrow bed, a washstand, a table heaped with books and a low chair with a rush seat upon which an untouched tray with a roll, a jug and a cup had been left. There was a smell of cold coffee and damp linen.

Henry was in bed but he'd raised himself on one elbow and even in the darkness I saw the eager brilliance of his eyes and that his hair had grown so long it flopped over his brow. We stared at each other. Then I stumbled across the room, knelt by the bed and held him.

My bonnet was knocked sideways as he covered my face with hot kisses. I wept and seemed to flow out of myself when I felt his lips on my hair, ear and neck. Though I was distantly aware that the door behind us was closed abruptly and that we had been watched, I didn't mind. I clasped his too thin arms as his hands caressed my back and I helped him with my bonnet ribbons, wondering how I could ever have doubted that I did the right thing in coming here. I realised that I had waited most of my life to have Henry kiss my throat, even to let him fumble with the buttons of my gown and pull loose the neck of my shift. My skin contracted as his lips closed on my breast. His breath came in rasping pants between kisses.

I fell back on the pillow, smoothed his hair and felt him grow heavy in my arms. Astonishingly, he slept. For perhaps half an hour I didn't move though I lay half off the bed, my bonnet dropping from my neck, a draught swaying the curtain, the clop of a mule's hooves on the street below. Because my hair was caught by the weight of his head all I could see was a fragment of cracked ceiling, a broken frieze and the shifting blue-grey curtain. I kissed him again and again, tiny, weightless kisses on his hair, which was far softer than I had ever imagined, like a cat's fur, and I thought: All these weeks he has been alone, watching that curtain and waiting for me. I was afloat in the miracle of his touch, the strangeness of a male body half covering mine, the fact that this was Henry who I had missed so much in the past months that even the blood in my veins ached for him.

Then I tightened my hold because although never in my wildest imaginings had I expected such a loving, needy reception as this, nor had I really thought to find him so weak that he was confined to bed. I had always relished his energy and the hardness of his arm under my hand but now he was as frail as a bird. And he smelled entirely different to the Henry who never failed to delight me with his scent of good soap, balsam or camphor. Instead the odour of confined flesh reminded me of the governesses' home.

As he woke his breath grew uneven on my neck. When he moved his head my skin was damp and hot from where his cheek had rested on me. I closed my eyes as my breast tightened under his circling fingertip.

This is Italy, I thought, no one will know. And anyway, what do I care?

'My dear love,' he whispered, 'I thought you would never come.'

His finger was making a diminishing spiral on my nipple so my words were disjointed: 'I wasn't sure you would want me here. And yet I wouldn't be stopped, even by you, so I thought it best just to come without letting you know.'

'You are my love, my love.'

'Your letters sounded so lonely I thought I must come.'

He nuzzled his cheek into my bosom and pressed his face to my neck, drawing me closer and closer under him. I didn't mind that he had the smell of fever on his breath; I was scarcely conscious of anything except the heat of him as he murmured, 'I thought I might never see you again. I thought you were gone.'

'Of course you'd see me again.'

'But you never answered me. You never said a word. It was killing me.' He laid his head beside mine on the pillow and reached out to turn my face towards his. I had time to see how pale his skin was and that because his moustache had been shaved off his mouth was as full-lipped and boyish as when I first knew him. Then he said, 'Let me look at you at last. My Rosa. My dear love. Dearest Rosa.'

Chapter Two

London, 1840

Henry's mother, Euphemia, known as *poor* Aunt Eppie, was my father's cousin. After her marriage to Richard Thewell, a Derbyshire innkeeper, the pair moved south and for a few years managed a prosperous hostelry near Radlett in Hertfordshire. Their subsequent tragic history was spoken of only behind closed doors so I had to pick it up piecemeal.

Thewell, not astute enough to anticipate that the new railway running through the town would kill his business, took to the bottle. Meanwhile, soon after the birth of their only son, Aunt Eppie began to suffer from a wasting disease. The business duly failed and my father rescued the family by moving them into one of the little villas he'd just had built in Wandsworth, a mile or so from our house in Clapham. While the boy, Henry, was at school poor Aunt Eppie spent her mornings with us at Fosse House, working on the household linen and teaching me to sew. I never met her husband, whose drinking put him beyond the pale, although I once heard Mother describe him to her friend Mrs Hardcastle as *ineffectual.*

Eppie was a little, high-cheekboned creature who had nothing in common with Mother except that both were from Derbyshire and fiendishly hard-working. Mother couldn't stand sewing, Eppie was never happy without a needle in her hand; Mother was the daughter of a squire, Eppie of a tailor; Mother was too preoccupied to spend more than an hour or two on my lessons each day whereas Eppie taught me to crochet imitation guipure lace, work an edge of Plaited Slav stitch on a linen tablecloth and put pin tucks into the bodice of a muslin blouse. We worked side by side in the morning room, and I remember the smell of her perspiration, the way a girlish froth of hand-worked lace framed her fiercely parted hair and pallid forehead, the tension in her hands and back as she sewed. She reeked of sickness, her breath was rotten.

By the time I was eight she was too frail to come to the house though Mother took me to visit her once in the Wandsworth villa. She lay on a mountain of pillows, her face lost in the flaps of her nightcap, a bit of smocking with the needle threaded through dropped among the folds of her quilt. Her smile was apologetic and she couldn't speak because of her cough. After that she faded from my life altogether though I inherited her skill, her small collection of books on stitchcraft and a leather sewing case, containing needles, scissors, hooks and pen-knife, with mother-of-pearl handles. Mother was suddenly busier than ever managing the Thewell household as well as our own, arranging a funeral and seeing the widower dispatched north to an aunt who was to help him recover from the blow of his wife's death. Meanwhile we were *to take the boy in.*

When Henry took up residence in our quiet household he was a thin-faced youth with an unhealthy complexion and eyes blank with suffering. 'He'll be with us only while he finishes school or until his father's back on his feet,' said Mother. 'He'll sleep in the room next to yours and be out each day. We'll hardly notice him.'

But I did notice him, I noticed everything about him: the cautious sounds of his rising in the morning, his meagre breakfast of tea and toast, his easing himself out of the house as if afraid of making the air stir as he shut the door, his return at six o'clock and disappearance into his room as soon as the evening meal was over. I noticed that he had long fingers like his mother and that he was never without a book. Even at mealtimes there was one sticking out of his pocket and when he set off for school in the morning I ran to an upstairs window and watched him open a volume and begin to read. It was a wonder he didn't fall over but he was skilled at avoiding obstacles, even with his eyes on the page.

He and I had nothing to say to each other. After all, he was a boy and eight years older than me. And his dead mother, poor Aunt Eppie, shimmered between us. I assumed he was sadder even than I was about her death but I couldn't tell how much.

However, one wet afternoon I noticed that, despite my mother's reminder at breakfast time, he had forgotten to take an umbrella from the stand in the hail and I was very troubled because this was the kind of detail we used to get exactly right before he came. For an hour I sat over my tapestry, plotting how to remedy the situation. In the end I asked Mother's permission to go down the garden with the umbrella and open the gate for him so that he could cut a corner of the lane and have cover for the last few minutes at least.

'That would be kind, Mariella.'

So I ran along the brick path skirting the lawn and passed through what we hoped would one day be a wilderness, to the herbaceous beds. There were stepping stones across the border to the gate which was half covered in clematis and had a well-oiled bolt.

I stood in the shelter of the wall, trembling. Perhaps he wouldn't come this way home today, or not be pleased to see me. Perhaps I'd already missed him. A blade of grass at my foot bent from the weight of a raindrop.

At last I heard the squelch of footsteps and there was Henry with his collar up and mud on his boots, a wet satchel clasped to his chest.

'Henry.' He stopped dead, looked round and saw me under the arch of the gateway. 'I brought you an umbrella,' I said. 'And it's quicker through the garden.'

His bottom lip pressed against the upper and to my horror I realised that he was trying not to cry. But he bowed, took the umbrella and followed me up the garden, holding it over us both. When we reached the house he gave me his satchel while he shook the rain off the umbrella and folded it up. Awed by the responsibility of clutching the damp mass of his books in my arms, I took a discreet sniff of rain-soaked leather. As we swapped burdens he smiled into my eyes and afterwards I stood in the drying room amidst rows of damp sheets and didn't know how I would live until dinner when he might smile at me like that again.

Chapter Three

Italy, 1855

I ran out of Narni down the winding road to the valley floor where the air was unmoving and thick with heat and a track led through scrubland and vegetable gardens to the river. When I passed a spring with a metal cup on a chain I gulped some water before stumbling on. My clothes were tight, I was wearing five layers of petticoats and, as I'd left my bonnet in Henry's room, my hair flooded over my shoulders. The very thought of that bonnet, chosen with such care for this journey but now discarded on the floor beside his bed, made me nauseous. If I'd been able to breathe I would have howled with pain. At one point the words, 'No, no,' did burst from me but died away in the rocky sides of what had become a gorge.

Eventually I sank down under a tree but even then I couldn't stay still. I hammered the ground with my fists and kicked the bank with my heels. Again I cried, 'No, no,' and beat my hands until they were bruised. My eyes burned with unshed tears. If I could have fought my way out of my body I would have done it and left my skin on the river bank like a rag.

The scene in Henry's room replayed: his eager face, his touch, his kisses, his words of love. No. No. It couldn't be . . . How could Henry have taken so much of me, then betrayed me? How could Henry have been so full of Rosa that he hadn't even noticed that the woman in his arms was me? *Me.*

What had I failed to see all this time?

I tore fistfuls of grass away from the earth, hurled them into the water, and there she was on the far side of the river with her light hair and pale skin; tapering hands held out to me, low voice calling my name. Her body was supple and slender, so that her narrow bodice hung smooth on her waist and her blue gown flowed in clean lines down to her ankles.

'But I love you,' I said to the shade of Rosa.

I reached for her, pleading with her to come and put it right.

Rosa, after all, could probably walk on water.

I became aware that I was covered with dirt and the hem of my skirt was trailing in the river, that I was very hungry and that I should pull myself together and go back to Narni. But I had run much further than I realised and was faint by the time I came to the spring. A woman in dark clothes was seated beside it and even from a distance I could tell by the size of her bonnet that this was none other than Nora, who handed me first a cup of water, then my abandoned hat.

'I could have told you it wouldn't be easy,' she said as we set off back to the hotel.

My room, at three in the afternoon, was dark and cool. Nora had the servants fill me a bath and afterwards watched me eat. Her hair had been flattened by heat and the weight of her bonnet but she looked more cheerful than at any time in the year since I'd met her. I managed a few mouthfuls and pushed my plate aside.

'Whatever shall I do?' I said. 'He thought I was Rosa.'

She stared at me with sludge-coloured eyes.

'Why would he think I was Rosa?'

'When I saw him after you'd gone he didn't seem in a fit state to know what he was saying.'

'You went up then?'

'We both did when you came rushing out like that. We found him fallen half out of the bed and raving, so we gave him a dose and calmed him down. He's dreadful sick, the poor man.'

'He thought I was Rosa.'

'That'll be down to the delirium.'

'But why would he want me to be Rosa?'

'It's not a matter of wanting. It's a matter of what he thought he was seeing.'

'He *wanted* me to be her but I don't understand it. There was nothing between Henry and Rosa. They didn't even like each other. I am engaged to Henry. He's always been mine. Something must have happened at the war.'

'I know nothing about that.'

'Do you think they fell in love?'

'I can't speak for him. I only know that girl would do nothing to hurt you.'

'What shall I do? What shall I tell him? What if he goes on thinking I'm her?'

'Tell him the truth. Tell him you're not Rosa. Tell him we're all worried to death about her because heck knows where the wretched girl is now.'

Chapter Four

London, 1840

In all the four months that Henry stayed in our house I saw him cry for his mother once. A parcel came after he'd gone to school one day, addressed in cramped writing which turned out to be that of the aunt who had taken his father in hand. In a covering letter she announced that she had come south to clear away the dead woman's things so that father and son could eventually return to the family home and start afresh. She had found the enclosed items which the mother had left for Henry as a memorial.

My parents discussed the matter at breakfast. 'We can't interfere,' said Mother. 'Henry's old enough to bear it. He's almost a grown man.'

'Just when the boy was doing so well, this has come,' said Father. 'In my view we'd be best putting it away.'

'But he must have something of poor Eppie's.'

'He has his memory of her. That ought to be enough.'

All day I gave the parcel a wide berth on my journeys across the hall and I didn't say a word to Henry about it when I met him at the garden gate because I wanted to preserve his happy mood as long as possible.

By this time our trips back to the house usually took an hour or more. If the weather was hot we flung ourselves down under the cedar and lay with fallen needles pricking our backs, staring up into the complicated branches, or else he leaned against the trunk and read an anatomy book borrowed from one of his teachers. I wasn't allowed to peek inside because he said the contents weren't suitable for a little girl so instead I sat against his bony ribs and listened to the thudding of his heart. Once, when I'd been told to pick raspberries for dinner, he and I filled our bowls until I was dizzy with the smell of hay and sugar and had to sit in the shade while he carried on, occasionally reaching down to pop fruit into my mouth with his stained fingers. When it was nearly dinner time we went inside at last, dazzled by the outdoors, dumped the bowls on the kitchen table and clattered up the backstairs to the landing outside our rooms where he tugged my plait: 'Wash your face, Mariella. You're a disgrace to the family name.'

On the afternoon of the package I took his hand and led him to the hall. As soon as he picked up the parcel it was just as I'd feared; he withdrew deep into himself, went upstairs and closed the door of his room.

He didn't come down to dinner. Afterwards Mother went up with a tray and half an hour later sent me to fetch it. His door had been left open and his room smelled of cooked meat because of the untouched food. He was sitting on the bed with the contents of the parcel scattered round him. I picked up the tray and put it outside in the passage. Then I closed the door and went to the bed where I stood with my hands behind my back, waiting to be noticed.

He was not yet a very handsome boy; he was too thin, his skin, though more tanned than when he first arrived, was still inclined to spots, and his hair was lank. But I thought him beautiful because of his serious, all-seeing eyes and I mourned the light that usually came into his face when he saw me. Eventually I went right up to the bed, put my hand on his shoulder, twisted my neck so that my face was almost upside down under his bent head and stared into his eyes. Still no response.

'Can I see what was in the parcel?' I asked.

Nothing.

His pain was so palpable that I knew drastic measures had to be taken so I sat on his uncomfortable lap and put my arms round his neck. 'Show me,' I said.

He pointed to a miniature, perhaps four inches by three, in a plain wooden frame, of Eppie in what must have been her glory days, before penury. Her little face was adorned with glossy ringlets and her long neck rose from a bare bosom. She wore a high-waisted dress that somehow clung to her chest despite being cut in a wide V across the shoulders. Her head was quarter-turned so that she looked somewhere to the right of the artist, and she was smiling rather shyly, as if she'd prefer not to be in the picture at all.

The other relics of Aunt Eppie were a pair of white kid gloves with pearl buttons, just a little soiled about the fingertips. I gave them a sniff because I knew that perfume clung to gloves, and immediately I recalled the hint of rosewater and perspiration that always hung about her. There was a tiny jewellery box with flowers embroidered on top, silk-lined and with a mirror inside the lid. Eppie's engagement ring with its row of three small diamonds, familiar to me from my sewing days, was wrapped in a piece of crumpled tissue and there was a folded-up sheet of paper that fitted exactly inside the box. On it was written in a frail hand: 'For Harry. My darling, darling boy. Never forget your Mama, how she loved you.'

'She was very kind, your mother,' I whispered. 'She left me her sewing case. Did you know?'

He didn't answer. I clung to his neck and tried to hug him but he was unyielding; as spiky as when he first arrived.

Eventually I gave up and left him but as I reached the door I heard a dreadful tearing noise that came from the back of his throat and before I knew it I was sitting on the bed, his head was buried in my lap, my fingers were in his hair and the skirt of my cotton frock was hot and damp with his tears. His sobs came from deep within his body and he clawed at my arm and back.

At last he recovered enough to raise his wet face and look into mine. 'You'll have to be everything to me now, Mariella.'

Chapter Five

The Derbyshire aunt failed to work a miracle on Henry's father *(unfortunate* and ineffectual Richard Thewell) who was buried two summers later. Meanwhile Henry disappeared down the long tunnel that was medical training the hard way through an endless series of lectures and examinations in unreachable subjects such as chemistry and physiology. His ambition was to be a surgeon and I suspect my father paid many of the bills. Occasionally, on Sunday afternoons, Henry called to drink a hasty cup of tea, spill out snatches of information about plaisters, dresserships and thirty-six-hour stretches without sleep, and depart an hour later laden with cold meats and cakes plied on him by our cook.

Father's business thrived and soon he was managing several projects at a time and had been invited to serve on various boards and committees to do with planning and public works. Mother was busier than ever teaching at the Sunday School, raising money for the Female Aid Society and serving on a hospital Board of Visitors. I went to a day school where I learned pianoforte, French, arithmetic and deportment. Thanks to Aunt Eppie I shone at fine sewing.

And then, in the autumn of 1843, when I was nearly twelve, a letter arrived from Aunt Isabella, Mother's widowed elder sister, who wrote that she was about to marry someone called *Sir* Matthew Stukeley. As soon as she and her daughter, Rosa, were settled into their new home, Stukeley Hall, perhaps next summer, she expected Mother and me to travel to Derbyshire for a long visit.

Mother was somewhat in awe of her older sister and had christened me Mariella to combine her own name, *Maria*, with my aunt's, *Isabella*. While Mother had married a mere builder, Isabella's first marriage had been to a small landowner, name of

Richard Barr, Esquire, who had unfortunately died, leaving her penniless. But she'd barely been widowed six months before capturing the heart of Stukeley. 'Not that he's from old money,' Mother told Mrs Hardcastle. 'His fortune is based on lead and cotton.'

She was intrigued by the prospect of returning north but full of anxiety about the journey. There was no question of Father leaving his business especially as he'd just bought a slice of land in Deptford. I didn't want to go at all. I liked school, I would miss Father, and most of all I was afraid that Henry might want to call for Sunday tea while we were away. How would I bear two or three months without even the possibility of seeing him? And the prospect of meeting a cousin eighteen months older than me, not to mention a knight in a mansion, was very alarming. So Mother and I were preoccupied on the train journey during which I crocheted an uncomplicated mat for Aunt Isabella's dressing table and Mother wrote a list of all the people she would need to correspond with while she was away.

We were met at the station by a coachman in uniform who drove a carriage of awesome dimensions. For a while we lurched over cobbles between buildings of ugly grey brick but suddenly the world turned green and we were rushing along narrow lanes edged with stone walls and steep hills that climbed up into the sky.

After half an hour or so we came to a pair of handsome gates with a lodge, no less, on the other side. Perched on top of the left-hand gatepost and showing a great deal of thin calf was a girl in a blue dress with a flood of straw-gold hair, a colour I had always yearned for, my own being light brown. She waved frantically then somehow scrambled out of sight, though the post was very high, to reappear just as we rattled through the gates. All the way up the drive she kept pace beside us, beaming at me through the window.

'That must be your cousin Rosa,' said my mother. 'What a girl.'

Stukeley Hall was a monstrous mansion complete with towers, turrets, pinnacles and gables. Mother and I stood on the dizzily geometric tiles of the entrance hail and were properly awed. There was a fleet of servants to fetch our bags and show us the way but already Rosa was on the first landing, her hair hanging over the banister like a rippling sail. 'Come on,' she called. 'Come.'

Aunt Isabella was seated in the drawing room beside an immense marble fireplace with an elaborate screen instead of a fire, it being a warm day. She did not get up but extended a white hand and said, 'I am very low today.'

'Forgive me, sister,' said Mother humbly, 'they should have told us, we could have waited until later . . .'

Now that I'd met her, I couldn't understand how Aunt Isabella had managed to attract even one husband, let alone two, including a title. She was a puffy woman whose complexion was perhaps her best claim to beauty, being powder soft.

Mother and I sat side by side but Rosa stared at me and wagged her head meaningfully towards the door. 'Come on,' she said. 'Mama, I want to show Mariella everything.'

'Then do,' sighed Isabella.

I didn't want to be led off into a world not governed by Mother. It seemed to me, as we ran along the passageways of Stukeley Hall, that I was about to tumble over a precipice called The Unknown.

Rosa flung open one door after another: 'This is the saloon, this is the gallery, this is the blue room, that's the library – I've been *banished* from there, would you believe it, the one room I'd spend every minute in given the chance.'

'But why?'

'Oh no reason. Just because my stepfather doesn't like me, I suppose.' Off we dashed again. 'This is the billiard room . . .' She even showed me her mother's bedroom – 'Come on, there's nobody here' – and I peeked at a vast bed bedecked with floral curtains and a flounced quilt, all in shades of pale blue and pink, in which must lie my cushiony aunt and the as-yet-unseen Sir Matthew. Thank goodness there were no indentations of their heads in the lace pillows.

'Come over here. Let's see,' said Rosa, dragging me across to a long mirror where we stood pressed together, staring at our reflections. 'Yes. We are very alike. Sisters almost.'

Actually I thought we had little in common. My hair was darker and straighter, my nose shorter, my eyes grey rather than blue and my jaw more rounded. I was terrified in case we were caught trespassing on such private territory and relieved when we went pounding down a narrow staircase and burst into a stone passage that led to the outside.

'So what do you think?' she demanded, walking backwards in front of me so that she could watch my face.

'Of what?'

'Of it all. Isn't it hideous? I wish I were dead. I wish I could go home,' and suddenly her voice broke and she cried: 'I'm sorry, I'm sorry, it's such a relief to be able to say it but I miss my father so much, I really do. You can't know what it's like, you're so lucky, your family is complete, you don't have to put up with stepbrothers called Horatio and Maximilian – can you imagine? – and a stepfather who never speaks to me except to tell me what I mustn't do . . .' I found myself abruptly placed in the role of comforter as she threw her arms about my neck so that my nose was buried in silky hair fragranced with lemons. Then she flung herself away, grabbed my hand and kissed it, smiled into my face, her blue eyes overflowing with tears, and said, 'It is so wonderful that you are here. I'll show you everything. I'll show you all the secret places I have discovered. Come on. Come.' And she rushed off with her hair flying and her blue skirts kicked back from her ankles and I followed at a pace which caused my unaccustomed heart to beat very fast and my spirits to lift higher and higher because already I had fallen head over heels in love with Rosa.

Chapter Six

Italy, 1855

Nora and I set out again for the Via del Monte the following day. This time I was dressed in my cream cotton gown with the broad horizontal stripes and single flounce, and I carried my parasol. Rather than rush ahead I walked sedately alongside Nora, my eyes heavy and dry with lack of sleep and my breathing rapid and shallow. When we reached the house I waited while Nora fetched Signora Critelli, who led us upstairs as before and knocked on Henry's door.

The room was altogether different: the shutters were open, the curtains tied back, the table tidied and the floor swept. A chair had been placed in readiness for a visitor. Henry was dressed and seated in a position I knew well with one leg crossed over the other, his arm thrown along the back of the chair and his head supported in his hand. Though he held a notebook his eyes were fixed on the door.

I said very clearly and slowly, 'Henry, it is I, *Mariella*, come to visit you.'

His back was to the light but something changed in his face and tension went out of his body. After a moment he gripped the table with both hands and stood up so that the sun shone through his shirt and I saw the skeletal outline of his body. 'Mariella.' He kissed my cheek and pulled back the chair for me while Nora sat on the bed. I looked into his eyes, which were full of sympathy and warmth, and I could not detect, even by the merest glimmer of consciousness, whether he remembered what had happened yesterday and the awful mistake he had made.

'Mariella, whatever are you doing so far from Clapham?' he said.

'I was disturbed by your letters. It seemed to me that someone should come out here and make sure you are being well looked after.'

'How did you get here? Who is with you?'

'Nora. That's all. You remember her, don't you, my aunt's companion and nurse? She seemed the best choice because Aunt is so much better and Nora has experience of journeys.'

'Of course I remember. But still I'm amazed that your parents would let you come so far without a male escort.'

'Mr and Mrs Hardcastle were travelling to Rome. We were not alone.'

'I thought you found Mrs Hardcastle a little overbearing.'

'It was a sacrifice I was prepared to make for you, Henry.'

As a reward for my feeble attempt at light-heartedness he leaned forward and kissed my hand. 'You are cold, Mariella. How can anyone be cold on such a hot day?'

Throughout this conversation my spirits had been sinking, if possible, even further. Henry was completely changed. Aside from the extreme loss of weight there was an air of abstraction about him that made me recoil. It was as if he were behind a thick sheet of glass and every speech and gesture was a huge effort for him because his attention needed to be on something else. Altogether he was totally unlike the passionate being who had seized me in his arms yesterday, mistaking me for Rosa.

Equally disturbing were the contents of the room. Half hidden behind a curtain was a huge, soiled sheepskin coat and piled on every available surface were dog-eared papers and ledgers. The only ornaments were the miniature of his mother, propped up beside his bed, and beside it, pressed flat by Henry's two old volumes of poems by John Keats, Rosa's unframed portrait of me.

'You've been working,' I said, pointing to his notebook. 'Surely you should rest.'

'Impossible to rest, Mariella, when there is so much to do.'

'What is there to do?'

'Army business. You know. I have become an expert on the proper preparation of the army medical services for war.'

I picked up Rosa's painting of me in which she had given my

mouth an elusive smile and put a gloss to my hair. When I saw an earlier version I had complained that I looked much too shy so she had adjusted the expression in my eyes until I was gazing more directly out of the canvas. It was signed with her usual vigorous initials: *RB, September '54*.

I said quietly, 'In one of your letters you mentioned that you'd seen Rosa. We are worried because we haven't heard from her for weeks so I wonder, do you have any recent news of her?'

His eyes had followed intently the passage of the portrait from its place on the bedside table to my lap. Otherwise he was utterly still. 'Rosa?'

'Yes, you know. You said in a letter that you'd met her one day, unexpectedly.'

'Unexpectedly. Yes, indeed. Very strange that was. You see I had no idea she was in Russia at all.'

'Not all my letters reached you, then?' I tried to keep my voice steady. 'Did you spend much time with her?'

'There was never any time to spare, Mariella.'

Nora said suddenly, 'The truth is, sir, it's been more than two months, and nothing.'

'A letter from Mother was waiting for me when I got here but the news is that they still haven't heard from her,' I said. 'Mother writes that Aunt Isabella is beside herself with anxiety.'

When he put his thumb and index finger to his forehead I noticed a tremor in his hand. 'Not heard from her? You should have done. Things are much improved; there's a railroad, telegraph even.'

'The mother will be worrying herself and everybody else to death,' put in Nora.

'Not heard from her,' he said again. 'Not heard. Someone should try to find out where she is. Your father could pull strings, surely.'

'We tell ourselves that there must be so many people in unexpected places in a war,' I said. 'We tell ourselves that she is probably safe, but unable to write.'

'And Rosa would be in an unexpected place, I suppose.'

'She would, Henry.' I spoke without expression because I could never have believed it possible to suffer so much and still go on breathing. There was no ignoring the precision with which he spoke, the pretence at disinterest when every inch of him was tuned to the name of Rosa.

He loves her, I thought.

'Mariella?' He leaned forward, hands loosely clasped between his knees, apparently waiting for an answer to a question I had not heard.

I tried to look away but he caught me in his affectionate gaze and spoke distinctly, as if to a sick child. 'I said, shall we go on an excursion tomorrow to see the ruins at Ocriculum? While you're here you should see something of Italy.'

'Are you really fit enough to be planning an outing?'

'My doctor, my good friend Lyall, said I should take plenty of fresh air so I'm sure he would approve. In fact he'd come with us if he were here; he's a great one for antiquities. As we speak he's probably chipping bits off the Forum in Rome.'

'Rather than taking care of you.'

'The poor man needed a holiday. I must weary him to death. And I don't require much looking after.'

He was looking at me in a travesty of the old Henry-like way: confident, smiling, arms folded, head thrown back. I stared at him, then pretended instead to be absorbed by the view of a shuttered window across the street.

I will surely die of this pain, I thought.

PART TWO

Chapter One

London, 1854

My father's reward for his unflagging support of Henry was to see his protégé rise rapidly to the heady rank of registrar, a role that involved supervising students and writing reports for the hospital board, and then to become an assistant surgeon on three hundred and fifty pounds a year. By the time he was thirty Henry had a national reputation as a teacher and surgeon, exceptionally skilled with the knife. His lectures were so popular that his friends boasted of how students crowded in the doorway and even stood on chairs outside an open window to listen. Unlike many of his contemporaries, said Father proudly, Henry was never satisfied with relying on tradition, so he spent his hard-earned salary on trips to Europe to find out what was going on there. Henry wanted to be at the forefront of medicine; he wanted to be the best. Henry, in short, was a man after my father's own heart.

By the summer of 1853 Henry had bought a plot of land in Highgate and Father was advising him on architectural plans for a new house. Then, just after Christmas, as yet another sign of his growing status, Henry was asked to join a group of military doctors and advisers who were to travel to Turkey and ensure that all was in place for the treatment of wounded soldiers should there be a skirmish with Russia. It seemed that 'The Eastern Question', a recurring theme in extracts from *The Times* read to us by Father after dinner, was after all likely to be settled through war rather than diplomacy.

Henry was away nearly a month and on his return wrote that he'd inspected the progress of the new house in Highgate only to find that there was a problem with the drains and the garden was a swamp. Could Father give him a spot of advice? And as the windows had at last been glazed and a hearth installed in the drawing room, perhaps the ladies would like to go too.

Mother and I drove from Clapham to Highgate through a ferociously wet February afternoon. She was dressed in brown silk bought against my advice; in my judgement the glossy fabric made her skin sallow and diminished her features. Having to sit still for so long and do nothing was torture for her and she kept notebook and pencil at the ready in case of ideas. She was currently secretary of a committee of ladies whose mission was to open a home for retired or distressed governesses, an enterprise thought up by Mrs Hardcastle, whose strong-minded daughters had worn out a succession of teachers, one of whom, a quarter of a century later, inconveniently came begging in frail old age.

After half an hour or so of stop-start travel we had still barely crossed the river and Mother drew out her watch. 'Surely the omnibus would have been quicker.'

'We'll be glad of the carriage on the way home.'

'I told your father that a carriage in London was a dreadful extravagance. I've never minded walking. Or a cab.'

'Father will enjoy riding about.'

'He knows nothing of horses. He should have taken more advice. I hope this one doesn't go lame. It has stumbled three times already; I've been counting.'

Beyond the murky glass Hyde Park was a green blur and the pavement bobbed with black umbrellas. My breathing was restricted because the bodice of my afternoon gown measured seventeen inches at the waist, one and a half inches less than usual, and the triple bow of my blue bonnet meant I had to keep my chin abnormally high.

'Are you nervous?' Mother said suddenly.

This was so unexpectedly prescient that I was irritated. 'Of course not. Why ever would I be nervous?'

'This is your first glimpse of the house. You've not seen Henry for a while. I just thought . . .'

Heat rushed up my neck and face. 'As if I'd be nervous of Henry. And after all we're just going to look at his new house. It doesn't mean anything.'

'*I* am sometimes nervous of Henry, as I am even of your father sometimes. I always think there is so much more to men than we realise.'

By now both of us were gazing studiously out of opposite windows. She said, 'I never imagined when I took Henry in what he would become. He seemed such a shy boy then.'

'He was in mourning. We couldn't tell at first what he was really like.'

'And yet who would have thought he had it in him? Of course your father suspected it, after all he has an eye for quality and talent. But you must not think that Henry is the only possible one for you. That's my worry, Mariella. There are other men, equally suitable, I'm sure. You have been very fixed in your ideas.'

'There's no question of being fixed, as you put it. Henry is like a brother to me.'

Her brown-gloved hand pressed my fingers. 'Something more than a brother, I think.'

Henry's new house, called The Elms, was built on the site of an ancient farmhouse. We drove at last between gateposts set in an old wall, relics of the past. When I pulled down the window to take a better look rain dashed into my face. 'What a lovely brick,' I said, using an expression learned from Father. 'And look, there's even a turret. We might almost be at Stukeley.'

The house had two wings extending at a slight angle on either side of a gabled porch. Henry was waiting at the open door, with a maid behind him ready to take our cloaks. 'My dear Aunt. Mariella. You are brave to venture out in such foul weather. I was sure you wouldn't come.'

He took Mother's arm and led her into a near-empty room where a fire had been lit and four chairs were drawn up round a little table. The miniature of Henry's mother stood in solitary splendour on the mantelpiece.

'How proud poor Eppie would have been to see you here,' said Mother.

'I hope so.' We were all silent a moment. 'We will have tea and then I will show you the rest of the house. You mustn't mind our very primitive arrangements.'

I unfastened the five buttons of my right glove and peeled it from my fingers. Despite the fire the room was gloomy because beyond the French doors rain was drumming on the roof of a conservatory. But that was all I noticed; the shock of being in Henry's presence made me blind and deaf to anything else. He was dressed very formally in a frock coat and cravat. When I was absent from him what I remembered most vividly was the way his abundant hair sprang from his forehead, the horizontal crease above his confident chin and the surprising gentleness of his voice. In the flesh he was always a little taller, broader, altogether more a man of the world than I expected.

Father, who was late for every engagement, did not appear, so the three of us had a cosy tea. Mother poured and Henry passed me a cup with a ceremoniousness that made us laugh. 'It's the first time of thousands that we shall all drink tea in this house,' he said, 'and you are my first guests so I must start as I mean to go on.'

'This is a beautiful tea service,' said Mother. 'I've not seen it before.'

'It was Mother's. I've had it packed away all these years. This seemed the right moment to unearth it.'

My hand shook as I held the shell of pink porcelain. 'Constantinople,' I said. 'You've told us nothing.'

'What would you like to know?'

'Everything. What you saw. Who you spoke to. Your mission was even mentioned in the paper. Father read it out to us. We were very proud.'

'Yes, I gather *The Times* got hold of the story. There are no secrets from the press any more. As you can imagine, Mariella, I felt a considerable burden of responsibility. At one point I even wondered whether I was the right man for the job, but they'd wanted a surgeon of my experience, I had met Herbert at a dinner, so there it was. We have established that there is provision for a large hospital in Constantinople and we have ordered massive stocks of lint and plaster and so on to be sent out there. It's the best we can do. But I wish your father could have been with us. The main hospital, should it be required, will be a vast old barracks and I have reservations about the state of its floors and drains. Uncle Philip would have been the ideal person to advise us.'

'Were the army doctors satisfied?'

'We all were in a way. The accommodation is certainly adequate in terms of space. But of course so little can be done until we know more about where or even if the fighting will begin. And the army doctors are entirely optimistic because they say the military is used to building something out of nothing. Certainly I was impressed by the speed and efficiency of the steamships. A wounded man could reach hospital in a matter of hours.'

'And what about Constantinople? Was it as you'd expected?'

'Colder than I'd expected; a different type of cold to here, more dense and penetrating altogether. I stressed in my report that we were planning for a summer campaign, and that if the war were to be delayed until winter things could be quite different. With rough seas, wounded soldiers would have a very uncomfortable time. But in summer all will be well.'

'It must have been so difficult,' said Mother, 'when you don't know the language. Did any of you speak Turkish? What a business it must be, preparing an army. My goodness, I am having difficulties planning a home for fifteen women, let alone tens of thousands.'

'How is the home, Aunt?'

'Oh, we are still as far from opening as ever. I never know what the next difficulty will be. The committee is currently researching the most hygienic type of mattress – we have been offered any number of second-hand beds but I can't help thinking we must be sure of their provenance.'

Henry leaned forward and took her hands in his. 'I tell you what, dear Aunt, we can't have you worrying about this type of thing. Why don't you leave me a list of queries and I'll answer them as best I can. Would that help your committee?'

We began our tour of the house in the conservatory where a fluted marble fountain had been installed, although there was as yet no running water. The windows were elaborately arched to allow a view of the garden, which at the moment was little more than a water-logged meadow graced by three enormous elms.

'Perhaps it was a mistake bringing you here,' Henry said. 'In this weather it's hard to imagine sunny afternoons on the lawn. But I am being asked to think of everything, wallpapers, plantings, pavements, paths, arbours. How can I do it alone? I need help.'

Mother eyed an array of pattern books and swatches of fabric set out on a broad sill. 'Do you know,' she said, 'I think I'll sit by the fire and work my way through these while you and Mariella look at the house. When Philip arrives we'll come and find you.'

I was amazed at her for sending us away on our own. Surely she was too guileless to orchestrate a proposal? We watched as she pulled her chair nearer the fire and opened a pattern book.

'So, where shall we start?' Henry said, rather too briskly.

'I'd like to see the turret.'

'Aha. The turret, my dear Ella, is a flight of fancy on the part of the architect. I hadn't the heart to curb his enthusiasm. It promises more than it delivers, I think you'll find, but follow me.'

I caressed the intricate globes and twists in the newel posts on the stairs and savoured how the unused boards of the first-floor corridor creaked underfoot. When Henry opened the last door a draught blew it shut behind us. The room had windows on two sides and a peculiar circular bay in one corner which was in fact the turret. 'What a shame. I'd hoped for a spiral staircase and a dark little tower room at least,' I said.

'It's a very modern turret, I'm afraid, but there'll be a wonderful view if it ever stops raining. I'm thinking of making this my library. What do you think? And at night I hope to have time for star-gazing.' He moved self-consciously round the room, poked his head up the chimney and pulled on the picture rail as if testing its firmness.

'I presume it won't always smell of plaster,' I said.

'Paint will be the next thing. I only hope it will be finished by summer. This place takes up so much of my thoughts and time that the sooner I can move in, the less of a distraction it will be. And perhaps when it is filled with furniture it will feel less vast and ostentatious.'

'Hardly ostentatious. You've earned every brick of this house. Nobody on earth works harder than you.'

'But then you would say that. You are too loyal and uncritical.' He came a little closer and smiled at me in the boyish way that quickened my blood.

A blast of wind drove raindrops against the glass. He offered his arm, squeezed my fingers and led me back along the passage. 'There are two bathrooms, one for guests, one attached to the main bedroom. We have cold piped water, of course, but the hot is more of a problem. They tried to persuade me to have a geyser but I resisted. Your father says they're very unreliable.' We peeked into a cavernous bathroom with a great, claw-footed bath in the centre and suddenly found ourselves on such impossibly intimate territory that I was a little faint. The house was so beautiful and untouched. If only I could fill it with my handiwork. If only it could be me who drew the curtains at the windows, lit the lamps and waited for him by the hearth at night.

'This is the main bedroom,' he said, moving on. 'In summer the sun will flood in here because it's south facing. And there is even a view, you see, to the heath. The architect thought of everything. There is a dressing room on one side leading into the bathroom, and this other little room could be a kind of parlour, perhaps. What do you think, Mariella?'

'The light is so good that it would make a wonderful sewing room.'

There was a pause. Perhaps I had been too forthright. Again we stood within inches of each other. The tension of being alone in a room with Henry after nearly two months apart was unendurable. In the end I sank down in the window seat with a puff of my skirts and put my forehead to the glass.

After another long silence he said, 'Yes, that's how I always think of you, with your calm brow and steady eyes. In those chilly nights on the ship when I looked at the stars I wondered if you were gazing up at the same sky. You have no idea, I think, how much it means to me, knowing that you are here.'

It was coming, surely. He reached out his hand, I gave him mine and he brought it to his lips in a soft, slow kiss which afterwards went on burning my flesh. Then he helped me up, tucked my hand through his arm and looked into my face. His eyes were a dark grey, like mercury, with yellowish flecks and this close I could see that his complexion was a little weathered from his recent journey. 'Mariella, there is so much uncertainty. I find the prospect of war very unsettling and then next month I am off on my travels again to a hospital in Hungary where I want to meet a doctor whose practices might have a significant impact on the way we run our own hospitals. Thanks to the government's interest in me, if I can make my mark, perhaps with these new techniques in the operating theatre, I could at last . . .' He kissed my hand again. 'You are, and have been, very patient with me. I think we both know – I at least have always known . . . Can I ask you to be patient with me a little longer?'

My lips were trembling so that I could hardly put words together. 'There's no need . . . I ask nothing except—'

At that moment there was a great clatter of the door knocker followed by the maid's footsteps in the hall, then my father's stamping feet and the flapping of his umbrella. 'Is my wife here? Where is she? Ah, there you are, Maria, my love. I'm late of course but I was needed at King's Cross. Where are the others? What's this problem Henry wrote to me about?'

Henry squeezed my hand and kissed the side of it at the base of my little finger; we looked into each other's eyes, smiled then grew sober because of what was behind the laughter, but the moment was gone.

Chapter Two

Three days later, at five in the morning, the new carriage was again brought to the door of Fosse House and Father and I, muffled up in coats and shawls, bundled inside and rode off to watch the Grenadier Guards march to war.

'It's a small sacrifice, Mariella, rising so early, but it's the right thing to do, a chance in a lifetime to turn out and see troops setting off for a foreign campaign. You'll remember this for ever. I was very small when I saw a regiment march through our village on their way to fight the French, but I've never forgotten it.'

'Did you ever want to be a soldier, Father?'

'Couldn't afford it. The army's no career for an ambitious lad with no connections.'

'You know that Maximilian Stukeley is going to this war. Or so Aunt Isabella said in her last letter.'

'Maximilian. The difficult stepson, as I recall. I thought he was in Australia. Well, at any rate a war will bring him into line. Perhaps we'll see him this morning. He'll most likely be with a northern regiment but you never know.'

Half a mile from Buckingham Palace the street was so congested that we had to get out and walk. Though all the crowds were rushing in the same direction it seemed to me that my own particular reason for being there was more momentous than other people's. This war, after all, was connected with Henry, and Father said that war brought rapid promotion to those who performed well.

The morning was dirty and cold but my steps were sprung with joy because of my private love. Besides, I sensed that I was part of something glorious and I was very happy to be out alone with Father. Before he became grand enough for dinners and clubs he and I used to be frequent companions on jaunts into town. I loved to feel the thick fabric of his coat under my arm and the full force of his attention. He wasn't tall, except when his top hat made him so, but his hair was thick and silver-white, his voice powerful with a strong Derbyshire accent, his face ruddy and his teeth excellent. Being with Father was to be with *someone.*

At the palace gates we waited in the midst of a large crowd, our breath misting the air and our hands plunged deep into our pockets. Some women had brought rice to fling at the troops, others smiled bravely though their lips quivered and their eyes were red with tears. Then there was a beat in the pavement, the crowd pressed forward and there they were, the first lines of immaculately marching men throwing up their feet and turning eyes left to face the balcony where the Queen had suddenly appeared, a speck beside her tall husband. I gave a half sob, waved, shouted, 'God Save the Queen!' and abandoned myself to the cacophony of sound and movement: the stamp of marching feet, the bellowing of the crowd, the band playing 'The British Grenadiers', the flurry of handkerchiefs, the proud, uplifted faces of the men.

I felt as if I were part of every soldier. My whole being cried out to their courage, the neatness of their packs, the ruffle of breeze in their bearskin hats, the precise angle at which they carried their rifles. Neatness, order, purpose were qualities I understood perfectly. Behind them came the cavalry, the horses reeking of polished flesh, the riders bolt upright with their boots gleaming and their elbows pressed to their sides. Though the crowd yelled even harder neither horses nor men took any notice.

I didn't see Max Stukeley, fortunately. In any case, given that I'd not set eyes on him for more than a decade it was unlikely that I would have recognised him; I didn't even know if he wore a moustache, how tall he had grown or in which regiment he served. But I avoided looking in anyone's face too long, just in case.

'Well,' said Father, 'we've done our duty. They'll remember that we were all here. What I admire about soldiers, Mariella, is that they're not fighting only for themselves, whereas most of us work mainly for our own advancement. When you're a soldier you rely on other men as your brothers. And you are fighting for something that will go on and on into the future, long after you're dead. It's a noble calling, I think. Those cavalry horses, for instance – what most people don't understand is that they are trained not to stop.

Once you get one of those horses galloping it can't be turned. That's what the cavalry's about – an unstoppable force. Imagine riding one of them great horses into the thick of battle.'

We walked back to the carriage through the suddenly deflated crowd. 'How must it feel,' I said, 'to be the sister of one of these men, or the wife or mother? To know you may not see them again.'

'That's not how they think, I'm sure. They trust that their men will come back. And in any case, preserving a life isn't everything, Mariella. Not for a man. This is a just war against a barbaric enemy. In order to lead a valuable life one has to throw oneself forward, to make a mark. No, I envy them.'

Chapter Three

That afternoon Mother and I were due at the church to plan an Easter Garden competition for the Sunday School children. It was likely to be a difficult meeting because Mrs Hardcastle had suggested that the children should add Turkish, French and British colours to their displays but Mother was shocked by the idea. Easter, she said, was a time of hope, not conflict.

'Surely Our Lord being crucified makes His resurrection even more pertinent to us this year,' argued Mrs Hardcastle. 'The Easter story is all about the triumph of the righteous.'

The weather was blustery and in preparation for our walk I draped a heavy merino shawl over my shoulders but couldn't resist wearing my newly trimmed bonnet. As I was halfway down the stairs the doorbell rang. The new maid, Ruth, sprang across the hall to answer it and I was left stranded with my bonnet untied and my hand on the banister waiting for her to deal with our visitor, a tall young man in full military dress the glamour of which rendered Ruth speechless.

'Captain Max Stukeley. Ninety-seventh Derbyshires. I wonder if Mrs Lingwood is at home.' Then, catching sight of me on the stairs, he took an exaggerated step backwards. 'Well, I do believe this must be Miss Mariella Lingwood.'

I gave him my hand, which he took and held. 'Do you know, you look even more like your cousin Rosa than before, Miss Lingwood. Not the hair, perhaps, but the features. Astonishing.'

I pulled my hand away, sent Ruth to fetch Mother and showed our visitor into the drawing room. Actually my knees were shaking. Last time I saw Max Stukeley he was sixteen or so and I was twelve. Then he had been a harbinger of doom, now he was tall and broad in his tight red tunic and dark blue trousers, all braid and gilt buttons, his dark eyes as disconcertingly keen as ever. In his large left hand he held a small basket of primroses. Father would not have approved of the dandyish flourish of his moustache.

While we waited for Mother, Max and I held an awkward conversation. He was entirely out of place in our drawing room because he wore strong colours, was very tall, and possessed, as I well remembered, pent-up energy that vented itself with constant movement, a restless prowling about the room and sudden lunges to pick up a book or ornament, to play a crashing chord on the piano or to dart a forceful, black-eyed glare at me. The drawing room, on the other hand, was designed for slow, small gestures, being decorated in pastel shades and crowded with delicate furniture.

I sat down and folded my hands. 'You are off to the war, then, Captain Stukeley.'

He balanced the primroses on the arm of a chair but didn't sit. 'This very evening, if they can find a ship large enough to cram in our horses. None of us will be separated from our beasts.'

I was about to ask: 'Are you looking forward to the war?' but decided that this was hardly an appropriate question. Instead I said, 'Father and I went to Buckingham Palace this morning to see the march past.'

'Did you indeed? I'm sure the men will be very gratified that you took the trouble.'

Every second I was remembering more of Max. After all, his eyes had exactly the same expression as when he was a boy, dangerously unsteady, flashing about as he took in every detail of his surroundings but then focusing abruptly on my face. This last remark of his, spoken with considerable irony, suggested that his manners had not improved at all.

'Is your family well?' I asked. 'In her last letter Rosa told me that your father had a bad accident with his horse.'

'An accident? Oh indeed. And he's not recovered. As a matter of fact none of my family is doing well at all, except Horatio, of course. Which is why I'm here.' He glanced at the clock. 'Will Mrs Lingwood be long, do you think?'

'She is dressing. We were about to go out.'

'So I see.' He raised an eyebrow, gave me a hot, sudden glance and nodded. 'That bonnet is certainly very fetching, Miss Lingwood, especially with those ribbons undone.'

I ducked my head to hide the flush that immediately climbed my neck. 'I understand you've been in Australia. How fascinating.'

He threw back his head and laughed, again a sharp memory. His rare laughter began as a chuckle and then, if he was really amused or if others joined in, his laugh became full-throated and prolonged. 'Fascinating. Absolutely. No other word for it. Sand and sky are *fascinating*, especially after a month or two of looking at nothing else.'

At that moment in came Mother, so burdened that she cracked the spike of her umbrella against the door frame and threw herself off balance. Her bonnet dangled from her hand, as did a capacious bag in which she carried the minutes from last year's Easter Garden meeting and she also clutched her gloves, cloak and a folded altar cloth because it had been our week for laundering the sacred linens. Max darted forward to help her and there was a flurry of laughter and movement as she disentangled herself, accepted the primroses with extravagant gratitude and glanced shyly into his face.

The ensuing conversation was conducted with breathless haste Both Mother and Max were in a hurry because if we arrived late Mrs Hardcastle would certainly use the extra few minutes to hold a private talk with the vicar, and Max behaved with the urgency of one who was rushing off to fight the entire war single-handed. He refused a seat and kept glancing at the door. 'The fact is, Mrs Lingwood, my stepmother begged me to call. She made me promise not to leave London without seeing you.'

'Ah, how is Isabella? I've not heard from her for weeks.'

'Your sister is not well, ma'am, but then she never is, in my experience. And she now has an additional burden of anxiety in that since his fall my father has been very ill with some debilitating disease of the gut . . . I don't expect him to be alive when I return from this war.'

Mother made sympathetic noises but Max shrugged. 'The trouble is that my brother, Horatio, will inherit Stukeley and as he plans to marry soon there will be no place for your sister or Rosa. The timing is unfortunate. Were I home I would do my best to provide for them. As it is, to be blunt, my stepmother doesn't trust Horatio to look after her and I'm afraid, from a brief conversation I had with him, her fears may be well justified.'

'But won't she be provided for in her husband's will?'

'He will make some small provision for her, I'm sure, but he's always been adamant that the estate should be left intact. The difficulty is that her health has declined so much that she needs constant nursing and because Father has scarcely been conscious for months he may not have left her a sufficient allowance. I'm not sure he has a proper grasp of just how desperate her situation might be. Hence Isabella's urgent request that I call on you.'

'But what can I do? Should I go to her, do you think? Would I be welcome? Now that Sir Matthew is ill, perhaps there would be no difficulty . . .' I could tell that Mother had mentally begun the process of cancelling her meetings and packing her bags. The news that Maria Lingwood had *gone north* to care for her sick sister, though inconvenient, would cause a gratifying flurry on the committees.

'I'm sure your sister and niece would be very happy to see you, but I think on the whole your presence would only add tension to an already difficult situation. At the moment Rosa is indispensable because oddly enough she is the only person my father will allow near him. Isabella's maid, Nora, is more than competent and willing to nurse him, but he has taken against her. There. You see, he's simply not rational. But when he dies . . .' He had the grace to look embarrassed.

'So what must we do?' asked Mother.

'Wait for news. There is no need for urgent action, but I fear it won't be long before your kindness will be called upon. I came to warn you, and I suppose to reassure myself that here at least Isabella and Rosa, and perhaps their maid, will be kindly received.'

He glanced into our faces, tucked his hat under his arm and looked so correct and handsome as he shook Mother's hand that for a moment I thought I had underestimated him. But then he stepped across to me, clicked his heels and kissed my hand so enthusiastically that I distinctly felt the brush of his ostentatious moustache, the pressure of his open lips and, as the kiss became prolonged, the hardness of his teeth. When he raised his head he winked at me. 'Wonderful bonnet, Miss Lingwood, it does my poor soldier's heart good to see how you have blossomed. I shall carry the image of you in that hat when I march into battle.'

Mother laughed but I was annoyed. Even when we were outside where the wind plucked at our skirts and blew our agitated conversation across the common the audacity of that wink and the fervour of his kiss still rankled.

Chapter Four

Derbyshire, 1844

Rosa's heroine was a young lady called Miss Florence Nightingale, who was ten years older than herself and had persuaded her father, a mill-owner in the next valley, to open a school for the children of the poor. Whilst in Derbyshire – her family had two other homes, in Hampshire and London – Miss Nightingale spent her days nursing the sick and her evenings teaching mill girls how to read.

'Everyone talks about her,' said Rosa, 'and I hope to meet her this summer. I want to be like her. Imagine what I could do one day, if Stepfather would let me. I could become someone who really made a difference.'

As a step towards this goal she lost no time in signing me up for a new-formed committee of the Society for the Improvement of the Conditions of the Sick, Needy and Uneducated at Stukeley of which she was the chairman and I was appointed secretary. Together we constituted the entire membership and we held our meetings in what was known as the Italian Garden where paths radiated from a central sundial, fountains played in each corner, a peach tree grew against one wall and there was a white pavilion.

At the end of June, some six weeks into our visit, a meeting had been arranged to draw up a curriculum for a prospective school. Aunt Isabella was unwell that day and after breakfast Rosa was summoned to her mother's room, so I went to the pavilion and waited for her. I felt very tired and low-spirited, the air was warm and breezy, and after half an hour or so I lay down on one of the cool stone benches and nearly fell asleep.

When I became aware that someone was watching me I didn't immediately open my eyes. But in the end I squinted up and saw

Rosa's black-haired stepbrother, Max, who was leaning against the pillar at my feet, hands behind his back, staring down at me. For a moment I lay still, dazzled by the combination of his intense dark eyes, the white pillar and the blue sky. He had placed his feet on either side of my calves and the expression in his eyes, tender, pitying even, pinned me to the bench. Then he was gone.

I turned my head and watched his progress across the garden. At one point he sprang onto the rim of a fountain, balanced for a moment and jumped down. When he reached the door in the wall he didn't look back but raised his left arm and let it fall to his side.

Meanwhile Rosa had appeared at the top of the wide flight of steps on the opposite side of the garden and was walking down, very slowly. When she reached me I saw that she was crying. She swept the back of her hand across her nose and eyes but tears kept spilling down her cheeks.

'You've got to pack your bags and go,' she said.

I sat upright so suddenly that a headache began in my temple. 'Why?'

'The stepfather says so. Evil man. Called you spongers. Mama's too ill to speak.'

'We're not spongers.'

'Of course not. We love you being here. We need you here. I can't bear it, Mariella.'

'I thought he liked us.'

'Well, now he's changed his mind. Typical of him. He's ordered the carriage. We've got to pack your things straight away. Your mother's waiting for you.'

'No, no, this isn't right.' I ran towards the house, the word *sponger* pounding in my head. I had to see Mother and find out the truth. But Rosa caught up with me, seized my arm and held me in a violent embrace. 'I can't bear it. I can't live without you. Please say you'll write every day, Mariella.' Her body shook as she cried into my hair while I stood very still and waited numbly for her to let me go.

Chapter Five

London, 1854

My next contribution to the Russian war was to make an album. Though this was originally Father's idea I took it up with enthusiasm because I was an expert on collecting, arranging and pasting. My last album, 'The Great Exhibition', had included programmes, tickets, detailed plans of the glass structure and sketches of exhibits. I had also made an album called 'Our Railways', and one coyly entitled: 'Miss Lingwood's Guide to Stitchcraft'.

But the front page, created on 15 March, turned out to be the new album's greatest triumph. First I cut red, white and blue ribbons to make a collage of a Union Jack on top of which I pasted the print from the *Illustrated London News* of the Scots Fusiliers waving their busbies to the Queen. Round this masterpiece I worked a pen and ink border with symbols of the war: the Russian bear, the Crucifix, a Minié rifle (drawn by Father), the Union Jack and the fleur de lys, all entwined with daffodils, crocuses and roses (the latter unseasonable but one of my few areas of expertise as an artist). Next, on 29 March, I cut out the thrilling headline: 'Declaration of War'. After that I ran out of ideas because the war had stuttered to a halt.

Henry called to say goodbye at the end of March before setting off on his trip to Budapest. As he gave us no warning of his visit, Mother was out with Mrs Hardcastle. A house for the governesses had been identified, a lease signed and now the ladies were measuring windows so that a final decision could be made about lace (second-hand, because it so happened that Mrs Hardcastle was replacing all hers) or muslin (new) for the curtains. I was at work in the morning room, restless because outside the sky was a riotous blue and white, trees tossed their budding branches and women held on to their bonnets. When the maid brought Henry up I was taken unawares and stood foolishly with my sewing clutched against my skirts. We were both shocked, I think, by the suddenness with which we found ourselves alone together.

He had brought an armful of daffodils. 'I have just been at the Elms. The garden is full of these, going to waste because there's no one to see them. But the painting has begun and there's a range in the kitchen so things are moving forwards.'

He spilled the flowers into Ruth's arms, took a seat on a distant chair and accepted my offer of tea though he could stay barely quarter of an hour. 'Yet another commission,' he said. 'This one about public health and hygiene. I'll see if I can get your father a place on the board. He knows more about sewers and suchlike than anyone else. They have heard I'm going to Hungary and they want me to report back on the state of that nation's public health. I've told them it is scarcely my field but it's surprising how, when one has become a known authority in one thing, one is expected to be an authority on everything.'

'You must be very proud,' I said.

'Proud? I don't know. A little daunted. The awful thing is one runs out of time for the really important things. Best of all I like to be in the theatre with my patients and students, and I ought to do more reading and research. The use of chloroform, for instance, to put patients asleep during an operation is an area that I believe will transform surgery, but I've had no time to analyse the latest findings on its dangers and effectiveness. Instead I rush from one meeting to the next. Being in Hungary will at least give me time to study and reflect.'

When Ruth brought first the daffodils in a vase, then tea, Henry lay back and watched me pour, his legs stretched to the fire and his foot inches from my own. After she had gone he said, 'I always rest when I'm here. With you I can be utterly myself.' Then his tone changed. 'But tell me, Mariella, what have you been up to since last we met? Not resting much either, I'm sure.'

'I have been making a war album but I refuse to show you because it's such a feeble thing so far. And these are a set of pillowcases for our governesses. Each is to have a matching pair with different flower motifs in the corners. Crocus, daisy, lily-of-the-valley. Mother is working me very hard.'

'And after the home is open, what then? I can't believe that you and your mother would ever be idle.'

'Oh I can hardly think that far ahead. The fund-raising will go on, I suppose. If it's a success there's talk of opening another house in a different part of London, this time for seamstresses. And we still don't know when or if Aunt Isabella and Rosa will come to stay.'

'Ah. The famous Rosa. I shall be intrigued to meet her after all these years.'

'Perhaps she will have changed and will turn out to be very ordinary after all.'

'I hope not. I would be very disappointed.'

The room held us quietly with its ticking clock and lick of flames in the hearth but still he said nothing significant about our future. When it was time for him to go I reached for the bell-pull in the dreary knowledge that soon I would be alone at the start of yet another lengthy period of doubt and longing. But as my fingers touched the tassel he made a sign to stop me and drew me up so that we stood between the tea table and the fire while I looked at the high polish on his shoes and he studied my face. 'You are my ideal,' he said. 'So utterly content in your own world. So selfless in your service of others.'

'But I do nothing. What is a pillowcase here or there compared to what you achieve?'

'The essential, I think, is to be an expert, to give oneself wholly to the task in hand. You are an expert at being Mariella. Your regard for detail adds up to one dedicated whole. You create around you an oasis of calm. Never change, my dearest girl.'

He took my face in his cupped hands and leaned forward to kiss my forehead where my parting began. My eyes closed and I felt his lips on my nose, then, very softly, on my mouth. 'Mariella.'

Almost before I realised that he had at last kissed me on the lips he was gone; his feet clattered on the stairs, the front door slammed and when I ran to the window I saw him walk rapidly away across the common.

I stood in a stupor of joy, staring at my own reflection in the mirror above the hearth. My body was aching, my face flushed, my eyes bright. I buried my face in the daffodils and my head was filled with spring. When I took up my sewing I didn't care that my fingers left a smear of pollen along a seam.

Chapter Six

We read in *The Times* that the navy was threatening Russian ships and ports in the Baltic Sea which, as Father showed me on the globe, was miles from what he called the *seat* of war, but I stuck in a sketch map, still somewhat unclear about what was meant by the Baltic States: Finland, apparently, Latvia and fortresses at Sveaborg and Kronstadt which protected the Russian capital, St Petersburg. It gave me a thrill to consult a globe because I could track Henry's journey to Pest. But nothing much else happened in the Baltic, either. Our navy's job, said Father, was to *crush* the Russian fleet. I imagined a flotilla of little wooden boats all in splinters. Our troops, meanwhile, were landed in Constantinople (upon a sheet of parchment, soaked in tea, I wrote a recklessly abbreviated history of that ancient city). At the end of April Father suggested I draw another map, this time of the Mediterranean, with arrows to mark the trade routes, showing why the Russians must not be allowed to take Constantinople from the Turks. If they did, he said, our *entire* empire was at stake, including India, because bullying Russia would be able eventually to march away with the lot. On the next page I drew a steamship. A journey to the Black Sea took eight days by steam, a month by sail. A long explanation by Father followed, including a diagram, labelled by me, of how the giant screws were turned by steam to work the paddles.

After that I lost interest and instead returned to the much more rewarding project of sewing flower motifs on the governesses' hand towels to match the pillowcases. The opening of the home had been put back to early July because no reliable relief matron could be found, which gave me more time to prepare a little entertainment for the assembled residents and dignitaries. I had chosen to sing 'Where'ere you walk . . .' though the accompaniment was very tricky. These particular lyrics were appropriate, we thought, to the governesses, particularly the trees crowding into a shade, though not perhaps the implied romance. When I thought of green glades I imagined the garden at The Elms on leafy summer afternoons.

And then a black-bordered letter arrived from Aunt Isabella which put the disappointing war, the governesses and even, for half an hour or so, Henry, completely out of my head.

Stukeley Hall
12 May 1854

My dear sister,

I have dreadful news. My husband is no more. [Tears had fallen on the word 'more' making it almost illegible.]

I believe Max told you, whilst in London, that we had little hope. Perhaps, even then, I underestimated the severity of his illness. Since December, when he fell from his horse in that unspeakable lane, he has required constant nursing and scarcely left his room. I am worn to a shadow of myself.

The terms of the will are not in my favour. I am bearing up, I expected nothing, but it seems very hard, after all [more tears, the next line an illegible smear]. *The estate, Stukeley, all goes to Horatio and, as you know, over the years that young man and I have had our differences. Maximilian is to have a small income but Rosa and I, it seems, are nearly destitute. We have what we stand up in, little more. It's very hard . . . I don't understand how . . .*

Dear sister, I am so weak I can scarcely raise my head from the pillow but I cannot bear to live in this house another minute where I am not welcome and where I have so many, many memories which rise up to torment me at every turn. You would think, after all I've done for his father . . .

Rosa urged me to write. A change of scene, she says, may be my only hope. We are coming, dear sister, to London. I never thought . . .

Here my aunt's writing faded out altogether. Instead, in a much firmer, larger hand, cousin Rosa had written:

We are sorry to give you no warning. The truth is we can't stand it here another minute. We'll take the nine-fifteen train from Derby on Friday next (19 May). We won't be any trouble because Mother will bring her maid, Nora. We should be with you by early evening.
Rosa

Since Mother was preoccupied with the governesses, preparations for our visitors were left to me and the task was daunting. Rosa and her mother were used to the airy spaces of Stukeley Hall and its marble floors, Turkish rugs, vistas of spreading lawns, gushing fountains and walled gardens. Fosse House, Clapham, built by Father to accommodate the three of us and a handful of servants, couldn't possibly live up to such splendour. Besides, unless Rosa had changed completely she would want to explore every inch of the house from attic to cellar and expect me to know the history of each item of furniture.

Ruth, though inclined to drift about and break things, was useful if given clear instructions. She and I took up the carpets so that the scullery maid could beat them while we cleaned and polished the boards; we lifted down the books in the drawing room, wiped the leaves and spine of each volume and dusted the shelves; we used stepladders to reach the pictures so we could clean the frames and wash the picture rails. We sent the table-covers, antimacassars, doilies and runners down to be washed; we had vinegar and water brought up for the windows which we cleaned in every room on all floors despite the sun blasting through and half blinding us; we swept under beds and aired the eiderdowns and we polished the cabinets and plumped the cushions. Then I rushed out to the garden and cut armfuls of white roses, columbines and forget-me-nots because unlike at Stukeley we had neither hothouse nor conservatory and must therefore put up with seasonal flowers. I thought even Rosa and Aunt Isabella would be impressed by the perfume of beeswax and petals and by the new braiding on the cushions. But in the event, nobody noticed. In the event, the state of the house was the last thing on anybody's mind.

Early on Friday evening Mother and I sat nervously in the drawing room waiting for Father to bring our visitors from the station. Despite our nerves we managed to discuss quite calmly, for perhaps the tenth time, how much mourning was appropriate for a brother-in-law and uncle-by-marriage visited only once a decade ago. As I didn't have any black I was wearing my midnight-blue taffeta but mother had shaken her black satin out of mothballs. However, as a compromise, after consultation with Mrs Hardcastle, she wore a white collar and a grey velvet ribbon threaded through the lace of her cap. 'The last thing I want is to be too ostentatious. After all, I scarcely knew Sir Matthew and didn't take to him that time we were there.' She paused. 'Of course, he was fond of you, I always thought.'

I was embroidering a quilt with tendrils of ivy; the design, pricked out with a pin, required five different shades of green. 'I don't think he paid much attention to me.'

'Oh but he did, surely you remember.' She watched me for a moment. 'But he struck me as a very difficult man, I'm afraid. I hope he mellowed in later years and has been kind to Rosa.'

There was the sound of carriage wheels on gravel, the bell rang, then there were voices in the hall. We sprang to our feet and tucked our work out of sight, glancing at each other in a moment of rueful admission that everything was about to change. First to appear was Ruth, very self-important, then Aunt Isabella bedecked from top to toe in black crêpe, her eyes brimming and her face plumper than ever. Rosa stood on tiptoe, craning for a sight of me over her mother's shoulder. She too wore black and the tucks in her bonnet framed a face grown even more beautiful than when she was a young girl. Her features were finely drawn, her dark blue eyes ardent and her moist lips trembling.

She dodged round her mother, rushed to my side, fell to her knees and flung her arms round my waist. From deep in my skirts I heard her muffled voice: 'Now, I think, I shall begin to be happy again.'

For a moment I was bewildered by this sudden onslaught then I bent down, took her by the elbows and raised her up. We stared into each other's face, laughing and tearful, until she pulled me towards her and kissed me.

Meanwhile Father was in the doorway, shifting his gloves from one hand to the other. 'The traffic was atrocious. An hour and a half, it took us. Still, if you're all settled I'll get back to work. There are some plans I have to look at before dinner . . .'

Rosa sprang forward and seized his arm. 'Uncle Philip, it is so, so kind of you to have us to stay. I don't think you have any idea how grateful we are.'

Father flushed and held out his hands as if to ward her off. 'There. It's nothing. My wife and Mariella will love you being here, though I must warn you that before you know it they'll have you up to your eyes in some project or another. But look, we have empty rooms in this great house. It's high time they were filled...' His eyes were dewy with sentiment as he strode away across the hall to his study.

After he'd gone Ruth appeared with a tray of tea. She and I had agreed to use the best set with gold trim and a rosebud design. But just as Ruth had embarked on the perilous journey between the miniatures' cabinet and the end of the chaise, my aunt gave a moaning sigh and fell back on the sofa. Her bosom heaved, her gloved hand fluttered feebly and her complexion went livid. This so startled poor Ruth that the tray jerked in her hand, cups toppled over on their saucers and the sugar basin rolled off altogether and smashed against a table.

'Dearest,' cried my mother. 'Dearest Bella.'

'Oh good Lord,' said Rosa, springing across to the window where she scooped back the lace curtain and flung the French door wide open. Then she hauled her mother's feet, shoes and all, onto the sofa, untied her bonnet, dragged her cape from under her and unfastened her blouse. 'A doctor?' said my mother. 'Shall I call a Doctor? Ruth, put down that tray, for goodness' sake.'

'Give her time,' said Rosa, 'she'll come round. It's her heart.'

'Her *heart*.'

'Some condition that means she must have no sudden exertion, no excitement, no travel. The doctors warned us not to come.' Rosa took a bottle of salts from Mother and thrust it under Aunt's nose. The result was a terrifying fit of gasps and splutters during which my aunt spread her legs and arms and, when she could speak, begged for water.

'Call for Nora,' said Rosa. 'She knows what to do with her.'

Nora was a squarish woman with a thick Irish accent, dense skin the colour of curds and sparse hair. She and Mother half carried Aunt upstairs to the best guest room while Ruth, with a heartbroken glance at the tumbled porcelain on the tea tray, gathered up the pieces of sugar basin and Aunt's discarded cape and bonnet; I swabbed the spilled milk with a napkin and Rosa poured tea and cut herself a slice of fruit cake.

Once she and I were alone I felt as shy as when I was a child. She shared with her stepbrother Max the knack of concentrating all the energy of a room on herself. Yet, compared to the glamour of her shimmering hair and slender figure, her adult voice, deeper than I remembered, was almost shocking for the prosaic words it formed. 'She's always doing that,' she said.

'Is she very ill?'

'Lord knows. I'm so used to it I presume she'll go on for ever although we all act as if she may drop dead at any moment. Ironic, isn't it, that in the end it was *he* who died? Mama never thought she'd outlive him. She was forever apologising to him because she said he'd be a widower for the second time.' She finished the cake, brushed down her skirts, sprang to her feet and began a tour of the room, picking up ornaments and picture frames, adjusting mats, flicking through a heap of piano music and playing a few trills and arpeggios. When she came to the war album she paused to turn the pages. 'Is this yours?'

'Father likes me to take an interest in world affairs.'

She peered a little more closely. 'Are you *sure* about that Prussian border? I would have thought the Russian Empire extended further west than that ... So, are you for or against the war?'

'Against? Nobody is against the war.'

'I am. Of course I am. You surely can't be for it. Nobody has yet given me a coherent reason why we are at war with the Russians.'

'In my album there's a cutting from *The Times* that gives our reasons. The Russians treat their own people abominably and they threaten our very freedom.'

'How?'

'They want a foothold in the Mediterranean.'

'How do you know?'

'Well, it's obvious. Father says they will break up Turkey and take everything. And then there's the question of Jerusalem.'

'What about Jerusalem?'

'Well, I mean, we can't allow the Holy Places to fall into the hands of Russia.'

'Why?'

'It's to do with Christian—'

'The Russians are Christian.'

'No they're not, they're Orthodox.'

'Christian. The Turks, on the other hand, are Muslim.'

'I know. I know.'

'And to cap it all we are also siding with the French. Have you considered how odd that is?'

'Father says that is another excellent thing about the war; that for once we are not squabbling with our nearest neighbour.'

'But what do you think our real motives are? Have you considered?'

'I've told you. Russia—'

'Politics. The government doesn't have the wit or the will to stop it. And of course we are all supposed to be bored because we haven't been at war for forty years. And everyone says our great and glorious country should strike a blow against oppressive Russia, never mind the fact that masses of our own population are half starved or slaving in factories sixteen hours a day.'

'The Russians have serfs. That's different.'

'Mariella! Thousands of people will die in this war, including, incidentally, Max. You haven't come up with anything that justifies that.' She stood at the window, held aside the lace curtain and peered out.

How dreadful, I thought. She's scarcely been in the room ten minutes and already we've argued. I was pierced by feelings I had not experienced for years: the sense of being absolutely in the spotlight, the desire to impress coupled with the fear of falling short of expectation.

She was as still as a sculpture in her black gown, her hair loosely wound over a ribbon and tumbled down her back. Was it the fact that she came from the north, I wondered, that made her so indifferent to fashion? Though she certainly wasn't poor, her dress had no petticoats to speak of so the skirt fell in a straight line from a high waist and I could clearly see the shape of her bosom and hips. I had been rather contented with my own appearance, apart from the vexed question of whether or not to wear black, but suddenly I felt trussed like a chicken in my corset, full sleeves and tight collar. My hair, even if allowed to fall loose, would never achieve those thick ringlets.

I picked up my sewing case, unfastened it, selected medium moss-green silk and separated three strands.

'I didn't realise it would feel so rural here,' she said. 'I thought you were much closer to London.'

'We are quite near. Sometimes I walk to the river. Or we can take an omnibus, or the carriage.'

'Tomorrow, will you show me the sights?'

'I'm afraid I don't know London that well.'

'You've lived here all your life.'

'Yes, but I don't go to the city much.'

Her blue, bright gaze was fixed on my face. 'But why not?'

'I hardly need to.'

'But it's there. London is *there*. I thought you must go all the time.'

'Oh I've hardly any time. We're so busy.'

'Why, what are you doing? How does your time get filled up?'

'There are so many things to do. Mother likes me to help in the garden, and I do all the household accounts. And then I am sewing for the Distressed Governesses.'

'The who?' She stared at me in a mix of disbelief and amusement.

'We have raised money for a house in Bloomsbury. All that remains is for the house to be furnished.'

'How wonderful. Could I help? Can we go there?'

'We can, yes. If you like.'

'I want, so much, to be useful.' She lightly tapped her toe as I went on sewing. 'I can hardly believe that I am here. All these weeks, months, years this is what I've wanted more than anything else – to be in the same room as you again.'

'What do you mean? You can't mean it.'

'Nobody else gives me this feeling. What is it? Completion. The sense of being in absolutely the right place with absolutely the right person.'

'But you had so many friends in the north. Your letters were full of parties and outings.'

'Nonsense. All shallow, except for a very few exceptional people. There was no one to replace you. When I see you bent over your work like that I remember your little brown head when we were children, your hair dropping onto your hands, the way I could never find out what was going on inside you however hard I tried.'

'There was nothing to discover.'

'Oh there was. Oh Mariella.'

I stared into her blue eyes and recognised that her features were exquisitely spaced. It was as if some artist, Alfred Stevens perhaps, had made deft marks with his charcoal on the perfect oval of her face.

'Mariella, am I sharing a room with you, like we did before?'

'We thought you'd prefer your own room.'

'But don't you remember the fun we had? I was fully expecting that we'd be sleeping together again.'

'We have plenty of rooms and my bedroom is small. We thought, as you may be with us some time, you might like somewhere of your own.'

'I've had years on my own. You saw how vast and empty Stukeley was. I was always lonely there. Or is it that you don't want to be with me?' Dismay and uncertainty lurked at the back of her eyes.

'I thought you would find me dull and our house too small.'

'Small? No. Not small at all. It's a home, full of loved things, I can tell. And dull? You? You were never dull. Mariella, this last year has been like living in a dark tunnel with no glimmer of light at the end. And then when Stepfather was dying Max and I thought of asking you to rescue us, and all of a sudden I was full of hope. I've held on to all your letters, and to the memory of those weeks we had together, the only time in my life when I've had a proper friend of my own age dearer than a sister.' We stood breast to breast, her cheek against mine. Even though I didn't quite believe that she could feel so much for me, it felt wonderful to tightly held. I put my hand on her shoulder and kissed her, just below the ear.

Chapter Seven

Derbyshire, 1844

When Mother and I first arrived at Stukeley neither of the stepbrothers was home. The older, Horatio, was just completing his first year at Oxford and the younger, Maximilian, was at boarding school in Malvern. 'He'll be back any minute though,' said Rosa. 'You'll see. He never stays anywhere for long.'

In the meantime she and I spent hours on our own. We had duties to our respective mothers, Aunt Isabella needed occasional nursing even then, and I was required to continue with my cursory education; otherwise we were free. Rosa used to hook her arm through mine and lead me to one of her secret haunts: a box hedge, hollow inside like a green cave; a turret with a view over half of Derbyshire; and a dressing room attached to her bedroom where we sat under the dangling hems of her frocks. She had an obsession with being hidden away in a confined space that meant I soon knew her intimately – the way her hair sprang in an irrepressible curl on the right side of her forehead, the fact that one front tooth was fractionally longer than the other, the angle at which the stem of her throat rose from the loose neck of her gown. When she was excited it was her habit to weave the fabric of her skirt over and under her fingers, then pull them out and dig them back into the little tunnels they'd made, and I became familiar with the grassy scent of her clean breath.

'Why do you like hiding places so much?' I asked.

'They're not *hiding* places, completely the opposite. I like being where nothing can distract me from myself or you. In a secret place I can be sure of being what I want to be. As opposed to what others want. Especially *him*, that man, Stukeley. I never want him to find me.'

The box hedge ran in a neat square round the outside of the water garden, broken in places to allow paths to run through the gaps. We entered it at one end and, by crouching down, tunnelled our way to a little open space right in its very heart. The first time I sat there with Rosa, cross-legged, knee to knee, she leaned forward and clasped both my hands. 'Tell me all about your life at home.'

'Oh there's nothing to tell.'

'There must be. What do you like? Who do you like? How do you spend your days?'

I told her about my sewing and showed her the smocking on my blouse and the embroidery on my pocket.

'Would I be able to do something like that?' she cried, peering intently. 'I can't believe you made those tiny stitches.'

'It would take a while for you to learn. Perhaps we should start with something quite simple, like a needle book. You see I was taught by an expert, my aunt Eppie, who was a professional needlewoman. She practically supported her family with her needle, right up to her death.'

'Ah, so she's dead.'

'She is.' I took a deep breath. I couldn't help myself, I had to speak his name. 'And since then my second cousin, Henry, has become like a son to my father and mother. He lived with us for a while and he still comes to our house whenever he can. Father takes a great interest in his education.'

'How old is this Henry?'

'Now he's nearly twenty.'

'And if he's like a son to your parents, does that mean he's like a brother to you?'

'A brother? Well. Perhaps. I don't know what brothers are like . . .'

'Stepbrothers are not much use to anyone.'

'Henry's not like that. Henry, I'd say, is more than a brother. When he stayed with us I was only eight but I spent hours with him and we talked all the time.'

'What did you talk about?'

'Everything. Medicine quite a lot, even then. He's studying to be a doctor.'

'I wish Max would do something worthwhile, but he won't, I'm sure. If he became a doctor, for instance, at least I could help him by being his housekeeper. Mariella, you're so lucky.'

'I know.'

'Do you love him?'

'Of course I love him.'

'Like a husband?'

'Oh no, not at all. Not like that. In any case, he's much older than me.'

'But you love him, I can tell. Oh Mariella, please don't love this Henry more than me. You won't, will you?' She cupped my chin in her hands and rubbed my nose with hers until I giggled. 'I love you better than anyone else in the world,' she whispered.

Chapter Eight

London, 1854

The day after Rosa and Aunt Isabella's arrival I was woken early by a commotion downstairs: a brisk knock on the front door followed by Mother's voice in the hall. Rosa was still asleep in the bed we'd had carried in from another room. With her hair spread over the pillow and one arm bent behind her head, she might have been modelling for a painting of the kind displayed at the Royal Academy.

I tiptoed onto the landing, peered down and saw that the doctor was being shown into my aunt's room, though it was barely seven o'clock. Mother would never dream of putting him to such inconvenience unless Aunt Isabella was dangerously ill.

I dressed in the room intended for Rosa. The air was perfumed with the flowers I'd picked for her, and mats with edges of hairpin lace, crocheted by me, were scattered about to receive her bottles and brushes. Ruth and I had buffed the barley-twist bedposts and dusted every last bit of moulding on the mantel. The windows overlooked the garden with its winding path under the rose arch to the wilderness, although this last now seemed a somewhat vainglorious name for a quarter acre of shrubbery. Our entire Clapham plot would have fitted into the Italian garden alone at Stukeley.

After half an hour I heard the front door close so I crept downstairs to join Mother at breakfast. She told me that during the night Aunt had suffered severe palpitations and was still fighting for breath. The doctor had ordered that she was to be kept in complete seclusion, preferably bed-rest, for the next week at least. The long railway journey, coupled with the strain of recent widowhood, had put an intolerable stress on her heart and nerves.

'It's unkind of me to say this, I know, but it's inconvenient,' said Mother. 'I have so much on.'

'I can help.'

'Of course you can. And there's Rosa, and their maid.'

'What did Father say?'

'He said we must do everything necessary, of course. But he was in a hurry. There's been a problem with the Wandsworth site to do with the proximity of the railway. The drains are affected.'

Rosa appeared in a flowing white dressing gown that swirled round her feet when she stooped to kiss us. She threw into sharp relief anything in the room that was old or shabby yet when she touched a chair-back or a napkin they suddenly became part of the graceful picture that was Rosa. She was blooming after her long sleep. 'You cannot imagine how wonderful it is to be here. I woke up and thought: I can't believe I have actually got away. That house in Derbyshire had become a mausoleum.' She reached across the table for the coffee pot and spread a lavish helping of butter on her toast. 'So tell me,' she said, 'what shall we do today?'

'Your mother is ill, Rosa, dear,' said my mother. 'We called in the doctor.'

'There was no need. She'll soon pick up.'

'He thinks not. He said she'll need constant nursing. It's always a worry when the heart is affected.'

'Nora can do it. That's why we brought her down with us.'

'Nora was up all last night, she needs to sleep.' Rosa had stopped eating and was watching Mother attentively. 'For the time being at least, while your mother is so sick, I think we must be sure she gets proper care. And I feel it would be inappropriate to bring a nurse in from outside, the moment you arrive.'

Rosa pushed back her chair and got up. 'I'll nurse her, of course I will, it's no trouble. I'm used to it. I wouldn't want us to be a burden on you. Perhaps Mariella and I could just step outside for an hour or so to get some air first, if you wouldn't mind, dear Aunt Maria, just taking care while we . . .' She dashed away tears. 'I'm sorry, I'm sorry. I'm a little weary of nursing, that's why I'm being selfish. My stepfather had a dreadful illness, some kind of growth in the gut. Mama couldn't bear to be near him and he was so bad-tempered the nurses wouldn't stay, except Nora, but he disliked her. And he was good with me, he seemed much calmer when I was there. I never mind being with sick people really. In fact it's how I'd choose to spend my life, if I could be of proper use. I'll go up to Mama immediately . . .'

She flew out of the room. We heard her pause in the hall and draw a long, shuddering breath, then her light step on the stairs.

An hour later she and I were in the omnibus heading for the river while Mother stayed at home to nurse her sister. 'I have only to cancel a short meeting this morning. It's nothing. Poor Rosa deserves a little holiday.'

Nevertheless Mother's sacrifice weighed heavily on my conscience as Rosa and I sat knee to knee with an elderly gentleman in a dusty hat, and a nursemaid holding a young child, all three transfixed by Rosa, who was peering hungrily out of the window and whose glinting hair provided a fetching contrast to her black gown, shawl and bonnet. 'First we'll go to Marylebone,' she said, 'where I have an appointment.'

'An appointment? But how could you? We didn't know what would be happening today.'

'I wrote to my friend, Miss Barbara Leigh Smith, that I'd call this morning if possible. She'll be expecting me, I'm sure. Come on, let's walk, we're missing too much,' and she dived across the knees of the other passengers and strode out in her serviceable boots while I tottered along in my smart shoes and was jostled by the crowd. She asked the way in her ringing voice and then away she dashed again, dodging handcarts and perambulators as if she had been a Londoner all her life.

'Who is this Miss Leigh Smith? I didn't know you had friends in London,' I panted, catching up with her at last.

'Apart from you? Well, this is someone I've been writing to for a couple of years, a cousin of our Derbyshire acquaintances, the Nightingales. I found out through their aunt Julia that they never acknowledge this Barbara because she's illegitimate, even though she is just about the most accomplished and brilliant woman in the country. She's a close friend of Dr Elizabeth Blackwell. *Surely* you've heard of Elizabeth Blackwell, Mariella, a real, qualified woman doctor in the United States.'

She marched up the steps of 5 Blandford Square and rang the bell. 'We mustn't stay long,' I whispered as the door opened. 'Don't you think we may be needed back home?' I was still reeling from her casual use of the word *illegitimate.*

The house reeked of oil paint and Miss Leigh Smith received us in a first-floor sitting room arranged as a studio; sheets were draped across the furniture, the curtains had been pinned back, an oil cloth covered the floor and an easel was set up by the window. She wore a voluminous wrap-around apron and her auburn hair, definitely her most beautiful feature, was pulled firmly from a jutting forehead. At first she looked puzzled when Rosa introduced herself. 'Miss Barr? I'm sorry . . . I don't . . .' Then seized both her hands: 'Rosa Barr. Of course. My correspondent from the north.' Her handshake was disturbingly firm and she held a brush in her other hand. Although she whipped the covers off chairs so we could sit down, we had obviously disturbed her work. 'I belong to a society of painters and we set ourselves challenges by picking themes. For next month we have chosen the subject of *Desolation* and I am right at the beginning.'

'Goodness,' said Rosa, peering into the canvas.

'Yes, well, it's a theme that suits our mood. There is plenty of desolation in our world at the moment. One doesn't have to look far. What do you think?' Rosa and I stared at a landscape so full of the rushing movement of wind, clouds and sea that I felt a tremor of excitement, as if Henry had touched me.

'It's wonderful,' said Rosa. 'The sky is brilliant, those racing clouds . . . I paint, but only pastels. I would have no idea how to use oils like this, layer on layer.'

'I took classes at Bedford College. Have you heard of it? I think having proper lessons and the influence of other people make all the difference. My friends help me – I have wonderful friends. Have you heard of the artist Gabriel Rossetti, for instance? He is my inspiration.'

'But how do you find these people? Can anyone attend that college? Is it very expensive?'

The doorbell rang and in came two gloomily dressed women who hugged and called each other by their Christian names, Marian and Bessie. I pushed my chair back a little. My gown was far too elaborate compared to theirs and their talk frightened me, especially when they asked Barbara about a paper she was writing on married women who divorce. Until that moment I had never even heard the word *divorce* uttered in public.

Rosa said, 'What is the argument of your paper?'

'We have a friend called Caroline Norton,' said Bessie, 'whose husband took her children away from her because he and she had quarrelled. Ever since then she has been fighting for the rights of women to see their own children even after separation from their husbands.'

A hot blackness was coming upon me. We shouldn't be here. Mother really would not like me to be among these people; if Mrs Hardcastle found out we would never hear the last of it. The long-faced woman called Marian turned to me suddenly and said, 'And what do you do, Miss Lingwood?'

'Do? Well, I—'

'Mariella and her mother are founding a home for retired governesses,' said Rosa. 'I'm hoping to make some small contribution myself. Mariella's sewing is exquisite. I have never seen anyone so fast and neat with the needle.'

'But I am looking for a needlewoman, Miss Lingwood,' exclaimed Barbara. 'Do you also do plain sewing? I need ladies to come and help out in the school I am setting up. We want the children to learn useful as well as creative and intellectual skills. Perhaps you would consider teaching for me, it need only be an hour or two a week.'

'Oh no. I couldn't teach.'

'Well, my school won't be starting for a few months yet. There is plenty of time for you to think about it.'

'But in the meantime your home is very timely, Miss Lingwood,' said Bessie. 'These single women, too old to work and after a life of service, deserve better than to die hungry and alone. What wonderful work.'

'Do you know, I believe that's what my cousin Flo is up to at present,' said Barbara, 'managing a home of a similar kind. And I do mean managing.'

'And you, Rosa, what is your field of work?' asked the insatiable Marian.

'I have no field. I suppose my dream would be to become a proper nurse, or even a doctor, if only that were possible. Mariella has a cousin who is a very highly respected surgeon. I'm hoping that now I'm in London, I might gain some introductions through him, at least get the chance to observe an operation and maybe attend one or two lectures.'

'That's a courageous and wonderful ambition,' said Bessie. 'Perhaps we can help you in some way. If my cousin Elizabeth Blackwell comes back to London you must meet her. What is the name of your relative, Miss Lingwood? We are interested in finding doctors who will promote the cause of women in the medical profession.'

I could barely keep my voice steady. 'My cousin?'

'You know. Henry, the one you always used to talk about when you came to Stukeley,' said Rosa. 'The one you often write to me about.'

'You mean my *second* cousin, Henry Thewell? The surgeon. But he's away.'

'How disappointing. He was one of the reasons I came to London,' said Rosa. 'Well, when he's back, I'm hoping that he'll show me the work of his hospital.'

I stood up and made a sort of lunge towards the door. 'We must go. We promised to be back for lunch.'

'Come again,' said Barbara, 'any time. Please.'

Still Rosa wouldn't leave. She loitered in the room, studying one painting after another until she came to a pencil drawing of a woman with full lips and flowers in her hair. 'Wonderful. If only I could sketch like this.'

'Lizzie Siddal,' Barbara said. 'Have you heard of her? The mistress of the artist Gabriel Rossetti I was telling you about. We were with them in Sussex recently but she seemed very ill to me. We all wonder if he'll marry her or not, or if she'll live long enough . . .'

Never in my life before, or perhaps not since my last evening at Stukeley, had I so wished to escape my present situation. Blood had rushed to my face, my clothes pinched me and my heart pumped violently. 'The time,' I murmured and then at last we were in the hall, out on the sunlit street and walking away.

Rosa gave a series of little skips and thrust her arm through mine. 'Wasn't Barbara amazing? Isn't she the most fortunate woman in the world? To have her own household, to have such friends. Perhaps one day you and I will have a home together like hers, just the two of us, where we can paint and sew and talk about important things with other women. Everything seems possible to Barbara.'

I said nothing.

'Look at me compared to her,' she said. 'I'm nearly twenty-four. What have I done with my life? You're different. You have a purpose, Mariella – the governesses' home.'

'It's not my purpose. You shouldn't have said it was.'

She stopped dead. 'You're upset. What have I said?'

'The governesses' home is not what I do. I sew for it, that's all. But it's not my life. You should have told them the truth. It's as if you were ashamed to say I simply live with my parents.'

'But I did tell them the truth. You are always busy. Your letters to me are full of the latest garment you've made or lecture or concert you've been to. I, on the other hand, when I'm in Derbyshire, never drive five miles beyond Stukeley. And in those five miles there might be a dozen families with whom we are on speaking terms, and most of those bore me to tears. Whereas here, within five miles or so of your house, you are in reach of the most thrilling people alive today.'

'Rosa, where are you going? We haven't time to visit a park. We ought to find an omnibus and go home.'

'Oh not yet. Please. Your mother said we should take as long as we liked. Look at that little boy rolling down the slope. Do you remember there was a bank in the woods at Stukeley we used to run down?'

She had her arm tightly linked through mine again and before I knew it we were walking in step and suddenly my irritation left me and I had that old sensation of speed and danger that came with being alone with Rosa. On we walked, faster and faster, hip to hip, with the breeze in our faces and our legs swinging forwards like those of the soldiers in front of Buckingham Palace.

But at last I persuaded her that it was nearly two o'clock, well past lunch, and we really should go home. So we recrossed the river on the old Westminster Bridge where she paused, peered dreamily down towards the dome of St Paul's and quoted in a quiet, precise voice: '*Dull would he be of soul who could pass by / A sight so touching in its majesty* . . . Yes. I see now. Of course the fields have gone, and Wordsworth's air was smokeless, I suppose, because it was early morning, but yes, I see, it's the contrast between the river and sky and the city that he noticed. The way we all fit into an ideal whole.'

'He didn't mention the smell of the river, though,' I said, pulling her away. 'And some days it's even worse than this.'

When we reached home, Ruth opened the door almost before I'd put my hand to the knocker. Still untrained in London ways, she yelled over her shoulder: 'They're back, Ma'am.'

Mother's head appeared over the banisters. 'My dear girls, where have you been? Oh thank God.'

We flung aside our bonnets and sprang across to the stairs thinking that Isabella must be dead. Then we saw that Aunt was in fact trailing down towards us in a voluminous nightgown, her head encased in a cap with floating ribbons, both hands clinging to the rail. 'Rosa! What happened to you?'

'We were out for a walk,' said Rosa. 'The time passed quickly. Whatever is the matter?'

Isabella sank down on the stairs, buried her face in her hands and sobbed. 'You will be the death of me. You have no idea what happens to young girls in London. I could not endure another loss. Rosa, promise me it's not going to begin again, all the running around and not saying where you are. Promise never to go out alone again. I have been worried sick.'

'I wasn't alone, I was with Mariella. Mama, you're not well, otherwise you'd see there was no need to worry. It is a beautiful day. Why don't you come outside and sit in the garden for a while? You'll soon feel better.'

'I thought you were dead.'

'How could I be dead? What could possibly kill me? Here I am, safe and sound. Come now, perhaps you'd prefer to go back to bed. I'm sure dear Ruth will bring us up some tea.' Rosa's voice was soothing but she handled her mother firmly as she and Ruth took an arm each and escorted her back upstairs.

Mother hurried me into the breakfast parlour, the damp patches under her arms a sure sign that she was flustered. 'You missed luncheon. I waited as long as I could. The Thorntons are expecting us at three, didn't you remember? I'll have to go alone. Fetch my bonnet and gloves quickly. And tell cook that you and Rosa will eat now.'

I kissed her cheek and watched her walk across the common.

She had become a little stooped, her skirts were bunchy because she refused to wear many petticoats and the fabric of her bodice was strained at the back. With all my heart I wished I hadn't got home too late to go with her.

She didn't turn and wave so I closed the door and stood in the hall, listening to the tick of the grandmother clock on the first landing. Then I crept down to the kitchen where cook had her feet up on a stool and was sipping tea. She said our lunch had been kept back in the pantry and she supposed that Ruth could bring it up in ten minutes, if I would go and wait.

Ruth's manner, as she served me an unpleasant meal of cold meat and potatoes, was self-righteous. Rosa, she said, was not hungry and anyway couldn't leave her mother.

Afterwards I sat on the terrace and worked chain-stitch borders onto a set of tray cloths. My feet were blistered and my body and mind exhausted by the foray into London with Rosa. I had spent innumerable afternoons sewing on this shady terrace but never in such turmoil, never so lonely.

It had happened again, exactly as before: after a morning in Rosa's company I was left shaken and uneasy but desperate for more.

Chapter Nine

Derbyshire, 1844

Apart from the nerve-racking conversations in the wardrobe or box hedge, I also had to endure Rosa's dangerous sorties into forbidden territory. The most daring of these was to her mother's bedroom, which drew her back time after time. I never ventured far in but Rosa roamed about opening doors and drawers as if she owned them.

'I'm not doing anything wrong,' she said, unstopping a cut-glass bottle and sniffing its contents. 'After all, she's my mother. I spent most of my life in her bedroom when Father was alive.' Talking about the late Squire Barr always made her cry. 'You would have loved him, Mariella. He was just quiet and gentle and what he liked more than anything in the world was taking me for walks on our land. He didn't say much but when he held my hand I was . . . I used to climb on his knee and push my head inside his waistcoat and then I felt so . . . I can't understand how Mother could possibly have exchanged him for that evil old—' She pressed her lips together, circled the bed and ran the fabric of its curtains between her fingers. 'Can you imagine them in here, my mother and Sir Matthew Stukeley with his bald head and brown teeth and slithering hands? Can you imagine what they *do*?'

I hung on to the door knob, ready to bolt.

'When we first arrived here after their wedding I was lonely in the night so I came looking for her. I opened the door and she was on the bed like this with him underneath.' She sprang up suddenly on all fours and peered round at me, her eyes bright with bravado between tumbling locks of her hair. 'Can you imagine?'

I shrank away. 'Don't, Rosa. You mustn't. Please.'

'Oh all right, then. Never mind.' She bounced off the bed and

I hurried over to straighten the pillows. 'We'll go and look at something else.'

She seemed to think that while her stepbrothers were away it was her right to familiarise herself with their possessions too. In Horatio's room she had discovered a collection of rude pictures at the back of a drawer. My insides did peculiar things when she flicked through the prints of women in frilly undergarments with their legs and bosoms exposed.

'You see,' said Rosa, 'these are just what I'd expect of Horatio. He's disgusting. He likes to brush against me whenever he gets the chance, and touch me here and here as if by mistake.' She pressed her thigh and the side of her breast. 'When he comes home you must take care never to be alone with him.'

Afterwards I washed my hands. The murky odour exuded by the rug and curtains in Horatio's room clung to my hair. When I met him at last I understood its source; I shook his damp hand and thought that Rosa was right, he was *disgusting*: a gangling boy with overgrown arms and legs, who spent his time doing things like shooting pigeons, or shuffling papers with his father in the library. Once I met him unexpectedly at the bottom of the servants' staircase peering up at someone. When he caught sight of me he adjusted his collar and the waist of his trousers and walked off without a word.

The only thing that interested Rosa in the other brother's, Max's, room, was a picture of the first Lady Stukeley and her two young sons, aged about three and six, who clung to her skirts and gazed up into her face. Aunt Isabella's predecessor had been a winsome lady with a cluster of shining ringlets either side of her high brow, an odd sort of veil headdress that swept across her shoulders, and a low-cut gown similar to that worn by poor Aunt Eppie in Henry's miniature.

Rosa pointed out disdainfully that when the portrait was painted the sitter had been plain Mistress Stukeley, but that Matthew Stukeley even then had pretensions to grandeur, and had probably commissioned the picture because having one's wife and children painted was a sign of *being* someone.

Apart from the picture, Max's room, as Rosa said, had *nothing* in it other than functional furniture and a row of uninteresting books about wild animals and other countries. 'The thing about Max is that he's never indoors so he doesn't care about possessions.'

As predicted, about a fortnight after our arrival Max came home suddenly, under a cloud due to an incident concerning a mill pond, a dead rat and some village lads. Rosa confided that she thought there had been naked swimming involved. This word *naked* was so forbidden that after Max and I had exchanged a brisk, bony handshake I gave him a wide berth.

Until an alternative school could be found he was kept at home with a clergyman tutor who came three times a week and seemed to spend most of his time playing the piano with his pupil; tempestuous duets came thundering from the music room until Aunt Isabella said they must stop, they made her head ache. The rest of the time Max roamed wild except when brought up short by yet another shouting session with his father because a fresh misdemeanour had been discovered.

One night I was woken by a tapping on the bedroom window. I sat up in bed, transfixed with fear while Rosa slept on. A male figure was silhouetted in the moonlight behind the half-drawn curtains. When the tapping came again I finally plucked up the courage to creep across and look out. There was Max, on the sill. Rosa's room was above the porch and he must have shinned up one of the pillars, crossed the canopy and heaved himself up. He signalled for me to open the sash.

In a moment he was in the room and had laid his hand, which smelled of stone, over my mouth. 'Ssssshh, don't say a word. My father will kill me if he discovers I got myself locked out.'

I was pressed against his hot body, held more by the laughter in his eyes than by the pressure of his hand. 'Will you keep this a secret?' he whispered, his breath warm and beery in my ear. 'A million thanks.' Then he gave my hair a little tug and headed for the door.

Afterwards I lay awake, eyes wide open, reliving the incident: the sudden arousal from sleep, the terrified crossing of the room, the scrape of the sash and Max's hand covering my lips. I even glanced across at the window from time to time in the hope that he would come back again.

The next day his sin was discovered because the precious new plasterwork on the porch had been damaged and a culprit was sought. The only thing to be said for Max, said his father, was that he was never afraid to admit when he was at fault.

Now that Max was home he often came bounding across the terraces to join Rosa and me on our trips to the far reaches of the estate. Another of Rosa's favourite places was a rope swing, constructed by Max, with a seat made of three narrow planks bound together, attached to an oak branch at the top of a high bank in the woods. The swing flew far out above a rushing stream and Max had a heart-stopping trick of hurling himself off at the highest point in its arc and landing among trees on the opposite side. Rosa loved to be pushed out and then to fly back and forth with her hair streaming and her skirts blown up to reveal the frilled edges of her drawers.

'It's *brilliant,'* she yelled. 'You've got to *try* it. Come on, Mariella. I'll give you a really gentle push. You needn't swing high. Just try. You'll regret it if you don't.'

'Come, Mariella,' said Max holding out his brown hand. 'I'll hold you. If you like we can sit together.' He took my arm and urged me across to the swing. Just for a moment I was tempted and allowed myself to be drawn onto his knobbly lap. He took both my hands, wrapped them round the coarse rope and covered them with his own. 'Trust me,' he said.

He pulled back and was about to launch out but then I came to my senses. 'No,' I screamed. 'No. I don't want to. Don't make me.'

He laughed, let go of my hands, straightened his legs so that I slid off, and invited Rosa to swing with him instead. I sat under a tree, arms wrapped tightly round my knees, and watched as they plunged across the ravine, dropping themselves backwards so their necks were exposed to the rush of wind. Lucky, lucky Rosa not to mind the danger. If only Henry were here, I thought. He and I would swing gently together; *he* would look after me properly.

Meanwhile Max and Rosa had grown wilder. He stood and she sat and they flung themselves out over the bank. 'How do you know it's strong enough?' I squealed. They took no notice but spun round and round on the end of the rope until Rosa went green.

'Anyway,' she said, marching away from him and sitting down with me, 'I don't want to share a swing with you any more. I can't respect you for being expelled. If I had the chance to get an education, any education, I'd jump at it. And you just throw it away.'

'The education they offer isn't worth having.'

'But how are you going to get on if you keep giving up?'

'I don't give up. The schools give up. They won't let me learn the things I want to, so I have to leave.'

'What *do* you want to learn, Max, exactly? Why do you have to be so different to other boys?'

'I can't stand sitting still. I don't want to learn Greek. There's no point. I'm not going to be a cleric so it's a waste of time.'

'It's what it leads to. We all have to start somewhere. Greek and Latin are the beginning of everything, medicine, law, the lot.'

'You've never been confined to a classroom in your life. You don't know what it's like.'

'I wish I did. What chance have I to learn anything? Nobody will ever take me seriously whereas you have the chance to change things. You're so selfish. Think what you could do at Stukeley if you got yourself educated.'

A sullen expression came to his eyes. 'I don't want anything to do with father's businesses.'

'That's not a responsible attitude. It's your duty to be involved.'

'It's Horatio's duty. Father won't listen to me anyway.'

'That's because he doesn't respect you. Why should he? Come on, Mariella, we're wasting our time here. Why should we bother with someone so ungrateful?' I risked a backward look at Max, who lounged on the swing, head down, before I was led off first to the kitchens where Rosa stuffed her pockets with thick jam sandwiches, then out of the front gates and along a track running through the valley between dry stone walls. The hillsides were covered with racing cloud shadows and my spirits lifted because I was alone again with Rosa.

'It's beautiful here,' I said. 'Don't you at least love these hills?'

'You wait.'

The further we walked from Stukeley, the less sweet the air became until after a while it reminded me of London on a foggy day. 'Stay here,' said Rosa, handing me the squashed sandwiches. 'I'll be back in quarter of an hour or so.'

'Where are you going?'

'You'll see.'

She left me by a gate so I climbed up, sat on top and looked out over a stream winding between trees in the valley floor, sheep grazing on the hillside opposite, a skylark pulling itself higher and higher until it was a black speck among the clouds. But the smell of the air, wafted in fits and starts by the breeze, clogged at the back of my throat and I wished she hadn't left me so long.

When she came back at last she was burdened by the weight of an infant who clutched her by the hair while another child clung to her hand and a small boy trailed behind. All three were grubby and sallow-skinned, smelling of unwashed bodies and worse.

'I've brought some new friends to see you,' called Rosa. 'We are going to play games and give their mama a rest.'

The children looked much too stupid to play. The youngest, Davey, though well over a year old, had to be propped against a wall, where he toppled sideways and wailed. At this the others started to cry messily, noses running, saliva dripping from their mouths. Only the bread and jam restored them and they crammed in gobbets as if they'd not eaten for a month. I drew Rosa aside and whispered that I'd noticed lice crawling through the lank hair of the little girl, but it didn't stop her sitting cross-legged on the grass, inviting the child onto her lap and kissing her.

By the end of half an hour the two oldest were joining in with the occasional words of a nursery rhyme and had even been induced to try a jumping race, though neither could manage to get both feet off the ground.

'Their mother, Mrs Fairbrother, is a widow,' said Rosa, 'and there is a six-year-old who is very ill.'

I offered to help take them home but she wouldn't let me. 'The mother might not like it. Wait here.'

Somewhat to my relief I was left alone again on the hillside. The sky had now clouded over completely and I was cold. To pass the time I composed a letter to Henry in my head – I would tell him about the village children, perhaps, but not the swing.

A week later our hair had to be treated with an evil-smelling lotion by the housekeeper at Stukeley, and when Aunt Isabella found out she raised herself from the sofa and informed us that Sir Matthew had *absolutely* forbidden us to go near those children again.

Chapter Ten

London, 1854

As soon as Henry came back to England at the end of May he wrote and asked if he could call the next evening.

Rosa and her mother were by now so well established in Fosse House that they had ceased either to be treated or to behave as guests. The household revolved around the needs of Aunt Isabella, who could not be left for more than a few minutes, her state of health, said the doctor, being too precarious and her state of mind too fragile. In the late afternoons she was helped out of bed and brought downstairs in time to eat a substantial meal and afterwards reclined in Mother's place on the sofa with her feet up on a cushion I'd embroidered with two peacocks, beak to beak. She held a copy of Mrs Gaskell's *Cranford* but I never actually saw her turn a page. Instead she stared at each of us in turn and sighed, as if drawing attention to the fact that she too would be usefully occupied, if only she had the strength. This particular evening, presumably in honour of our visitor, she was wearing a flirtatious lace stole and an ostentatious sapphire ring.

Father read *The Times* under a lamp. At one point he muttered: 'Still at sea, many of the troops ... Appalling journey for horses ... Carried under sail rather than steam ... Don't understand it ...'

Mother was writing a letter arguing the case for the installation of a lift in the governesses' home so that hot food might be conveyed swiftly from the kitchen to the dining room and Rosa was making a sketch of me.

Despite what she'd told Barbara, Rosa's education in art, as in so many other subjects, was vastly superior to my own because she had sat in on the tutorials arranged for Max during the many spells when he was between schools. Her folder contained sheaves of half-finished work and when she first arrived she had leafed hastily through, pulled out the occasional sheet and flashed it in front of me: 'What do you think? Perspective's all wrong, wouldn't you say?' She thrust it out of sight before I had the chance to form an opinion. I glimpsed Max standing up on the swing with his long frame idling against the ropes, a cluster of cottages in the village, Isabella reclining on a couch set in the drawing-room window and me, little Mariella, in the Italian garden. I looked very glum and Rosa had caught my childish timidity with what I suspected was unnerving accuracy; the slightly concave posture as I put my hands behind my back and leaned on the wall, head to one side.

She said she wanted a new picture of me in which she hoped to invest a little of what she called Barbara Leigh Smith's *energy*, and had therefore begun a series of studies. She was perched on a low footstool, back very straight, skirts pooled around her feet. Her charcoal squeaked, her hair slipped forward and had to be pushed behind her ears with a careless movement of her left hand, and either her head was gracefully poised over her work or she was tilting it back as she glanced at me. Her gaze was unfocused so that she seemed to be looking into, rather than at me, which made me feel transparent. That night in particular I did not want her to find out what I was thinking because of course my whole being was concentrated on Henry.

Aunt Isabella watched Rosa with a proud glare like a mother cat's. She said, 'A *Doctor* Thewell, is calling this evening, you say.'

There was a pause as Mother's attention shifted from the composition of her letter. 'Henry is a surgeon, sister, not a physician. I'm afraid it's no use discussing your symptoms with him, I doubt he knows a great deal about conditions of the heart.'

'Rosa tells me he is very highly thought of in medical circles.'

'He certainly sits on a number of government boards and committees to do with health. He was especially selected to go to Turkey before the war and oversee arrangements for any wounded soldiers.'

'He must be quite old, then, to have achieved so much.'

'Not so old. Thirty.'

Aunt was silent for a moment but her gaze swivelled from Rosa to me. 'I forget the exact family relationship between Mariella and this Dr Thewell.'

Mother's tone was a little exasperated. 'They are second cousins, as I've told you.'

Another silence while Mother's pen dashed across the page. We were braced for the next question. 'What was it she died of?'

'Consumption, I believe. We were never sure.'

'Ah.' A long silence. Glancing up I saw that a faint smile had quirked the corner of her mouth. 'We see such little company here, sister, I can't help taking an interest in the few visitors we do have. At Stukeley we were scarcely alone for a day at a time. Sometimes carriages had to queue at the door in the afternoons.'

'Ella, you've moved again,' said Rosa. 'Chin up, please, and look a little further to the left.'

When the clock struck eight I glanced at Mother for permission to leave the room, threw my shawl round my shoulders and went down the garden to unlock the gate. Then I walked back and forth, taking deep breaths of the May air as the hem of my gown brushed a border of lavender and a grey moth fluttered in the ivy. I might just hear Henry's footsteps in the lane but otherwise I would have no notice of his arrival until the gate opened.

A snick of the latch and there he was, half hidden by leaves, hat under his arm, jacket slung over his shoulder. I could hardly catch my breath, he was so beautiful and so distinguished with his expectant gaze and moustache clipped in a new, possibly Hungarian, style.

He hugged me like a brother, kissed my hand and drew it through his arm. I now registered other alterations; there was a tick in the muscle of his jaw that came and went like a pulse and though he looked tired he was quite tanned, presumably from the sea voyage. I measured the kiss he had given me against all the others I had received from him and knew that it had been more lingering than usual but by no means as presumptuous as Max Stukeley's. He smelled of sunshine, sweat, soap and, inevitably, of sickness.

We stood in the seclusion of the wilderness while I told him about our visitors. 'My aunt is keen to discuss her symptoms and my cousin Rosa wants you to take her on a visit to the hospital and turn her into a doctor.'

'Does she indeed? Then let's stay out here for the evening where there's just you and me and nobody wants anything.'

'You wait until you meet Rosa. She's extraordinary. I'd forgotten how dull she makes me feel.'

'How dare anyone make my Mariella feel bad about herself? No, I want to see your Rosa less and less.'

We took the longest possible route up to the house through the wilderness and over the lawn. A thrush ran across the grass ahead of us and our feet trod a carpet of needles under the cedar. 'Was your trip to Pest successful?' I asked.

'Definitely, yes. I shall be writing a paper for the *British Medical Journal* and have been invited to deliver a public lecture. But whether I'll get anyone at Guy's to change their practices is another matter.'

'What changes would you like to see?'

We had made a slow rotation of the lawn and were now hidden from the house by the cedar's great trunk. 'Let me look at you,' he said as I stood with my back to the tree, my eyes on the rose arch behind his left shoulder. A lock of my hair had blown loose and ruffles of my muslin gown were flying up in the breeze. Beyond the cedar the garden faded into dusk.

'Mariella.' I risked a glance into his eyes and was a little frightened. 'Whenever I am away, you draw me back. I hope that will always be the case. I hope that you will always be a beacon, guiding me home.'

He took my hand and drew me closer until I was pressed to his chest and his other hand was on my back. With a pang of grief I understood that he would never touch me again as the friend who used to gallop my eight-year-old self across this same lawn and swing me up into the cedar so that I perched, helpless with laughter, squealing to be lifted down. For one dizzy moment I thought that if I looked up I would see my own white-stockinged legs in the tree above.

'Mariella?'

His face was so near mine that I felt his breath on my forehead. The expression in his eyes was part smiling, part heavy and distracted. For a moment the kiss was suspended between us and his fingers, gripping my hand, were crushed by our bodies. The juxtaposition of two times confused me; at that moment I was both child and woman and there was something in the heat of his hand on my back and the pressure of his leg amongst my skirts that made me hesitate. His moustache pricked my skin but his lips were soft, he tasted of tea and his tongue jabbed insistently between my teeth. I was so shocked that it was all I could do not to jerk my head away. Afterwards I hung in his arms and turned away my face. 'I'm tired of waiting,' he whispered.

I nodded, he drew my hand through his arm and we walked on, just a very few steps across the lawn, over the paved terrace and up the three steps to the house.

'At last,' called Mother, pushing aside her letter and putting up her cheek to be kissed by Henry. Father flung down his paper, Aunt Isabella held out a limp hand and Rosa sprang to her feet so that her drawing materials went rattling to the floor. 'Finally, the medical second cousin,' she said, looking him in the eye and shaking hands with a vigour learned from Miss Leigh Smith.

Henry helped gather up the charcoals then surveyed the room fondly as if to check that everything was in place. Lamplight fell on the patterns of roses in the pale green carpet, on the swags and tassels which held back the pink summer curtains, on the little round table at which my mother had been writing her letter, and on Rosa's golden head. Meanwhile, dazed by what had happened in the garden, I sank down in my chair, picked up my sewing and made a succession of bad stitches.

Father at once engaged Henry in a conversation about the war. 'They are hanging about,' he said, 'Gallipoli, Malta, Constantinople. They should be taking up strongholds along the coast of Russia itself. Inaction is poison to an invading army. When you were out there, could you see any reason why they would become so entrenched?'

'Only that Constantinople, and Varna in Bulgaria where the troops are based, are both very beautiful places. Perhaps our generals prefer to go sightseeing rather than to battle. At any rate, it's surely better that nobody is killing each other yet.'

'Apparently you were sent to ensure that proper arrangements had been made for casualties. What were your recommendations?' asked Rosa.

There was a moment of surprised silence at the boldness of her clear, feminine voice. Henry stared at her for a moment and I was afraid that she had offended him. 'Nothing extraordinary, as I recall, Miss Barr. Everything has changed with the advent of steamships. The wounded soldiers can be transported home in a matter of days so emergency field stations are all that's required. But there may not be any major battles to speak of. Warfare is so different now – the threat of our superior firepower may well be enough.'

'Of course there will be battles. It's hardly likely the government will go to the great expense of sending thousands of troops out there only to bring them home again.'

'Token battles, we hope. The Russians are in for a tough time, given the sophistication of our weapons. Our new rifles, for instance, are lethally accurate from a considerable distance.'

'A great opportunity for those young men,' said Father. 'I wish I was twenty years younger.'

'And yet the generals in charge, as I understand it, are all old men,' said Rosa. 'Lord Raglan is sixty-five years old, and has got only one arm, for goodness' sake. Isn't it the case that most of them served under Wellington in the wars against Bonaparte forty-odd years ago?'

'Experience tells more than youth, Rosa. You'll learn that in time. My niece is a very impatient young lady,' said Father fondly. 'She has shaken us all up.'

'But in a war when, as you say, there are new weapons, what good will these old men be?' Her voice rang out and she put her head on one side as if to challenge Henry.

'I can't comment,' said Henry, laughing. 'I'm a medical man, not a tactician. Though it's certainly the case that in medicine we young men long to shake up the system but are kept down by the caution of our old masters.'

'The truth is,' said Rosa, 'no one knows what will happen in a war. My stepbrother Max told me that. He said that facing the unexpected was one of the reasons he liked being a soldier. And yet you speak as if the outcome were certain.' She picked up her sketch pad as though there was nothing more to say on the subject.

'Poor Max,' put in Aunt Isabella, who had never shown any feelings other than disapproval for her stepson until this moment, 'I do worry about him. He's in the Ninety-seventh Derbyshire regiment. The trouble with Max is he will get himself into trouble.

When he went to Australia he nearly died of thirst walking in the desert. Until he's home safe and sound, I shall never get a wink of sleep. But you, Dr Thewell, you must know some very influential people if you were sent out to Turkey by the government. Back on our Derbyshire estate, Stukeley, I was used to all kinds of company. My late husband was a justice of the peace and a great landowner and industrialist. We knew every good family for forty miles. I've found life very quiet since we came to Clapham.'

'You've hardly been well enough for company, sister,' said Mother.

My aunt smiled woefully and shook her head.

'I have always rejoiced in the peace and quiet in this house,' said Henry and went to look over Rosa's shoulder first at me, then at my picture so that my cheeks burned.

'You won't credit it, Dr Thewell,' said Isabella, 'but in my younger, healthier days I was used to entertaining forty people to dinner and holding balls and garden parties for a hundred. Rosa has been brought up to hold her own in the highest circles.'

'That Derbyshire could offer,' put in Rosa.

Henry was still behind her and I wondered if anyone else noticed the expression in his eye when he studied the picture. 'It's wonderful,' he said. 'You've absolutely got her.'

'I haven't seen it myself yet,' I cried. 'She wouldn't let me look.'

Rosa laughed and held the portrait at arm's length. 'Come and see.' But when I stood beside Henry I couldn't say whether or not the sketch was like me. All I cared about was that our upper arms touched, that his breathing was rapid as if he had been walking fast, and that a quarter of an hour ago his tongue had played across mine. When I was able to pay more attention I saw that in Rosa's portrait I had eyes like those of a fawn glancing nervously away from the painter, my face seemed small above my wide white collar and my mouth a little peevish. 'Is that really how I look?' I asked.

'When you're being pensive, yes,' said Rosa. 'Or when you're a bit afraid. Which is quite often.'

'I've never seen Ella afraid,' said Henry.

'That's because you've not dragged her round London. I don't believe there's a sight we've missed in the past few days, including the new station at King's Cross that Uncle Philip has helped to build.'

'Then you're ahead of me,' said Henry. 'You'll have to show me some day.'

'And I've taken her to see all sorts of wild and wonderful people, haven't I, Mariella? You'll find that I've turned her into quite a radical since you've been away.'

'Which people are these?' demanded my aunt. 'You haven't told me about any wild people. Who do you mean?'

'Oh I only mean the friends I'd been writing to. You know. Barbara Leigh Smith. Bessie Parkes.'

'The Leigh Smith related to the Nightingales in Derbyshire? Didn't I say you shouldn't pursue that correspondence? I hope you are not doing yourself any harm, Rosa.'

'Hardly. We talk, that's all.'

'Rosa is always so extreme,' said Aunt. 'She wants to change everything.'

'Does she?' said Father. 'Does she want to change me?'

'Nobody would want to change you, Uncle Philip,' said Rosa, reaching over and grasping his hand. He smiled down at her and for a moment all eyes were on her slender throat, her delicate wrist exposed by the falling sleeve and her rippling hair. The moment of danger, when she might have talked more about our visits to Blandford Square, was averted.

'Tell us about Hungary,' I asked Henry.

'Well, I met an astonishing doctor, Semmelweiss, who has transformed practices in the obstetric wards. Now everyone must wash their hands before they go near an expectant mother.'

'But surely,' said Rosa, 'that's nothing new. Our local midwife says cleanliness is everything in childbirth.' She spoke with incredulous authority, as if her knowledge was equal to – or better than – Henry's.

'Yes, Miss Barr. You would hope that midwives and doctors did wash their hands frequently. But not all of them do, I regret, and in hospitals, when there is so much pressure of time, when it's difficult enough even to have an adequate supply of clean water for drinking, let alone washing, cleanliness often gets overlooked.'

'I thought it was common knowledge by now. I read an article by Addison, who writes about the formation of pus and how a wound is unlikely to become infected if it is clean. In my work with the villagers . . .'

'Oh don't bring in those interminable villagers,' sighed Isabella.

'In any case,' said Henry, 'I've been asked to give a lecture on my findings. You are very welcome to attend.'

'I should like that,' said Rosa, 'and I was also wondering if I might see what happens in a London teaching hospital.'

'Well, of course, you can visit any time.'

'I don't want to visit just the wards. I want to know what goes on in the laboratories and operating theatres. You see one day I want to work as a doctor, or a nurse, but preferably a doctor.'

'I'm sure those are very commendable ambitions, Miss Barr, but personally—'

My aunt sat bolt upright and swung her feet onto the floor. 'No. No. Don't listen to her, Dr Thewell. I absolutely forbid it. She knows that.'

'You can't forbid me visiting a hospital,' said Rosa, smiling calmly. 'Good heavens, Aunt Maria is always visiting hospitals.'

'Because she is on the committee of visitors. She doesn't want to *work* in one. Rosa, I don't want you going near a hospital.'

'Hush,' said Mother. 'I'm sure Rosa is only showing an interest because Henry is here. When he comes the conversation always gets out of hand. He does have this regrettable habit of bringing the wards with him into the drawing room.'

'And speaking of wards, I must be gone,' said Henry. 'I promised I'd look in on a patient this evening.'

'Surely it's far too late to be working tonight,' cried Mother.

'I performed an amputation on an elderly woman this morning. She's very sick, I'm afraid. I must check on her.'

Rosa was transfixed with sudden admiration. When he said goodbye she didn't get up but smiled into his eyes. The neck of her gown had a slight V and I saw his gaze flicker from her face to the hollow that was just visible at the base of her throat.

I took his arm and escorted him to the hall where he stood under the gas lamp and looked back to the drawing room. 'How changed your life must be, Ella. What a difficult girl she must be to live with.'

'Difficult, yes. But don't you think she's amazing?'

'I find her exhausting.'

'Could you bear to show her the hospital if we can persuade Aunt Isabella?'

'She can come and visit by all means. Why not? I'd like you to see where I work. And Ella,' he kissed my hands, then the palms, 'I prefer this living, breathing girl to that portrait Rosa has drawn. Your cousin is undoubtedly very clever but even she cannot capture your dear, gentle soul.' He glanced towards the half-open drawing-room door and for a breathless moment I wondered if he would dare to kiss my mouth again.

That night Rosa and I left the bedroom window open so the room smelled of grass and roses. In a glimmer of moonlight she lay beside me with her arms behind her head. 'Shall we talk about Henry?' she whispered.

'What is there to say?'

'I can see why you love him, of course. He's different to most people. More serious-minded. In fact very serious-minded. My only concern would be, does he ever laugh properly?'

'Of course he laughs, he was laughing tonight.'

'He was laughing *at* me tonight. He thinks me ridiculous, I can tell, because I'm a woman who wants to know so much.'

'He found you extraordinary.'

'No. He could hardly be bothered to argue with me. But that's all right as long as he's kind to you. As long as he makes you laugh sometimes, like I do. I mean, would he ever make you laugh like this?' She lunged under the bedclothes, took hold of my bare foot and pressed the sole with her fingertips so that I writhed. 'Or this?' and she clenched my thigh and tickled my stomach until I was howling with laughter and my legs were tangled with the sheets.

'Stop it. Stop. You'll wake the house.'

After we'd recovered she stroked my hair and studied my face. 'So do you think you'll marry him soon?'

'I've never thought of it.'

'Don't pretend with me, Ella. I knew you were on tenterhooks all evening until he came. You can't hide from me, and he spent ages staring at my picture of you. Of course he loves you. How could he not? You will be Mrs Thewell and drift about in pastel silk with your hair smoothed over your ears and your voice never rising above a murmur. The pair of you will raise perfect children and you will forget all about your Rosa, grubbing about in the dirt, looking for something to do with her life.'

'I won't forget you.'

'You will because I won't fit. I'll be an uncomfortable visitor frowning and fidgeting over the tea table. The pair of you will tolerate me as an eccentric poor relation, wheeled out to make up the numbers from time to time.'

'Stop, Rosa. You know I'll never think of you like that.'

'Oh don't cry, Mariella.' She hugged me close and I wept against her shoulder. I couldn't explain this sudden outburst of grief except that I was still shaken by Henry's kiss. Rosa's caresses reminded me of how he had traced the curve of my spine with his thumb. We were wearing summer nightgowns and our bodies, released from the daytime layers of fabric, were shockingly soft and pliable and I felt confused to be lying in her arms so soon after standing in Henry's. 'Why are you crying, silly girl?' she whispered.

'It's all so complicated. Every time I see Henry I think he will actually propose and he never does. And now you say I'll lose you if I marry him.'

'You won't. I was teasing you.'

'I lost you once already, remember, when your stepfather sent us away. Rosa, why did Sir Matthew send Mother and me home so suddenly when we came to stay? Did you ever find out?'

She ran a lock of my hair between her lips. 'He was like that – full of moods and dislikes.'

'At the time you said he thought we were spongers.'

'Did I? Well, maybe that is what he thought.'

'But who would have put that idea into his head? Why did he turn on us?'

'It's surely not important now, after all these years.'

'I keep thinking about it. I've never forgotten.'

'Good heavens, Stepfather's dead.' She extracted herself from my arms and went back to her own bed. 'I don't want even to think about him. I spent most of my life trying to avoid him and now I've finally escaped for good I certainly don't want to waste time talking about him. Really, does it matter now?'

I lay in the half-light, wishing she would sleep in a different room for once so I could think. Instead of being full of joy that Henry had nearly proposed I now felt sour and sad. The burden of words that had yet to be clearly spoken was very heavy. No wonder I had remembered being exiled so abruptly from Stukeley. That dread of being caught off guard had gone very deep.

Chapter Eleven

Derbyshire, 1844

Only once, apart from on the last day when he stood over me in the white pavilion, was I alone with Max Stukeley. One evening – my last, as it turned out – I came out of the library, closed the door behind me, and found myself face to face with Max, who glanced first at me, then over my shoulder at the shut door. 'Hello, little Mariella.'

I was about to run away but he held me by the arm.

'Hello, Maximilian,' I said.

'What have you been up to in there?'

'Nothing.'

'What's that book under your arm?'

'Your father said I could borrow it.'

'Is Father in there?'

'Yes.'

'Why?' I tried to escape but he hauled me off to a tucked-away alcove under the stairs where I sat like a frightened rabbit, trying to steady my shaking lips and hands. I could feel Max's wiry arm next to mine and smell his boyish breath. 'Why were you in there with Father?'

It was the first time I'd ever seen him close up in daylight. His eyes were chocolate-brown, almost black, and he had enviably dark lashes. Now that he was concentrating fully on me it was like being caught in the beam of a lighthouse lamp. 'I don't know any Latin. Your father offered to teach me.'

He seized the little book. 'Catullus. Which poems?'

'Only a couple so far.'

He flicked through the pages then read a line aloud as if he knew exactly what it meant, even though, according to Rosa, he had attended school so little that it was a wonder any learning had gone in at all. '*Nulla potest mulier tantum se dicere amatam / vere . . .* What does Father teach you about these poems?'

'Nothing. I'm learning how to translate them.'

He nodded several times, very fast. 'Is he teaching Rosa too?'

'Rosa already knows Latin. A bit.'

'Does my stepmother know about these lessons? Does your mother? Does Rosa even?'

I didn't reply.

Max peered into my face. 'Father never gives me lessons.' He was scrutinising my hair, face and clothes. Every time his gaze fell on part of my body I shivered. 'I wonder what use you'll make of this old Latin,' he said, slamming the book shut so hard that I jumped. He threw it aside, leapt up and gave me an elaborate bow, which involved swinging one hand behind his back, the other across his middle and making a heel. But as he walked away he turned. 'Are you all right, Mariella?'

'Of course.' I bit hard on the inside of my cheeks so that I wouldn't cry, slid across the bench, ducked under the staircase and scurried up to where Rosa was lying face down on the bed making sketches of her own hand. The book she'd been reading was tossed aside on the pillow.

'Where did you *go*?' she said. 'I've been waiting ages.'

'I've been talking to Max.'

'*Max*. Why?'

'Because he bumped into me. Because he was there.'

'What did you talk about?'

'This and that.'

'You're wasting your time talking about anything to Max. By now he'll have forgotten that he even spoke to you.'

Neither Max nor his father was at dinner that evening. The next day Mother and I were banished from Stukeley.

Chapter Twelve

London, 1854

Rosa wouldn't rest until she had visited the hospital. She persuaded her mother that in fact it would be churlish not to go, given that Henry was my father's protégé. But the nearer we came to the appointed day, the more anxious I felt. There was no question of Mother chaperoning us because, as Isabella put it, her head was too full of those *wretched* governesses who must now perhaps wait until September for their new home, due to yet another hitch, this time with the gas supply. Mother had to be there every day to give instructions to the workmen.

It was a pity I had never visited Henry at the hospital before. I didn't want to share the first time with Rosa. Overall, my feelings were so complicated that I would much rather have stayed at home and practised my song for the governesses. I worried that my ignorance would be exposed and that I would show shock or displeasure instead of calm acceptance, ownership, almost.

Rosa said we should take suffering seriously and not set ourselves above either patients or nurses by decking ourselves out in elaborate muslins or silks. As none of her gowns could have been described as frivolous this decree was obviously aimed at me. She and her stern lady friends such as Barbara Leigh Smith tended to ignore fashion, which I took to be a choice made for artistic or intellectual reasons. I, by contrast, had to dig deep in my wardrobe for anything suitable. We both wore plain white cuffs and our hair was wound tightly at the back of our heads. Rosa borrowed a petticoat to give a conventional bell shape to her gown which was cinched at the waist by a narrow belt.

After we were dressed we linked arms and stared at ourselves in the mirror. The Quakerish arrangement of Rosa's hair allowed a glimpse of her fragile neck, and the simplicity of her dress provided a fetching contrast to her luminous skin and eyes. I, on the other hand, was made shrunken and plain by the loss of decoration and volume.

'You don't look plain,' she cried. 'Never call yourself plain. You are like a beautiful woodland creature, delicate and quite wild, if you only knew. Besides, if you're plain, I must be too. We're so alike.' Perhaps we were in some ways, but the slight differences in our features meant that Rosa was beautiful and I probably wasn't.

The drive through London was uncomfortable because we were wearing heavy dresses in the midst of a heat wave and I was being carried somewhere I by now didn't want to go at all. Worse, I knew from experience that my companion was decidedly untrustworthy when it came to sticking too rigidly to her mother's orders, all of which I was very happy to obey: 'Don't go near any of the patients. Don't touch anything. Don't allow yourself to be drawn into conversation with one of those nurses. I need hardly say that you should only look at the women's wards, though I wish you'd keep away from the sick people altogether ...'

Rosa was worryingly pensive, hands folded in her lap, an expression of quiet determination in her eyes. It was as if she was about to be admitted to a convent as a postulant nun. This was Rosa on a higher plain, driven by forces in her nature which were nobler than anything I would ever experience. Her mind, presumably, was fixed on the hospital, whereas my own thoughts were focused on the fact that within an hour we would be seeing Henry for the first time since the night he kissed me under the cedar. Of course, there would be no opportunity today for intimate conversation, but perhaps there might be a glance or a touch. My worse fear was that when we met I'd receive no signal from him.

From the outside Guy's hospital looked very grand with imposing gateposts, gabled fronts and ranks of high windows. It had the appearance of a palace, rather than a hospital for the poor and destitute and it even crossed my mind that Rosa might have miscalculated and we should have dressed a little more grandly. Beyond the front doors was a panelled entrance hall with portraits, over a sweeping staircase, of jowly men in stiff cravats. But there was also a smell of unpleasantness covered up and sounds of distant activity that I found very alarming.

We were ten minutes early for our meeting with Henry and after a while Rosa grew restless. From time to time a man in a frock coat, orderlies in their shirtsleeves and women who were either nurses or servants crossed the hall. I backed away to the oak staircase, picked up my skirts with one hand and discreetly put my handkerchief to my nose with the other.

Rosa strode about and glanced up at the clock. Ten past twelve. Next she ventured along one of the corridors which opened on either side. 'Come on,' she said. 'There's no harm in looking.'

As I didn't want to be left alone I had to follow. She marched down a stifling passageway through a series of doors until we were actually in a ward where one glance was enough to convince me that Aunt Isabella had been absolutely right and we should have nothing further to do with the hospital. The smell almost knocked me over. Overflowing privies. Vomit. Worse. I thought of my aunt leaning against her stack of pillows with her tray of tea and a lightly boiled egg, the interminable excretions that had to be dealt with, and it seemed to me that all these other sick men – dear heavens, it was a men's ward – were some dreadful extension of her.

Although nobody raised their voice except for the occasional yelp from one of the patients, there was in fact a great deal of noise: doors opening and closing, heavily shod feet on bare boards, activity on the floor above, the slosh of water, the clink of bottles. At first glance, the ward was quite tidy with rows of beds on both sides but there was dirt everywhere, stained sheets and bandages, tarnished utensils, unkempt, low men. My gaze kept drifting to those dreadful bare chests and arms, some hairy, others pallid and flabby-skinned. A memory flickered – that smell, the feeling of guilty revulsion.

The nurses moved from bed to bed in a weary ritual of attendance but they seemed bored and careless. Flies bothered the patients, sun baked through the broken blinds. Meanwhile Rosa walked fearlessly up to a dumpy little nurse and put out her hand (thereby breaking two more of my aunt's rules). 'We are friends of Dr Thewell. My name is Rosa Barr. I am thinking of becoming a nurse.' The nurse gave a sort of half curtsey and hurried past me. She smelled of drink, I noticed.

Rosa's ringing voice had caused heads to be raised from nearby pillows. She even approached the first bed, stooped down and took the patient's hand. 'Is there anything I can do for you?'

I backed away in an agony of embarrassment and distaste. It was as if she had actually climbed onto the stage in the middle of a play. From my former place at the bottom of the stairs in the hall I watched the hands of the clock move on a few minutes. At last Rosa joined me. 'I looked for you but you'd gone.'

'We shouldn't intrude.'

'We're waiting for Dr Thewell. It's not intruding. If nobody took an interest, this place would have no funds at all. It relies on public donation.'

'But you're not giving anything,' I said, knowing that she never had any money.

'Who knows what I shall give one day? A nurse just told me there is another outbreak of cholera and it's expected that the hospital will soon be inundated with victims. Five cases have already been brought in. They're going to empty one of the upstairs wards to use it for isolation purposes. She says they're sure to need more nurses.'

Cholera. Horror was heaping upon horror. Cholera. Then we would all die. My head was hot and my bones turned to water. The miasma in this hospital was already enough to kill me in minutes, let alone if cholera patients were admitted too. Images of my deathbed flashed through my mind, my mother pausing long enough in her work to hang over me and become infected, then Father, Aunt and Rosa.

'We should leave straight away,' I said.

'Why?'

'Cholera is very contagious. We shouldn't stand here in the middle of a crisis and invite disease. It's sinful to put oneself in the way of trouble. We might take cholera back to Clapham. Your mother, being so ill, is particularly vulnerable.' My voice was high with panic. We ought to have been in the morning room at home, hemming snowy sheets for the governesses.

'There is always a crisis of some kind in a hospital. Can't you see? That's why I so want to work here. I want to intervene at the point in people's lives when they most need me.'

At that moment the entrance doors were thrust open and a crowd burst in carrying some kind of stretcher, followed by a further troop of onlookers and a woman holding a baby of about a year who howled mournfully. The crowd also brought a gust of hot air with them, and the stench of a London street. No one was properly dressed but wore bits of clothes frayed at the neck and hem, tied on with string. Rosa and I were pressed higher up the stairs by the crush.

On the stretcher was a boy of about twelve. His upper body was covered by a ragged shirt, his complexion was greenish and his eyes huge. Worse, his feet were exposed and filthy with uncut nails curled over the big toes, and the trouser of the right leg had been cut away to expose a dreadful wound. The thigh was snapped so that jagged bone actually protruded through the bruised and bleeding flesh. All this I glimpsed in a second or two. Though I turned away it was too late, the image was seared onto my mind.

I dragged Rosa's arm. 'We should go.'

She wrenched free and climbed higher so she could see above people's heads and at that moment Henry appeared, formally dressed but without hat or gloves. I started forward at the sight of him but he didn't even notice us. Instead he asked people to step aside so that he could be allowed through to the patient, gave low-voiced directions to an orderly about sending the crowd away, and asked for a chair to be brought for the boy's mother, who was a poor little creature, round-bellied and stooped at the shoulder, altogether too scrawny to be carrying such a large baby.

'I sent him out for milk,' she said. 'He couldn't keep away from them new drains. I told him time after time. He always was too inquisitive.'

Henry drew her aside so that they were immediately beneath us, under the banister. 'What is your son's name? . . . Well, Mrs Lee, I'm afraid that we have no choice but to take Tom's leg off. In a case such as this where the break has severed flesh, we have no choice. Infection will set in otherwise and he will die of gangrene.'

It took a while for her to take in what he was saying. The baby writhed and arched, its mouth a wet O of misery. 'No, no, don't take his leg. Oh no, my poor boy. Don't do that. Don't. He loves to run.'

'He will run still. We will make him a new leg.'

'But he'll be a cripple. What good will he be? Oh God, when I think of him running around this morning driving me to distraction.'

Henry took the woman's hand in both of his. 'My dear Mrs Lee, don't let him see that you are frightened. Find the strength to take care of him.'

He looked into her eyes and gripped her hand until she pulled herself up and nodded. Henry held out his arms and took the baby, who stopped crying in amazement while the mother stooped over the stretcher and kissed her son's forehead. His eyes flew open and he began to wail.

'I'll take care of your son,' said Henry. 'I promise.' The baby changed hands again, Henry smoothed the boy's hair and spoke his name, then nodded to a couple of orderlies.

The mother tried to grab the stretcher as it was borne away but she was held back by a nurse. I discovered that I was gripping the banister in both hands because I had never seen Henry as tender as he had been with that woman. It was as if he loved the mother and her children more than anyone in the world and he had handled the baby so competently that it calmed down and played solemnly with his watch chain. My heart contracted at the thought that one day he might hold his own child in that way.

Then I wished that I too was sick, that I could fall at his feet and be taken up in his arms and have the light of his compassionate gaze on me.

Rosa had grabbed my arm. 'Come on. Come.'

'Where are we going?'

'We should follow Henry.'

'But we can't. You heard what he said. They're going to operate on the child.'

'Operations are open to public viewing. Come on. It's my dream to see an operation,' and then we were actually rushing along the corridor in the wake of the stretcher and a gathering crowd of young men.

I thought someone would surely put a stop to it, we would never be let in to see the operation, but everyone was in such a hurry that they didn't seem to notice us. A whisper was flying about that Thewell was going for a record seven minutes, the fastest amputation above the knee in history. I was weeping and murmuring under my breath, 'No, no, no,' but we were suddenly squeezed through a low door and actually at the top of an arena looking down over a mass of heads at a cluster of men in frock coats and the child on the stretcher. We were forced forward so that we hung over the edge of the gallery and a voice behind us said, 'Thank God, the new nurses are a sight easier on the eye than the last lot . . .'

The heat was atrocious. Sun blasted through a skylight and the room stank of butchery. I would have fainted but for the horror of falling into the arena below. I forced myself to breathe deeply, to disconnect myself from Rosa, who I loathed passionately at that moment for getting us into this situation and who was now gazing avidly down.

A high-pitched whimpering could be heard above the general hubbub. From somewhere Henry had acquired a long leather case which he passed to a man behind him. Then he approached the table, lifted his arms and drew them backwards, as if performing breaststroke. The effect was to cause the circle round the boy to open up, for light to fall more strongly from the skylight above, and for me to be able to see exactly what was happening. The boy was propped on his elbow as if he would bolt if only he could. His trousers had been cut off and a towel thrown carelessly across his genitals.

Don't look, Mariella, I told myself. You mustn't. You'll never forget it if you do.

But of course I couldn't help myself. I had to see.

There was a slow gathering of quiet and the child's weeping became more audible, a sort of whining snuffle like that of a young dog.

'So, my dear young lad, Tom. Tom.' Henry's voice was low and caressing. Meanwhile the boy's head was held by another doctor and brown liquid dropped between his lips until his gaze became unfocused. Henry's assistant unpacked the case rapidly, laying instruments one by one out of sight behind the patient's head. The boy's wrists and good ankle were strapped down. And all the time Henry went on speaking, even as he rolled his cuffs and flexed his fingers: 'So I hear you and your friends were playing leapfrog near the building site on the Mile End Road? Bad luck to fall like that. I've asked someone to tell the authorities to see about that site being fenced off in future. I hope your mother doesn't give you too hard a time for it. She's outside. You'll be seeing her in a moment and then I'm afraid you'll catch it. So, Tom, what I want you to do is watch the eyes of this gentleman here, see, do you know he's called Thomas too . . .'

It dawned at me at last, above the zooming flies, the raucous shout of someone in the street below, the horror of being there at all, what I was about to witness. Dear God, dear God, I thought, the child doesn't realise what is going to happen to him.

Henry now spoke to his colleagues in a dispassionate voice I'd never heard before. 'I wonder if anyone can tell me why I don't choose to employ chloroform with this particular patient.'

Silence. Tom whimpered. Someone said, 'Too young, sir.'

'Precisely. It would be very difficult to administer a safe dose to such a slight child. So. Are we all set?' There was a moment of great tension as Henry lifted his head and looked about him; I distinctly felt his piercing gaze fall upon first me, then Rosa, and saw one eyebrow raise a fraction before I turned my face away.

'You can start the clock,' he said and whipped off the towel. He laid two fingers on the pulse in the child's groin, put out his hand and received a shiny instrument, waited an instant for a basket to be kicked closer to the bottom of the table, then became utterly intent. My mind fogged and I swayed against Rosa. I remembered the child's mother and how she had sent her son out for milk. When I looked again Henry's assistants were stooped over the boy and I couldn't see anything but I heard a noise that took the strength from my legs altogether. Smashed bone, it could only be, and then a high-pitched, dying howl. An eerie silence fell, the men around us pressed closer and Henry's measured voice said: 'The essential thing is to tie off the artery with all expedition, loss of blood being the chief cause for concern . . .'

Afterwards I was half carried by Rosa into the passage outside where she propped me against a wall, her arm locked through mine.

I heard Henry's voice through a mist of faintness: '. . . these two women are doing here. Extraordinarily inappropriate . . . loss of concentration.'

Then he was actually in front of us, a black column smelling of blood. I pulled myself upright and found that he had taken my hand although his fingers barely pressed mine and his voice was so chilly that I scarcely recognised it as his. 'Mariella. Miss Barr. I had quite forgotten that I arranged to meet you this morning. Forgive me. There was something of an emergency, as you see. I'm afraid that you have come at rather a difficult time. Perhaps another day we could give you a more detailed tour of the hospital.'

'Thank you,' said Rosa, 'but I don't want just to tour, I want to be useful.'

'So I remember. Well, I'm glad to hear it. We don't have enough ladies prepared to take an interest in our work here.'

He moved away but her voice rang out: 'I would like to take more than an interest, Dr Thewell. As I said, I should like to work here. Tell me how I can do that.'

'I see.' Henry's voice was clipped. 'The chapel is close by. It will be cooler there and I'll have some water brought for Miss Lingwood. But I'm afraid I have only a few minutes to spare.'

The chapel was mercifully empty and civilised with a gallery and pillars. It even smelled of plaster and flowers, like a proper church. I sank into a pew and pretended to sip from the glass although in fact I wouldn't consume a drop of anything in that place. There was a brownish smear on my white glove above the index finger. Blood, surely, transferred from Henry's hand to mine.

'What will happen to the boy?' asked Rosa.

'He will possibly survive but it is by no means a definite outcome. Shock, loss of blood or infection, perhaps all three, will probably do for him.'

'You sound as if you scarcely care. In fact, you all seemed more interested in breaking a record for speed than in saving the boy. Isn't it the case that the real reason you didn't use chloroform is that it would have slowed you down?'

Even in my befuddled state I could tell that Henry was still far from his usual self. He was very pale and his eyes, which had smiled so warmly at the patient and his mother, were expressionless. 'It's true that there are certain, rash doctors who might have used chloroform in this case but the process is still relatively untried and the last person I'd experiment on is a young boy, already in shock. But whatever decisions were taken by my colleagues and me, I believe we all had the best interest of our patient at heart.' He paused. 'I must say, though, I was amazed to see you both in the theatre.'

Of all the experiences that morning, the most terrible was realising that Henry now disapproved of me. Rosa, however, was undaunted. 'Why? We simply followed you.'

'You were a distraction. Operations are private affairs and students are only allowed at the discretion of the surgeon.'

'I wanted to see if I could bear it. If I am to be a student here—'

'I am not thinking about you, Miss Barr, so much as the patient. And Mariella. Look at her. She is faint, as any lady would be. It was a brutal thing to expose her to. I must wonder at your motives.'

'My motives?'

'Are you sure it was not just sensation you were after?'

'How dare you?' She too was white-faced and her voice was low and passionate. 'I suspect that you are angry because you object to us women experiencing what you have seen dozens of times. How did you know that you wanted to be a doctor, except by seeing what doctors do?'

'I went through the proper channels; I studied for years; I earned access to the operating theatre through my work with patients and my knowledge of anatomy.'

'And what about me? I wish to go through the proper channels but there are none for a woman interested in medicine. How will I know whether the hospital is to be my vocation if I am not allowed to see the worst or the best that it has to offer?'

They stared at each other. It was as if neither was prepared to give ground by shifting their gaze. 'What you say is unanswerable,' Henry said at last, 'except for two things. In the first place I cannot help thinking that you have abused your acquaintance with me. When I invited you to the hospital I by no means gave you permission to enter its private rooms. In the second place, the operation was performed on a child who may die. At the very least he will be a cripple. The attention of all should have been on the patient. The essential issue, at that moment, was not testing whether or not you could withstand the sight of such an operation, it was thinking about what was best for the child. I therefore propose that we should talk carefully about how you can be introduced to the work of the hospital a little at a time, in the future, and what will be of benefit to all parties. Come and visit my clinic, if you wish, and I will explain how you might be of use. But please, there is a proper time for everything. It is a matter of respect.'

For a moment she went on staring at him and I expected her to argue further but she said nothing more.

'Well, I will accompany you to the carriage,' he said, and held the door open for us.

We walked in silence down the hateful corridors, each far apart from the others. The building repulsed me with its echoing shouts and rushing feet. Every breath I took, it seemed to me, was rank with disease. I didn't know Henry in this place and when he handed me into the carriage my glove barely brushed his fingers.

Chapter Thirteen

Rosa and I rode in silence, seated side by side so that we couldn't see each other's face past the brims of our bonnets. At first the shock of what had happened seemed an external thing like a punch in the stomach but gradually it filled me up so that I was nauseous and aching. Hope was dead. By being present during the operation we had humiliated Henry before all his colleagues; he would become a laughing stock for being followed about the hospital by a couple of women. We had ruined all his chances of promotion. The shame, the shame. I pressed my hand to my mouth and kept my eyes tight shut to blot out the anguish.

Then, as we ground to yet another halt amidst the traffic on the Clapham Road Rosa said, 'I think the truth is that your Henry does not want women in his hospital. And I can see why. He wouldn't know how to behave with women in that male domain. It would make everything different.'

Outside the carriage a couple of dogs engaged in a fierce fight and were soon joined by their owners. The carriage shifted as the horse grew nervous.

'Well?' she said. 'What do you think, Mariella? Will your Henry be persuaded? I mean, if I can't make any headway with someone I know, what are my chances of breaking into the world of medicine at all? I can't afford to wait too long, I'm already twenty-four. Perhaps I should consider working in Barbara's school, if she'll have me. But then, is teaching what I want to be doing, really?'

At last I said quietly, 'Surely it would be foolish to begin something you can't finish. Presumably you will be going home soon.'

'Home? What do you mean? I have no home apart from with you. I couldn't bear to go back to Stukeley. Besides, I'm quite sure Horatio has no intention of accommodating us there. He'd rather hide us away in a cottage and leave us to starve.'

I wondered how I could endure another half-hour in the carriage with her. Surely she could see beyond her own ambition to my pain? Still we didn't move and the sun scorched down on the roof. In the end I said, 'I can't bear this. I'm going to walk home.'

'I agree. I'll come with you.'

'No. Alone. Please.' I fumbled with the latch but she held me back.

'Mariella.'

'No.' I threw her hand off my arm.

'Mariella.'

'Please, I beg you, don't speak to me.'

'I don't understand. This isn't like you. Why are you angry?'

At that moment the carriage jolted forward and I fell back against the seat. I was so full of rage and grief that I couldn't find any more words so we drove the rest of the way in total silence and once there Rosa went immediately up to her own room – the one originally intended for her – and shut the door.

I refused lunch but asked Ruth to fetch hot water for a bath while I removed my clothes. My gloves, I told her, should be burned, my skirts cleaned, my boots treated with carbolic, including the soles, and my petticoats and undergarments boiled and bleached. Never mind if they were shrunk or discoloured as a result; it was a risk I would have to take. I then stepped into the bath and scrubbed myself violently from head to toe though the touch of my own body repelled me. I thought of myself as a bundle of messy organs liable to become diseased at any moment. The smell of the hospital was still in my nostrils and I imagined it spreading like an inkblot inside me until it had penetrated every last cell.

My thighs were heavy with the recollection of the boy's exposed groin. He and the patients in the ward had reminded me rather of the carcasses of pigs hung up outside butchers' shops than of human beings.

Then I thought of the formality of Henry's touch as he helped us into the carriage. He had been a different man to the one who kissed my lips. So remote, so cold. I wound my wet hair into a tight knot and put on a light muslin dress, all the time avoiding the sight of my scrubbed face in the mirror. This is how I will live the rest of my life, I thought: untouched, untouchable.

I went down and sat with Mother and Aunt in the morning room where the shades had been drawn to keep out the sun. Though a slight draught blew from door to window it was still very hot. Click-click went a fly on the glass. I was working on festive caps for the governesses whose home at last had a definite opening date in late September.

Of course Aunt took a ghoulish interest in the hospital so I told her that I had been impressed by its architecture and the dignified quiet of the chapel. Glimpses of a ward, I said, had confirmed my view that those who worked there must have strong constitutions. I explained Rosa's absence by suggesting that she probably had a headache, due to the heat.

'I trust it won't bring on one of *your* headaches, Mariella. You look very pale,' said Mother.

'Well, perhaps at least Rosa will be convinced now that a hospital is no place for a lady,' said Isabella. 'What do you think, Mariella?'

I said nothing.

'Do you think she will want to go again?'

'I don't know, Aunt, though perhaps it would be unwise to go back. There was a rumour of cholera.'

Consternation. Even Mother laid aside her pen, while Aunt gave up all pretence of working and fanned herself furiously. 'It's the Indians,' she said, 'we were never under threat until the Indians gave us this dreadful disease.'

'Philip was saying that our troops are also suffering from it in Varna,' said Mother. 'I don't understand how it got all the way to Bulgaria as well as here. Did the men take it with them? Is there no cure?'

'I don't know,' I said. 'I remember Henry once telling me that a colleague of his is convinced it's to do with dirty water.' There, I had mentioned his name quite calmly and at that moment I really thought I could let him float away from me on the slow river of my new hopelessness.

'Nonsense. Bad food, bad air, dirty people – everyone knows that these are the causes of cholera. In fact, all the reasons I said you should not go near that hospital,' said Isabella. 'Well, that's it. From henceforth Rosa doesn't leave my sight. I won't listen to any more arguments. Dear heavens, if she died where would I be?'

All the long afternoon memories of the hospital surged through my mind however much I tried to keep them at bay by concentrating fiercely on the lace trim of a cap I was sewing, on the swaying shades at the window and on the way Mother ground her teeth as she worked.

Father was out that evening at a meeting of the local society for the Encouragement of Arts, Manufacture and Commerce, of which he was currently chairman. This was a pity because it meant that at dinner there was no topic of conversation other than the hospital. Rosa came down late, wearing her plainest black gown and her hair loosely tied in a ribbon. She looked ill, her lip trembled, she ate only a mouthful or two and couldn't be persuaded to talk about what she had seen. All she said was that she had found the experience of visiting the sick every bit as moving as she had anticipated.

The result of this behaviour was that all eyes were upon her. Aunt Isabella repeated several times that if only she'd been listened to in the first place the hospital visit would never have happened and that the chances were that Rosa would be dead from cholera within a week. 'I've already been wrung raw this year by the death of my poor husband and now I am to lose a daughter. For the life of me I cannot see what I've done to deserve such bad luck.'

'Rosa isn't dead yet, sister,' said Mother.

'It's a terrible thing to outlive one's only child.'

Like Rosa I had no appetite but unlike her I couldn't bear to draw unwelcome attention to myself so I had to swallow mouthful upon mouthful that might just as well have been dust in my mouth.

After dinner Aunt declared that she was too exhausted to think of working so she dozed on the sofa while Mother wrote yet another letter begging a distant relative's financial support for the replacement gas pipes in the home. Rosa sat at the piano and played the opening bars of Mozart's Sonata in A. She rarely performed but when she did it was with passion and clarity, though I had still never heard her play a piece all the way through. I took my sewing out onto the terrace believing that I would be left alone.

Even late in the evening the air was warm; low rays of sunshine shuddered on the lawn, perfume steamed from a cloud of roses and birdsong fluted in the still air. I lifted one nightcap after another from a heap and attached white ribbons but my mind would not be soothed; instead I replayed the scene in the chapel.

After a few minutes the music stopped and Rosa joined me. 'Do you mind? I shan't say a word.'

I gave a reluctant shake of the head so she sat beside me, spent several minutes staring out into the garden then began writing notes in a book I'd never seen her use before. Her silence was so unusual that it weighed in the air more heavily than if she'd bothered me with incessant talk. I was conscious of the slight sound of her hand brushing the page and the way her hair fell like a veil across the side of her face.

The moon rose, a sliver of pearly light over the poplar trees marking the boundary of our garden.

Then I realised that her attention, like mine, was elsewhere: we were both waiting for Henry. I was sure that he would come even though he never paid surprise visits. The knowledge that he was on his way grew and grew until I could not help but look up from my work every minute to see if he was there.

Faintly we heard the doorbell, then nothing more until Henry was standing in the open French windows wearing a summer waistcoat I'd never seen before, his hair damp on his forehead and his jacket slung over his shoulder. He was still very pale and the expression in his eyes was one I remembered from his first arrival in our house: fear of intrusion.

Rosa sprang to her feet, notebook clutched to her chest, and backed away a few paces while I gave Henry my hand. He squeezed it affectionately and smiled into my eyes. 'Are you well again, Ella? Have you recovered?' Yes, he had forgiven me. It was over. I was so relieved that I had to sit down abruptly in order to hide my tears. Meanwhile he offered his hand to Rosa. 'Miss Barr.'

She said nothing but let her hand slide through his, then sat at the greatest possible distance from us, half turned away, writing in her book.

Henry fanned himself with one of the nightcaps. 'I thought you'd like to know that the operation was a success, as far as it went. The boy lives but I don't know for how long. He's very sick with a high fever. We can only hope now.' He seemed entirely his old self and I was amazed by his generosity, that he could treat us so kindly after we had invaded his world.

'Do you think he still might die, then?' I asked.

'I'm afraid it's likely. In a child that young infection spreads rapidly. But then on the other hand if he's healthy he may yet fight back. So much depends on state of mind.'

'It's terrible that he should lose his life in so trivial an accident. Is there nothing that can be done for a broken limb except amputation?'

'Well, now this is where I differ from some of my colleagues who will whip off a limb if it's so much as bruised. I have learned from my travels abroad that it is possible to save a limb with careful setting and dressing of the wound, if only infection doesn't set in. But where the flesh is broken and the bone protruding as in young Tom's case there is no hope other than through amputation. But Mariella, it's a perfect evening and I've been cooped up in the hospital all day. Won't you and Rosa walk with me as far as the wilderness?'

I got up and we both waited for Rosa. I thought she would refuse; I willed her to go on with her writing but at last she sighed and tucked her pencil between the pages of her book. 'I am keeping a note,' she told us, 'of any activities that might be described as medical. It is my poor attempt at organised study.'

I took Henry's arm while Rosa walked ahead of us, hands clasped behind her back and the trailing hem of her skirt sweeping the path. When we emerged from the shade her hair, which had tumbled from its ribbon and spilled to her waist, turned to gold. We ducked beneath the rose arch and crossed the lawn to the wilderness where the azaleas, long past their best, had left a scent of decay in the air. Rosa, still ahead, swayed as she walked and reached out to brush her hand over low branches. A loose flower twirled from a bush of mock orange and caught in her hair.

'Miss Barr,' Henry said, 'I made enquiries. It seems that volunteers may indeed be required at the hospital if there is to be a cholera outbreak.'

She did not turn. 'Surely I am not fit for such work, being so unskilled.'

'You could be trained. But I must warn you the work is dangerous.'

'Oh, then it can't be suitable for a woman.'

She spoke so bitingly that I thought he had every right to be angry again but he said quietly, 'For certain women, it is. I am partly on your side, Miss Barr, believe me. Although I happen to think that the study of medicine, being such a long drawn-out business, should probably remain a male preserve, I have seen for myself that some women are natural nurses and that we could improve the care of patients considerably if there were more trained women in charge of the wards. For instance, there is Mrs Wardroper at St Thomas's hospital who runs a marvellous team of nurses.'

'Well, in any case,' said Rosa, 'there is no question of my taking the idea any further. My mother won't hear of me working in a cholera ward, or indeed any other kind.'

'It's understandable. Given the possibility of infection, the work is perhaps best left to those without family ties.'

'Is it true,' she said bitterly, 'that none of the doctors who look after these patients has family ties? Or do you think that those women who do nurse are of such low class that it scarcely matters if they become infected?'

'That's not what I think, Miss Barr. I have the highest respect for women who nurse, as I've said.'

She turned on him suddenly. 'But you can have no respect at all for me.'

'On the contrary—'

Her voice was now full of tears. 'You must think me selfish and impetuous.'

'No.'

'You were right. I was entirely to blame because I was thinking only of myself when I came to the hospital today. It's just that I have waited so long. But that's no excuse. How could I have behaved so badly?'

'It was a moment of great tension for us all. Nobody thinks clearly in such circumstances.'

Her head was drawn back, a tear brimmed on her lower eyelid and her lips were pressed together to prevent herself from breaking down entirely. 'At any rate,' she said, 'please don't hold it against Mariella. I forced her to come with me.'

'As if I would ever hold anything against Mariella.' We all laughed and this time when we walked on Rosa linked her arm through mine so that I was supported on both sides and we had to keep close together to negotiate the narrowness of the path until we emerged back onto the lawn.

'The truth is,' said Henry, 'I have a great deal on my mind. There is the lecture next week, which I know will provoke a great deal of hostility. And then things are not going well with the army. The troops have been so long in Varna, in Bulgaria, that cholera has set in there as well. There may be an epidemic and of course we didn't anticipate that.'

'How could you?' I said. 'You were sent to consider the situation for wounded soldiers, not diseased men.'

'And yet there are precedents,' said Henry. 'I have since looked them up. Soldiers often die of typhus and other diseases. We've seen it happen most recently in India. We know that cholera has been the scourge of our century and that wherever a great many people are gathered together sharing the same air, infection will spread. Yet I didn't foresee the danger because I simply couldn't imagine a situation where thousands of men would be encamped in hot weather at close quarters. Perhaps that's why I was so angry today. It wasn't your actions so much as anxiety and frustration with myself for not looking ahead. I deeply regret that you two innocent women should have suffered because I was angry with myself.'

'You are too generous,' said Rosa. Tears still shone in her eyes and she stood apart from us, chin high, face half averted. 'The truth is that the one person above all others I would never want to hurt is Mariella and I deliberately put her through a dreadful ordeal.'

I was so unused to being annoyed with anyone, let alone her, that now it was over I felt as if heavy chains had dropped from my heart. My body filled with heat and light as she kissed my hand and held my palm to her wet cheek.

Henry's eyes were fixed on our joined hands. 'Well, perhaps we should progress with your medical education in easy stages, Miss Barr. My lecture on the experiments being performed in Pest by Dr Semmelweiss will be a start. I do hope you will come.'

'Of course. If I am allowed. If Ella will come too.'

'Oh I'm sure she will. And I'm hoping Uncle Philip will attend. Public health is a subject that I think is of great interest to those whose work is to plan and build.'

By the time we reached the house he and Rosa were talking so animatedly about the spread of disease among the poor that it was as if the morning incident had never been. Or rather the incident, instead of driving us apart, had given us a shared understanding that had not existed before. When we returned to the drawing room Henry sat next to me while Rosa curled up on the sofa and rested her head on her mother's shoulder.

'I hope you didn't catch a chill in that damp garden,' said Isabella.

Rosa kissed her. 'It's not damp. It's a wonderful evening.'

'Go up and fetch a shawl, Rosa, your hand is very cold.'

'I'm not cold. It's just that yours is very hot. But still, if it would reassure you, I'll wear a shawl,' and she flew out of the room to collect some concoction of silk and lace which settled round her shoulder like cobweb and mingled with her curls.

When it was time for him to leave Henry kissed each lady's hand. To Rosa he said, 'Miss Barr, allow me,' and lifting one of her curls, he picked out the little white flower that had fallen there and handed it solemnly to her.

I went with him to the door where he gripped my hand in both of his. Then he held me in his arms and stroked my hair. My face nestled in the warm space beneath his chin, my ear was pressed against his collar and all the pain in my heart was soothed away. We laughed as he released me at last, then pulled me back against him one last time.

Chapter Fourteen

The day after the hospital episode Aunt Isabella was too ill to get up and the doctor was called again. He told us that she had suffered a severe relapse causing irregular heartbeat and a possibly fatal weakness in her limbs. The only hope was bed-rest and vigilant nursing, night and day. Apparently to someone of her delicate constitution the threat of cholera was almost as prostrating as the disease itself.

We took it in turns to watch over our patient so that Nora, the Irish nurse, could have time off to sleep or take the air. She and I rarely spoke because she made me uncomfortable with her smell of stale bed sheets, her pale, watchful eyes and an air of thinking a great deal more than she was saying. Her position as Aunt's special nurse gave her a different status to the other servants, and I wasn't sure how I should behave towards her. Mother deferred to her almost as much as to the doctor, while Rosa treated her more as a relative than an employee. Sometimes they even had tea together.

'After all, I've known Nora for eight years,' she said. 'Often she was the only friend I had at Stukeley.'

'Friend?'

'Certainly. She has been very good to me. And more than loyal to our family even though she has no cause to be; the opposite, in fact. You can have no idea how much we all relied on her. And I respect her as a professional nurse, which is what I want to be after all.'

One afternoon Rosa took this Nora McCormack on an outing to see the Crystal Palace in Sydenham, leaving me alone in the sickroom where I sat in the window initialling a pile of towels, hardly daring to snip a loose end for fear of disturbing my aunt. The sliver of daylight from the partially drawn curtains gave the room an air of gloomy withdrawal whereas I had always thought this bedroom, with its crimson paper and overstuffed armchairs, the most elegant in the house. When my patient asked for water I leapt to my feet, fearful of getting something wrong. I supported her hot back so she could drink, made minute adjustments to the window in order to admit just a little more air and bathed her face with lavender water.

'You have a gentle touch,' she sighed. 'Sometimes Rosa is too impatient and splashes me. A little lower, dear. Cool my throat.'

I hadn't seen such quantities of skin before or had any reason to handle another person's body. When my knuckles brushed her breast as I raised her on the pillows I came closer to her than I had to any other human being except Rosa.

I hated the sickroom. Aunt commented on every sound in the house and every movement I made. There was always something to be done: a fly was causing irritation . . . She fancied a little barley water . . . Could I say when she might expect the doctor to call? . . . Perhaps I might read some Tennyson, if it wasn't too much trouble . . . At Stukeley there was always a supply of iced water but in London it was probably more difficult to obtain . . . Where was Rosa?

'She'll be in at supper time, I'm sure. She's taken Nora on a little outing.'

'Then where is my sister?'

'Mother has gone to call on Mrs Hardcastle.'

'But what if I should be worse? Oh I feel so ill and alone.'

'I am here.'

She turned her head on the pillow. 'I'll try to sleep until Rosa gets back. It's dreadfully hot. I can't help thinking of my room in Stukeley where it was always so cool . . . If you were to fan me for a few minutes, Mariella, I might doze off again.'

We couldn't even go to Broadstairs that summer because Aunt Isabella was too sick to be moved and we thought it unkind to leave her and Rosa alone at Fosse House. In any case, thanks to Henry, Father was engaged with a new committee called the Consolidated Commission for Sewers, which was planning a healthier, more modern drainage system for London. Meanwhile Mother was beside herself with worry over the home because two more disasters had put back its opening still further. The first was that nobody in their right mind would encourage frail old ladies to move in together during a season of cholera. The second was that the installation of new gas pipes had revealed another problem; one of the ancient sewers under the house was leaking, so more money had to be raised for repairs.

To make up for the missed holiday, Rosa and I went on outings to the new Battersea Park, to the Palace of Westminster and to the British Museum. One day she even persuaded me to take her to Highgate and show her The Elms.

'I must see where you are to live, so that I can fix you there in my mind.'

'But nothing's actually been said. I'm not—'

'Nonetheless, I want to go because, whatever happens, that house is important to you.'

We made the trip through London by omnibus and on foot, despite the sultry weather. We found the gates ajar though there was no sign of any activity in the house or drive. I thought it would be indelicate to go in when Henry wasn't there but Rosa marched straight up to the front door and rang the bell.

Nobody answered so she took several steps back and admired the frontage. 'It's much grander than I'd expected. Six bedrooms, you say. Goodness, Mariella. Can we look at the garden? What wonderful trees. Well, now I see why it's called the Elms. Yes, you have my formal stamp of approval. I think this is an entirely suitable house for my lovely cousin.'

'Rosa, we shouldn't go any further. It's almost trespassing.'

'Why? Even if you don't actually have a ring on your finger Henry is a close relative, isn't he? Of course we're entitled to be here. But it's so hot. Let's sit down for a while and imagine what your married life will be like.'

She spread her shawl under an elm and we leaned against the trunk. The dining room had double casement doors opening onto the terrace and with a rapidly beating heart I saw myself on the other side, flinging them open so that Henry and I could take a walk together, arm in arm. And in the winter the conservatory would be an ideal place to work on sunny mornings, provided it was adequately heated.

'Mother received a letter from Stepfather's solicitor yesterday,' said Rosa. She had closed her eyes, her head had fallen back and her hands rested in her lap, giving her an air of unusual resignation. 'Now Max has gone to fight in the Russian war, Sir Matthew's affairs have been settled. I didn't like the tone of the letter at all. It's as if Max has been written off, somehow.'

'Max will come back safely, I'm sure.'

'It makes no difference. One way or another Horatio wants Mother and me out of his life for good, so he has made us an annuity each – two hundred pounds for her, one hundred for me.'

'That doesn't sound very much.'

'Exactly what Mama says but I think it's more than enough and I hope that by Christmas we will be in our own house. Your father told me that it's possible to rent a very nice villa in Putney or Wandsworth for seventy pounds a year.'

'But you can't leave us. How will you manage to look after your mother by yourself?'

'I'll still be able to employ Nora. Mariella, I *must* take this step. The longer I stay at Fosse House, the harder it will be to leave.'

'We don't want you to go, Rosa.'

'Soon you'll marry Henry. Look how this house is waiting for you. I couldn't go on living at Fosse House without you, I'd miss you too much. In any case, we can't impose any longer on your family.'

'It seems a terrible prospect for you. How will you bear it?'

'I wanted to be a nurse. Well, I can. Mother is my patient, my vocation.' Her voice was too bright and she jumped up, gave me her hand and hauled me to my feet. 'Come on, do you think we'll be able to see anything if we peer through the windows? I especially want to have a glimpse of the scullery; you can tell a great deal about an establish—' and she darted away round the side of the house.

I followed more slowly but as I reached the corner I heard her laughter, then a male voice, Henry's, and there they were, face to face as if they had actually collided. He was gripping her elbows to help her regain balance, and was so startled that for several moments he could do nothing but stare and shake his head.

'I'm so sorry,' I cried, 'you must think we are intruding.'

Now that he'd recovered he greeted us more light-heartedly than I'd ever known him and offered each of us his arm like a shy boy. 'It is wonderful to find you here. What a coincidence – it so happens I had arranged to meet the architect at half past three, otherwise I would never have visited in the middle of the day. I am so used to coming alone that I have lost all pleasure in the place. Now I shall be able to share it with you.'

He ushered us into the porch, unlocked the door and stood back to let us in. Immediately the house enclosed us with its smell of new paint and trapped air. We walked from one room to another admiring the proportions, the polish on the wooden floors and the light flooding through the casement windows. But my pleasure was marred by my consciousness of Rosa's pain, though she was as full of question and comment as ever. This, after all, was my future. How bleak hers must have seemed by comparison.

As we were about to climb the stairs she said, 'Do you know, I'm so hot I think I'll wait outside under the trees. You go on.' She backed away and disappeared through the open front door.

Henry's foot was already on the fourth stair but now he hesitated. 'Perhaps it is late. The architect will be here any minute.' He seemed hurt, and as we went back outside to join Rosa I hoped she hadn't offended him by her abrupt change of mood. But perhaps, despite my initial disappointment, it was a relief not to have visited those impossibly private upstairs rooms again with Henry, knowing that she was outside.

A few minutes later the architect arrived and I insisted we leave at once. Henry, though very courteous, seemed abstracted and I again blushed with embarrassment that he had come upon us so unexpectedly. If only he and I had been formally engaged, all would have been well.

His final words, however, were reassuring. 'I hope to see you both very soon, at the lecture. I cannot tell you, Mariella, Miss Barr, what a pleasure it was to find you here. Now, I think, this house has become a home in my eyes.' As we reached the gates and looked back he was still in the porch. Rosa waved and he made a slight gesture in reply.

Chapter Fifteen

The cholera epidemic delayed Henry's lecture, entitled 'Death or Clean Hands?', until the end of August. When we finally received an invitation to the Willis's Rooms, St James's, Father insisted how wise he'd been to buy a carriage which would transport us quickly and comfortably across London late in the evening. Even though his starched evening collar made an angry red mark on his throat he was too impressed by the occasion to complain.

Mother volunteered to stay at home with Isabella who would hate to be left alone with just Nora. It was no hardship, Mother said, because knowing Henry's bluntness the contents of his lecture were bound to be distasteful and she relied on us to report back anything that might apply to the management of the governesses' home. But actually I knew that she would have given a great deal to attend the lecture. Her capacity for self-sacrifice, I realised, was far superior to my own.

Rosa was ready in ten minutes. Her black silk gave her the austere beauty of a stained-glass saint as she lay among the pillows of my bed and watched me dress. I was to wear my ice-blue evening gown, cut low to reveal a risky quantity of neck and shoulder.

'I won't put my body through that,' she said, as I laced the front of my stays. 'Why do you do it? You already have a tiny waist.' She sprang up, circled me with her hands, pressed her cheek to mine and planted kisses on my shoulder and chin. 'Lovely, lovely Mariella. I wish I could put essence of Mariella on a handkerchief to ward off the bad things in life. But why torture yourself?' She swayed me back and forth in front of the mirror.

'I like the shape the corset gives me and I would feel undressed without it.' She was a couple of inches taller, willowy and ivory skinned while I looked tiny and demure despite the low-cut bodice.

I tried to cover myself with a lace stole but Rosa whisked it away. 'Throw back your head and lift your elbows a little. If you let your shoulders sag you'll be lost. No wonder Henry finds you irresistible.' She massaged the top of my spine with her thumbs. 'What you need is a necklace, something blue to match your eyes. I have just the thing – I was going to give it to you anyway.' She held out a velvet-covered box. 'Now it's yours.'

The box, as I well knew, contained a heart-shaped gold locket set with a sapphire and with a lock of her father's hair inside. 'I can't take your locket,' I said.

'I want you to have it. I do. How else can I repay you for all you've done?'

'There's no need for this, Rosa.'

'There is a need. Don't think I'm not aware of what a trial it's been sometimes having us here. So do let me, please, give you this. For my sake. Look inside.'

She had replaced the little curl of greying male hair with a tiny plait, wound so that it was a coiled spring of brown and gold. 'I cut a strand of your hair while you were sleeping. Yours and mine. Now don't go weeping, Mariella.' She took my face in her hands and kissed my forehead, cheeks and lips.

'It's too precious. What about your father's hair?'

'I have that still. I don't need the locket to remind me of him.'

'I won't be able to wear it. What would your mother say?'

'She needn't know.'

'I hate secrets of any kind.'

'The locket is mine to give. Don't spoil my present, Mariella. And anyway, what's wrong with you wearing it? Everyone knows that we share everything. If Mama notices we can say you've just borrowed it for the night. Let me fasten it for you.'

She sat behind me on the bed and her breath fell on my neck as she fiddled with the clasp. For a moment the backs of her fingers rested against me as she leaned her forehead on my bare shoulder. As we ran downstairs she floated ahead in her shimmering black silk, her bonnet tumbled half off, ribbons streaming.

The lecture hall was intimidating because the clannishness among the gentlemen seemed unassailable, and there were few ladies present. Even Rosa was a little subdued as we watched the arrival of what she called *the great and the good*. Father dived in and out of the crowd to report on who was there; not only luminaries from the medical world, including Dr John Snow and Sir James Clarke, both of whom were known to have attended the Queen, but a member of the aristocracy, Lord Ashburton, the author Mr Carlyle and the politician Richard Monckton Milnes, who was a particular favourite of Henry's because they both admired the poet John Keats.

I was so nervous, the hall was so hot and my bodice so tight that I felt a tick in my forehead – the beginning of headache. There stood Henry in a flare of gas light, soberly dressed in frock coat and gleaming shirt front, hands clasped behind his back, barely referring to the notes on the lectern as he spoke for three-quarters of an hour about a theory which he said might change surgery for ever. I tried to see past this man with his meticulously brushed hair and thick moustache to the boy who used to sit on the drawing-room sofa, one leg tucked under the other, absorbed in some impenetrable text. While he read his left arm was flung round my eight-year-old shoulders and his fingers occasionally played with a lock of my hair as I leaned against him and stitched a sampler.

The shadows came and went in the hollows of Henry's cheek. I loved his voice which, though strong and authoritative, was at the same time measured, with no edge of harshness or patronage. After a while I had to glance away in case he became aware of how attentively I watched him and how, when he half turned his head to address another section of the audience and the lamplight caught his lip, I remembered that those same lips had kissed mine under the cedar.

'Semmelweiss has been more or less banished from Vienna,' he said, 'where he performed his ground-breaking research, but he continues his work in St Rochus's Hospital, Hungary. This is what he noticed: in a ward of women who were delivered by midwives less than three per cent of the patients died of puerperal fever, whilst in a similar ward served by medical students the death rate was as high as thirteen per cent.

'Semmelweiss, like everyone else, at first struggled to see what the connection might be, but after careful observation he realised that the medical students began their day by performing autopsies, and then went straight into the labour wards to examine and deliver expectant mothers. The midwives, on the other hand, never performed autopsies. From this Semmelweiss concluded that the young students were passing infected matter from the corpses to the mothers, hence the high death rate. To rectify this situation he insisted the students wash their hands in a solution of chlorinated lime before attending a birth, that clean sheets should be issued to each new patient, and that the labour wards should be regularly cleaned. As a result the death rate came down almost immediately to just over two per cent.

'Now we, in our hospitals, move from one patient to the next and from one operation to another without washing our hands or cleaning our utensils. The premise that I would like to put to you is that if we were to adopt Semmelweiss's measures, we too would see a dramatic decline in the death rate associated with both surgery and childbirth.'

Though I was listening to Henry with unwavering attention I could not help being aware that there were restless elements in the audience, a good deal of coughing and whispering was going on and a couple of men had crossed their arms and thrown back their heads derisively. The mutter of pain in my temple had become an insistent jabbing. It had never occurred to me that anyone could disagree with Henry but when he finished speaking the applause was thin and a gentleman with a bald head and immense whiskers leapt to his feet. 'What *proof* is there that infected matter is passed in this way from the dead to the living?' he demanded.

'We have no absolute proof. Only the dramatic decline in the death rate once the medical students had changed their habits.'

'Or perhaps, knowing that they were under scrutiny, they simply took more care. They were only students after all, while the midwives were probably old hands. We understand that Dr Semmelweiss has never published his research. Doesn't that suggest to you that he might have something to hide, or at the very least some doubts in his own findings?'

'Dr Semmelweiss is not the easiest man to deal with. Perhaps with reason. He has endured ridicule and opposition and therefore doesn't trust his colleagues.'

Dr Snow stood up. 'Members of the audience will know that my investigations into outbreaks of cholera have convinced me that infection is somehow ingested through the mouth rather than from the air. The medical profession, including, I might say, the distinguished Dr Henry Thewell himself, has refused to give proper credence to my ideas, and the cholera continues to kill thousands of our population. Apparently we would all rather blame bad smells and piles of rubbish than believe that food, water, or indeed droplets from another person's mouth might be to blame. But sometimes, as in this argument of Dr Thewell's, the cost of not taking action, when it is possible to do so, is too great. We cannot always wait for statistics and experiment to prove a theory beyond doubt. Even if Semmelweiss's findings cannot actually be proved, what harm can there be in adopting his methods?'

'Because they are founded not on modern scientific research based on sustained observation and experiment but on a hunch. Dr Thewell seems to be suggesting that there is something poisonous in the flesh of a dead person. Is this not a little old-fashioned? The days of evil spirits associated with corpses are long gone.'

'I am suggesting that it is the body that is the cause of infection, not the spirit,' said Henry.

'Have you given any thought to how much it would cost to implement these types of changes, to have such measures in place for every nurse, orderly and doctor, to have the wards cleaned in this way just in case some fanatical Hungarian's theory happened to be right? How many patients would we have to turn down in order to accommodate Semmelweiss's ideas?'

'Perhaps it is the case that though fewer patients could be treated more lives might be saved.'

'Dr Thewell, if we carry your arguments to their logical conclusion, you are suggesting that countless deaths have been caused by the very men who trained for years to become surgeons and physicians and thereby save lives. In fact, you are calling your colleagues murderers. I'm amazed that you would venture to spread such ill-founded and dangerous ideas among the general public.'

I was perspiring even in my light gown and the headache had become like the blade of a knife through my cheekbone and jaw. Why do they speak so savagely to each other, I wondered; where is their humanity and comradeship?

After the lecture the hall divided into two distinct groups, those for Henry's argument and those against, and my father went about anxiously testing their opinions. 'The good thing is,' he murmured, 'that Henry has provoked controversy. They may not like what he says but they will remember it. In the short term, maybe, it might do him no good, but in the long term, if he is proved right . . .'

I gripped Rosa's arm. 'What do you think? Will it have damaged him?'

'Hardly. He is in many ways brilliant and he has courage. You must be so proud that he is not afraid to take on the establishment.'

At last Henry came over and took my hands. My headache retreated a little at his touch. 'Ella, my dear. Do you know, when I saw you watching me so sternly, I remembered how when you were a little girl you used to test me whenever I had to learn a text by heart. She was very strict,' he told Rosa. 'She wouldn't let me get a word wrong even though she was only eight and had to follow the tiny writing, some of it in Latin, with her finger. I used to watch for the way her little tongue poked out when she was concentrating.'

'Oh you mean like this,' said Rosa, catching the tip of her tongue between her teeth. Henry glanced at her mouth and then looked away. 'She still does that. Your lecture made complete sense to me, by the way. I cannot understand why your colleagues are being so obtuse.'

'We all hate change. And the suggestion that at the moment we are actually harming patients cuts very deep. No doctor could find that easy to stomach.'

'What do you think of Dr Snow's point, that the same type of backward thinking applies to his work on cholera? I have read another report in *The Times*,' she added in a low voice, 'about the terrible losses among our troops from cholera. Can nothing be done?'

'The best cure would have been to move the troops away from what is obviously a very unhealthy spot, but that is down to our generals. At any rate, I believe the latest news is that they will set sail from Varna imminently.'

'They say thousands of men have already died. It's such a pitiful waste. I'd hate to think that my stepbrother Max's life might be thrown away in a bout of unnecessary sickness. He's survived the Australian desert, after all. How futile it would be if he now died of a contagion much closer to home.'

Why did she do it, I wondered. I had hoped that they were now good friends so why, on a night when Henry was fired up with the exertion of giving his lecture, had she raised the one subject guaranteed to make his eyes go bleak?

'The war office has not chosen to seek my advice again thus far,' he said, 'and if it did—'

'Must you wait for them? Couldn't you insist that they listen to you? After all if it's common knowledge that cholera is passed from one person to another in close proximity . . .'

'Common knowledge does not count as medical proof, as you've heard tonight. Even Snow isn't sure enough yet to publish a definitive report on cholera. I'm afraid it's not my job to advise anyone of the dangers to our troops.'

'But you were *out* there. You are responsible.'

I was dismayed she should speak so forcefully that her remarks had been overheard by many in the room. Henry's colour was high. 'I don't think I can be held responsible for every death in the Russian War,' he said quietly, then turned to me. 'And what about you, Ella, did you enjoy the lecture?'

'I did. You spoke so clearly, it seemed to me that nobody could doubt the truth of what you said.'

He took my hand and smiled lovingly. 'I think some of my colleagues would say you were mistaking truth for conviction.'

'Perhaps. But sometimes I hear something and immediately there is no doubt in my mind that it is true.'

He pressed my hand in both of his and glanced briefly at my bosom. 'I haven't told you . . . You are looking . . . What a beautiful necklace, Ella. I've never seen you wear it before, I think.' He reached out and picked up the locket so delicately that his fingertip barely brushed my skin.

'It's Rosa's,' I said. 'She lent it to me.'

He studied it for a moment longer, then let it fall abruptly and turned to a couple of gentlemen who were waiting to speak to him.

But still Rosa hadn't finished with him. 'Dr Thewell, I must just ask, how is the little boy Tom? The one who lost his leg that day in the hospital.'

He said curtly, 'Died the next day, rather as I feared.'

'How dreadful, to put him through so much, and then for him to die.'

I turned my head a little to the side and smiled at Henry, hoping he would understand that I was dissociating myself from Rosa's implied blame. Once his back was turned the pain in my face became so intense that I put my hand to my forehead and staggered. Rosa was full of concern. 'What is it, Mariella? Come outside. It's too close in here.'

She found me a chair in the lobby where I sank down and closed my eyes. 'You are so hard on Henry. Why do you speak to him so fiercely?'

'Was I hard? I don't think so. Mariella, you mustn't mind so much. There's no need to protect him. His whole professional life is based on argument and discussion. That's how doctors learn.'

'But tonight, at least, we should have supported him.'

'We are supporting him, by being here. We show him respect by taking him seriously but we don't have to agree with him.'

'We should be on his side.'

'Mariella, I am always on your side but that doesn't mean I think you're always right. Can't you see? The more we overcome our differences, the stronger our love.'

Chapter Sixteen

At the beginning of September the weather became so cool and unsettled that we took the summer curtains down early. Meanwhile news from the war was very exciting because our troops had embarked at last, were crossing the Black Sea and about to seize Sebastopol, the port where the Russian navy was based. For the past ten days I had been confined to bed following my attack of migraine and was still too frail even to undertake plain sewing. Work with paper, glue and scissors was less of a strain so I added another page to my album. I drew a map to show the relative positions of Varna in Bulgaria, and Sebastopol, at the tip of the Crimean Peninsula. My depiction of the Black Sea was of a ragged lozenge with Turkey in the south, Bulgaria in the west and the Crimean Peninsula, a squashed little diamond shape stuck at the bottom of Russia, on the northern side. The voyage from Varna to Sebastopol would be relatively quick under steam, perhaps two or three days, and I drew firm black arrows pointing from one to the other. It all looked so straightforward that I couldn't think why the generals had waited so long.

Down came Rosa wearing a dark green woollen gown, a thick shawl and her heaviest boots ready for house-hunting in Battersea, which Father said was an excellent location due to the new park and proximity to the river. Rosa would be gone the entire day because in the evening she was meeting Barbara Leigh Smith in the Hanover Square Rooms for a performance of Beethoven's 'Moonlight' Sonata. The carriage had duly been ordered to collect her at ten. I was glad that my recent illness gave me an excuse not to join them because Barbara worried me to death with her persistent requests for me to offer myself as a teacher.

Rosa leaned over the map and traced the route across the sea from Varna to Sebastopol. 'If the Russian navy is based at Sebastopol it won't be that easy to take, surely.'

'Their navy is very inferior to ours, Father says. The allies have steamships armed with rockets. And the Russians may not be expecting an invasion after all this time.'

'Of course they'll be expecting it. The whole world has been expecting it. That's why it's so ridiculous that there's been all this dithering. By now the Russians will have their defences ready.'

'Our generals must have thought of that.'

'Don't you believe it. Your father says they have no respect for the Russians, and he's worried that they won't have planned for what will happen if there is real resistance. Max used to tell me stories of how Napoleon's army was devastated by its invasion of Russia in 1812 because even he, a magnificent general who would have run rings round our poor old Lord Raglan, underestimated the sheer size and obstinacy of the Russian army, and on top of that had no idea how to survive the Russian winter.'

'What a pity the war office never thought to consult Max.'

'The war office, he says, consults only men who have been in the system for decades and therefore have no idea what's really going on. But wish me luck, Mariella, I have a list of half a dozen houses to look at, none of which will suit Mother. I only wish you were well enough to come with me – you have such a knack of making a room into something more than itself.'

I kissed her. 'Don't look too hard. Stay in Fosse House at least until the spring. And if you must go out, take an umbrella. Father thinks it will rain again later.'

After she'd gone I worked on the Crimean map and then went to the window and pulled back the lace curtain. The air was liquid clear and the pavements glittered with sunshine on wet stone but I was fretful and cold. Perhaps I should have made an effort and gone with Rosa; it was unkind of me to let her face such a weary trek alone. I would definitely go tomorrow. Though I put more coal on the fire the flames were sluggish and when the sun went in the room was gloomy.

I should have gone up to see if Isabella needed me but the thought of climbing the stairs, of easing open the door and peeping in, of finding her awake and perhaps demanding a game of backgammon was too dismal to contemplate.

When the doorbell rang I didn't stir because Ruth had been told that while I was convalescent I was not at home to callers. But then I heard hurried footsteps on the stairs, the door was flung open and there was Henry, hair tousled by the wind, smelling of autumn.

My eyes were heavy because I'd been indoors for so long, my hair, though neat, had not been washed for over a week and I was wearing an old gown with a wide collar which, according to Rosa, made me look no more than sixteen. When I got to my feet and held out my hand the ghost of headache murmured in my temple.

Henry refused to sit down although he did say he would drink a cup of tea. His manner was altogether so strange that I grew nervous. As we waited for Ruth I sat with my hands folded, wishing I had a bit of sewing to occupy me, while he went to the window and looked out into the street. We talked about the lecture and how it had provoked much discussion but little change amongst doctors and students at Guy's, and when Ruth at last came in we both watched with excessive interest as she placed the tray on the table, dropped a little curtsey and departed, though not without first giving me a significant stare.

I poured the tea but everything made too much noise: the liquid trickling into the cup, the clink of the spoon, the sudden rattle of the window as a strong gust beat against it. And then when I held out the cup Henry seemed not to notice but looked away as he suddenly enquired after the whereabouts of each member of the family.

'Mother is sifting through applications for the post of matron at the home, and Rosa is house-hunting. Then she's off to a concert.'

'A concert. On her own?'

'With her friend, Miss Leigh Smith.'

'Ah yes, the radical friend, as I recall. But house-hunting, you say?'

'In Battersea.'

'Battersea. Do you know, I cannot for the life of me imagine Miss Barr in Battersea. She seems to me to be a woman who needs a great deal of space, who mustn't be confined.' He started forward, took the cup and saucer from me but then immediately set them down and returned to the window. 'So, she has gone out for the entire day. I see.' He and I were now separated by the tea table, Father's armchair and a plant stand holding a ceramic pot decorated in the Chinese style with a dragon and temple, from which sprouted a thriving maidenhair fern. I took a sip of tea.

'Don't you find it hard to imagine that a war is being fought for our sake halfway round the world?' he said suddenly. 'I do, especially when I'm in this room with you.'

These last words were spoken with such shaky tenderness that it was as if he had reached out and stroked my breast. But his hands were actually clenched on the sill and he turned his face away so that I could see only his profile: chin held very high, slightly hooked nose, deep forehead. 'Mariella, I have decided to travel out to Turkey again. As you know, there is a plan to lay siege to Sebastopol. There are bound to be casualties and the main army hospital is near Constantinople, three hundred miles across the Black Sea. When I was last there, as I've said, I didn't envisage that the war would be fought this late in the year so we didn't take account of how stormy the Black Sea might be in autumn and winter, or how unreliable the steamships. As both these factors will affect the care of the wounded I should like to be there to help.'

'Surely the army has its own doctors?'

'So it has, and more have volunteered. But it's impossible to estimate how many doctors will be needed. So much depends on information we don't have. How long, for instance, will the war last? How many battles will there be? How far superior to the enemy are we in terms of weaponry and manpower? At any rate, as you know, I have some skill as a surgeon. I can't help feeling, I am arrogant enough, I'm afraid, that I could be of particular use.'

'Father says that the Russian army is primitive and ill-disciplined so there will be only a few casualties on our side.'

'Let us hope that he is right. At any rate, I came to tell you that I'll be leaving in the next couple of days and I shall be gone a few months, perhaps until Christmas.'

I looked at my hands and thought: He doesn't realise that my entire life is in suspense every second that I am not with him.

After a few more moments I became aware that we had both been silent for so long that it would soon be impossible to speak. Then he said, 'There are five, six, seven rabbits on the front lawn.

What will your mother say if they get into her vegetable garden?'

At first I couldn't understand why we were to waste time talking about rabbits. Then I realised that in fact he was inviting me to join him at the window so I got up and manoeuvred my petticoats between the table and the plant stand, and past the back of the armchair. For a moment we looked at the rabbits, then he suddenly clasped my hand.

My first thought was: So he really is going to propose. Then I registered that my fingers were actually aching because he was squeezing them so hard and I shivered as heat passed from my warm hand to his cold one. He brought my hand to his lips, kissed my knuckle and spoke very decidedly, as if making a well-rehearsed speech. 'Mariella, I'm sure you know what I am going to ask you. My sweetest memories, since Mother's death, are of the times I have spent with you. I made my decision early in the summer, as you know. I thought then that I could foresee a period of stability in my life. Now, however, I am going away again and even though I am probably being very selfish it seemed impossible to leave without saying, without telling you, that I hope you will agree to be my wife.'

I said at last, 'It sounds as if you are only proposing to me because you are going away.'

'I am asking you to marry me because there suddenly seems to be great uncertainty in my life. In fact for the past few weeks I have been in turmoil. I mean ... prior to this summer I had felt very clear about the progress of my career but when I gave that lecture I realised that my path was not necessarily going to be a smooth one. And who knows what I shall have to face with our troops in Russia? I feel as if I need to secure you as the one constant in my life, to make sure that you will be here when I get back. Is that very selfish of me?'

'I have always been here waiting for you and always will, whether you wish to marry me or not.'

He nodded but the tension didn't leave his face. 'Yes. I know. My dear Mariella.' When the wind gusted again the rabbits kicked up their heels and bolted for cover. I shivered. Henry and I seemed fixed in our stiff positions and my heart was aching. Love. *Love* was the missing word. Why didn't he say the one thing that would make me happy for ever?

I leaned forward so that a huff of breath passed from his mouth to mine. He put his hand on the back of my head and pressed me against his neck. 'My dear,' he said. 'My dear one.' Then he put his lips to my forehead, almost as if he were blessing me, and at last kissed my mouth.

I heard the clunk of the mechanism in the clock as it prepared to strike the quarter. There was restraint in every muscle of his body and I told myself that it must be because we were in the morning room at Fosse House, where he and I had once been children together. In the end I leaned further forward and opened my lips under his but instead of prolonging the kiss he gave a deep sigh and crushed me fiercely against his chest. 'Is that yes? May I speak to your father tonight?'

'Yes.'

'But you're trembling, my dearest girl, what have I done to you?' He led me to the sofa, poured me more tea though my hand shook so much it spilled into the saucer, and we sat side by side and laughed about how we had never imagined this, fourteen years ago. Except that I, of course, had always imagined it.

As promised he returned that evening after dinner to ask Father for my hand in marriage. While they were in the study I sat in the drawing room with Mother and Aunt, missing Rosa dreadfully. I felt as if I were playing the role of young-lady-awaiting-betrothal; I simply could not connect those minutes of suspense with the fulfilment of a lifetime's dream. The drawing room was the same as it had always been – the tassels and swags of the winter curtains, Richmond's portrait of my father looking benign with a pen in his hand and a plan spread before him, my mother under a lamp, apparently engrossed in writing responses to the candidates not selected for interview, although from time to time she glanced up and smiled sympathetically at me. The one difference was that Aunt stared at me jealously. Henry, though by no means a perfect match due to his being a member of the medical profession and having a consumptive mother, was at least *something*, he apparently had prospects, and most important of all, after tonight I would be spoken for. Isabella's own old age, by contrast, depended on Rosa, who was making herself ever more ineligible by flitting about London with the outcast Miss Leigh Smith.

Suddenly a door opened, male feet crossed the hall, and there was Father rubbing his hands and ringing for Ruth to bring up the Madeira while Henry was embraced by Mother and given a tearful kiss by my aunt, and there was I, blushing and demure, receiving a little glass, smiling into Henry's eyes, holding his hand for the first time in public.

We were duly toasted and I presented him with Rosa's portrait of me, wrapped in waxed paper and tied with a blue ribbon. He unrolled it carefully and stared at it for a long time. 'Are you sure I can have this?'

'Of course. Rosa gave it to me. She would be delighted if she knew you were taking it with you.'

'It's a pity we couldn't ask her first. She's still not back, then?'

'By all means wait—'

'No, no. I must pack. There is a great deal to do. I have been here too long already.'

Now that we were engaged I was allowed to put on my shawl and walk with him to the garden gate, in the dark. He put one arm round my waist and with the other reached for my hand. The wind gusted and the sky was so dark that I could hardly see his face. He spoke into my hair, above my ear. 'I wanted to give you this ring of my mother's. When I come back we'll buy you something new, if you like, but in the meantime I wonder if you would wear it for me.'

A cold band slid over my finger and when I held it up close I saw the three glittering stones that had once been Aunt Eppie's sole ornament. Henry kissed the ring then drew my hand through his arm and we walked on.

The garden was full of the ghosts of all that he and I had ever been to each other. I could track the progress of our love, the suspense of waiting for a visit, the self-conscious smiles and blushes, and after he'd gone my lonely revisiting of the places where we had sat together. Then, as we entered the wilderness, I heard Rosa's voice as she confronted him with folded arms and tears in her eyes: *But you can have no respect at all for me* . . . and the sudden crowding of the path, the jostling as we walked three abreast, the joy of reconciliation.

By the time we reached the door in the wall I was crying so hard that I couldn't hide it from him. 'I don't think I can bear you to go. You don't know . . . you don't know—'

'What don't I know?' He kissed my face and held me in his arms. It was glorious and sweet to be so firmly possessed and yet the pain of what was happening made me brittle. 'Hush, hush, my darling girl. You must bear up.'

'But after all this time, we've had only a few minutes. I feel as I've wasted all these years, not being able to show you, tell you . . . and now you are going away.'

'I'm only going away like all the other times. I want you to write to me every week if you will, and as soon as I come back we will be married. But please, Mariella, no more tears. This is not like you.' He pulled away and held me firmly by the upper arms. 'It will be three months at most. Dearest love, we must get better at saying goodbye or we shall never be able to bear it.' He kissed my hand, unclenched my fingers which were fastened tight round the key, took it from me and opened the gate. 'Send Miss Barr my regards. Tell her I'm sorry to have missed her but that I couldn't stay. Goodbye now, Mariella. Goodbye.'

'Henry,' I cried, but he was gone, his rapid footfall fading while the gate caught the wind and groaned on its hinges. 'Henry.' He didn't come back. I waited and waited but there was only the sound of the wind funnelling down the lane so I pulled shut the gate, crouched down, wrapped my arms round my knees and tried to understand why, on this happiest of nights, my heart was breaking.

When Rosa came in later I was already in bed. 'I went to say goodnight to Mother and she told me the news. Oh darling girl, you must be so happy. I'm so glad for you. But why are you crying?'

'He's gone to the war. He's proposed at last, after all this time, and now he's going away.'

'But he'll be safe. He's not going to fight after all.'

'You don't know what it's like. I'm forever having to say goodbye to him. You're not in love with anyone so you don't know what it feels like to be without the one person in the world who makes you truly happy . . .'

She released me and stood up. 'No. Perhaps not. But Mariella, try to be joyful, at least tonight. This is what you have been wanting all your life, isn't it? Only the very few ever achieve that.' She stood over me for a moment longer. 'I'll leave you in peace, then, shall I? I expect you would like to be alone tonight.'

Chapter Seventeen

We read in *The Times* that less than a fortnight after landing in the Crimean Peninsula the allied army in Russia had won a great victory at a village called Alma and that Sebastopol had fallen. Up to two thousand English soldiers had been killed or wounded but we all agreed that a short, sharp battle had been just what was needed to ensure a speedy victory and to show the Russians our metal.

Though Henry couldn't possibly have reached the Crimea by 20 September I read and reread the war reports in the newspaper for mention of how the medical services had performed. A few days after the Battle of Alma there was a disturbing indication that things hadn't gone quite as smoothly as they might have done:

> *When I was looking at the wounded men going off today, I could not see an English ambulance. Our men were sent to the sea, three miles distant, on jolting arabas or tedious litters. The French – I am tired of this disgraceful antithesis – had well-appointed covered hospital vans, to hold ten or twelve men, drawn by fine mules.*

What a pity, Mother said, that Henry hadn't been there in time to put things right for the wounded. But at least the war was bound to end any moment now. He would soon reappear in the drawing room for all the world as if he had been on a trip to Edinburgh or Oxford rather than Turkey.

I began sewing a trousseau. My allowance had been increased on my engagement and I bought yards of cambric muslin to sew undergarments and nightgowns fit for the the Elms. Folders of paper patterns piled up in the morning room and at night when I closed my eyes all I could see was a froth of lace and broderie anglaise. Rosa used to unwrap my latest creation, hold it up to the light, marvel at my tucks and frills and press her face to the cloth because she said she loved the scent of fabric fresh from the roll.

But it then turned out that the news reports had been very misleading, that although the allied forces had certainly won a battle, Sebastopol had by no means been taken, and in fact now our forces were digging in for a long siege which would probably last all winter. I had been faithfully filling my album with clippings from *The Times*, and on 10 October, when I collected the previous day's paper from Father's study, I was confronted with the words:

> *Our victory was glorious ... but there has been a great want of proper medical attention; the wounded were left, some for two nights ... on the field. The number of lives which have been sacrificed by the want of proper arrangements and neglect must be considerable.*

'... *the want of proper arrangements* ...' Though I put the paper down hurriedly and took up my sewing the words shrouded me like a wet cloak. Surely Henry wasn't to blame. He was always right about everything so it wasn't possible that he could have been wrong about this. Someone else must be responsible, the military men, probably, who, according to Rosa, planned things piecemeal, reacting to each new crisis as it arose. In the end I cut out the article but didn't stick it in, thinking I would wait until the news was better so that the unpleasant words of 9 October didn't spoil the album.

But a couple of days later, on the twelfth, Father came in just as we were going to bed. *The Times* was folded on its tray waiting for him but he already knew what it contained. 'This is very grave,' he said at once. 'Has anyone told you the news? I'm afraid I can't spare you,' and he read us the latest article.

> *It is with feelings of surprise and anger that the public will learn that no sufficient preparations have been made for the proper care of the wounded. Not only are there not sufficient surgeons - that, it might be urged, was unavoidable; not only are there no dressers and nurses – that might be a defect of the system for which no one is to blame; but what is there to be said when it is known that there*

is not even sufficient linen to make bandages for the wounded? The greatest commiseration prevails for the sufferings of the unhappy inmates of Scutari . . . Not only are men kept, in some cases for a week, without the hand of a medical man coming near their wounds . . . but now, when they are placed in the spacious building, where we were led to believe that everything was ready which could ease their pain or facilitate their recovery, it is found that the commonest appliances of a workhouse sick ward are wanting, and that the men must die through the medical staff of the British army having forgotten that old rags are necessary for the dressing of wounds.

Mother seized her pen as if she would immediately dash off a letter of protest; Aunt Isabella pushed her upper body out of the cushions and stared about the room; Rosa sat with her head in her hands and her hair covering her face.

Finally Isabella said, 'Yes but this can't be true. I thought your Dr Thewell went out specifically to get everything ready.'

'It looks so bad,' said Father. 'The country will feel it and the government will struggle to survive. The trouble is that when a nation goes to war it does so on the assumption that it is going to win.'

'We are winning, I thought,' said Isabella.

'Not just the physical battles but the moral ones too. It's hard for a nation to sustain a shock like this. The people will come to hate the war. Confidence will suffer and business will be affected. We'll all feel it.'

Another silence. 'But what about Henry?' I said.

Rosa lifted her head and gave me a strange, dreary look. 'He couldn't have known, he'd never been on a battlefield so he won't have imagined thousands of casualties.'

'Well, what were the other, the military doctors thinking of? They knew what war was like.'

'I doubt it. One or two of them might have been present at a few spats in India maybe.'

'But you said there would be no casualties, Father,' I cried.

'*Few.* Few. I thought few casualties. It's not my job to predict what's going to happen in a war. Now don't get upset. The Russians can't hold out for long against the combined forces of British,

French and Turks, for goodness' sake. And as for the medical matters, now the authorities have been alerted to the problem it can only be a matter of days before it's all resolved. Modern transport is very fast and our manufacturing trade is second to none. Before we know it those hospitals will be better stocked than any in the world. I'll have a word with a couple of colleagues, see if we can get things moving forwards.'

Mother laid down her pen and blotted her work. 'We can help. I'll speak to Mrs Hardcastle. We can cut bandages. I have masses of sheets upstairs we never use. Together we can sort it out.'

Chapter Eighteen

By Monday 16 October, a sewing circle was established in the morning room at Fosse House. Even Isabella was included; the plight of the wounded soldiers in Russia seemed to have done more to improve her health than any amount of bed-rest and it turned out she could manage an adequate hem stitch and produce thirty or so linen arm supports a day. Mrs Hardcastle, a leading member of the group, sat in her green satin, surprised brows arched high under her cap, cutting triangular bandages. As she reminded us regularly, she and her husband had made a double sacrifice for the troops, first by all this work (in addition to the sewing she was doing, Mr Hardcastle managed a bank and was engaged in financial transactions to do with funding the military campaign), then by having to postpone their departure for a well-earned trip to Europe that had been planned.

Only Rosa was missing from the circle. Her sewing was hopeless, and because Isabella was for once both healthy and occupied her daughter was free to leave the house more often than usual.

In fact Rosa was obsessed by the war. Since she had always opposed it, she seemed to feel culpable for not making her protests more widely heard, and turned her bedroom into an office so that she could mount a one-woman campaign against the iniquitous government that had first engaged our troops in a spurious conflict, then murdered them by cholera or neglected battle wounds. Out went the cushions, the lace cloths and the potpourris I had arranged in preparation for her arrival. In came an upright chair and deal table borrowed from an unoccupied bedroom in the attic. By her bed she kept a collection of cuttings from *The Times*, far more businesslike than anything I had managed, each one annotated and referenced with pages of notes alongside. Night after night she scribbled letters to officials protesting about the conditions of the troops and the fact that women and children were among those trapped within Sebastopol. '*And what is the reason for all this misery? War should surely have been the very last resort, not an activity we tumbled into for want of any better idea . . .*' During the day she met with Miss Leigh Smith and her friends in the hope of gaining allies who would protest against the war.

Late that Monday afternoon she burst in on our sewing circle just as we had broken for tea, took one look at Mrs Hardcastle and ducked away, leaving a tantalising perfume of fallen leaves and a flashing memory of her tousled hair and dark blue gown.

When it was time to leave the ladies spent several minutes in the hall adjusting their rustling skirts, re-tying their bonnets in front of the glass and arranging the date for the next meeting during which we were to pack the sheets and bandages ready for transportation. Mrs Hardcastle, I noticed, kept glancing up the stairs, as if expecting Rosa to appear and apologise for her rudeness. After they had all gone at last Aunt Isabella announced that she was exhausted and would go upstairs to lie down, so Mother and I were left alone.

I was working on a cut-stitch trimmed blouse for Mother to wear at the home's Gala Opening, now scheduled for 3 January. Mother, worn out with the labour of organising the ladies of the sewing circle, a task that required a precarious mix of deference and authority, sat over her writing desk with her head in her hand. After a few minutes, Rosa came in quietly, closed the door and knelt by the hearth. She had discarded her shawl, brushed her hair and knotted it at the nape of her neck although one strand had already unwound and was dangling down her back.

She turned her hands in the heat and spoke in a low, urgent voice. 'They are looking for nurses to go out to the Crimea; I heard it from Barbara. They are to leave in three days' time. Her cousin, Miss Nightingale, will lead the party. Interviews are being held at a house in Belgrave Square.' Mother lifted her head. I thrust my needle into a layer of cambric and took off my thimble. 'It feels as if I've been preparing for this moment all my life. I cannot bear the thought of leaving you all, I know it is a great deal to ask, but I have to go.'

The gas popped in the lamp. Rosa caught hold of the loose strand of hair and twisted it round her finger.

After a long silence Mother said, 'I really don't understand what you are talking about.'

'The war. Our troops are dying of neglected wounds. Women are needed to nurse them.'

Mother spoke in the tight voice that used to frighten me as a child because it was the nearest she ever came to anger. 'But this is out of the question. I wonder why you have even allowed yourself to think that you might go, Rosa. Are you sure you heard correctly? It seems very unlikely that ladies will suddenly be required in the Crimea, of all places. And then, I wonder how you could possibly consider yourself in any way qualified. You are very young and inexperienced.' She paused. 'And in any case, there is the question of your mother.'

I replaced the thimble and held my work to the light. Meticulous counting of threads was required for cut-work and I wished I had been working on something less complicated.

Rosa so rarely met with opposition, least of all from Mother, that for a moment she had no words. 'It wouldn't be for very long,' she said at last. 'I was hoping that you and Mariella could take care of Mother. Given the cause.' Her voice wavered on the last phrase.

'But you are due to move out next month. I thought you had as good as signed the lease on a house in Battersea.'

'Yes. Indeed. Certainly if I were to go to Russia I wouldn't be able to take on that particular lease. But there will be other houses, I'm sure. A home for Mother and me is perhaps not as urgent as our sick soldiers in Russia. Don't you remember, I read out the article from *The Times* that said: *The manner in which the sick and wounded are treated is worthy only of the savages of Dahomey* . . . ? Aunt, I'm so sorry to ask this of you but I have no choice. It is *meant* that I should go. This is more than just a wish, it's a calling. When I look at my life so far it seems to me that it has all been a preparation for this moment. Year after year, when I could, I visited the cottages at Stukeley to help with the sick. Then, when Stepfather was ill, nobody else could stand being in the room with him. I can't describe to you the degraded state he was in sometimes, but I never minded because I am not afraid of anything to do with illness. I must be as qualified as any other woman in Britain, as Miss Nightingale herself, in fact. I know her, remember? I met her in Derbyshire. Do you understand? This is not my choice. I was born for this moment. Oh I don't really believe in destiny but now I *know* this is what I must do. I can't resist this.'

All the time she was speaking I rotated my engagement ring, conscious of the heat of the fire on my knees and the awful weight of Isabella in bed on the floor above.

Rosa suddenly scrambled to her feet and stood with her hands on her hips, gazing into the flames. 'But if it's a matter of my mother, yes, I see, it's an impossible burden for you. Yes. Of course. Well, perhaps I'll sign the lease on the Battersea house after all. There's Nora, between them they could manage . . .' But even Rosa knew that Nora and her mother could not be consigned to an unfurnished house in Battersea. She dropped her head in her hands and began to cry.

Rosa often cried in a passionate burst of joy or sorrow but I had never known her despair. She cried beautifully, of course, her hair shifting from its pins, her nose dainty as ever, the tears dropping through her fingers. 'Aunt, I am utterly selfish, I know it. And yet how can it be selfish to want to relieve suffering? I know my mother is ill but does she really need me as badly as those hundreds of soldiers?'

'Isabella is your first responsibility and you are her only daughter. It's always easier to help those to whom we're not related, in my experience. On the other hand there must be thousands of unfortunate women with no family or ties, who are able to go to Russia.'

'But if there's a choice – if she could be left here, if you could look after her – aren't we all doing our duty? I could use Mother's annuity to hire another nurse to help Nora. Neither you nor Mariella need concern yourselves much with her.'

'Henry has gone,' I said and they were both startled that I had spoken at last. 'We have already given Henry. Isn't that enough?'

'I know, Mariella. You are being asked to sacrifice too much. I've thought of that. But Henry has gone for his own reasons. I have nothing to do with Henry. I simply want to get down on my knees and scrub floors and give our men warm beds and clean water. There is nothing noble in what I can do. And yet I must do it. To leave you will be like leaving half of myself. But I have no choice.'

Rosa, the unstoppable, went up to tell her mother that if arrangements could be made she planned to go to Turkey and an hour later Aunt Isabella came down to dinner with dishevelled hair and a dead-white face. She managed two mouthfuls of soup before dissolving in tears. 'I have told her that I shall die while she is in Turkey but she is still determined to go. I swear it will break my heart.' And she flung down her napkin, pushed back her chair and sat the rest of the evening on the sofa refusing tea and gulping back tears.

Even Father was miserable. He deplored the fact that Rosa would be putting herself in a dangerous and sordid situation, he thought nursing was probably best left to older, less refined women, but after all he was a patriot and his opinion was that as Miss Nightingale was from one of the highest families in the land, Rosa could only gain from association with her. And it never occurred to him that we should mind about Isabella, whose presence in the house made little impact on him.

As for me, I was numb with shock. That Rosa would think of leaving me at all, let alone abandoning me with her mother, seemed like a betrayal more terrible than the time that we had been banished from Stukeley. How could she do it? And without consulting me.

That night we lay flat on our backs side by side like a knight and his lady on a tomb.

'You think I'm being very selfish, don't you?' she said.

I didn't reply.

'I know you do. I know I am. The point is, I have no choice. It's as if suddenly the purpose of my life has been made clear. I was blundering along on a journey and now at last I see the direction I was travelling in. I cannot bear to think that any human being should suffer if I can do something about it. And now I can, and so can you. Can't you see? If it wasn't for the fact that I know you will be here to help look after Mother I would have no choice. You have given me a choice.'

'But you didn't ask me first. You didn't give me a chance to say no.'

'That would have put you in an impossible position. You'd have been forced to agree to let me go because you'd have had to take the burden all on yourself. At least this way it is your mother who has to decide. But yes, I am selfish, I know it. But I can't not be. This chance will never come again. Never.' She raised herself on her elbow and turned my chin so that I had to look at her. 'Say something. Anything. Please.'

'All right. I'm thinking . . . It was bad enough when Henry went. How will I bear it if you go too?'

'But can't you see? You have Henry. He is your first priority. You will marry him the minute he comes home. And what will I be left with then? Oh please, Mariella, please try to understand.'

Something broke inside me. I knew I would have to let her go and with the end of resistance came a kind of relief. 'Go. Go. Just go,' and we lay cheek to cheek, locked together.

In the morning I went down to breakfast, unfolded my napkin and placed it neatly across my lap. 'I am happy to look after Isabella, if she will let me,' I told Mother. 'I think Rosa should apply to be one of Miss Nightingale's nurses. Today she and I will put her name forward.'

Chapter Nineteen

Rosa borrowed a small round bonnet, a plain collar and my new horse-hair petticoat to puff out her skirts. The pleated lining of her hat was a perfect foil to her luminous complexion and I had never seen her look so subdued and ladylike. Before we left we paid a visit to Isabella's room where I drew back the curtain and Rosa stood in a shaft of light to be scrutinised by her mother and Nora.

'You look dreadful,' said Isabella. 'Like a nun. I suppose the next thing is that you will cut off your hair and become a Roman Catholic.'

'Why would I do that, Mother?'

'Because you seem intent on doing everything you can to displease me.'

'What do you think, Nora?' asked Rosa.

Nora shrugged. 'I think that the silk, in whatever colour, is hardly suitable for the nursing.'

The house in Belgrave Square, home of Mr Sidney Herbert, Secretary of State for War, was very grand with white marble steps and a high-ceilinged entrance hall complete with impressive chandelier. A disdainful footman showed us to a line of chairs where two women were already waiting, one clutching a voluminous carpet bag, the other barely sixteen and with the red hands of a laundry maid.

'I thought there would be hundreds of ladies here,' said Rosa loudly and introduced herself to the others, who answered in monosyllables. Rosa, of course, persisted; I knew that she was viewing them as future companions and as such was determined to find possibilities in each.

A door opened and out came a blousy-looking woman with untidy hair and a bright red spot on each cheek who had obviously not been given an encouraging reception. The woman with the carpet bag was shown in, the doorbell again rang and two frail-looking elderly ladies with crucifixes prominently displayed on their bosoms took seats beside us.

Rosa said in a low voice, 'I think it would be better if you came in with me, Mariella. I shall explain that you are here to support my application in case there are questions about my family situation.' One of the religious spinsters took out a small black prayer book. The scullery maid picked at a bit of dead skin on her index finger.

The carpet-bag woman emerged, looking very pleased with herself, and in went the laundry maid. Rosa struck up a conversation with the elderly ladies, who had devoted their lives to private nursing and had even met dear Mrs Fry – had we heard of her? – but had never been in a hospital. I could tell that Rosa was torn between anxiety that they had seventy-odd years of experience between them and relief that they must surely be much too old for the hospital in Skutari.

But when at last we were shown into a formal parlour where four ladies, each wearing an austere morning gown and plain cap, were seated at a round table covered by a green cloth, it dawned on me that we were for once in a situation where social contacts, youth, enthusiasm and beauty were of no value, and that all the anguish of the previous night had been wasted because Rosa was doomed to disappointment. There was a distinct atmosphere of suppressed impatience and I sensed that the ladies, having glanced at us, had largely withdrawn their attention.

Lady Canning, whom I had met at various charitable functions, said, 'Miss Lingwood, what a delightful surprise. How is your dear mother? You've surely not come to volunteer your services.'

'No. But my cousin, Miss Barr, would like to be among Miss Nightingale's nurses.'

The distinguished eyebrows shot up into the frill of her cap. One of the other ladies sighed.

Rosa sat in the vacant place at the table and a lady introduced as Lady Cranworth entered her details in a book. 'What is your age?'

'I'm twenty-four.'

'Then you are too young,' said a Miss Stanley at once. She was the youngest of them all, perhaps in her thirties, with a prominent nose and bulging eyes.

'Surely youth is needed to endure the hardships ahead. I know that we shall have to work long hours and that there will be none of the usual comforts. I don't mind any of that and I've never had a day's illness in my life. You could write to the doctor at Stukeley and he will vouch for me, and tell you that—'

'You are too young and too attractive, my dear,' said Lady Cranworth. 'Have you any idea of the kind of peril that you would face being amidst so many common men, most of them deprived of female company for months on end? Have you ever been in a hospital ward?'

'I have—'

'You would be eaten alive, Miss Barr. We are sending, at great expense, a party of nurses to relieve the suffering of thousands of sick men. It is imperative, for the sake of Miss Nightingale's reputation as much as for the wounded soldiers, that the expedition should be a success. Even if you had experience running a ward in one of the great teaching hospitals, and I doubt that is the case, you would be rendered unsuitable by the beauty of your face and your youthfulness. Miss Nightingale is adamant about the type of lady she is not prepared to take. You would be seduced within a week and then we would have the worry and expense of caring for you and shipping you home. I'm sorry to speak so bluntly but there are of course other ways in which you and your cousin might consider supporting us. We are in great need of money, and of bed linen—'

'Please,' said Rosa. 'You tell me I am too young and attractive. Well, I do know how to manage myself among men because I was brought up with two stepbrothers. Could I not speak to Miss Nightingale in person? She is a family friend and I know that she is herself a very attractive woman . . .'

Here she had made a bad mistake. 'Miss Nightingale is thirty-four and has the backing of the foreign office itself. Miss Barr, your going to the Crimea is out of the question.'

No further notes were made. Miss Stanley sprang to her feet and opened the door. 'Good luck, my dear, in whatever enterprise you finally choose. I'm sure that with your great spirit you will succeed in doing magnificent things.'

There were now six or seven women in the entrance hail who stared at us avidly as we walked past, heads high, and stepped out into the square.

Chapter Twenty

Balaklava
1 October

My dear Mariella,

A brief note to say I am safely arrived at Balaklava Harbour, seat of the British operations. The journey was uneventful, on relatively calm seas. There is certainly plenty of work for me. I am to accompany wounded troops across the Black Sea to our hospital at Skutari. As I reported in the spring, the hospital there is very large but I'm afraid, given the number of casualties, more space may yet be needed.

Mariella, we parted quite coldly. You were sad and unlike yourself. I don't think you can fully understand that I am not at my best when saying goodbye; I dread partings, in fact. Those last few minutes were agony for us both, and in retrospect I should have left you in the drawing room, with your family. My memories of you in that garden are the sweetest and saddest I know. I remember my desolation after Mother died and that the sight of you each afternoon, waiting for me at the garden door, was both a sharp reminder that she *would never welcome me home again and the first glimmer of hope that there could be others in the world who might love me.*

Will you understand if I tell you that as I travel further from you in time and distance, I love you more?

My love, I was distracted that evening. Our future life together mustn't be tainted by all this.

Dear girl, pray for me. Write soon. Perhaps if you have time, you and your cousin might visit my - our - house again, and see how it goes on and imagine us all in the summer garden. I should like to think of you there.

I am not often at leisure, but I shall endeavour to write regularly. As I have not been over-impressed with the military organisation of affairs here I have little faith in the postal service.

Your affectionate,

Henry

Chapter Twenty-One

London, 1854

Two more battles were fought, Balaklava and Inkerman. The names became part of our daily conversation, evoking feelings of both pride and horror. We wanted a glorious, clean finish to the war, like at Waterloo, but instead, despite repeated assertions by the papers that on both occasions we had heroically repulsed the enemy, we made no real headway. The Russians were still firmly entrenched inside their city of Sebastopol and though our armies were camped outside the town the siege was incomplete. Supplies of weapons and food could still get through. Henry would certainly not be back by Christmas.

The only glimmer of hope was Miss Nightingale's party of nurses, whose progress through France was documented every inch of the way by a fascinated press. Poor Rosa read every detail, as if deliberately to torment herself. A great deal rested on the shoulders of those nurses who had become the one romantic spark in an increasingly bleak account of the war and provided an endless source of conversation for our sewing circle. In Mrs Hardcastle's opinion the inclusion of Roman Catholic nuns was a disaster for all concerned. 'What proper Englishman would wish to be nursed by a Roman Catholic?' she demanded. 'Irish women, at that, probably. If I can call them women.'

'Perhaps they are the best-qualified nurses we have,' said Mother in the falsely jovial voice she used when risking an argument with Mrs Hardcastle. 'Our own Nora McCormack, dear Isabella's Irish nurse, is excellent.'

'The exception to prove the rule. You're fortunate if she isn't a secret drinker. When Mr Hardcastle was struck down with his gout again last winter I hired a fine nurse, as you know. Sober and honest to a fault. From Devon. She could have gone to the war. I wonder if she thought of it.'

'The nuns will be well schooled and obedient, at least.'

'Obedient to their own,' said Mrs Hardcastle. 'To the Pope in Rome. That's who they obey. And what he's after is souls. I'm surprised Miss Nightingale has fallen for such an obvious plot. The Catholics will stop at nothing to convert everyone in sight.'

Rosa was never part of our sewing circle because she was engaged on a mission only I knew about. She redoubled her efforts to be accepted as a nurse until her outpouring of letters rivalled even my mother's. She wrote to the war office, to Miss Nightingale's family, to our member of parliament and our local vicar, detailing every scrap of nursing she had ever done at Stukeley. To the ladies of the committee who had rejected her she protested: '*Your greatest charge against me seemed to be that I was too young. I may be young, but I am determined. This was no whim on my part. I know what I am doing. I have compiled a list of my credentials as a nurse and I believe few women can have done more . . .*'

One evening she came into my room holding a bundle of clothes, closed the door and gazed at me, eyes ablaze.

'Mariella! You won't believe it. I have news. Oh Mariella, watch.' She dragged at the buttons of her gown with trembling fingers, pulled it off and stood in her narrow petticoats and chemise. Then she put on a hideous dress made of flecked grey tweed, far too wide at the waist and shoulders and ending three inches above her ankles, and a plain white cap. The ensemble, which would have made me look like a washerwoman, transformed her into some lovely maid in a Dutch painting.

'It's the nurse's uniform that I am to wear when I travel out to Constantinople. I am actually going on the first of December. I've done it. The war office has decided that because the nation has been so enthusiastic about Miss Nightingale and her nurses, they must send out more. Miss Stanley is to lead the party. She is Miss Nightingale's closest friend and she remembered me, she says, for my *great spirit*, whatever that means. Today I went to Belgrave Square and received these clothes and a lecture from Mr Sidney Herbert. He said: "If you behave yourselves well, there will be provision for you. If not, it will be the ruin of you."' She laughed delightedly. '*Ruin*. I should so like to be *ruined* at Skutari Hospital.

Do you think it will happen? Oh Ella, please, please be happy for me.'

I tried to smile and I murmured that of course I was glad for her. But actually I felt more desolate than if she had actually left a month ago with Miss Nightingale. I had steeled myself for her going, I had made myself be brave, but then the danger passed and I had believed myself safe.

The days that followed were full of tears, mostly Isabella's. The rest of us had little time for private sorrow. The government was in a great rush to send more nurses out to Turkey because the news was that soldiers were dying by the hundreds in understaffed hospitals. A disastrous hurricane had struck supply ships in Balaklava harbour and thousands of winter coats, boots and food supplies had been lost, which meant that our troops were now suffering from the frostbite as well as sickness associated with poor diet and dirty water.

We were in a frenzy of packing, although Rosa's luggage was restricted and she would be forced to wear her uniform on the journey as a clear sign to everyone else on board that she belonged to Miss Stanley's party. We had to go shopping for galoshes and a thick cloak and I sat up far into the night sewing replacement linings for her bodices, muslin under-sleeves and half-sleeves, dark petticoats, woollen blouses and plain, high-necked nightgowns so that if necessary she could wear layer upon layer of clothes to protect her from the cold.

I tried not to dwell on what my life would be like without her but couldn't help thinking in the midst of each routine action – as I watched her plunge her face into the basin of warm water in the morning, press a towel to her skin with her near-translucent hands, fiercely brush and plait her hair, as we ran down to breakfast together: This will be the last time, tomorrow she will be gone and yet I can't capture this. I can't bottle it or sew it and frame it. Tomorrow there will be no more Rosa.

Father, Mother and I accompanied her to London Bridge where she was to take the train to Folkestone. Aunt Isabella, prostrated by the prospect of her daughter's departure, was unable to raise her head from the pillow.

Rosa's hair was severely parted and gathered into a net at the back of her head under a dark bonnet with a white pleated lining.

Hidden under her clothes was the sapphire locket which now contained her father's hair as well as our own. After much argument we had agreed that she should be the one to wear it as a talisman while she was away.

She immediately met up with Miss Stanley, who looked very anxious and held a sheaf of papers. Already Rosa didn't belong to us but talked about the time of arrival in Boulogne, arrangements for being met in Paris, and the fact that their companion, a small, sandy-haired female who I feared would have a difficult time in a Turkish hospital, had brought far too much luggage.

When Rosa turned to us, just for a moment there was a look of detachment in her face. Then the old expression of ardent affection returned. 'Goodbye, my dearest, dearest, Aunt Maria. Take care of Mother for me ... But I know you will. Of course you will.' Then she embraced Father for whom she had no words, just a tearful glance and a lingering kiss on each cheek.

Last, me. She held me at arm's length and looked into my eyes. 'I will write. I will tell you everything. I can scarcely bear it. I know what I am asking. I know. But I will be thinking of you all the time.' She showered me with kisses and I smelled her perfume through the stench of soot and steam.

I kissed her smooth, high cheekbone. 'You might see Henry. Oh Rosa, if you do, tell him I am thinking of him.'

The station was thronging with travellers, the train was chuffing and fuming, there were a great many officials, men dressed in stove-pipe hats and black coats, a group of nuns, some rough-looking older women and scurrying children.

Rosa flung her arms around my neck one last time and I held her, the precious, warm, pliant length of her, then she pulled away and snatched up her two light travelling bags. 'Mariella,' she cried, and couldn't say anything else. Instead she ran between the skirts of her companions and drew them after her into the train. We next saw her in the carriage, standing at the window. 'Go,' she mouthed, laughing through her tears. 'Please go.' But we stayed until the whistle blew and the train at last began to jolt forward in a great commotion of smoke and stink and Rosa's features became ill-defined at the window. Then I turned away and took Father's arm.

PART THREE

Chapter One

Italy, 1855

I tried to dissuade Henry from the picnic because the overcast sky threatened rain but he would have none of it. He hired a carriage and the three of us were driven along the wooded valley south of Narni and then began the slow climb up into the hills above the plains of Lazio. The fortified medieval village of Otricoli was perched high on a slope with bird's-eye views from the parapets. Our carriage squeezed through the gateway, along a crazily winding street and then down to the valley of the Tiber where wealthy Romans had once built their summer playground.

Henry and I sat shoulder to shoulder facing forward, with Nora opposite. I couldn't take my eyes off his hands because I was haunted by the memory of how his fingers had struggled with the buttons of my gown, and I was on fire with longing and suspicion. Had those hands caressed Rosa's breasts and threaded their fingers through her silky hair?

At last the carriage halted amidst a clump of trees. Nora said she would stay put, that it was far too muggy for looking at ruins. She had brought her knitting and there she sat, for all the world as if she were beside my aunt's bed in England.

Henry and I walked at a tortuously slow pace because he paused frequently, fighting for breath. Gradually what had seemed simple meadowland reformed itself into the site of a city. A series of mounds emerged as an amphitheatre with pillars and arches which had once supported tiers of seating. We rested on a bank where the Romans had crowded to watch plays, or athletes pitched against each other head to head. Now the only activity was the wind in the grasses and the flitting of a little brown bird.

Henry fell back on his elbows and took sucking breaths of the moist air as if he had run a mile. His forehead was knotted in concentration and his cheeks were sunken under his eye sockets.

'We should go back,' I said, in my new, cold voice. 'It may rain. The last thing you need is to get wet.'

He opened his eyes and brushed my elbow with the joint of his index finger. The blood juddered in my veins. 'The last thing I need is a fretful Mariella.'

'Are you really feeling better today?'

'I'm gaining so much strength that sometimes I wonder what I'm doing here. If I was working I wouldn't have time to think about my health and then I'd get better instantly. I've a good mind to go back to the war.'

'Yes, I quite understand how difficult it is to be inactive when so much needs to be done. I've read in the newspapers that the summer is proving very difficult for our troops.'

'I like the heat. It was the cold that did for me. I should go back to the Crimea. In any case, is being healthy the most important thing? I need to be useful. If I can't work, I wonder what is the point of being alive?'

'It seems that some of us must fling ourselves into whatever excitement the world has to offer while others must be content to stay at home and keep quiet.'

'My dearest girl, you sound very bitter. I don't despise those who stay at home. Far from it. Each of us has his own vocation. But I can only tolerate myself when I am endeavouring to make things – people – better. It has been my mission in life to try and make a difference.'

'You sound like Rosa.'

After a moment's silence he held out his hand. 'I think you're right, it really is going to rain.'

I pretended that I was drawing on his strength as I got to my feet though had I actually pulled on him he would have fallen over. We walked amidst a flock of evil-eyed goats through an orchard of young trees and down a lane that had definitely, said Henry, been made in the time of ancient Ocriculum, look at the way it had sunk beneath the level of the banks on either side. We found a well and the remnants of the old Via Flaminia where Roman carts had left their wheel marks, and we saw across to the Tiber where rich Romans had spilled out of their barges and sought shade and refreshment after their hot journey up river.

'I'm trying to see them,' said Henry, 'but I can't. It amazes me that there are no ghosts even in somewhere as untouched as this. I can imagine them surging out of their boats, the noise, the jostling into place of the slaves and lower orders, the screeching of tired children, but they're not here, are they, in any sense?'

'There'd be no room for us all if we were surrounded by ghosts.'

'Yet, sometimes, I think we must be moving through an invisible soup of the dead.'

'Is that what it felt like on the battlefield?'

But again he didn't answer.

The theatre where the bloodiest battles had been fought was the best preserved of all, with arches through which the gladiators had rushed from the dark interior. Henry said, 'I expect a hoard of doctors used to come here to attend the frailties of spoiled Romans on holiday.'

'I presume that's a dig at your colleagues back home.'

'Of course. But after all, I have profited from rich patients myself. Look at the house I'm able to build because of the fortune I've amassed through medicine.'

'I thought you were pleased with your house, *our* house, as it was to be. And you always said that if you didn't treat the rich you wouldn't be able to cure the poor.'

'Did I use that word, *cure*? I think now I never affected a cure on anyone.'

'You have saved hundreds of lives, I'm sure.'

'I hacked off body parts and called it surgery. Dear God, I could have saved so much pain, in my time, had I been issued with a pistol so that I could have shot all my patients in the head and had done with it.'

I glanced into his face thinking that I might be expected to smile incredulously but he was in deadly earnest. We were under a formidable bit of Roman engineering: arch upon arch leading to the labyrinthine cells and passageways backing the theatre. There was an ominous trickle of falling stone and a smell of dank earth and goats' dung. Ferns grew high up in the walls, their lurid green foliage proof of moisture and shade but no exposure to sunlight.

'Shall we walk on?' I said. 'I'm very cold.'

'I'm amazed. I find it too warm.' He took my arm and we walked out into the yellowish light where his jacket was immediately misted by a fine drizzle. After a few more paces he sank onto the remains of a wall and buried his face in his hands. 'Ella, I can't keep up this pretence. I have never been able to hide from you.'

Yes, yes, I thought. It will be much better if everything is in the open. I need to know the truth.

He shoved his hands in his pockets and stared at the ground so that his too-long hair flopped across his eyes. 'I shall never be able to practise as a doctor again. They thought I stopped working at the hospital because I was ill. In fact I found that I couldn't bring myself to inflict any more pain. The sight of blood appalled me. I couldn't make an incision of any kind because of breaking yet more flesh. That's what made me incapable.'

I sat beside him in the rain with my hands folded on my lap. My pink silk was bound to mark, it would not stand up well to a drenching. 'You are ill,' I said wearily, 'too weak to make any such decision. When you are well again, when we have returned to England . . .'

He gripped my wrist. 'Mariella, I won't have you tied to me. I am useless, worse than useless. Culpable.'

'Of what?'

We stared at each other. His eyes were red-rimmed, his nostrils bluish; he put up his cold hand and pressed it to the side of my face. 'Mariella, don't love me. I'm worthless. And I won't be coming home. Look at the state of me. Dear God, the state of me.' He seized my hand, kissed it and kept his head bent low. 'Mariella, I can't keep my promises. Forgive me.'

'Forgive you?'

'Oh God. God.'

'Forgive you for what? Tell me. Henry, you wrote that you'd met Rosa. What happened?'

'Mariella.'

'I think you are in love with her. Do you love her?'

'Mariella.'

'Please, Henry, tell me. Are you in love with Rosa?'

But there was no answer because he had fallen against me.

Chapter Two

London, 1854

Fosse House. Minus Rosa. Minus visits from Henry.

Fosse, meaning ditch or trench. My father's joke. 'That's what I do,' he said. 'Dig ditches, lay pipes, make foundations. Every building must begin with a ditch. What better name to give a builder's own home, then?'

He had designed the house himself, its large windows, crenulations above the porch and broad white steps to the front door, which is where he deposited me at nine-thirty on the morning of Friday 1 December, after we'd waved goodbye to Rosa and taken a long detour to leave Mother at the governesses' home. Father was on his way to a site in Putney so when the carriage pulled away there was no one left at home except the servants, Aunt Isabella and me.

I watched until the carriage, jaunty green and black, had swept round the edge of the front lawn and out of the gates. The morning had begun clear and frosty but already puffy white clouds had collected in the north. Ruth came to the door and took my hat and gloves but I said I would keep the shawl because I was cold.

The hall was noisy with the tock of the grandmother clock on the landing, the clip-clop of a cart on the road beyond the gates, a clatter of cutlery from the kitchen, a stair that creaked though nobody came down. I knew that many things were awaiting my attention: in the morning room was Mother's unfinished blouse; my writing box had been left open, ink pot and blotter at the ready so I could write to Henry; I had promised Mother that I would practise a selection of Christmas carols as a treat for the governesses when the home opened; and in the kitchen was my aunt's breakfast tray which I would have to take up at ten o'clock. In fact she was probably awake, tears seeping down her cheeks, waiting to learn the details of Rosa's departure. Across the common was Mrs Hardcastle's house on the Pavement where I was due to call that afternoon to plan the next phase of our sewing circle's campaign to equip the hospital for our wounded soldiers in Skutari.

Rosa must be nearly at Folkestone. Perhaps she was staring out at soggy green fields and thinking of me. Or was she too immersed in conversation with her companions?

Nora had appeared at the top of the stairs. 'Did the girl get off all right?'

'She caught the train, yes.'

'So. Your aunt will be wanting her breakfast.' She leaned on the rail which ran round the first-floor landing and rested her chin in her bosom as she stared down at me. Stray hairs sprang forward from under her cap and her skin had the greyish tinge of one who has been up most of the night. 'She has been very restless. Scarcely slept for the loss of her daughter.'

As we stared at each other it struck me that my own home was full of strangers and this was one of them. Her eyes were almost lashless, unblinking, with a glutinous quality which made it difficult to distinguish between iris and pupil.

'At any rate,' she said. 'I'll be off to bed now.'

A bell rang. My aunt's. Pause. Then again, more emphatically.

I pushed through the door leading to the kitchen where the fish had been delivered and cook was gutting them at the sink. A row of sorrowful heads lay on the table.

I took a pot-holder, made Aunt's tea, sliced bread for toast, removed the crusts, buttered it and poured milk into a jug. Then I carried the tray up two flights of back stairs and knocked on her door. The room was very dark and the air smelled of stale linen. I started to open the curtains but Isabella called from the bed: 'Just a crack. I can't stand much light this morning. I thought you'd all abandoned me. My poor girl. She came into the room to say goodbye but I was barely conscious. Did you actually see the train leave the station? Did she send me any messages?'

I slid my arm under her shoulders and helped her sit up, placed the tray on her lap and spread a napkin over her bosom. She took a sup of tea. Ruth had followed me in and was raking the ashes.

'This tea tastes of fish,' said Isabella. 'In fact I can *smell* fish.' She sniffed her toast and pushed the tray down the bed. 'I cannot eat that.'

'I'll bring you another cup of tea.'

'Don't trouble yourself. I couldn't drink anyway, with my daughter going to Russia. How am I to bear it?'

'It's a shame you weren't at the station. I'm sure she would have been glad if you'd come to wave her off.'

'I wish I could have been there. It's very hard, to be cursed with ill-health. One feels so helpless.'

I went to the window and pulled the curtains back sharply, one after another. Thin sunlight poured over the bare trees and into the room. Isabella put up her hand and squinted in the sudden glare. Ruth looked round. 'Then don't be so helpless,' I said. 'Don't be.'

Isabella turned her head into the pillow. 'Oh, oh. I don't know what you mean. Oh shut those curtains. Fetch Nora. I feel so ill.'

'What are you doing, lying there day after day? Get up out of bed and lead a life like anybody else's. I'm sick of you behaving as if you're half dead.'

Ruth's poker crashed against the grate and Aunt put her hands over her eyes. I was terrified because I had no idea where the rage came from but I couldn't stop. 'You think of nobody but yourself. Do you suppose Rosa really wanted to go to the war? Maybe she was driven to it because it was her only hope of escaping you. If you hadn't been so selfish and her life had been more bearable, she might have stayed. As it is she's gone and I've been left behind to take care of you. Well, I won't become your slave. You can ring your bell as much as you like but nobody will come. Nora is asleep. Mother is out. The other servants are too busy to look after you. If you want food or drink then get up and sit at the table and eat like a normal person.'

I was shaking so violently that the words came jolting out of my mouth like marbles. Ruth picked up one lump of coal after another in her bare hand and placed them carefully in the grate. Aunt's head flung from side to side on the pillow and she clutched her throat.

'So there you have it, I shall be working in the morning room, should you want me,' I said. 'Ruth, Lady Stukeley will not be needing a fire today, I believe. And as she doesn't want any breakfast perhaps you would take that tray downstairs.'

I wrapped my shawl tight round my shoulders and marched away, down the main staircase, across the hall, through to the kitchen passage where I collected a key, out of the back door and into the garden. The morning air was like a dousing in cold water; a leafless rose bush clung to the arch and the azaleas in the wilderness were covered with frostbitten leftover buds. My feet smacked down the wet paths and the movement of air amidst the wan vegetation sucked warmth from my skin. The clematis had died back, exposing the garden door. I unlocked it, stepped into the lane and walked up and down. My feet were soon caked in mud and my uncovered hair tangled. I muttered under my breath, 'What have you done? You've murdered her.' I imagined writing the news in a letter to Rosa and discovered I didn't care. Good, good, I'm glad she's dead. And anyway, Ruth had been present in the room all the time. She knew I never laid hands on her. There's no law against losing one's temper.

Then I came to myself and saw the arch in the wall where I used to wait for Henry, and I realised what a sight I must be and what a terrible thing I had done, shouting at my aunt on the very morning that her daughter left. So much for my promises to Rosa. And what about my poor mother? How would she feel when she came home and found Aunt dead or, worse, gibbering accusations about her wicked niece? And then there was Henry, who thought he was marrying a kind, quiescent person. Surely he would end our engagement if he discovered I was capable of such cruelty to a sick woman.

I locked the gate, walked slowly back up the garden, changed my shoes and went to the morning room where a fire had been lit. I opened my workbox, took out a reel of pink cotton and a pair of scissors.

As I pushed the needle into the fabric I heard a low moan. My hands went up to my eyes and I started to rock but no tears came. The pain of knowing that Rosa was in a train hurtling further and further away from me was as if a steel belt had been wrapped round my heart and was being pulled tighter, notch by notch.

Chapter Three

16 November 1854

My dearest Mariella,

I am writing once more from aboard ship, this time the Jason. *I thought you might have heard news of the hurricane that struck here two days ago, and that I should reassure you about my safety, though it is a matter of luck, purely, that I am alive. Ships moored outside the harbour were dashed to pieces and many men were lost. The water, even in this sheltered place, boiled, and we saw, rising up from behind the headland, spray from breakers thrown upon the other side of the cliffs. At one point the ship was so tossed about that we considered running for safety by scrambling from one deck to the next and thereby reaching the quay but we would probably have been crushed or drowned. One of our supply ships is lost, which will be very bad news for our men.*

I have never known weather as changeable as in the Crimea. I think when I first wrote we had been basking in a kind of Indian summer. Since then we have had endless wet days, then freezing cold, then more wet. Perhaps you have heard that a party of women has been sent from England to the hospital in Skutari. We are all amazed that such an experiment should be tried in time of war though both Russian and French armies are said to tolerate female nurses. It's odd that we should now be attempting to model ourselves on our enemies -former enemy, I should say, in the case of the French. I fear that the poor souls will not find much of a welcome. Our army doctors, like their civilian counterparts, recoil from any suggestion of change. What an odd, turbulent period of history we live in, a clash of conflicting ambitions, great and small.

I had a letter from you, with the flourish on the M that I would recognise anywhere on earth, and the rather shy good wishes at beginning and end. Don't be afraid, my love, that I shall be shocked by words of affection.

If you have a moment, Mariella, write to me again soon. I want to know if the governesses' home is open at last. And how is your dear family? I think of you often. In fact, I have a memory of you all that I take out at night, for companionship.

The memory is of the drawing room at Fosse House. I was just back from my trip to Hungary, and a little irritated, as I remember, because you had met me in the garden and told me that there were visitors. Visitors, I thought, but I want the Lingwoods to be as I have always known them, with only one place left in their family circle, to be filled by me. I followed you through the glass doors and into the drawing room, and you went and sat in your usual place and took up your sewing. I don't think I'd realised until that moment, when I found two additions to your family circle, how much I had treasured the tranquillity of that drawing room and how selfish I had been. It was almost as if I expected you to fill your time entirely by waiting for me. Because your cousin Rosa was sketching you I saw you for the first time through somebody else's eyes, your down-tilted head, your soft hair, the gentle, reflective expression in your eyes when you looked up at me. I have that picture with me now, a most treasured possession, and I unfurl it often.

I keep that moment in the drawing room in mind, most especially the long, dreamy look you gave me as I stood behind your cousin Rosa. It seemed to me that you were speaking to me from your soul.

Goodnight, my dear Mariella.
Your affectionate
Henry Thewell

Chapter Four

London, 1854

Aunt Isabella didn't die of shock on the morning that Rosa left to join Miss Nightingale's nurses although relations between us were frigid for a while. When I entered a room she flinched and she never spoke to me directly. The phrase that she repeated over and over again within my hearing was: *I don't want to cause anybody further trouble.*

She did, however, get up each morning at a reasonable hour, heave herself down to breakfast and then do nothing all day but hem the odd pillowcase, wipe her eyes on a lace handkerchief and sigh. I was thereby punished one hundredfold for my outburst because it was I who had to endure her company for longest. Nobody except me noticed her martyred behaviour because we were all much too troubled by the terrible news from the war. Not content with killing our troops by cholera and untreated wounds, our government had now chosen to freeze them to death in the siege trenches.

On Christmas Day the leader in *The Times* read:

> *If we have transported England to the Crimea in one sense, we have not in the sense of English humanity, prudence, mechanical genius, and variety of resources. Will it be believed that the authorities in the Crimea will neither take proper care of the sick and wounded themselves, nor allow others to do it for them? The chaplains, who at first gladly distributed the comforts procured by the fund at our disposal, have been peremptorily forbidden to do so any more, and it appears to be thought more in accordance with military discipline that an English soldier should perish from hunger or cold than that he should be clothed and fed by a private hand.*

We couldn't understand it. Our circle of friends, our governesses, the church ladies and servants had been knitting furiously until our hands ached through turning out mittens, stockings, hats and vests; I had donated my trousseau allowance to *The Times* fund; Mrs Hardcastle's nephew at Oxford had sent three waistcoats and an overcoat and still soldiers were dying in their hundreds in the trenches above Sebastopol because they were starving and their toes were dropping off.

'*Surely*,' said Mrs Hardcastle, whose European trip had now been postponed until late spring, 'what with steamships and railways and telegraphs and factories, it is not beyond the wit of man to get a few pairs of socks to Russia and then have them distributed through the proper channels. I've heard that the French soldiers have huts while all our British troops have to sleep in tents and most of those were torn to shreds or blown away in the hurricane. *Surely* anybody would know that you can't go camping in December.'

Father went to numerous meetings in Westminster to get things put right. He said our factories were churning out hospital beds, nails for huts, frames for stretchers, tracks for the railway and more and more shells and bullets (courtesy of Horatio Stukeley's lead, presumably) at a rate unprecedented in history, so it was outrageous that our men hadn't yet knocked the Russians into the sea.

But although our troops had thus far been singularly unsuccessful above Sebastopol, they had achieved one astonishing victory at home in that Aunt Isabella continued to make a miraculous recovery. She was dressed by nine-thirty each morning in one of her boundless black silks and thereafter installed herself by the fire with the sewing circle, or set herself apart to write letters. It transpired that she had other acquaintances in London beside ourselves, connections of the grand Derbyshire families she had known through her round of dinners and afternoon teas, and she now roused herself to pick up every thread, however tenuous.

Before another week was over calling cards began to arrive and Ruth was sent flouncing into the drawing room to announce an assortment of lady visitors. Within a fortnight Isabella was borrowing the carriage to return their calls; by the end of three weeks she had achieved a dinner invitation to a house in Fitzroy Square, and a couple of days after that we learned that a gentleman had called to see Lady Stukeley.

Chapter Five

Constantinople
17 December

Dearest Mariella,

I'm writing this from on board the good ship Egyptus *where I'm sorry to report we have been stranded for days. On very choppy Bosphorous. Within sight of the Barrack Hospital wherein dwells Miss Nightingale, her clutch of nurses and a thousand or more wounded soldiers who surely could do with a little attention from us. Every day a new ship arrives from the Crimea that we know contains mortally sick soldiers but we can't get near them. We wait, with varying degrees of patience and our sleeves metaphorically rolled up, but it seems there is a problem.*

The problem is simple.

We are not welcome. We travelled out here under the delusion that we were to be part of Miss Nightingale's team but it transpires that she did not ask for us, in fact had said specifically that she wanted no more nurses and so now we are arrived she will have nothing to do with us. Miss Stanley gets us into huddles and tells us she cannot understand what is the matter with Miss Nightingale, her dearest friend, and that the misunderstanding will be resolved any moment. But Miss Stanley's hair, I notice, is less trimly dressed than before and her smile has become very fixed. In fact I rarely see her when she is not smiling and this bothers me.

Some of us are indignant and blame Miss S. and Sidney Herbert for not letting Miss N. know we were coming. Others blame Miss N. for being ungrateful. Others (please don't tell Mrs Hardcastle there is a large contingent of Roman Catholic nuns aboard) retreat to a dry part of the ship and rattle their beads.

Sometimes we are indignant, sometimes we weep, sometimes we crack jokes, some of us drink, others go on sightseeing tours. I don't, because I have a dread of not being here at the very minute I am needed.

Miss Nightingale doesn't want us and in my opinion this cannot bode well. I am remembering much more vividly my encounters with Miss N. at Lea Hurst tea parties. The other women ask me: 'What was she like?' I say: 'Very charming. Very rich. Very self-controlled.' I do not add: 'But there was no reaching her.' I remember trying to get her to take an interest in my little endeavours among the cottagers but it was impossible to engage her in a cause that wasn't her own.

I am horrified by a rumour currently circulating that she may send us a consignment of shirts to mend. Nobody asked me if I could sew when I applied to come here.

Also our money is gone. Where?

Does this letter sound desperate? I am nearly desperate. Not quite.

This is what I do, my own love. I imagine you at home in Clapham. I can see you quite clearly at the turn of the stair, holding a lamp that makes your shadow very long and sheds light on your chin and forehead. You carry the lamp to your room and set it down on the dressing table. Then you unpin your hair so that it falls dead straight, in a way you hate, but which to me is a miracle and you take up your brush and begin your hundred strokes. Soon we are both in a trance. You are in a stupor of familiarity because this is what you have done each night of your life but I am enthralled by the beauty of your hand, and the way the light ripples through your hair, how one or two strands separate themselves and cling to the brush. This image of you makes me nearly happy because I know that were you in my shoes you would find yourself a quiet spot, take out your needle and produce some exquisite, useful item and the thought of your tranquil acceptance makes me calmer.

Incidentally, unless it's already too late, can I beg you please, please not to tell Dr Thewell that I joined Miss Stanley's party, or where I am now. He might feel duty bound to seek me out and the thought of his discovering that I am trapped in this stinking ship on the Bosphorus makes me squirm. He will disapprove of our venture, start to finish, and I cannot stand any more disapprobation, from anyone.

But write soon to me, Ella, anything at all.

Happy Christmas, darling girl.

Your coz.

Rosa

Chapter Six

London, 1855

The governesses' home was finally to be opened at the end of January by Lady Furlong, a friend of Mrs Hardcastle. Our cook made a celebratory sponge cake and Mother asked me to ice the top with a pattern of rosettes and to inscribe some suitable words of congratulation.

On the day before the opening I duly went down to the kitchen where cook had left the cakes on cooling trays while she took her afternoon nap. The trouble was that all I cared about was when next I would hear from Henry or Rosa. Every minute I yearned to know what they were doing and whether they were safe, and this life of speculation was much more vivid to me than anything in Fosse House. Normally I could rely on my hands to perform deftly any small domestic task but now icing sugar flew from the sieve and made me sneeze, and after I'd added glycerine and lemon juice I slopped in far too much beaten egg white so that the icing was a puddle. The more sugar I poured in, the more it dissolved. In a mood of reckless despair I spooned the white syrup onto the cake and watched it slide across the top and down the sides. When I tried to scrape it back with a spatula I succeeded only in breaking the surface and mixing crumbs into the icing.

Cook woke up and found me weeping into the wet mixture. 'Well, I'm not making another cake,' she said, 'and there's no serving that.'

The next afternoon at the governesses' home Lady Furlong cut a length of pink ribbon and shouted into the frail ears of the grateful inmates over tea and scones in the crowded parlour. There was no cake.

That same day *The Times* reported that parliament had voted for a select committee to investigate the conduct of the war in the Crimea. The prime minister duly resigned and by early February Lord Palmerston had been invited to form a new government though he was the Queen's third choice and Mrs Hardcastle didn't approve: 'What with the dear governesses, and poor one-armed Lord Raglan in the Crimea, and now Lord Palmerston as prime minister I feel as if I never want to see another septuagenarian. I do wonder how these dear old people can go on so long, especially in such a bad winter . . .'

Father also had mixed views about Lord Palmerston, whom he called opportunistic ('Takes one to know one,' he added), but it was generally agreed that at least Palmerston would bang heads together. And in any case the newspapers reported that the newly opened railway line between Balaklava harbour and the British camps above Sebastopol would mean efficient transportation of food, warm clothes and fuel. Sheepskin coats had arrived, admittedly so late that the men sweated inside them, but night duty in the trenches surely must be much more bearable. And the weather was apparently so much better that the troops were being treated to sudden displays of wild flowers, including crocuses and hyacinths just like in English cottage gardens, and it was said that the men were better fed than if they'd been at home and were growing fat and lazy.

Father's business was now doing so well that we were able to employ a footman who took over Ruth's more formal duties. His name was James Featherbridge. ('Probably christened plain Jim Bridges,' said Aunt Isabella. 'I know that trick.') Poor Ruth was in a sulk because she was no longer allowed to answer the door. We also had a proper vegetable gardener who promised Mother we'd soon be eating strawberries and asparagus by the sackful, and cook employed an additional kitchen maid to help with the dinners which were now held regularly for Father's important colleagues. He was rarely in the house except for these events and spent much of his time in the carriage hurtling from committee to building site. Henry's colleague Dr Snow had given evidence to parliament that cholera was spread by dirty drinking water rather than by unsavoury smells in the air, and if this idea caught on, said Father, it would have serious consequences for the building trade because new regulations about waste pipes and water pumps would have to be rushed through. Although everyone wished to live in a more sanitary city, it was best to get on with the latest projects before any such costly laws came into force.

We received regular letters from Henry but only one more from Rosa, a scribbled note from Koulali Hospital, near Skutari, dated 2 February.

Thanks to you, Mariella, I have achieved my heart's desire, and I am in a hospital nursing soldiers. You would think I should be happy but I spend most of my time rigid with panic. Imagine a building the size of one of your new London railway stations, just as empty but a hundred times dirtier and older, the only provisions a handful of bedsteads, a few sacks and a dozen bottles of port. Imagine that a couple of steamers come puffing and snorting up to the ramshackle jetty outside and discharge three hundred wounded men, each in need of warmth and sustenance and skilled nursing. Imagine that what they find instead are half a dozen Rosas and a clutch of nuns, all more or less empty-handed and in a state of shock. That's the hospital at Koulali.

My only hope is that I won't be here long. A party of nurses is to be sent to the Crimea at the special request of Lord Raglan himself and I shall apply to be one of them. It seems to me that I must get to the heart of this war, wherever and whatever that is or I shall never be satisfied.

Miss Stanley is in charge of this hospital and she has a notebook and a ruffled brow and cries a lot but that's about it. The nuns are much more useful and have taught me how to dress wounds and feed a sick man through a gap in his bandages.

Miss N. up at the Barrack Hospital is better organised but she is not prepared to either share her nurses with us or help us manage things more efficiently, although Miss N. incidentally is as much a transition point between the battlefields and the graveyards as are we. Very few emerge from either of the hospitals alive.

Miss Stanley, quite frankly, ain't up to the job. Miss Stanley, when under pressure, just smiles more and puts out her hands, like a preacher trying to quell a rebellious congregation, and says: 'This is not why I came. I had no idea of being in charge of a hospital. I thought I could do good, but if she *won't co-operate . . .'*

Please write again soon to this address, in the hope that your letter might reach me before I leave. Tell me what colour your newest ribbon is, which hymns you sang in church last Sunday or whether Ruth has a young man yet and I will read it all with an insatiable appetite to know every minute detail about you.

My bed here is hard and dirty and full of fleas (please don't tell Mama that detail). I ration myself five minutes a night only, when I am allowed to think of you at Fosse House. I ache so much to see you, to touch you, for the scent of you, the sound of your voice, your slow deep smile that I curl into a ball and bite my lousy pillow.

Are you thinking of me?

Your Rosa

Chapter Seven

Balaklava
6 March 1855

My dear Mariella,

I am in the midst of arguments with the authorities here, who wish to send me home. I have developed what they are calling a pulmonary infection and they insist that my health is in great danger. I argue that everyone is sick and I am certainly no sicker than most, less sick than many. Scurvy, cholera, dysentery, frostbite, hypothermia, these are the ills that affect us all in some measure. But a pulmonary infection is just a grand name for a cold and at home I would not even take to bed with anything so trivial. So I'm hoping they will see sense and let me stay.

I have found that I prefer to be outside, whatever the weather. In fact I hate the hospital hut and can't breathe within its musty walls. I have been issued with a sheepskin coat which reaches the floor and when I am tightly belted in, and wearing your cap and gloves, not a bit of this slushy wind can reach me.

Last week the weather was so much improved that the men held a race meeting on a bit of flat ground well within sight of the Russian defences. They could have been picked off by sharpshooters one by one as they mounted their horses. As if the war isn't dangerous enough they have to hurl themselves into a foolish race. For fun, is it? I went up to one of the captains, Stukeley, a relation of your aunt's by marriage, as I realised when I recognised the name. I said: 'You know, we are almost related. I am to marry your stepmother's niece. I beg you therefore to have a care for your own neck, and those of your men.'

He was on horseback, a great chestnut beast, healthier-looking than most of the poor nags who have survived the winter, though scarred about the flank and neck. Anyway this Stukeley grinned down at me through a very black beard, and I saw that there was fire in his eyes, a kind of fanatic enjoyment of the race that was driving him so hard I would never reach him. 'You're Dr Henry Thewell, ain't you? What's that you say about my stepmother?'

'Her niece is Miss Mariella Lingwood, whom I am to marry.'

'Is that so? Mariella Lingwood. My stepmother and stepsister, Rosa, went to stay with the Lingwoods when my father died. Did you ever meet them there?'

'I did. But that's hardly the point. The point is I want you to stop these races. You risk breaking yet more limbs . . .'

'If you ever get back send Rosa my love. Tell her I was thinking of her. And thanks for the warning, Doctor. You're a good man. I've heard all about you.' He grinned at me again, kicked his spurs, and was gone. I saw him later flying across the plain ahead of a dozen or so others, yelling at the top of his voice.

So there you have it. Everybody is intent on killing either each other or themselves. Nobody listens to me.

The odd thing is that this topsy-turvy world of war has become more real to me than any other. England, the well-paved London streets, the prospect of a comfortable bed, all these have shrunk to almost nothing. In my mind's eye I see you at the Elms, Mariella, and your cousin, running towards me round the side of the house as through the wrong end of a telescope. Very small, very clear.

Dear girl. Are you really still waiting for me?

Henry

Chapter Eight

London, 1855

When Rosa stopped writing we weren't unduly alarmed at first. The post from the Crimea was so erratic that people wrote to the papers protesting how in our modern times of steamships and telegraphs it was disgraceful that families had to wait up to a month for news. But as the days passed and still no letter came we grew anxious. Mother wrote to everyone we could think of including the English ambassador in Turkey, the war office, Miss Nightingale, then every point of contact in the Crimea from Lord Raglan to Captain Max Stukeley. We even disobeyed Rosa's instructions and wrote to Henry that she was perhaps nursing in Balaklava, and could he look out for her.

In the end Father discovered that Miss Stanley was back in London and at once paid her a call, but managed to speak only to her brother, an archdeacon, who gave a brief, mournful interview during which he said that Miss Stanley was too ill to speak.

Three days later a letter arrived written in a quavering female hand.

> *Do not ask me of the whereabouts of dear Miss Barr, who was heroic in her efforts to nurse the sick, even against all the odds. She chose to leave us and go to Balaklava of her own free will. It was nothing to do with me. Lord Raglan asked for some nurses to be sent to the heart of the war at Balaklava, and she pleaded to go. I cannot see you, I am too ill. I suffer a great deal.*
> *I am your obedient servant in Christ,*
> *Mary Stanley*

We told ourselves that no news was good news, and that knowing

Rosa she would be in the midst of some extraordinary adventure but anxiety made my sewing coarse and erratic, I couldn't be bothered to keep the reverse side of my embroidery as immaculate as the front and the criss-crossing of loose ends frustrated me so much that I once slashed an entire afternoon's work to pieces with Aunt Eppie's little scissors. I didn't care if my hair needed washing or my gloves mending and when I went with Mother to the governesses' home I found the smell of ancient bodies so oppressive I had to wait outside in the carriage.

Father was so concerned about my low spirits that one afternoon he made time to drive me across London to The Elms but the trip was unfortunate because the gates were locked and he had forgotten the key. I peered through the bars at the blank windows and noticed that clumps of daffodils had sprouted on the lawn and some were already brown. When we arrived back at Fosse House Featherbridge told us that Lady Stukeley was serving tea to a gentleman in the drawing room.

In the months since Christmas Isabella had altered her mourning by degrees so that now cascades of lace spilled from her throat and wrists, and jewels (those she had saved from Horatio Stukeley's clutches) sparkled on her fingers and breast. A further lace creation was perched atop her softly coiled hair which, released from her widow's cap, was revealed to be a tender shade of grey blonde, and her complexion was powder soft and pink. She looked matronly and genial, her plump bosom ripe with promise.

She introduced the gentleman, Mr Shackleton, as a distant relative of Mr Hardcastle's. 'Mr Shackleton and I discovered at once,' she said, smiling guilelessly from her nest of shawls and pillows, 'that we share an interest in Nature.' Today, in response to her supposed nostalgia for the abundant specimens of flora and fauna on her Derbyshire estate, Shackleton had rushed round to show her part of his moth collection, twelve creatures in all, pinned inside a glass frame.

The visitor was so short that when he got up to shake my hand the top of his head was level with my nose, and so small and bony that his frock coat would have fitted me. His ginger beard stuck out like the blade of a spade. As soon as was politely possible he sat beside Isabella again, leaned close to her shoulder and allowed his hand to stray near her breast as he pointed out the markings on what he insisted was a particularly handsome cinnibar moth.

I noted that Isabella had ordered the best tea service and this shameless appropriation of Mother's treasured porcelain was the last straw. 'Is there a letter from Rosa yet?' I asked.

Sure enough her lip quivered and her eyes filled. Mr Shackleton took the cup from her shaking fingers. 'No letter. None from Rosa. Oh Mr Shackleton, forgive me. I don't know how I shall carry on.'

Chapter Nine

On the morning of 2 May, Featherbridge brought me a letter on his salver. The envelope was addressed in an unknown hand, postmarked in Italy a week ago. I took it upstairs to my room, closed the door and sat down at the dressing table.

Of course I knew that the letter could bring only bad news. I would have been a fool to expect anything else. Throughout that winter, wherever we went, bad news hung in the air like a miasma. Everyone was afraid of catching it. When I glimpsed my face in the mirror I saw that I was deathly pale.

The first sheet of paper, which enfolded all the others, was written by a stranger.

House of Signora Critelli
Via del Monte
Narni
24 April 1855

Miss Lingwood,

I am writing to give you the sad news that Dr Thewell is critically ill at present. He arrived here in a state of collapse, and though somewhat improved, his health is certainly precarious. A colleague, knowing that I am here in Italy and something of a specialist in these types of cases, wrote to me asking if I would undertake the care of him.

I found the enclosed letter, addressed to you, in his belongings with the other fragments. Under the circumstances I assumed that you would wish to know where he is and have therefore taken it upon myself to write.

Be assured that I will continue to give my patient every attention.

My apologies for what must seem to you a strange and troubling intervention.

Your servant,

Dr R Lyall

Next, a crumpled envelope with no stamp, addressed to me in Henry's writing.

April

My dear Mariella,

I find myself on another ship, on calm seas.

This was not my decision. I was bundled aboard and carried away almost without my noticing. It feels all wrong to be on the Mediterranean rather than the Black Sea, far away from the war.

Why is the Black Sea called Black, when I have seen it grey, green, blue and brown but never black? Pirates, I was told; there was always the fear of pirates in the old days.

As I write a little cohort of troops under Canrobert's Hill is digging another trench to accommodate the night's dead and a surgeon at the Castle Hospital is hacking off the foot of a man caught by a Russian bullet. And I lie under a blue and white striped awning on this ship full of wealthy officers invalided out of the war, and sightseers and businessmen returning home. I watch a loose strip of canvas swing in the breeze. There is one cloud, very steady and quite flat underneath, on the horizon.

A colleague of mine recommended Italy and that is where the boat is taking me. I am to be met by an English doctor who will arrange my accommodation. I will send you my change of address.

Henry

By the way, I saw Rosa. Your cousin Rosa.

Very strange affair. Shocking, in fact. It was a while ago now, when I was still allowed to work in the trenches. Perhaps I mentioned it in a previous letter. I can't remember. One morning, at dawn, I went forward as usual, after heavy firing from the Russian batteries. A more furious cannonade than we had been used to for days. I suspect because the cold had lost its grip Russian hands were more nimble at loading the rifles. Same with us.

During an armistice we rush forwards to pick up the wounded. We mingle with the Russians, sorting the bodies. Two for you, one for me. A man writhes. I stoop down. He is Russian. He has only lost an arm. He could live. I wave to the Russian orderlies and they come and pluck him off the field.

I move on. The day is very wet - a steady drizzle is falling. I see something bright hanging over one of our wounded men. It is a woman's light-coloured hair. She is wearing a soldier's great coat, and most of her hair is bound up in a blue knitted scarf which she has also wound round her neck. She is crouched over the body of a soldier whose head lies in a pool of blood and tissue. His eyes are fixed on her face. She must see that he won't live but she takes his hand and strokes it. Then she becomes aware of me and raises her head. It is your cousin Rosa. Of all people. I can't work out what she is doing there. It can't be true. No. Perhaps she is some kind of fantasy or mirage. The rain dashes into her face. She looks thin and her nose is red because it's so cold. Her hands, which are bare, have chilblains. Two of her fingertips are completely yellow. She should take more care of herself. She really should. If the weather was a degree or so colder she'd be in danger from frostbite.

'Dr Henry Thewell,' she says very slowly, as if the name comes to her a little at a time. Then she shakes her head. 'Your services are not required here.'

We both look down at the boy, who has that abstracted look of the dying. Rosa bends her face close to his. I hear her murmur words of comfort.

Then someone yells my name. I'm wanted twenty yards away, where perhaps there is hope for a wounded man, if I can get there soon enough. I move on.

When I look for her again, she is gone.

And finally, a few scraps of paper that scattered on my lap like confetti.

Dear one, dear girl,
Can't see you. Can't touch you.
Please write.

Just to convince myself that you were real. Cannot tell. Cannot remember which is the truth.

No word from you. I thought you were bound to write. If you don't write, I shall die. If you don't write soon it may be too late.

All I have is the volumes of Keats. You are there, in all his poems. I didn't realise until now.

If only I could get back to you. In the Clapham garden. Or indoors, the lamplight falling on your hair.

Sometimes I am terrified by your utter faithfulness. You humble me. I know, in my bones, you will be loyal to your dying day.

> . . . Still, still to hear her tender taken breath,
> And so live ever – or else swoon to death.

Write. I think it may already be too late.

For the rest of the day I didn't leave my room as I read and reread the contents of the envelope until the words of Henry's last, scribbled notes were as part of me as flesh and bone. I fumbled through volumes of Keats until I found the 'Bright Star' sonnet from which he'd quoted and by midday I'd learned it by heart. Then I sat in the window and watched the May sun climb higher in the sky, the shadows shorten, the cedar glitter and ripple in new greens, the changing quality of light in my room.

Punctually at four o'clock I heard the doorbell. Next came the voices of Mr Shackleton and my aunt as they emerged onto the terrace beneath my window, then the chink of tea cups.

As the afternoon advanced the light grew warmer and the garden dipped into a late springtime haze of blossom and new leaf. Everything shifted under the golden wash of the sky. From my window I couldn't see much past the cedar, except the beginning of the wilderness and the edge of the vegetable garden where the new gardener stooped and straightened, stooped and straightened.

Early in the evening I dressed for dinner. When I opened my door I was immediately aware that the ears of the house were alert.

Nora appeared at the top of the staircase. 'You've had news,' she said.

I nodded.

'Rosa?'

'Dr Thewell. He is very sick.'

'Does he mention her?'

'He does. He saw her, but a long time ago.'

She came a step closer and a light glimmered at the back of her eye. 'I hope now we shall take action,' she said.

At dinner I took no part in the conversation. Father was in for once, and Aunt was still up, though on the brink of tears because of Rosa. Mother filled the silences with the news that premises had been found for a second governesses' home in Fulham; all that was needed was seven hundred pounds though Mrs Hardcastle wondered if it was the right time to embark on such a project, given that she was herself about to leave for the trip to Europe.

Father joined us in the drawing room as soon as we left the table. Aunt, too distracted to work, lay back on the sofa with her hands clasped under her bosom, rotating her thumbs round each other. A window was open and a draught ruffled the frill on her cap. The grandmother clock began its wheezing build-up to the hour and struck nine. Mother's pen squeaked. Father turned the page of *The Times* but said nothing about the war. I was working on a simple patchwork quilt for one of the governesses because straight lines and plain seams were all I could manage.

Despite the thaw in relations between us, Aunt had not quite lost her habit of speaking about rather than to me. 'I see Mariella is using the striped flannel after all,' she said. 'Maria, I see your daughter is disregarding all our advice that flannel will not wear well. That old shirt of Philip's has been washed too often.'

Mother's pen paused and she smiled attentively but I could tell she wasn't listening.

'I'm surprised there is enough fabric even for eight small squares. Well, I hope she's allowing more than quarter of an inch for the seams. I've noticed that Mr Shackleton wears . . .'

I stood up and the quilt went rolling the length of my skirt onto the floor. Afterwards I discovered the needle still pressed between the index finger and thumb of my right hand. 'I am going to see Henry,' I said but my voice was no more than a whisper and at that moment Featherbridge came in with the tea tray and placed it on the table in front of Mother. 'I will need some money,' I added after he'd gone. 'I'll ask the Hardcastles if I can go to Italy with them.'

I was shaking so much that my knees actually knocked against each other. Aunt said, 'Stir the tea before it stews, sister. I don't know what the girl is talking about. Maria, can you make sense of what your daughter . . .'

Father let his paper drop into his lap and Mother laid down her pen because I was still standing by the tea table saying in a querulous voice, 'So, Father, I wonder if I might have a few pounds for the journey.'

'Journey?' said Mother. 'Where are you going?'

'Henry. I must see Henry.'

'Oh that's it,' said Isabella. 'Here's another girl wanting to up sticks and abandon us.'

'Follow me,' said Father, and ushered me into his study, a room I scarcely ever entered now, though as a child I'd been allowed to go in and borrow one of his thick rubbers for my drawing, or peer at the faultless pencil lines of the plans spread out on the drawing board.

I sank down in the one armchair and started to cry while he paced about. 'What is this, Ella? What are you talking about?'

'Henry is ill. He is in Italy. I think he may be dying. I must go to him.' I held out the letters and covered my face.

He didn't speak for a long time though I heard the slight rustle of paper as he placed each page on his desk. At last he said, 'My dear child, I hardly know what to say. This doesn't sound like Henry at all. I would not have believed him capable of anything so . . .'

'How can I not go to him, Father?'

He stared at me. Then he coughed, folded each sheet into four and handed them back to me. 'And it seems that he met Rosa, but so long ago it scarcely helps. He might have let us know before. Mariella, what of all this uncertainty about Rosa? And then there is the question of a chaperone. Who would be your companion?'

I sat open-mouthed, nose running, tears dripping off my jaw and onto my bosom because something extraordinary had happened;

Father was discussing the obstacles rather than forbidding me to consider the plan any further.

It had never, for an instant, occurred to me that I might be allowed to go.

PART FOUR

Chapter One

Italy, 1855

The next morning Nora and I set off once more for Henry's lodging. Though the air was warm, it was still raining and the street was slippery with dirt.

Signora Critelli was actually at the door and as soon as we were within earshot shouted at me: '*Il medico … inglese … Roma …*' and bustled me up the stairs. An unpromising stranger emerged from Henry's room and peered down at us; his florid complexion was due, from the smell of him, to a partiality for wine. This was the English doctor, Lyall, back from Rome at last.

'Was it you who encouraged him to go out yesterday?'

'There was no encouragement. He chose to go.'

'Madness. What is the point of all my hard work if it's to be undone in a matter of hours? Getting a consumptive patient wet is as good as signing his death warrant.'

'Consumptive?'

'Was there ever any doubt? You must have known. Dear God, no wonder I choose to live away from England. No one admits the truth there.'

'Is he much worse?'

'I'm amazed he survived the night. Well, in you go. I presume you're the woman he's been talking about. Tormenting himself. You can't do any more damage, after all.'

'What do you mean, tormenting himself?'

'You'll no doubt be gratified to have him in thrall. Isn't that every woman's dream?'

Henry was lying much as I had first seen him except that he didn't even raise his head but flung it back and forth as if trying to escape the pillow. The shutters were closed and there was no daylight, just the glow of one candle.

When I knelt by the bed and took his icy hands he stared at me blindly, as if he was in the midst of a dream. 'Henry, it is I, Mariella.'

He seemed not to know me, then suddenly gripped my hand. 'Mariella.'

His beauty took my breath away; the tumble of hair on his forehead, the sculptured curve of his nostril, the fullness of his lips. I longed to press my mouth to his breastbone, visible through his translucent skin. With his burning eyes fixed on my face the knot of pain loosened inside me. I thought: He's dying and I must forgive him everything, there's no time for blame. 'I love you,' I said and kissed his forehead.

He clasped the back of my head and put his lips to my ear. 'Help me. Find Rosa.' It was as if he had struck me in the mouth. 'Mariella. Please. Please find her.'

I sat up poker straight.

'Mariella. I beg you. There are terrible deaths. Thousands of unmarked graves. You must find her.'

'I'll write her a letter,' I said at last.

'No. Find her. Tell her to come to me. I think she will, she must. I see her. I hear her voice but I can't reach her. I should never have closed my eyes.' His grip was so tight on my hand that my fingers hurt. 'Find Rosa.'

I was as cold as stone though he was hunched over towards me with tears oozing down his cheek. 'Mariella. Find Rosa.'

'Where shall I look, Henry?' He fell back on the pillow. 'What happened? Please tell me.'

He pushed my hand away. 'Find Rosa. Hurry.'

After that Nora and I walked back without a word to the Hotel Fina where my room was so dark that I had to grope my way to the bed. She unlatched the window, lifted the bar and flung open the shutters to admit a flood of moist, grey light. 'Well?'

'I want to be alone.'

'And later?'

'We'll go home tomorrow.'

'You're never intending to leave him?'

'I'm not wanted here.'

'Then you're to abandon him?'

'I've told you. He doesn't want me. All he can think about is Rosa.'

'It's true then, what's being said. The woman downstairs insisted he'd been speaking her name, over and over.'

I untied my bonnet, threw myself back on the pillows and covered my eyes with my forearm.

'They met at the war,' she said. 'There's no more to it than that, so he'll be wanting to know if she's safe.'

'He's obsessed with her.'

'Well, it seems to me he's right. Someone should go looking for Rosa. This silence from her isn't natural.'

I sat up and gaped at her. 'Nora, she's in the Crimea, in Russia, in the midst of a war. How could I get there?'

'We'll find a way.'

'I'm alone. The Hardcastles—'

'I'll go with you. For Rosa's sake.

'I don't want you to come with me. We're going home.'

'Then I'll go by myself.'

'And leave me here?'

'You have Dr Thewell to care for, after all.'

'I don't want you mentioning his name again. He's in love with Rosa. I can't bear to think about either of them. Leave me alone.'

'Now don't you be thinking ill of that girl. She would rather cut off her hand than hurt a hair on your head.'

She marched out of the room, leaving me shipwrecked on the bed. But then an hour or so later back she came with a cup of tea. 'I presume you'll be wanting to make some arrangements for the journey. We can't just stand at the door and expect a carriage to arrive and carry us off,' she said.

I wouldn't meet her eye. 'We'll go to the Hardcastles in Rome, as arranged. Mr Hardcastle will take care of the rest.'

'I've been enquiring at the desk and of Dr Lyall. We will be able to take a carriage to the coast, to Pescara, and from there a steamship to Turkey. Or to Civitavecchia and sail round the bottom of Italy. It can be done.'

I rolled over on the bed, buried my head in the pillow and felt a familiar snake of pain in my temple: headache, brought on, no doubt, by distress. I understood that I had three choices, each more unthinkable than the last. First I contemplated the long journey home beginning with an interrogation by Mrs Hardcastle in Rome, the arrival at Fosse House, the climbing the stairs to my bedroom and the removal of my cloak and bonnet. Then what?

Or I could stay in Narni and endure Henry's anguish that I wasn't Rosa.

Or I could pick up my skirts, dash across Europe, find Rosa and beg her to tell me the truth.

Chapter Two

Next morning Lyall came with money sent by Henry. Pain thrummed under my bonnet and his features were a blur. Then I was handed into a carriage and driven rapidly downhill across Narni's unforgiving cobbles. As we journeyed through Terni and into the hills it grew insufferably hot, my head rolled on my neck and the pain behind my eye was so bad it made my mouth drop open. I was too nauseous to eat but Nora held me against her bosom and dribbled water between my lips. At night we shared a room in some dark little inn where I writhed on the narrow bed and she slept on the floor. Towards dawn I fell asleep and when I woke she had pushed the shutter open a chink and was sitting up with her eyes closed, fingering a string of green beads.

In a port called Pescara we found a steamship bound for Constantinople from where we would be able to sail to Balaklava. That night, while we were still in the dock, Nora opened the porthole of our stifling cabin and I smelled the sea. In the morning my headache faded and I had a flicker of happiness when she brought me a cup of tea because though it was tepid and milk-less, I could drink it without feeling sick.

All that day, as the engines juddered to life and the racket of paddle, piston and rushing water began, I lay in a bunk with my eyes shut, held tight to the sheet and wondered how it could possibly have happened that I was being carried towards Turkey and a war. Nora appeared from time to time but we didn't speak. In any case, I didn't care where I went. Now that my headache was gone and the excitement of departure was over there was no hiding from the fact that Henry had fallen in love with Rosa and the great dream of my life was therefore over.

The community of the ship impinged itself slowly. Through the queasy first days of the voyage I listened as other bodies moved above, beside and beneath me, lurching against my cabin wall when the ship tipped, the soles of their feet walking the boards a foot from my face until I couldn't stand the confinement any longer, I had to get away from that anonymous, busy flesh. So I rose from the bunk, wrapped myself in a shawl, covered my lank hair with a bonnet and crept up on deck.

The world turned out to be blue, rushing and sparkling, water and sky, swaying, rippling, flashing blue. I was too ill to go to the saloon for dinner so instead Nora brought a meal of bread and soup to my chair. When I took a mouthful I discovered I was ravenous.

I liked the fact that the ship was so economical and neat in its fitting and furnishings; the bathroom had brass taps, an ample supply of towels and an adequate water closet. After the third day I discarded a few petticoats because I was too hot and the gangways and cabin were so cramped. The ship juddered and stank its way into the Aegean Sea among a hundred little islands. With Greece on one side, Turkey the other, I was actually inside the map I had stuck into my Russian war album.

Small rituals gave me a degree of comfort such as the removal of clothes before sleep, the brushing of my hair, though this last reminded me of Rosa's obsession with watching me. 'I listen for the crackle,' she used to say. 'I think there is more of Mariella in her hair than in anything else about her.' At all other times, when I wasn't quivering with shock and despair, I was consumed with panic. When I lay down at night my heart went into palpitations and thudded against my side.

By day I sat on deck with Henry's letters in my hand, the ones he'd written me and the last, delirious notes which must have been meant for Rosa. After all, I thought, who, faced with a choice between that thrilling girl and her doll of a cousin, wouldn't choose Rosa? Now I saw everything differently. Now, as we sailed down the coast of Greece, as I watched a relentless blue sky slide overhead, as there strolled past me men with extravagant moustaches and military dress, and women in floating muslins with the shadows of their parasols bobbing on the deck behind them, I thought only about Henry and Rosa and how despite his having once, as a child, pressed his head into my lap and sobbed, despite the hours I had spent trimming my gowns, arranging my hair and moistening my lips in preparation for his visits, despite the fact he and I had stood in the turret of his new house and gazed into the future together, he had still fallen for Rosa's dazzling smiles, just as I had fallen for them the minute she turned the blaze of her attention on me from the top of the gatepost at Stukeley.

Chapter Three

As we arrived at Constantinople a purple dusk rolled over the water and obscured all but the skyline of the city. The sudden end of vibration and engine noise made us stagger and rush to the deck. There was an uncanny silence which filled immediately with a thousand other sounds: voices, feet, cartwheels, dogs and the insistent Muslim call to prayer. It seemed to me that the timing was deliberate. 'You are in a foreign place,' wailed those off-key voices. 'Mar-i-ell-aaaaaaaaaaa, you have nothing to do with us.' Needle-like columns with odd little bulges on top, domes, towers and chimneys pierced the fading sky. The city smelled of smoke and sewage and ahead of us, as we glided into our berth, was a tumbling crowd of humanity wearing the wrong clothes, speaking the wrong language. In a moment of panic-stricken forgetfulness I looked for Rosa. If only I could spot her elbowing through the crowd, springing up to get a better look, her eyes lit with joy.

But no one came to rescue me. However, the Italian crew had taken a liking to Nora, presumably because of her Catholic leanings, and the first mate found us a steamer, the *Royal Albert*, which was to sail the following evening for Balaklava carrying soldiers who had been sent across the Black Sea to the English hospitals at Skutari and were now fit enough to return to battle.

Our transfer from one ship to another went so smoothly that we scarcely had to touch Turkish soil except for a brief scurry along the dockside behind a servant who contrived to carry our entire luggage, consisting of two trunks and five or six bags, on his back, head and under his arms. The new ship seemed quite clean, though noisy because it had just taken on a cargo of chickens and geese as well as crates sent from England, some of which might contain, for all I knew, the mittens Aunt Isabella had knitted at such cost to her nerves and mine.

My idea was to send notes to Lady Stratford at the embassy and to Miss Nightingale at Skutari Hospital enquiring whether they had heard of Rosa but Nora, without consulting me, had already arranged for a boat to take us across to the hospital at Skutari first thing in the morning. She said that notes, in her experience, could easily fall into the wrong hands or get ignored. We must go in person and knock on doors.

From what I had heard of Miss Nightingale I thought she would be very irritated by the sight of my pink travelling dress so I unearthed my plainest blouse (eight vertical tucks each side of the buttonholes and a three-layered ruffled collar) in which I would be far too hot, a summer shawl and my large-brimmed bonnet. There was a scrap of mirror in my new cabin and I saw that I looked entirely unconvincing as a sophisticated lady, being merely a pale version of Mariella Lingwood, the broken-hearted daughter of a builder.

I barely slept. The night was very warm, I had scarcely eaten any supper – the meat had been tough and the bread sour – and as darkness settled it became apparent that I was sharing my bed with insects. *Fleas*. I lay in the dark with tears falling into my pillow, pinpricks of pain piercing my hands and neck. What troubled me almost more than the physical discomfort was this slide towards the abyss. Fleas, inedible food and a close association with a Roman Catholic were all part of my disappearance from the known world.

Next morning one of Nora's Italian sailor acquaintances escorted us to the pier where we would take a boat to Skutari. I gripped Nora's arm as we entered a Turkish crowd and kept my eyes fixed firmly on the pavement, or rather on the collection of large boulders that passed for a pavement and across which humanity, animals and cartwheels lurched and staggered. There was a racket of other tongues and a blur of strangely draped clothes and bare feet, a sudden flash of embroidery worked in gold thread and then we came to a rickety jetty where a Turkish boatman was waiting to take us across the Bosphorus in his gaudily painted boat.

To my horror the Italian, who by now seemed like our last friend, was not to accompany us on our voyage so off we set in that flimsy vessel rowed by a heavy-shouldered Turk with a permanent smile and very white teeth. I huddled in the stern while

Nora struck up a conversation that was mostly nods and smiles from both parties because he was too ignorant to know English although he nodded repeatedly and uttered the word '*buono*' as if it covered every eventuality.

After a few minutes I realised that he was a proficient boatman, that he was trying to please us, and that far from abducting us we were in fact heading towards what was unmistakably the Barrack Hospital, a colossal building a thousand times the size of the dwellings clustered under its walls. I had never seen so many windows in one structure and wondered what Father would have made of it. There must surely be practical difficulties in managing the maintenance of the pipe-work in such a place.

The boatman gave me his warm, rough hand and I climbed ashore, aware that this wide jetty of new wood and the well-laid path up the slope to the hospital were not at all like the nightmarish picture that had been painted in our newspapers at home. The sun shone, the ground was firm, a smell of seaweed came from the Bosphorus and the water seemed clean enough despite a slick of rubbish. Along the path we passed natives and soldiers who stepped back and removed their caps with great deference. The Turkish women were shrill-voiced and dressed from head to toe in bright colours but their faces were heavily veiled. I envied their obscurity. My own face, by contrast, seemed as prominent as a white moon in the dark frame of my bonnet.

Once through the gateway to the hospital we suddenly entered deep shade. Here the noise was more concentrated and purposeful: running water, brisk footfalls, the clop of a mule, the rasp of a saw. Inside was a vast courtyard, wide enough for ten parade grounds, with huts scattered about, groups of loitering men wearing fragments of uniform, and dogs slumped in the shade. A couple of men dressed in shirts and trousers and with two bare feet between them lolled on a bench against a sunny wall. They took off their hats when Nora asked the way to Miss Nightingale's office and the smallest sat up eagerly. 'We can take you up to her quarters but she's not here. She went to the Crimea. And she's got terrible sick. Surely you've heard.'

My spirits fell still further. Aside from the inconvenience of her being away, it crossed my mind that if the indomitable Miss Nightingale could get ill here, what hope was there for me? Meanwhile the men had covered their tousled heads, heaved themselves onto crutches and prepared to be our guides.

The hospital consumed us with a dankness unique to stone buildings in hot countries as we climbed a staircase and entered a long corridor lined with beds. I remembered that Rosa had compared the hospital at Koulali to a railway station and here indeed were high-arched ceilings, many-paned windows set deep in the walls, row upon row of doors, and down the courtyard side of the corridor, lines of beds, and in each bed a sick man. I thanked God that at least I'd had a glimpse of a hospital in London so that I wasn't too horrified by the sights and sounds of collective sickness. We saw only men – patients shuffling from bed to bed, orderlies carrying pails or trays, some officials in army uniforms, a man in a frock coat. Anyone who was conscious stared at us, and one or two of the patients invited us across to their beds.

Then, in the distance, I saw a gown the same sludge colour as the one Rosa had been given and my pulse quickened. But no, the woman was at least three times the girth of Rosa and by the time we reached the end of that particular corridor, thanks to the tortuous pace of our escorts, she was gone.

Finally we met a nun wearing yards of black and a limp headdress covering all but her puffy cheeks and beady eyes. She smelled initially of camphor but when she moved all the other, less desirable smells of the hospital flowed from her skirts. 'Well?' she said in a flat voice with an Irish lilt. 'Can I help you?'

How could I tell whether she was Catholic or Anglican? She wore a large crucifix with the image of the dead Christ stuck to it, which perhaps suggested she was a Papist. 'I am looking for my cousin who was nursing in Skutari at one time, Rosa Barr,' I said.

Not much of the nun's forehead was visible but one eyebrow lifted and she blinked. 'Rosa Barr. I know the name. She's not here now, for sure.'

The ward shattered into fragments and reassembled itself. *Rosa Barr. I know the name.*

'We think she went to Balaklava. The fact is we haven't heard from her.'

'And you've come all this way to look for her, is it? Isn't that a wonder? I certainly hope you won't be disappointed. Well, you just sit yourselves down and when I've done my errand I'll see what I can do.'

It was a long wait. The nun, who was heavy on her feet, first had to walk the length of the corridor and disappear through one of the doors. After several minutes she came back, pausing at a couple of beds on the way, then disappeared into the stairwell behind us. Meanwhile the business of the ward went on. Some sort of meal was being served; a huge pot was brought to the far end of the corridor, a few of the patients raised themselves on their elbows in anticipation and a smell of broth wafted towards us. So they're not starving and they're not dying in droves, I thought; perhaps the great effort of knitting and self-sacrifice back home had in fact been unnecessary.

Meantime our escorts had propped themselves either side of Nora. 'So what happened to the pair of you?' she asked in her new, forthright manner.

'Oh you know. The usual. A touch of dysentery. Then the frostbite.'

'Frostbite? In this weather? It scarce seems possible.'

'The weather's changed.'

'Did you both lose limbs through frostbite, then?'

The most talkative had a wiry frame and a sickening scar on his cheek where the flesh had been gouged away and healed piecemeal. 'Actually, I blame Halford here and he blames me. We was on duty together in the trenches, quiet night, fell asleep, which admittedly we shouldn't have done. The cold makes you sleep. Woke up and the soles of our feet was glued together with ice. By that time we never bothered with boots – broken and worse than useless and the devil's own job to get on and off. Both of us was chilled to the bone so we got close, couldn't tear us-selves apart. They had to carry us down to the hospital in a cart, both of us howling and shrieking till they tipped a bucket of rum down our throats. Next thing we know we're side by side in a heap and there's a doctor hanging over us and he puts his hand on my leg, higher and higher up until I can feel him pinch me and he says, "You've both got to lose a foot because I assume neither of you will want three, two of them dead meat, so who's going first?" In the end we lay side by side and held each other's hands like babies and Halford here lost the toss. We haven't been apart since and we mean to go home and make a fortune by displaying us-selves at shows.'

Halford, lumpen and red-faced, nodded approvingly but said nothing. Nora asked why on earth the soldiers hadn't been issued with decent boots. The men replied that their regiment expected one pair of boots to last a year and any extras were docked from pay.

At last the nun came back with a ledger. Her manner had chilled and she stood at a distance. 'That's it,' she said briskly. 'We've found your cousin's name. As a member of Miss Stanley's party she wasn't given a place here, but first went to the hospital at Koulali, a mile or so away, and then chose to go to Balaklava at the end of January. We've not seen her since.'

'Did you ever meet her?'

'I may have. I can't remember. A few of Miss Stanley's women did come here and try to gain an interview with Miss Nightingale, but things were very overstretched and we had no time to accommodate untrained nurses.'

'So how will we find her?'

Her pale eyes scanned my face. 'You could send a note across to the General or Castle Hospital at Balaklava. But I've been speaking to my sisters. They think that Miss Barr may be one of the women who would not stay put in the hospital. Not all of them do.'

'Then where would she go?'

'Who knows? You see, this is the trouble. One is never quite sure, with some of these young women, what their real intentions are in coming out here.'

'Rosa Barr's intention was to nurse,' said Nora.

'Perhaps so. I cannot speak for her. But there are other examples of those who don't choose to accept our discipline. One of them, for instance, went off with a Highland Regiment. We think she is there still, up among the men. The reputations of us all are affected by such thoughtlessness. I hope your cousin is not in a similar condition.'

'Is there anyone else who might know more about her?'

'Miss Nightingale would certainly have been the one to ask but Miss Nightingale is sick and cannot talk to anyone. And in any case she is still in Balaklava. You could not have come at a worse time.'

'Then what do you suggest I do?' I cried.

'Well, dear Lord above, girl, shouldn't you have thought about that long ago, before you set out? I cannot think what you're doing so far from home. And now you're bound to get sick, they all do, the ones that visit from England, and we'll be having you to look after as well.'

There was no denying, now she had drawn our attention to it, that the hospital reeked of disease. I could almost see sickness hanging in the air: greenish, with tendrils that reached into my pores.

'Well, what about the other hospitals here? Is it possible that she came back to Constantinople? Should we enquire?'

'You can, but you'd be wasting your time. We know exactly who is employed in hospitals in Turkey. It's the Crimea where we have difficulty keeping an eye on things.' She gave a nunnish bow, cast a sharp eye over what was taking place in the ward behind me and moved away, ledger tucked under her arm.

When we returned to the ship we found a note from Lady Stratford who said she'd seen Rosa's name on a list, may even have met her during Christmas festivities, but had no knowledge of her present whereabouts. She invited me to tea at the embassy next Tuesday but I replied regretfully that the *Royal Albert* was sailing that evening. Tea at the embassy sounded like a remarkably safe proposition compared to our journey to the Crimea.

Chapter Four

The Black Sea turned very choppy and the new ship, much smaller than our last and dangerously overcrowded, smelled very unpleasant after an hour or two – of sewage below deck, soot, oil and poultry above. There were so many passengers that we had to dine in shifts in the tiny saloon although the food was poor and I felt so ill that in fact I scarcely sat down to a meal throughout the voyage. I spent most of the two days' journey first along the Bosphorus and then across the Black Sea either confined to my bunk or on deck with my bonnet blown back and my battered complexion exposed to the glare of the sun, tormented by the incessant thwack of the paddle wheels and gusts of black smoke while I strained nervously for a glimpse of the infamous Crimea.

I avoided the soldiers, some of whom were so young their complexions were greasy and whiskerless, others older than Father. Nora of course sought out the Irish contingent and before long was in the midst of a loud group, more animated than I'd ever seen her. She'd hold a man by his arm while she asked where he was from, when he'd *come across* from Ireland, what had happened to the rest of his family and if they might have acquaintances in common either fighting in the war or back home. Names were reeled off: Mc this and O' that and families were picked apart to see who was related to whom and whether Paddy or Cathy or Jim or Shelagh somebody or other had been heard of since 1846.

One or two men asked me whose wife I was or if I was going out to be a nurse like those other *good ladies* of Miss Nightingale's. I told Nora to pass the word around that I was engaged to a doctor.

'You should speak to them yourself,' she said. 'How will we ever find Rosa if you don't ask questions?'

'I have never approached a strange man in my life.'

'You wouldn't have to approach a strange man, for goodness'

sake. One smile and they'd be like bees round a honey pot. And in any case, in what way are they strange? You know exactly who they are. They are brave men going to fight another battle in this wretched war. It would be a kindness to distract them from what lies ahead.'

'I would have no idea what to say to such people.'

'What do you mean, *such people*? Well, I have no such inhibition. I'll be talking to them.' I watched as she moved back along the deck, absurdly hurt that she should prefer their company to mine.

When I later asked her what the soldiers had said she was curt. 'I have learned nothing definite.'

'What do you mean, definite?'

'One thinks he may have been nursed by a woman of Rosa's description when he was half dead of frostbite and pneumonia up at the General Hospital in Balaklava, but he had been too ill then to say for sure now.'

'What about Dr Thewell? Have they heard of him?'

She sniffed and shrugged. 'You should ask them yourself. War, it seems, breeds unpleasant rumour. I'll say no more.'

What I had expected of Russia was treacherous cliffs, barren plains, *foreignness;* what I first saw of the Crimea was as green and lovely as a wooded bit of Britain, fresh-looking and tranquil across the blue water. But then we saw to the west a cloud, which one of the soldiers said must be cannon-fire above Sebastopol. As we sailed closer we heard the rumble of guns. The soldiers went still and, when I glanced into the face of the nearest, a square-faced country boy, I saw that the same deathly look had come into his eyes as I used to see in Nora's when she emerged from a long night in Aunt Isabella's room.

I went down to my cabin and wept until Nora found me.

'Good Lord,' she said. 'So whatever is the matter?'

'Oh nothing.'

'Well, that's a deal of fuss for nothing.'

'Leave me alone.' The trouble with Nora was that she took such requests at face value and the last thing I really wanted was to be on my own. She retied her bonnet and made for the door. 'We will die when we get there,' I said.

'I have no intention of dying.'

'Everyone is dying of cholera. *The Times* said so. Or we'll be shot. We will be in a battlefield, undefended. We have no idea what to do when we arrive.'

'Find Rosa, of course.'

'How, exactly? We've never discussed what to do. We've no plan.'

'We will make a plan, when we've seen the lie of the land.'

'Did you not notice how strangely that nun looked at us in the hospital? What if something terrible has happened to Rosa? What if she's dead?'

We stared at each other nervously. 'Then we'll find her grave, the poor girl, but at least she won't be left unmourned.'

'Neither of us knows a word of Russian.'

'Well, I'm hoping we'll not be meeting many Russians. If we do, it'll be a sure sign that the war is over and they have won, or that we've made a terrible blunder and got ourselves the wrong side of the lines.'

'Aren't you afraid, Nora?'

'Afraid? Good God, Miss Lingwood, why would I be? What can touch me these days?'

In the event we had to anchor outside Balaklava for another night while the boat tipped sickeningly up and down on the waves, its boards creaking and grinding and its fleas biting while we waited for an official to sail out and meet us. In the small hours I woke to the distant murmur of gunfire and was terrified that battalions of Cossacks would attack us from the cliffs, that the instant we stepped ashore we would be shot or taken prisoner and my life would end in chaos and carnage.

I wondered how this sad news would be received at home. Poor Father would have to abandon his business and follow me out here to ask questions and have a proper stone erected. The thought of him sifting through a heap of bodies under the violent heat of the sun, his second-best top hat perched on the graveside, brought more tears to my eyes. Perhaps, when she'd had confirmation of the news, Mother would go up to my room and finger my embroidered cushion covers. Would the governesses be issued with black crêpe bands? And of course the situation would be made worse by the fact that I had *brought it on myself*, a favourite phrase of Mrs Hardcastle's. In fact to die in such circumstances could be described as self-indulgent.

Then at last, an hour after dawn, an engine approached and the poultry set up a frantic clamour as a steamer came alongside. Soon the boat quaked with the stamp of official feet. I dressed, seized bonnet, shawl and a reticule containing our documents and money, and went up on deck where a light dew had made the boards slippery and the Crimean coast looked benign under a milky sky. The harbourmaster, heavily bearded but otherwise civilised, had come aboard, brandishing a sheaf of papers.

After a couple of hours of whisker-stroking, parading about and peering into crates we were at last permitted to steam forward again on what seemed to be a collision course for the coast. Then I saw a gap in the cliffs so narrow that we had to wait while another boat, a yacht, had edged out towards us and slipped by, presumably on her way back to Constantinople, before a couple of tugs took up the slack ropes and we slipped between walls of rock into Balaklava harbour.

'Good Lord,' said Nora, 'what a place. It's no bigger than your back garden in Clapham.'

We were in a stretch of water half the width of the Thames, hemmed in on three sides by steep hills, on a fourth by a cluster of buildings, and so full of ships that it was impossible to disentangle one mast from another. I had never seen anywhere more crowded or enclosed except perhaps the Strand at nine on a weekday morning. We had sailed from bright sunlight into deep shade, and there was a din of human voices, dogs, horses, wheels, machinery and again, in the distance, the heart-stopping thunder of cannon-fire.

I behaved as my mother would have done in similar circumstances; that is, almost paralysed with fear and without an idea in her head what to do next. I sat in my cabin with Nora and got out a notebook and pen. Then I wrote the following, in my most laboriously neat handwriting: *3 June 1855. The* Royal Albert. *Balaklava Harbour. Ten o'clock in the morning.*

And under that the word *Plan.*

'Well?' I said to Nora. 'What shall I put?'

'We must ask for Rosa.'

'Whom shall we ask?'

'Everybody. In all the public places. And in the hospitals, of course.'

'But it seems likely that she left the hospitals.'

'I would not have thought that a lady on her own, with hair the colour of Rosa's, would go unnoticed here or anywhere for long.'

So I wrote:

Item One. Ask for Rosa in stores and public places in Balaklava.
Item Two. Ask in hospitals for Rosa.
Item Three.

'The nun at Skutari said she may have gone among the troops,' I said. 'And Henry met her immediately after a battle.'

'Then we too must go among the troops.'

Item Three. Go among the troops.

'And there's Max Stukeley,' said Nora. 'He may know where she is.'

'Mother wrote to him. He never replied.'

'Nevertheless.'

'I don't know him well enough to approach him.'

'I do. There's no need to look at me like that. I was at Stukeley for eight years, remember.'

Item Four. Approach Captain Maximilian Stukeley.

Chapter Five

As the *Royal Albert* was not due to sail back to Constantinople for a week or so we were to use her as lodgings. The intention was that we would find Rosa quickly and leave with our ship.

I dressed in my third-best gown, hung my reticule over one arm and with my other hand held an open parasol to protect myself from the blistering sunshine. Even Nora, who wore a shapeless bonnet with a deep brim, approved of this arrangement. She said that we were so unused to the conditions that it was likely we'd get sunstroke if we weren't careful.

My first thought on stepping onto Russian soil was of Henry, who had stood on these same paving stones and set sail from this same cramped harbour with shiploads of wounded men. But it was hard to equate this bustling place with the muddy pest-hole described in his letters, and the very thought of Henry, which led inevitably to the memory of that dreadful episode in the Narni bedroom, made me wretched.

In any case I realised that I was attracting a great deal of unwanted attention. Nobody else held a parasol or wore cream muslin, flounced and beribboned over half a dozen petticoats; in fact, as far as I could tell, nobody else except Nora was female. Fortunately the captain had supplied us with an escort who was to take us to someone in authority but though men fell back on either side as we passed, nobody worried about gawping at me, particularly foreigners, whose filthy feet and knees were visible to me from beneath the fringed shelter of my parasol.

Eventually we came to a building which might once have been the house of a wealthier townsperson but had been allowed to fall into a state of near ruin and then roughly rebuilt. Shutters were missing, stucco had flaked away and the roof was patched. Soldiers were hanging about in the hall and when an officer came running down the stairs he gaped and then sent us to a waiting room in which papers flooded every surface and burst from files and boxes. After a while it grew so hot that I leaned against a heap and twirled the handle of my parasol. Nora went to the window but there was no view except of a yard filled with filth and rubble. Footsteps clumped up and down the stairs, men's voices called, mostly jocular and well spoken, some harassed or rough, and the business of the harbour rattled and clanged outside.

At last we were shown into a little office with a crooked desk and notice boards covered in maps scribbled over with notes, lists and information about ships, masters, regiments and purveyors. The smell of blocked drains was very bad but otherwise it was a reassuring enough place because it reminded me of Father's study. The official behind the desk was tall and thin with a long face and mournful eyes, like a well-intentioned mongrel, though his skin had an unhealthy grey tinge and his moustache drooped sadly at either end. He took one look at me and said under his breath, though distinctly enough for me to hear: 'Jesus Christ, what will they send me next?'

I was so offended that I plumped down on a rickety chair while he sighed, took a clean sheet of paper, dipped his pen and prepared to write. 'I'm Lieutenant Barnabus. In charge of arrivals. Your name, madam?'

I gave him my name and Nora's.

'How did you get here?'

'On the *Royal Albert*.'

He made a note. 'I will give your captain a reprimand. I assume you paid him an immense sum. Well, I won't have it. We can't allow just anyone to sail in and out of Balaklava as if it were Broadstairs.'

'I am looking for my cousin, Rosa Barr. She came out here to nurse and has gone missing.'

Barnabus's posture did not change but I was certain that his eyes widened a fraction. 'Rosa Barr, you say?'

'Miss Rosa Barr. Have you heard of her?'

'Since when do you think she's been missing?'

'We last heard from her at the beginning of February. Nothing since.'

He scribbled energetically in his notebook. 'Well, it's no use asking me. I'm new here.'

'You've heard nothing of her, then?'

'I arrived in April. But surely a simple telegraph from London would have sufficed for your enquiries. What is the point of coming all this way and putting yourself in danger? Who is your father? I'm amazed at him for allowing this.' He peered at me. 'I assume your father knows your whereabouts.'

'Well, of course my movements have not been certain . . .'

'But this is absurd. I can't be doing with this. People turning up here whenever they feel like it. Young ladies with umbrellas. Have you any idea of the dangers? Miss Nightingale couldn't stand it even. Crossed the Black Sea, was here five minutes and took sick with Crimean Fever. Can you imagine the fuss if she'd died? We have enough sickness on our hands without you women turning up.'

'I'm not sick.'

'You will be. Look at you. A puff of wind will blow you away, let alone a swig of bad water. There's nowhere for you to stay and no transport for you. All our energies should be directed against the Russians and instead I have to nanny hoards of women who drop in on all sides. I suggest you get straight back to your ship and sit tight until it sets sail again. In fact I'll put you aboard the next sailing. How's that? Get you back to Constantinople or some other safe port in double-quick time. And we'll send a nice telegram to your mama, let her know where you are, and before you know it you'll be home. Now, what's your address in England?'

At which point Nora said in her flat voice: 'Max Stukeley.'

Barnabus pushed back his chair. 'I beg your pardon?'

'We are also here because we were summoned by Captain Maximilian Stukeley. I assume you've heard of him.'

'Of course. Whatever does he want you for?'

'How will we know, until we see him? You see he is Miss Lingwood's cousin and Rosa Barr, the woman we have come to find, is his stepsister.'

'Stepsister. I see. Yes of course. But officers, even Stukeley, can't just invite people out here. Why would he do such a thing?' He stared at me again. 'Are you sure you're related? It's not some kind of . . . You're not in some sort of liaison . . .'

I was too appalled by Nora's foolish lie to give him an answer. *Summoned by* Max Stukeley indeed.

Nora said, 'That's quite enough. Maybe you'd send for him, so we could talk to him.'

'Why didn't you mention your connection with Stukeley at first?'

'Miss Lingwood is naturally most concerned about her other cousin, Rosa. She's the one uppermost on her mind.'

'Well, I suppose I could have a message sent up to Stukeley if that's your wish though it would take upwards of a day, there and back.'

'And in the meantime,' said Nora, 'perhaps we might pay a visit to a hospital.'

'Under no circumstances. Absolutely not. No. I've made an order. No more visitors. Absolutely. Since the business with Miss Nightingale we don't allow anyone up there who's new to the Crimea.'

'Is Miss Nightingale in Balaklava now? Might we see her?'

'Her ship set sail this morning.' His expression was a little too triumphant for my liking. 'I believe she's going back to some place in the hills above Constantinople where she can convalesce. Now I'm going to have you returned to the ship where you will stay until I send word. And in the meantime I'll arrange a passage for you as soon as possible. I've got it all here in my notes.'

In a matter of minutes Nora and I had been whisked back to our cabin where an envelope awaited me, addressed to 'Miss Lingwood, the lady passenger aboard the *Royal Albert*' and containing an invitation to call on a Lady Mendlesham-Connors, aboard the yacht *Principle*. Apparently despite – or perhaps as an explanation for – the fulminations of Lieutenant Barnabus, I was not the only female in Balaklava harbour. Nevertheless I decided not to accept the unknown lady's hospitality because the last thing I wanted was awkward questions.

Nora disagreed. 'I've said, you need to get among people and talk to them if you're intent on finding Rosa. Meanwhile I could make myself pleasant with the maid, who'll always know far more than her mistress.'

'Lady Mendlesham-Connors might be acquainted with Mrs Hardcastle. She'll think it's very strange that I'm here. It's bad enough that Barnabus will have telegraphed London by now. And incidentally, Nora, I should prefer it if you allowed me to conduct conversations—'

'You must write home, post-haste. Tell them you're doing fine and will be back soon. You don't want them following you out here.'

'It would only be Father. Mother couldn't leave Aunt Isabella.'

'I wouldn't put it past Lady Isabella Stukeley to insist on being brought on a cruise down here. She'd say t'would do her heart a power of good to be in the sea air.'

It was possible, given the glint in her eye, that Nora was making a joke. 'Then you'd have to go back to your old job of nursemaid, Nora. How would that be?'

'I think now I'd rather put my head in a cannon's mouth.'

That night I wrote a letter to my parents in which I gave them my profound apologies for taking such a momentous step without their permission and begging them not to worry. Henry had been too ill and too insistent to resist; there could be little doubt, in fact, that I was answering the wish of a dying man and his frantic concern for Rosa, which we all shared, had been an additional spur.

It was a letter that took many drafts and after it was done I lay on my bunk, in a now familiar posture of rigid unease, and listened to the clinking of masts and voices on shore. I wouldn't let Nora open the porthole because a place as hot and enclosed as Balaklava must surely be a breeding ground for cholera. In the distance was the ker-boom-boom of guns firing, and sometimes the rattle of smaller arms, perhaps the Minié rifles as described in my war album. Sometimes the ship swayed and knocked against its neighbour, sometimes there was drunken shouting. *Like Broadstairs*, Barnabus had said. If only. Sun on the sand, damp petticoats, a fistful of seashells. Father's legs stretched out as he snoozed behind a newspaper, Mother with a veil over her bonnet to protect her complexion from the sun, the only time I saw her read a book.

My chief worry was the coming meeting with Max Stukeley. Whatever would he say when he heard that Mariella Lingwood and Nora McCormack had come calling at Balaklava? Would he bounce onto the ship like he had into the drawing room at Fosse House and give my hand an impudent kiss? Would he be full of blame or praise, and what news would he bring of Rosa?

Then I began to wonder how much time Rosa had spent in Balaklava. Perhaps she too had listened to the sea birds and grown used to the incessant clipping of one vessel against another. A few words from her would set everything right. *My lovely Mariella, my amazing girl, I cannot believe you have come all this way to find me* ... I was sure that she would explain Henry's behaviour in a few dismissive words ... *fantasy* ... *delirium* ... *war fever.*

Where was she? Perhaps very close. The Crimea was surely not big enough to contain us both without her fatal magnetism pulling us together.

Chapter Six

The next day, in anticipation of Max's visit, I dressed with extreme care. Yesterday's gown had obviously not convinced Barnabus that my expedition to the Crimea was anything other than frivolous so in the end I chose a spotted muslin blouse from which I cut all the turquoise ribbons except for one bow at the neck, and a relatively narrow green skirt. I then settled myself on deck and embarked on the painful task of writing a letter to Henry.

The note was short and my tone restrained. Was I writing to the sick, obsessed Henry, or to my fiancé, the rational Dr Thewell? In the end I stated simply that I had arrived at Balaklava and was taking all possible steps to find Rosa.

My work was disturbed by the extraordinary bustle of the harbour. It was like being confined to an open hutch in the middle of King's Cross Station or another of Father's building sites. Somewhere in the distance was the racket of heavy crates being loaded, yet another steamer came in amidst shouted orders and greetings, carts rumbled along the quay and pallets were flung about. At one point I saw a series of wagons laden not with baggage but with wounded men. I glimpsed a bloodied blanket, an unconscious shape rolling from side to side at the bottom of a cart, and after that I gave up trying to write and took up my sewing instead. I decided to remove the lace trims and ruffles from two more of my gowns and thereby make myself less ostentatious in these foreign parts. Even my unsteady fingers could manage the snipping of stitches.

At about midday there was a clop of hooves and a very tall officer wearing a red jacket and tight trousers dismounted nimbly, threw the reins over a nearby post, looked about him whilst fumbling to do up his collar buttons, shouted questions to passing sailors and eventually ran up the gangway of the *Royal Albert* and yelled so loudly that curious heads appeared over the railings of the next ship: 'Miss Mariella Lingwood. Is she here?'

Nervous excitement was rapidly replaced by a mixture of chagrin and relief that my visitor was not Max Stukeley.

'Lieutenant George Newman, ma'am.'

I folded my sewing, got up and dropped a curtsey, noting the high polish on Newman's boots and buttons. 'I am Miss Lingwood. This is my maid, Nora McCormack.'

'I've been sent to tell you that Captain Stukeley is not in the camp. He's away on a mission.'

'When will he be back?' asked Nora.

'I'm not able to answer that, ma'am. He's been gone nearly two weeks, is all I'm at liberty to say. We expect him to be several more days at least.'

'Perhaps he's at Kertch,' said Nora mysteriously.

The officer gave his hat a half turn.

I said, 'Have you no idea when he'll be back? We can't wait here indefinitely. In fact we'll be leaving very soon.'

He looked at me unhappily and I guessed him to be no more than eighteen or nineteen. Nora said, 'Perhaps you'll be wanting a nice cup of tea after your ride, Lieutenant Newman?'

'Thank you.' When Newman and I were alone he sat with one leg extended in a touching attempt at grown-up military style and tried several resting places for his hat: knee, floor and nearby chair.

'And how do you find it, here in the Crimea?' Even to my own ears I sounded unnervingly like Mrs Hardcastle in conversation with one of the governesses.

'It's not what I'd hoped for, certainly. It was not what I'd envisaged.'

'What had you envisaged?'

'India. That's the place to be. Had high hopes of that. Mama and Papa were expecting India when they bought me a commission last year. But I mustn't complain.'

He leaned forward and posted his hat between his legs as if inviting me to say more but the admiring glint in his eyes made me too uneasy to press him further.

Nora came back with the tea and I poured, faintly amused to be holding a tea party in Balaklava harbour. Young Lieutenant Newman showed his genteel upbringing by the manner with which he lifted his cup. A rasp of sunlight fell on his exposed brow where the weight of his cap had left a line of angry pimples.

I said, 'Did the note from Barnabus mention that I was looking for my cousin who came here as a nurse? Rosa Barr.'

Newman's tea splashed into his saucer and a flush rose up his neck and cheeks. He looked away from me and his lips twitched involuntarily sideways, distorting the end of his nose. 'Rosa – Miss Barr. Was she your cousin? Is she?'

'My first cousin, yes. Our mothers are sisters.'

'I see. Ah. Rosa Barr.'

'You've heard of her, then?'

'Why yes. I've heard of her. I should say I have.'

I drew a deep breath. 'Where did you hear of Rosa?'

'Why at the camp. Of course I did.' Another pause. 'She was living there.'

Nora came a little closer to my shoulder. 'Ah. Now, is she still among you?'

'No, no. Wish she was. But no. Damn . . . 'Fraid she's not there any more . . . Never actually met her. She was gone a couple of weeks before I arrived.'

'I see. And yet you are familiar with her name, Lieutenant Newman?'

'Because they all talk about her. She lived in a little hut attached to our hospital tents. It was irregular but allowed because she was Stukeley's sister, sort of.' He looked unhappily down at his cap, now crushed between his knees.

'I'm surprised she was with your regiment. We had understood she might be working in one of the hospitals here. That's why she left Skutari, we thought, to work for a hospital in Balaklava.'

'I couldn't say, I don't know the full story. Only that she shared a hut with a couple of the wives who've stayed on . . . even though their husbands haven't quite made it, they don't want to go home. She had no time for the officers, said they had plenty of attention one way or another and didn't need any more. But my men say that if they were sick or injured, she was the one. They won't go near the hospital if they can help it. Can't blame them. Rumours abound of men who go in with an injured toe, carried out dead next day. She used to bait Stukeley, they say. Most of us don't like crossing him but she had no fear. If he came back with a brace of duck she'd have them cooked up for the men.'

'But by the time you arrived, she'd gone. Where?'

'Ah, no idea. None at all. Not the foggiest.' But I noticed that Newman would not meet my eye. 'She's said to have disappeared into thin air. Left all her possessions behind in a box. Stukeley won't have her name mentioned now.'

'What do you think has happened to her?' asked Nora.

'I don't know.' But Nora held him with her stern gaze until he stumbled into speech again. 'You do hear ... The truth is people do disappear. The cholera can strike a man down in a matter of hours. There's been talk of raiding parties, Tartars or Greeks. And then some men can't stand the incessant firing. The guns. In the end they go strange and wander off.' By now he was in a trance of misery.

I took up my sewing. Nora said briskly, 'Well, that's enough of Miss Barr. Tell us about yourself. What kind of a time have you been having here?'

'Not so good. Tedious mostly. Night after night in the batteries.'

'And what's that like?'

'Oh you know. Not much to it. Trying to stay alert; sending the men up to mend the barricades when they get smashed; dodging the shots that come over; returning as good as we get. Our regiment has had some heavy losses one way or another during the winter so a lot of us are brand new to the work. You lie about in the grass half the day, in the evening you dine with your friends as if it were the old days, at school say, then at night off you go to the trenches and the next morning three or four of you are gone. Can't quite get the hang of it, you know.' My sewing hung still in my hands as I noted that his eyes had filled with tears.

Nora poured more tea. 'I doubt you get much time for taking tea with the ladies so just you make the most of it. I wish we had a slice of cake to offer you. And in the meantime tell us about Max Stukeley. He seems to have survived all right for a year or more. But then that boy has a devilish luck on him.'

'He does.' Newman ran the back of his hand under his nose. 'He leads, we follow. We can't resist. He sweeps us up like it was a game of tag or some such. Whoosh, we're in. But some of the newest recruits are so raw even Max struggles with them. They're all over the place. Ask too many questions before they'll obey an order. I'm not used to it myself, like I say, but I've been trying to bring them up to scratch while he's away. Uphill struggle.'

'Of course the young mistress,' said Nora, wagging her head at me, 'is engaged to be married to one of the doctors who was out here, a Dr Thewell. You must have heard of him, surely?'

Newman sat upright, stared, then concentrated again on his cup.

'Or maybe you missed him too,' said Nora. 'He was taken ill and had to be sent away. We saw him in Italy just now. He'd had a bad time of it, seemingly. We did wonder if Rosa and he might have met up.'

It was intolerable that Nora should share my intimate life with a complete stranger. When I stood up Newman shot to his feet. 'You've been very kind taking the trouble to come here, Lieutenant.'

'Is there anything else I can do for you, Miss Lingwood?'

'Thank you. No.'

'How would it be if I took you on a little excursion next time I've got a free hour or so? I could borrow a pony for you perhaps and we could go up to the ruin, and Mrs McCormack too, if she likes. There is a wonderful view of the harbour from there, and very safe.'

'The ruin?'

'The old Genoese fortress – you see up there on the cliffs? It has a twin, over in Therapia. You might have seen it while you were in Constantinople. No? Well, I'd be glad to show you, I was always very fond of ancient buildings at home. I believe some of the other ladies have been there for a picnic and enjoyed the view.'

'I'm afraid I have no head for heights,' I said firmly, wondering what Barnabus would say if he caught me on a jaunt along the cliff with a young officer.

'I should like to go,' said Nora, 'if you'll take me.'

'I cannot spare you, Nora. What are you thinking of?' I said sharply. 'I'm sorry, Lieutenant, there is no question of either of us coming with you.'

Newman's eyes were heavy with disappointment and he stood about for a little longer glancing hopefully into our faces but neither of us spoke. 'Well, then,' he said, 'never mind. Not to worry. And of course when Stukeley gets back I'll tell him I saw you.'

Nora followed him to the quayside. 'How is Captain Stukeley in himself?' I heard her ask.

I didn't catch the reply, which was lengthy. Instead I marched down to the cabin, furious with her for making me look a fool over the expedition to the fortress. Mrs Hardcastle, I thought, would advise me to dismiss Nora but that was hardly possible when I had no other companion within a thousand miles. In the end I decided simply to tell her that if she persisted in contradicting me I would have to write home suggesting that her situation should be reviewed on our return to England.

After a while Nora came down and watched me. When I paid her no attention she shut the door and put her hands on her hips. At last she exclaimed: 'Oh for feck's sake.'

'I beg your pardon?'

'What the feck are you doin' here?'

'I will *not* be spoken to in that—'

'Oh no, you won't, won't you, but who's going to stop me?'

'Enough, Nora.' I ripped the gathering thread out of a ruffle and began winding the strip of material round and round my fingers. Meanwhile she had come to rest with her back to the door. Out of the corner of my eye I saw that her bosom was heaving under her brown serge blouse and she was watching me closely.

'I won't stop it,' she said, her accent much stronger than usual. 'I'll speak my mind now I've gone thus far. Do you want to find Rosa or not?'

'Of course I want to find her.'

'Then why did you send that boy packing? There's all sorts we might have learned from him.'

'I won't have you discussing my engagement with—'

'Why? What have you got to lose? Don't you want the truth?'

'Of course I do. But not at any price.'

'So the bottom line is that you don't care enough to know what's happened to your cousin. Well, I'll tell you something. *I've* not come here to waste my time hanging about while you make up your mind who you'll talk to and who you'll shun. I'm thinking of offering my services at the hospital. They can't be that overrun with nurses. I've been thinking that while I'm away from England

I should take the chance to live a little and it's hardly living being here with you and pandering to your every need.'

'I've not noticed much pandering. It will make no difference to me whether you're here or not.'

'Well, good then.' She began to sort through her possessions. 'I'll be sending for what's important in my luggage later. Most of my things will be down in the hold. I had been feeling a touch responsible for you, having come with you this far, but you're enough to try the patience of the blessed saints in heaven. I cannot stand it no more.'

'This is presumably what you intended all along, then, is it? You've had it in your mind since we left Italy to work in a hospital, like Rosa. Oh yes. I see. I can't think why you didn't join Miss Nightingale's nurses when they first advertised if that's what you've been wanting all along.'

'I would have done had it not been for your aunt. But oddly enough I had a sense of loyalty and attachment to her and I was sorry for her sickness, which perhaps you'd never understand.'

'If I had known you'd been harbouring these kinds of thoughts I would have got rid of you long ago. It's unfortunate that you have been dishonest enough to allow me to pay your fare, under false pretences.'

'Well, then, now you know the truth about me. So you won't miss me.'

'Of course I won't miss you. But I forbid you to abandon me like this. If you leave me I shall be forced to write about you to Mother and Aunt and you'll be turned away with no reference.'

'What good is their reference out here? Can't you see? We are in a different place, where we have to think differently and find ourselves a new way of being.'

'You're wrong. We cannot allow our standards to slip one inch. This is what I've been fighting all along. We must be what we have always been or we will be lost.'

'Your standards, as you put them, don't apply out here. Use your brain, Miss Mariella. Think about it. But no, you can't think because you've never really left the nursery in that Clapham house of yours. In all the last weeks you've not changed one iota or opened your eyes to nothing. How will you find Rosa if this is the way you carry on? It's quite obvious that the poor girl has got herself into some dreadful scrape and we'll have the devil's own job to find her, especially if Max has tried and been unsuccessful.'

By now I was weeping. She seemed in such deadly earnest, folding up her nightgown, dropping spare hairpins into a little tin, unlocking the box containing our provisions and removing packets of tea and coffee. 'I don't understand. Why are you talking to me like this? It's not my fault if nobody will help us.'

'Then whose fault is it? Look at you, sewing a frock while the world is at war. What do you care about your cousin Rosa or indeed anyone else out here?'

'I care. I do. All I want is to find her and then go back as fast as possible to Henry before it's too late. He's the reason I'm doing all this. And yet I've known all along that we should not have come. We aren't wanted. Nobody is willing to help us find Rosa.'

'No. I'll tell you what I think, really and truly. You don't want to find Rosa. You're not even prepared to try because you're too frightened to face the truth of why she came here and what has happened to her. Well, I'll tell you why she came. You squeezed her out with your attachment to that smug doctor of yours. You couldn't give her what she needed, you never could satisfy that terrible look of hers I've seen so often, of hope mingled with fear. Well, I don't want to please you. Why should I? I'm not sitting another moment on this ship waiting for you or anyone else to tell me what to do. I've seen my chance and I'm taking it.'

I was sobbing freely, wiping away the tears with the length of ruffle. 'What do you mean, squeezed her out? What are you talking about? And if you care about her so much, why are you going to the hospital? How will that help?'

'Oh I expect to discover all sorts once I'm among the nurses.'

'Go, then, if that's what you want. Leave me alone. See if I care.'

A fatal mistake this, because of course she went. And there was I, left alone on board the *Royal Albert* where a great many curious ears had probably heard every word of our argument. I was hot, hungry, tearful, bewildered, with no idea even how to acquire lunch.

Chapter Seven

Nora still wasn't back when I woke the next morning so I washed my face in yesterday's stale water, drank a cup of coffee and ate a piece of bread brought by the steward – or cabin boy, he could barely have been thirteen. It now seemed possible that Nora would not return immediately and that I had been right yesterday to suggest that she had been planning this defection for some time.

My eye fell on the calling card left the previous day. Apparently I had no choice but to throw myself on the mercy of this Lady Mendlesham-Connors.

The *Principle* was a private yacht, beautifully appointed with furled brown sails and highly polished brass fittings. As she was moored out in the harbour away from more workaday vessels I had to pay an exorbitant fee to be rowed there. I wore my best pink silk gown and for once had gauged my dress correctly; Lady Mendlesham-Connors, or Lady Mendlesham as I was invited to call her, a large lady perhaps a dozen or so years older than I with staring eyes, a violently weathered complexion and deep ruffles to her gown, watched my approach with approval.

She gave me tea under an awning and introduced herself as the wife of one of Lord Raglan's closest aides and a friend of Lady George Paget, whose husband had played such an heroic part in the Charge of the Light Brigade during the Battle of Balaklava. In return I told her that whilst travelling in Italy I'd heard that my cousin, one of Miss Nightingale's nurses, had strayed from her position in the hospital. Though I could stay only a few days in Balaklava my attempts to find her had been blocked by officialdom.

'Oh you don't want to worry about any of that,' boomed Lady Mendlesham, 'nobody really cares what anyone does out here. Where do you want to go? I can point you in the right direction.'

'But it seems rash to venture out of Balaklava on my own when I have no map and no idea where to go.'

'On your own? Surely your parents haven't sent you out here unprotected? Someone said they'd seen you with a maid. What was the name of your cousin? Perhaps I've heard of her?'

'Miss Barr. Rosa Barr. Daughter of Lady Isabella Stukeley.'

A gleam of avid interest came to her eye. 'Rosa Barr. Rosa *Barr*. But wasn't she up with one of the Derbyshire regiments? Wasn't she the one who disappeared into . . .? Well, I pity you, Miss Lingwood, you must be eaten up with anxiety.' She drew her chair nearer to mine, a tigress in for the kill. 'Were you very close? My poor love. When was the last you heard from her?'

'You're frightening me. You speak as if she were dead.'

'But my dear girl, you must bear up. For all we know she may be dead. Everyone talks about her. It's said that she was last seen on her way to Inkerman way back in the early spring.'

'But that doesn't necessarily mean she's dead, surely?'

'Oh don't cry. Oh I've been very tactless. I'm known for my blunt speaking, ask anyone. Of course she may have survived. She might be anywhere. But you mustn't raise your hopes.'

'Please tell me what you know. I've heard she was with her stepbrother's regiment but what else?'

'That's it. She broke away from the hospitals and went to join the Derbyshires. It's turning out to be a common story unfortunately. Take dear Martha Clough. She was once engaged to poor Colonel Lauderdale Maule, who died of cholera almost as soon as he set foot in Varna last summer, and they think that grief might have turned Martha a little mad. She came out with Miss Stanley's party and the next minute she's upped and left the hospitals and is living among the troops. Miss Nightingale is very hard on those nurses who don't toe the line. Quite rightly, in my view. We dine with the Nightingales twice a year; vital that the family name is not mired by all this nursing business. But as for your Rosa Barr, nobody is sure what happened to her, though there are all kinds of rumours flying about.'

'What kind of rumours?'

'I don't like to spread gossip but it's said she had a liaison out here. Just what Miss Nightingale feared. Apparently she went to the caves above Inkerman because she had an assignation.'

'An assignation . . . With . . .'

'I can't disclose a name. One learns to be careful, in my position. And as I say, this is all speculation but one way or another she was never seen again. It's all very terrible.'

Henry. Oh God, she could only mean Henry. 'Lady Mendlesham, what should I do? I am here for only a few days. I must try and find out for sure what's happened to Rosa. At the very least I should like to visit the Derbyshires. Is there any chance that you would be able to provide me with a guide?'

She seemed to be calculating how much status could be gained from finding out more about this marvellous scandal because suddenly she said, 'I can't help thinking it might be nice to have a jaunt away from the harbour and I'm very intrigued by the situation with your elusive Miss Barr. There's been little action up at the front for weeks, yet my husband keeps me on a very tight rein. Well, I'm sick and tired of it. I don't see why I shouldn't take you up to the plateau where you can have a view of Sebastopol at least. We'll go late tomorrow afternoon when the sun has lost a little of its heat. And in the meantime I'll put the word out among the men in case there's any more news of your poor cousin.'

The process of taking my leave, the need to retain my composure whilst being rowed the short distance back to the *Royal Albert* was intolerable. Had Rosa betrayed me, then? Was she as guilty as Henry? I couldn't believe it of her. And yet there had been an *assignation.*

But if she loved me, how could she bear to take him from me?

Lady Mendlesham was bound to find out that I was engaged to Henry Thewell. Then what? How could I endure her company tomorrow? And yet I had to go. Now that I had discovered a little, I must know more.

Then it dawned on me that there were other, more practical difficulties in the way of the proposed expedition, not least the fact that since my stay at Stukeley with Rosa more than a decade ago I had never ridden any distance at speed. The second problem was that I did not have a riding habit and even I knew that I couldn't mount a horse in a muslin frock. The third was that I had been ordered by Barnabus to stay on board ship.

In the end I chose to tackle the one problem I was equipped to solve. The only garments I possessed remotely suitable for riding were the tweed jacket which I had worn on the journey from London to Italy and a pair of stoutish boots. As Nora had deserted me I felt no qualms about using her clothes so I sent for her box and unearthed a dark skirt and blouse in heavy cotton drill. Next I needed plain petticoats but when I burrowed deeper I uncovered disturbing signs of her true nature. Out came a book with worn leather bindings and wafer-thin, well-thumbed paper called *The Daily Missal*; a rosary made of green glass beads; a little wooden box with a hook clasp containing what seemed to be a handful of soil – surely some dreadful relic; and, most surprising of all, out came a sketch of Nora, signed by Rosa.

This last gave me a shock because I found myself staring not at the taciturn Nora I had known in Clapham, but the defiant creature who had revealed herself since we left Italy. In Rosa's picture Nora was seated on a low stool and leaned forward with her chin supported by both hands and her elbows on her knees, resolute and a touch amused.

This sudden discovery of Rosa's work brought her abruptly close. *Rosa's* slender fingers had executed the sketch, *her* hand had smoothed the page, *her* blue eyes had smiled on the subject.

Who are you, Rosa? Do I know you?

Chapter Eight

The riding habit I created was nothing short of inspired. My scissors went slicing recklessly through Nora's black skirt until I had cut the waist down by a dozen or more inches. I took out gathers from the front, removed several yards of stuff and used the spare fabric to add a deep frill, complete with train.

My needle flew along the seams and with every tightening of the thread, every stab of the fabric, I thought of Henry: '*Bright Star . . .*' Or Rosa: '*But you can have no respect at all for me . . .*' Then, as the scissors went snip-snap through the waistband of Nora's petticoat, round I went again. Henry. Rosa. '*Her hair is bound up in a blue knitted scarf . . .*'

Rosa. Henry.

I planned how I would use my own jacket as a template and transform one of Nora's blouses into a riding coat, complete with wide lapels and brass buttons, but still their faces came back to me. '*I saw Rosa. Very strange affair . . .*'

'*I am terrified by your utter faithfulness.*'

It was past midnight by the time I'd finished the skirt and still Nora hadn't come. In the morning, I thought, I will show her what I've achieved. And though she will want to go with us up to the camps I won't let her. She has burned her boats with me.

By the time Lady Mendlesham arrived the following afternoon I had a blistering headache brought on by a sleepless night and a morning seated under the awning while I worked on my bonnet and jacket, but I said nothing about it in case my escort changed her mind about riding with me up to the camps. She sported a tailored riding habit, straining at the bust and trimmed with military-style braid and buttons, and she was leading a little pony ominously called Flight. He had bony haunches, a fly-blown coat shaved in places to reveal a couple of vicious scars, and a sensitive disposition. He took one look at me, felt my nervous hand on his bridle, threw up his head and stamped his back legs.

'He was the best I could find,' said Lady Mendlesham, who was mounted on a tall piebald mare. 'I borrowed him from one of my husband's aides who assured me that he will behave like an angel, as long as he is well treated. Do look after him because horses are like gold dust out here. Never let him out of your sight or he'll be snatched from you and whisked away to market at Kamiesch as soon as you can say knife.'

We wove through piles of crates lining the harbour amidst heavy traffic of carts, horses, mules, Turks, soldiers, Greeks, labourers and beggars. I concentrated on holding Flight steady and hoped that Barnabus, if he happened to glance through his dirty window, would not recognise me. 'Now that, over there, is the ordnance wharf,' said Lady Mendlesham. 'Did you ever see so many munitions in one place?'

I had never seen munitions at all, beyond pictures of the famed Minié rifle and the guns stored in the medieval-style armoury at Stukeley, but now I saw cannonballs stacked up like heaps of oranges, thousand upon thousand. 'How can there be so many?'

'What on earth do you mean? There's a war, remember. Although in the past couple of months there's been so little action one wonders if it's worth being here, if one's energies, not to mention one's husband's, might not be better used elsewhere. I've left three small children at home in Gloucestershire, not seen them since January.'

'I heard the guns firing all night. Wouldn't you call that action?'

'Oh they're always firing but nothing is achieved. A breach is made, a breach is mended. A head appears above the enemy barricades so we fire at it and vice versa. But now that we've taken Kertch I'm sure it will be much easier to starve them out. My husband says it's all a matter of morale.'

'What is this Kertch? I've heard it mention—'

'But surely you've heard of our great victory in Kertch? We have cut off a major supply route to Sebastopol and now command the Sea of Azov. The enemy crumbled almost as soon as they spotted our ships. Hardly put up a fight. A notable British victory managed despite French prevarication, as usual. We would have taken it months ago had it not been for the French but I can't give you details, obviously. In my position one has to be discreet.'

We began a slow climb up the metalled road out of the village with the new-built railway to our left. 'Horse-drawn trucks,' said Lady Mendlesham. 'As I say, we rely on horses for everything which is why it was such a disaster to lose so many in the winter.'

At the very top of the road leading to the harbour was a collection of broken stone cottages and an encampment of new huts. 'Kadikoi.' Lady Mendlesham stabbed her riding whip. 'One of our hospitals is here.' She lowered her voice. 'The British Hotel is that large building on the hill. Run by a Negro woman, name of Mrs Seacole.' The hotel was a two-storeyed hut with gables and glazed windows, goats and sheep tethered in the yard, chickens pecking round the door and a group of diners seated at a table under an awning. 'You are perhaps too young to be told what goes on in that place. So many people have come out here to exploit our men,' she added loudly. 'I'm afraid some people can't resist the chance to make a quick fortune. Armenians. Jews. They're all at it.'

The further we rode from the harbour, the more we were amidst a bustling community of tents and huts and the air was filled with the muted clank of pots and the murmur of voices of the kind that accompanies a village fete. From the lurid accounts I'd read in *The Times* I had expected chaos and squalor. Instead there was a smell of new bread, we passed piles of vegetables outside the cook huts, and on all sides was evidence of purposeful activity: men polishing boots, on parade or trimming their weapons. It was very hot and my riding habit, being black, soaked up the sun. From time to time Lady Mendlesham took a gulp from a flask of water. She didn't seem to notice that I had none and I was too shy to ask if I could share hers. The headache dug deeper into the side of my face.

With every forward movement of our horses the sporadic gunfire grew louder but as my companion didn't bat an eyelid I tried not to show that I was nervous. Instead I had a sense of disbelief that here I was, actually in the Crimea, and yet the sky was blue, the grass was covered with flowers and men were whistling. The only real discomfort was the lack of shade, although the men were able to shelter behind huts and tents. In places the ground was scarred where roots had been torn up or trunks roughly hacked down at ground level.

'In the winter,' said Lady Mendlesham, 'men ripped up all the trees because they saw them as convenient fuel. They didn't think ahead. But how much further do you want to go? The English camp extends as far as the eye can see; we could ride all afternoon and not reach the end of it.' She took such a careless drink from her bottle that liquid trickled into her collar.

'As far as you'll take me, at least to the Derbyshires,' I cried recklessly, though the crack of gunfire had grown uncomfortably loud, pain was coiling into my ear and my limbs were beginning to protest at the discomfort of being on horseback. The side saddle had a high pommel which demanded a particularly awkward stretch of my right thigh and meant that when the horse stumbled a sharp pain ran through my muscle.

The Ninety-seventh Derbyshire's camp was on the far side of the plain, and like everywhere else had a disturbing air of permanence about it: huts as well as tents, washing lines, even vegetable patches. From within one tent came the sound of raucous singing. '*Oh then Polly Oliver, she burst into tears / And told the good captain her hopes and her. . . .*'

'I expect the men are rehearsing one of their interminable shows,' said Lady Mendlesham. 'You would not believe the tedium but the poor boys have to be occupied somehow. We are occasionally expected to go up and laugh.'

We came across Newman on a low bench outside a bell tent, hunched over his rifle, shirt undone almost to the waist. He stared, scrambled to his feet, saluted and turned his back for a moment while he made himself decent. When he faced us again he was blushing deeply. 'I wish you'd given me warning, Miss Lingwood. I would have had tea sent over.'

'You mentioned that Rosa Barr had left a box here.'

He looked horrified. 'Oh no. I'm so sorry. You've come all this way. Captain Stukeley would have it but he's still away. Oh Miss Lingwood . . .'

'Well, there we go,' said Lady Mendlesham. 'At least we tried . . .'

'But I could show you her hut if you like, where she slept.'

'Why yes.'

Lady Mendlesham said she wouldn't dismount but one of the boys might bring her a lemonade, provided he could guarantee it had been made with boiled water. We left her giving instructions about the preferred method of cooking beetroot to a group of men gathered round a cookhouse.

Newman was rather too eager to help me over a succession of guy ropes as we walked between tents to where Rosa's hut was set a little apart from the rest in a row of five. Nearby a couple of women sat on shady ground with a heap of mending between them. They were coarse-skinned and their hair was hidden under scarves in the Turkish style. When Newman introduced me as Miss Barr's cousin conversation died completely.

Newman knocked on the door of the last hut, then, when there was no answer, pushed it open. The interior was hot and cramped though it contained just two camp beds and a pile of packing cases. The smell of rough-cut wood gave me a sharp memory of a potting shed at Stukeley, one of Rosa's secret places where she and I went sometimes on wet days to listen to the rain on the thin roof and peer through the half-open door at dripping greenery outside.

Newman's gaze shifted disconcertingly from my bosom to my hands and back again.

'Would it be possible to have some water?' I asked. 'I'm very thirsty after my ride.'

He looked mortified. 'Oh by all means. So sorry. I should have thought. Back in a sec.' At last he ducked his head and backed out of the little doorway so that I was alone in Rosa's hut. The air settled softly about me and sunlight shone through knot-holes onto shelves running at shoulder level round the walls, piled with shabby possessions: shoes, hats, boxes and labelled tins. I sat on a bed, half closed my eyes and tried to imagine Rosa there. Yes. She'd have liked it, a place where she could be among the soldiers but set apart. Between the clamour of guns I heard birdsong, the women's voices and a sudden burst of male laughter.

Then it dawned on me that the labels on the tins, SEWING, BISCUITS, TEA, MEDICAL, had been printed by Rosa. Soldiers' wives probably couldn't write and anyway there was no mistaking that confident print.

I took down the tin labelled SEWING and opened the lid. A couple of ants scurried over the neat contents; reels of black and white thread, a pair of scissors, a collection of buttons, a paper of pins, a thimble and Rosa's needle book, the very one she and I had made at Stukeley. It had been her first attempt at sewing; a fold of canvas lined (by me) in silk, with uneven red running stitches along the fold to attach a little square of flannel in which the needles were kept – there were three left, very rusty. On the cover were the cross-stitched initials RB, with a decorative cross at each corner in green. The whole enterprise would have taken me ten minutes but had occupied Rosa for two afternoons because she had scarcely touched a needle before in her life. I remembered sitting in the box hedge, a caterpillar traversing my shoe, the dappled shadow on Rosa's hair, the knitting of her brow as she sucked the end of the thread and tried to push it through the eye of the needle ('No, Rosa, do as I taught you: fold the thread over the needle, pinch it between finger and thumb and push the loop through the eye'), her frustration when I told her the embroidery would have to be undone because she'd not made all the criss-crosses go the same way. 'But who cares which way the crosses go? I don't. What does it *matter*?'

'It matters because in needlework the appearance exactly reflects the quality and durability of the finished product,' I said, repeating poor Aunt Eppie verbatim.

'But I think my cross stitch looks fine the way it is.'

'Turn it over. You see what a mess it looks on the back?'

'But nobody will see the inside after we've lined it.'

'Yes, but you and I will always know that the inside isn't right.'

She picked up the scissors. 'I like that,' she said. 'I like the way you say, *You and I will always know* . . . Because we will, won't we? We'll always know and we'll always be together.'

'You mustn't undo the stitches by cutting through them, Rosa. Unpick them with the blunt end of the needle so you can use the same thread again. Embroidery silk is expensive.'

She sighed dramatically. 'Such a fuss,' then darted her head forward to kiss me. 'Never change. Never let me persuade you these little things aren't important because they are.'

I wondered whether I should take the needle book with me but couldn't bear to remove it so I replaced the tin on the shelf and peeped into a few others, but found only a muddle of impersonal things. Then I sat on the bed and pictured Rosa lying with her arms behind her head, hair tumbled over the pillow, smiling because she was so happy to see me. But with a shock I recalled that Rosa's smile had perhaps been false and that even when she slept in this little hut she may have been plotting her seduction of Henry.

Had *he* been here? Had they lain together on one of these narrow beds? Is this where he had learned to caress the contours of *her* breast?

I pushed open the door and walked into a blaze of sunlight. Newman was approaching with a tray containing a carafe and a glass but I stumbled off in the opposite direction, unfastened Flight, climbed inelegantly onto his back and asked which way we should go next.

Lady Mendlesham set off at such a brisk pace that I was hard-pushed to keep her in sight as we trotted northwards up a gentle incline until the camp stretched away like a child's model.

'Look,' she said, 'that is where the battle of Balaklava was fought. You'll have heard the stories no doubt.'

When I moved my head the pain shifted as if it were a stone rolling within my skull. I couldn't equate this wide valley edged by low hills with the scene of the headlong charge by the Light Brigade into the very teeth of enemy fire, as described by *The Times* correspondent.

'My friend, dear Lady Paget's husband, was the unsung hero of that day,' said my guide. 'When every other senior officer had been killed or sloped off to safety, he alone was left to rally the men and bring them back along the valley. Now come and look the other way.' She turned her horse, trotted a little distance further up the hill and pointed ahead. 'Sebastopol.'

The name of the city quickened my blood because of its qualities of mysticism and notoriety. There, spread before us, was the source of all the trouble, the focus of the world's attention, the city under siege. It was both a Holy Grail and an enemy hell, we wanted it and we hated it, and here it was at my feet with the blue sea glinting beyond. What lay before me was so orderly and distant that I might as well have been watching a giant board game except that from one of the squares came real puffs of smoke.

Sebastopol – Henry had spelled it Sevastopol and pronounced it to me as Sebas-*to*-pol – was a sprawling port, built mainly on the southern side of a wide estuary and on several smallish jutting peninsulas of land. This was why, in an unsuccessful attempt to surround it, the allies had spread themselves so far. In front of the city were the Russian defences, artificial hillocks heavily fortified on top, linked by what looked like, from our viewing point, low walls or ditches. Between our hill and those Russian batteries were walls of sandbags that marked the snaking trenches of the allied forces, French, mostly, said Lady Mendlesham; the British were sandwiched in the middle facing some of the worst fire. The Turks, the thankless crew for whom we were fighting, were an ill-disciplined lot, according to her, and not to be trusted, and the Sardinians were dug in somewhere back there – she waved her left arm at some hills behind us – but better at playing music than fighting.

She surveyed the scene with the proprietary air of a squire's wife overlooking her estate, produced a little telescope from her pocket and peered through it. 'You'll get used to the names of the Russian bastions, the Mamelon, the Great Redan, the Malakov and so on. They are the bane of our army and the Russians are tireless in maintaining them, like beavers. No sooner do we make a bit of headway in breaking them down than they come sneaking out to build them up again. If you look hard to the north you'll see a line of spikes across the harbour, masts of the battleships sunk by the Ruskies to prevent us invading. And then beyond is our navy. D'you see?'

The telescope gave me sudden circles of close-up vision, like a peep show. Once I had adjusted the lens I saw that Sebastopol had white churches and gracious civic buildings with massive walls and windows. It seemed wrong to bombard a city with domes, apartments and parks, a bit like attacking a woman in petticoats and starched cuffs. The harbour looked like any other with ships and smaller boats steaming busily inland or moored in the docks, except that nothing sailed past the ghostly barrier of masts at the harbour mouth. And all round, neat as worm casts thrown up in the sand at low tide, were walls and barricades of stone, earth or wood, some many feet high, all of them bristling with black dots which I presumed were guns, although in one place the dots were blue, yellow and white, and seemed to float above the walls.

'What are those colours over the Russian defences?' I asked Lady Mendlesham.

She took the telescope, fiddled with the lens and snorted. 'Impudence. The Russian women like to fly their kites on the barricades.

It's supposed to be a gesture of defiance but I don't believe a bit of it. The Russian defences are crumbling as we speak, they've got a quarter the number of our guns, the ones they do have are out of the ark, and their morale is rock bottom. After all, they hadn't reckoned with the British spirit.'

'But it all looks so well established.' I shaded my eyes as I squinted at the floating flecks of colour. 'How are they surviving if the city is barricaded like this?'

'They won't survive for long once we've cut off their supply routes. Like I say, now Kertch is down they'll really feel the squeeze.'

The earth convulsed and from the ground between the allied and Russian lines came a rapid volley of rifle-fire answered immediately by a burst from the French batteries.

'What's happening?' I cried.

'They fire all the time. The Russians are mean little fighters. But they should watch out. We're all waiting for the final bombardment. You'll see. One day soon we'll be up and over those walls and then we'll flush the Russians out like rats from a water pipe.'

'When will the bombardment start?'

'We are waiting for orders from on high. And the trouble with being allied to the French is that just at the very minute we think their generals will finally act, along comes a telegraph from Napoleon insisting that everyone change their minds. The French never could stick to any one idea for long.'

The low sun burned on the brim of my bonnet, a skylark scooped an arc in the sky above me and a soft breeze brought a waft of sea air, gunpowder and dinner cooking. My right leg, hooked over the pommel, was numb and my head was shot through with migraine.

As I watched, the brilliant blue of the sky deepened and the sun sank a little lower. Then there was a shattering explosion from the allied trenches and balls of fire crackled over the Russian bastions to the north.

'And Inkerman,' I said at last, though I found I could hardly speak the name. 'Where is Inkerman?'

'Inkerman?'

'My cousin Rosa . . .'

'Ah, Inkerman. Over there to the north, do you see? Beyond

the river. Those low hills actually mark a complete change in landscape, a treacherous bit of land, deep quarries and ravines, caves, some man-made. We fought a battle there, the bloodiest of the war by all accounts – it was before my time. Inkerman is just outside the Russians' last defences.'

'Can we go there?'

'Certainly not. Much too far. And dangerously near enemy lines.' There was another shattering explosion, and another, sending up a spray of earth a hundred yards ahead. 'We should go,' said Lady Mendlesham, turning her horse's head. 'Things always hot up towards nightfall and I have a dinner with my—' An ear-splitting bombardment burst over the Russian defences, my pony bolted after Lady Mendlesham's horse and my head was filled with spatters of light.

Though we had left the camp only half an hour ago everything was different when we returned. The men were now in uniform, fully armed and hustling themselves into columns – battalions, said Lady Mendlesham. There was an air of controlled hurry, shouted orders, a scurrying about between the huts as if an ants' nest had been disturbed and an entire colony was preparing to march. Lady Mendlesham's head swivelled from left to right. 'What is happening? Has there been a raid? Is there news? Just a moment, my man . . .' But nobody stopped, even for her.

From Sebastopol came a steady jabber of cannon-fire and the June sky was extinguished by violent snatches of light and a slow drift of smoke. My ears were ringing and my wretched pony began to shuffle and drag his head from side to side, he sprang about on the spot and kicked his heels so that the pain in my head thundered. 'Lady Mendlesham,' I shrieked. 'Please help me. I don't think I can—'

'We must get back to the harbour at once,' she cried, smacking her horse sharply on its flank. 'If there is to be a bombardment, why wasn't I told?' She disappeared in a cloud of dust and I tried to follow but my own pony had other ideas or rather was too maddened by the racket to obey orders of any kind. He bucked and careered from tent to tent, faltering over guy ropes and then, as there began the rhythmic pounding of marching feet behind us and a devastating cannonade to our right, panicked in earnest.

I screamed at him to stop and dragged frantically at the reins, tearing at his mouth as he plunged his head down then up. The reins went suddenly slack but before I'd the wit to gather them he was plunging forward again so I lost my advantage and he was free to vent his frenzy by careering off the track altogether and galloping towards the guns, except that every time there was an explosion he zigzagged away. I bounced up and down on his back, each sobbing breath catching in my throat, my hands clenched on the reins, my thigh muscles aching with the effort of holding to the saddle and my flesh battered remorselessly as I landed on hard leather. Then, with every downward thump I began to slide until in the end I couldn't bring myself upright at all and was clutching the saddle with both hands. Dimly I saw that the grass was scattered with bits of shot and cannonballs rolled about as if left over from some demented bowls' match, that we were approaching a column of men and that ahead of us reared up a barricade of some kind from which smoke was pouring and guns were battering out fire. At last the pony realised his mistake and pulled away towards Balaklava and for a few minutes we flew on and on until we were almost among the tents but I couldn't keep a grip, the saddle twisted out of my gloved fingers and the next second I had slid sideways, was tossed up by the movement of the pony and landed with a crack on the small of my back that knocked the breath out of me and threw me onto my elbows.

Time stopped. My spine seemed to have hit my ribs and I could only croak and watch the sky splinter and feel the ground shake with the boom of cannon and the rack-a-cack of rifle-fire. My back arched, the sky went black, no breath would come, only a grinding from my tortured windpipe. Then suddenly my elbows gave way and I breathed again. The sky reformed into deep evening blue and at eye level were grasses and little grape hyacinths.

I lay still for several minutes, so fearful that some part of me was broken that I hardly dared test my limbs. The astonishing thing was that nobody seemed to have noticed my fall, which was a relief, given that my skirts were rucked up round my waist. Eventually I turned over onto my stomach, brought myself to my knees and tested my body. All in one piece. Then I stood upright on the unsteady ground, kept my head averted from whatever horror was going on in the trenches and beyond and began to walk to Balaklava. There was no sign whatever of my pony.

With the first step pain collected itself together in my head and began to pound only this time it shot tentacles into my stomach, stirred them about, made me retch and then stagger to one side and vomit into the grass. I sat down heavily and buried my burning head in my hands. Was it the fall that had made me sick? Fear? Typhus? No. *Cholera*. It must be. At last it all added up. The headache, the raging thirst, the sickness, the delirium. Cholera. Henry had taught me the signs, in fact everyone in London was stalked by the symptoms. And in the Crimea, we'd heard, the cholera was even more voracious; a man could be eating breakfast at eight in the morning, dead by lunchtime.

The odd thing was I felt relieved. At least I wouldn't have to go back to Narni and face Henry again or return home and deal with my parents' reproaches. But in the meantime I obviously couldn't just die there in the middle of the allied siege of Sebastopol so I stumbled on. A lock of hair tormented me by dangling in my eyes, my bonnet had fallen sideways but I had no energy to untie it and my leg muscles had been so stretched by the saddle that they could hardly support my body. After half an hour or so I found myself in Kadikoi and then began the slow trail back to the top of the steep incline leading down to Balaklava harbour.

Once in the little town I skulked past Barnabus's office, praying that he was not working late that evening, and came at last to the *Royal Albert*, as glad to see that verminous little steamer as if it had been my own dear Fosse House. I put my hand on the rail, climbed aboard and fumbled down to my cabin, which was in pitch darkness. I groped for a taper, took a flame from an oil lamp in the passage, lit the lantern in my cabin, seized the pitcher of stale water, left since morning, and drank deeply. Though my bed was rumpled and hopping with fleas I lay down fully dressed but the instant I was horizontal the cabin rolled about and shook loose the contents of my stomach again.

I reached for the wash bowl, then staggered up on deck to empty it. Wretched Nora. The headache was driving skewers down the side of my face. How many hours had I been ill? One or two? So I had at most four left to live and during those hours my stomach would evacuate its contents, then would come the agonising cramps and vicious sweats. I was surprised when I glimpsed my face in the scrap of mirror that though I was streaked with dirt and very pale I didn't yet have the livid complexion of a cholera victim.

Then I noticed that behind my reflected image three slips of paper had been pinned to my cabin wall.

The first was a transcript of a telegraph.

Come home. Immediately. You must. It is arranged.
P. Lingwood.

The second, in a neat official hand, was from Barnabus.

6 June. Encl. your father's telegraph. Have agreed that you should leave on first available ship. The Wellington *sails for Gallipoli 9 a.m. tomorrow. Have secured passage for you and maid. Kindly be on board in good time.*

The third was in a woman's well-formed copperplate.

Dear Miss Lingwood,

We have your companion, Mrs McCormack, up with us in one of the hospital huts. We regret that she is very ill, not like to last until morning. She asks would you kindly bring her things, that she would like to have around her.

God bless you, Miss Lingwood.
Sister Doyle at the Castle Hospital

I fell back on the bunk and clutched my head. It simply wasn't acceptable for a cholera victim to be faced with three urgent demands all at once, two of them entirely contradictory.

In the end all I could do in the face of these peremptory orders was turn my head on the infested pillow and try to sleep.

Chapter Nine

Derbyshire, 1844

Despite, or because of, the prohibition on going near the village children after the head-lice incident, Rosa insisted on visiting them again.

'You don't have to come if you don't want to, Ella. But I promised poor Mrs Fairbrother I would look after her. Nobody else will.'

'But your stepfather ... your mother said ...'

'Which is the greater good, to obey one's stepfather blindly or to try and help a woman who's been abandoned by everyone else? Her husband died last year. She's got nothing.'

'I'll ask Mother what she thinks.'

'Mariella, you've got to make up your mind whose side you're on. After all you're the secretary of our society. What if your mother tells you not to go? Miss Nightingale visits the cottages in her village and my mother thinks it's a social triumph to have the Nightingales to dine. So if Miss Nightingale is allowed to nurse sick babies, even when they have scarlet fever, why can't we?'

'Is there scarlet fever in the Stukeley cottages?'

'I shouldn't think so.'

'But what can we do for this family?'

'Well, the first thing is to show that we haven't forgotten them. And then look, I've collected a few things from the kitchen. Cook thinks we're having a picnic. And we have nearly three shillings to give them. That should go a long way for the Fairbrothers.'

I never broke rules and did not want to go to the cottages. Aside from the head lice, the Fairbrother children had been singularly unrewarding company compared to the bright-eyed Sunday School pupils I helped with after church in Clapham. We even had to take a circuitous route across the Italian garden, down through the water garden with its series of fountains, flights of steps and waterfalls, through the kiss gate and along the stream in the woods so that nobody would guess where we were going.

We came out high up in the valley above Sir Matthew's lead-smelting works and dropped down over dry stone walls and across fields of sheep until the air was rank with smoke from the factory and there were some cottages beneath us.

From a distance they looked picturesque, misted in brown smoke, of local stone and huddled deep in the valley by the river, but as we came closer I saw that the roofs were bowed and the windows unglazed. Beneath the eye-smarting stench from the lead works was the distinctive smell of poverty – I recognised it from the beggars who sat in the church porch and occupied the back pews on wet Sundays.

It seemed to me that the dereliction here was wilful. The yard was full of litter and the assorted children who stood about watching us were dirty-faced with sores on their mouths and tangled hair. I longed to take their clothes, have them boiled in a wash-house and then spend a day patching and darning. Nobody seemed pleased to see us.

Rosa tapped at the door of the nearest cottage and after a moment it creaked open. Outside, the light was brownish; inside, behind Mrs Fairbrother, it was almost pitch-dark. She was a little creature with a bent back, a bare, almost bald head, and the same dull expression as her children.

'Good afternoon, Mrs Fairbrother. We've come to see how Petey is getting on. This is my cousin Mariella, from London.'

When Mrs Fairbrother stood aside to let us in I didn't think it appropriate to shake her hand so dodged past without meeting her eye. The first thing I noticed was the drop in temperature, even though there was a fire in the hearth. Then the smell hit me, it was so bad that I covered my nose and mouth. It was a smell of old, dirty things, unemptied chamber pots, rotting potatoes. No, oh no, I thought. We shouldn't be here. This is not right. We can't do anything about this.

'How is your son, Mrs Fairbrother?' asked Rosa, and her bell-like voice was the only clean and beautiful thing in the cottage.

'Very poorly.'

In one corner a heap of rags revealed itself to be a small boy lying flat with his head thrown back. His mother stood at the hearth and looked across at Rosa, as if resigning all responsibility for her son. I was cowed by the knowledge that all we had to offer were three shillings and a parcel of cake.

Rosa knelt by the bed. 'Petey. Petey.'

''E can't hear you. 'E's not woken up for more'n a week now. 'E'll take a bit o' sommat now and then but I can't rouse him.'

'Has the doctor been again?'

'There's naught he can do, 'e says.'

'Mariella, why don't you come and talk to Petey? He might be glad that someone new is visiting him,' said Rosa.

I took three paces across the room and looked into the pinched little face. The child's eyeballs were visible under half-closed lids and his long hair was clotted on his forehead. A dribble of vomit had dried on his chin and every breath was an effort.

As Rosa stroked his hand his eyelids fluttered. Very softly she repeated his name, over and over.

'You try, Mariella,' she said.

The child's hand was as limp and cold as a bit of dead fish. 'Petey,' I quavered. He drew in a prolonged, mucus-filled snore and when he breathed out a trickle of yellow stuff came from his mouth.

The sight of him made me so nauseous that I got up, headed for the door and burst outside where I took deep breaths of the rancid air. The little girl who had given us head lice was hanging about near by.

I was so ashamed of how I'd behaved in the cottage that I wound my hair into a tight coil, thrust it deep under my sun bonnet and offered to mend her pocket. She approached a step at a time as I took out my needle and thread and began to sew. The poor little thing smelled very bad so I kept my head to one side. 'Do you remember you came to play with us?' I said.

She stared at me.

'We sang a song. Shall we try it again? *Baa Baa* . . .'

She looked blank. I gave up and went on with my sewing. By the time Rosa came out I had attracted quite an audience of gawping children.

'I didn't know where you'd gone,' said Rosa as we walked away. She turned to wave at the children but none of them responded.

'I thought I'd be more use outside. I couldn't bear it, I'm sorry.'

'Now you know why I have to go there. Someone has to do something.'

'It didn't seem right. All we could do was look.'

'I wasn't just looking. I was trying to be useful.'

'What about your stepfather? Can't he help?'

'Their father used to work at the lead works but he's dead. Stepfather says he provides them with a roof over their heads and when the children are old enough he'll find them a job in the mill. Mrs Fairbrother refuses to go in a workhouse and who can blame her?'

'What is the matter with the little boy?'

She was walking so fast up the hill that I couldn't keep up with her. The further we climbed, the sweeter the air became until we were at the edge of the Stukeley woods and the cottages had disappeared from view altogether. Instead the valley lay in late afternoon shadow like a scene in a painting.

'Rosa?'

'I can't tell you what's the matter.'

'Why not?'

'I don't want you to know.'

'Then why did you take me there?'

'Because it's my *life*. Now you've seen it all – my life on top, my life underneath.'

Chapter Ten

Balakava, 1855

When I woke it was still dark and though my stomach hurt, my head ached and my bones had been shaken half to pieces, there was otherwise not a great deal wrong with me and I therefore had no choice but to deal with the new day. I rang for the cabin boy to bring me clean water but it took him several minutes to appear and even longer to fetch the pitcher. He told me sullenly that it was scarcely past three in the morning. Poor boy, I had dragged him from sleep.

'The guns are still pounding, then,' I said. 'Even at this hour.'

'There is to be an attack, we think. We will storm the Russian bastions. Softening them up is what we're doing, with our guns.'

'How long do you think the bombardment will go on?'

'Days and days maybe. Who can say? I wish I was up there. What I would give.' He stared at me with rheumy eyes as if it was in my power to grant him permission to join the troops.

I told him to go back to his bunk, unpinned the three messages from my wall and lay watching the lamp tremble with the very slight movement of water in the harbour. Well, it seemed Nora's things must be sent to the Castle Hospital and my own packed up and transferred to the *Wellington*. There was no arguing with the tone of Father's telegram. Though his anger had never been directed at me I had seen him in a rage, notably when one of his suppliers tricked him out of a large sum of money and again when Mother and I reappeared at Fosse House having been banished from Stukeley. His complexion had been purplish with rage and his eyes pinpoints of fire. 'That's it. You're to have nothing more to do with him. *Sir* Matthew Stukeley. I won't have my wife and child treated like that. I've a good mind to go up there myself tomorrow and knock his teeth into the back of his head. In any case, your sister's little better than a—' Slam went the study door but my parents' voices, Father irate, Mother conciliatory, rose and fell on the other side for nearly an hour.

After the turmoil of my ride and the night of sickness I was like a shell scoured by the tide. But the noise was maddening, an incessant, irregular hack-hack of explosives and, underneath, the rumble of much bigger guns. No chance, therefore, of more sleep. The lamplight flickered, the guns boomed and my cabin revealed itself knee-deep in the mess of half-packed trunks and discarded bits of cloth from the riding habit.

In the end I decided to get up at once and start packing. I hadn't the heart to disturb the cabin boy again but when I went up on deck to find a porter I discovered that the harbour at four in the morning was as full of bustle as in broad day. The air was still crackling and beyond the white light of guns the sky had paled from deep purple to grey. The ordnance wharf was a hive of activity: lamps swaying, the rumble and smash of cannonballs being loaded onto trucks, the clang of metal. I realised that because everyone was busy I had no alternative but to take Nora's things up to the hospital myself. A couple of elderly men in ragged uniforms pointed to a steep, narrow path that wound between battered dwellings but I was so weak that I had to pause every few yards, put down the bags and draw breath. The further I got from the harbour, the more orderly it seemed when I looked back – ships neatly moored side by side, the straight line of the railway, the straggle of carts on the harbour road.

When I reached the hospital, which appeared to be little more than a row of huts, I hovered about for a while then opened the door of one at random and found myself at the top of a long ward. The air was filled with the unmistakable whiff of male sickness so I stayed on the threshold peering into the gloom. After a few minutes a lantern detached itself from deep in the interior and approached me. It turned out to be a simple lamp with a pleated paper shade to protect the flame, carried by a nun wearing layer upon layer of black, her homely, big-nosed face looming from a vast white cap.

She told me that nurses and nuns slept in their own row of small huts so I set off again under the now silver-gold sky and came to a collection of little sheds, like Rosa's. The first three were empty but in the next I found two women sleeping. The door to the last was shut but when I opened it I heard scratching and scurrying. As I pushed the door further back the flood of thin dawn light gave me such a sudden, vivid picture of what lay within that later I found it had been printed onto my memory like a daguerreotype.

The hut was arranged very like Rosa's with a bed on either side and a narrow space between. One of the beds was empty but on the other lay Nora with her head roughly shaved so that tufts of hair stood up above her ears. Her face was half turned away from me as she lay twisted on the bed with one knee drawn up. Her plump throat and upper arm were naked and her chest was covered by a strange darkness. At first I thought it was a crouched cat, then I saw that it had small, evil eyes and a disgustingly naked tail. A rat, eighteen inches long, had settled on Nora's breast as if claiming her.

The beast turned its horrid head and gave me an insolent stare. Meanwhile a dreadful smell bit the back of my throat. Nora raised a feeble hand as if to bat the creature away and at last I came to my senses, gave a little scream and threw the carpet bag containing Nora's things towards the bed. Fortunately I was so weak and my aim so bad that I fell well short of hitting Nora but the sudden movement and clatter was enough to shift the creature which scuttled off the side of the bed and into the shadows, its tail flicking out of sight like an afterthought.

Nora sank back into a torpor while I took another cautious step. Her flesh was sunken and grey and her breathing so laboured that she must surely be dying. Only two days ago when she raged at me in the cabin she had been indomitable; now she was so consumed by sickness that there was nothing left of the old Nora but this shell of a body. I remembered how ill I had felt the previous evening, vomiting into a wash bowl, and was ashamed. Though I had been disgusted and frightened it now seemed to me that, compared to this, I had been play-acting. I stumbled out of the hut and came upon a nun walking head down towards the hospital. 'There is a sick woman in this hut,' I called. 'She is obviously in considerable discomfort and needs clean linen.'

The nun looked at me with passionless eyes. 'I beg your pardon?'

'My name is Miss Lingwood. The woman in there is my maid. She should not be left in that state.'

'I presume you must be the young lady from the boat. You've brought her things, have you? Well, I'll show you where the linen might be, if there's any spare, and the clean water, and you can sponge her down. If you need to empty the chamber pot you'll find a line of trenches beyond the last hospital huts. Be sure to keep your hands washed. We insist on the strictest attention to hygiene here. If you follow me I'll show you.'

I tried to tell her that unfortunately I wasn't there to help, I was leaving on the next ship, but she ushered me back into Nora's hut, touched her on the hand and throat, murmured that she had done well to last so long, and again told me to follow her.

'I cannot stay,' I said again. 'My ship leaves at nine. I am not a nurse. There's nothing I can do for Nora.'

She led me outside into the shaking dawn. 'We warned her that she would probably get sick but she insisted that she would like to join us and proved to be an excellent nurse, for the very short time she was well. But now she is ill and there is nobody spare to look after this extra female. We've heard that there is to be a battle and there's much to do. My sisters need to sleep, ready to face the troubles that are sure to come. The most likely thing is that your woman will be dead in a few hours, and then you will be free. If she lives, she may be of use to us again. Either way, you should do your duty.'

'But what if I am sick too?'

She brought her pocked complexion close to my face. 'Were you responsible for bringing that poor woman out here?'

'She wanted to come. She insisted. It was nothing to do with me. I would not be here had it not been—'

'Whose money paid for the trip? If it was yours it seems to me that you are responsible.'

'But my father has arranged my passage home. I must go.'

'Then go. But I wouldn't have your conscience for all the world if she dies.'

I fetched a bowl of hot water from the cookhouse, as I had been told. Then I tore off the ruffle from one of my petticoats and tied it round my mouth and nose in the hope that it would protect me from infection. I had no idea how to handle a dying woman and was so nauseated by the task of cleaning her that at one point I had to leave the hut. When I went back to Nora I found her apparently wide awake and trying to get out of the bed. In fact her eyes were staring, her flesh was burning hot and she raved and fought me until I was actually leaning on her shoulders to hold her down.

'We have to get away,' she said, again and again. 'There is no point in us staying. We have waited far too long. Now we must get away . . .'

'We'll go just as soon as you're well,' I said, but she clawed at my hands to push me from her.

'. . . I will not listen to you any more. We shall carry them. I'm strong. I'll take them both. You bring the cart . . .'

'Don't worry, Nora. We'll manage between us. When you're well I'll arrange—'

'. . . One on my back. One in my arms.'

'That's it. That's right. We'll manage.'

'Well, we must go from here. Come.' Each time she tried to get up I put my hand on her chest and held her down while she tugged feebly at my arms. 'Give them to me,' she moaned. 'I can take them all the way. I promise, they're not heavy.' Her struggles grew more feeble but still she fought me until I caught sight of the bags I had brought up with me from the ship and pushed the contents into her hands one by one. She threw everything aside, the rosary, the missal, Rosa's picture, until she came to the little box of earth which she held against her cheek. I used the moment of calm to bathe her neck and forehead with a vinegary solution that had been left by her bedside, and to drop water between her cracked lips. She stared at me blindly for a moment then clutched the box and started rambling again. 'Give them to me. Let me take them. They are light as a feather . . .' Again I had to hold her down by pressing on her chest. I tucked the sheet around her, bathed her head and held her grasping fingers. This business of alternately soothing and struggling went on until I was in a fury of frustration and helplessness. I thought of Aunt Isabella, who had spent years reclining amidst laundered sheets and inwardly I remonstrated with her: You were a fake. This is proper sickness, this is a real struggle with death. How dare you waste our lives in that pretence of weakness?

I was horrified by the spectacle of a strong woman brought low by fever, and by the incessant quivering of the earth as the bombardment of Sebastopol went on and on. Something must surely break. And I was frantic because my ship had left without me and everyone would be in a rage, and all because these sly Roman Catholics had left me alone with a dying woman. *Bring her things*, they had written, that was the lure; they had got me here under false pretences.

It was now full daylight outside, the door had been left ajar and a shaft of sunlight revealed that the floor of the hut had been constructed so hastily that grass grew through the cracks in the boards. Shelves accommodated a motley collection of supplies, jams and pickles, tins, bottles, and bags of coffee and despite the fact that it was morning the rats still worried under the floor and their claws scratched as they made a sudden dash from one side of the hut to the next. I had never seen rats so huge or so hungry, even down by the Thames, and I tucked up my skirts to stop them climbing up my legs.

I crooned words of comfort to Nora as she moaned and fumed. 'You're safe now. There's no need to worry. I'm here,' though I reflected that there could be few people in the Crimean Peninsula less qualified to care for her. After a couple of hours my efforts were at last rewarded when she gave a deep sigh and subsided so abruptly into sleep that I put the back of my hand near her lips to make sure that she was still alive.

I didn't dare move in case I woke her. Instead I sat on the opposite bed with my feet off the floor. A wind got up and knocked against the roof so it was like being on board ship again and I felt shockingly lonely. If only Rosa would come. Whatever she had done, however much she had betrayed me, I would have given all I possessed to have her appear in the doorway, bright-eyed and powerful.

But when the door was pushed open a stranger came in, though dressed in a similar pepper-and-salt gown to the one Rosa had worn at London Bridge Station. She seemed unsurprised to see me but waited patiently while I got off the bed, then dropped onto it, turned her face to the wall and fell into a deep sleep.

By late afternoon the wind had strengthened but Nora and the other mysterious woman slept on while I sat hour after hour on the end of Nora's bed. The idea that I could ever have thought of leaving on the *Wellington* had become a distant dream. In the meantime I was ravenous, not having eaten since before my ride with Lady Mendlesham, so I crept across to one of the shelves, took down a jar at random, unscrewed the lid and dipped my finger.

Raspberry jam.

My mouth filled with saliva and my stomach was cavernously empty. The jam-maker, a Mrs Prior from Morpeth, as stated on the label, had left whole fruits amidst the thick syrup and my teeth closed round a nugget of sugary succulence so that suddenly I was among the raspberry canes in the garden at Fosse House, juice on my lips and apron and with Henry's shadow to protect me from the glare of sunlight. I watched his efficient fingers pluck fruit after fruit, as he pushed the back of his hand carefully through the leaves to avoid the thorns.

I took another mouthful and this time remembered Mrs Hardcastle and her sale of work in the church hall. The ladies moved between stalls of cakes, bits of crochet, books and knitted bed jackets, scrutinising each item as if they were about to pay a small fortune instead of sixpence. The jams, more often than not produced by the expert hands of the ladies' cooks, were arranged in ranks on the Home Produce stall. Behind the fragrance of raspberries I smelled floor polish, stewed tea and moth balls from the women's winter skirts.

Another mouthful. Rosa: her pink, moist lips, her white teeth biting neatly on fruit, her childish kisses when we shared a bed at Stukeley, the scent of her breath.

I improvised a spoon with the lid of the jar and put a smear of jam between Nora's lips. Her tongue came out and licked gratefully so I fed her a little more, convinced that as she was dying anyway a last taste of perfection could do no harm.

Then I was so deathly tired and so sated with that sudden dose of sweetness that I took off my boots, lay down beside Nora, my head to her feet, fitted myself carefully into the spaces left by her curled body and slept.

When I woke there was a distant rattle, as if someone was shaking dice in a box, then the sudden cessation of gunfire. The hut was pitch-dark and the rats were busier than ever. The jam jar was pressed to my bosom and I was cramped by the confined space created by Nora's body and the hut wall.

Then I realised that in fact the night, or evening, or early morning, whatever it was, was filled with other sounds than just the rats – the rattle of cartwheels, men's voices, snoring in the next hut. For the next hour or so I slipped in and out of sleep until I became confused about what was real and what wasn't. Dawn was definitely breaking, a dim light was shining through the knot-holes of the hut, and I was alone with Nora because the other woman had slipped away again. I dreamed that I was actually in my bed at Fosse House with the wind blowing the white curtains and my workbox so near at hand that I could reach out and touch the packet of new embroidery silks given me by my mother for my last birthday, all the shades of red from coral to burgundy, each with a name so evocative that I longed to thread my needle and transfer the colour onto crisp white linen: Cardinal, Cornelian, Dawn, Estruscan, Garnet, Moroccan, Fire, Raspberry. *Raspberry*, that was the one to choose. Raspberry. But before I could slide out an end, carefully unfurl it from the rest, snip an eighteen-inch length and separate three strands, gently, so that the other five didn't knot, I realised that Henry was in the bedroom doorway holding the frame on either side, his face slightly illuminated because he had placed a lantern on the floor at his feet. In a moment he would reach out, put his warm, sure hand on my cheek and run it sweetly down the side of my face and neck.

The man swayed slightly but made no other move. When I held out my hand, by way of invitation, he spoke at last. 'Well, now, I swear, I shall never be surprised at anything again.'

This wasn't Henry but someone so unexpected that I sat bolt upright with my blouse undone, my hair falling over my face and my mouth dry and rank. I recognised those clipped vowels all right, the nasal drawl of the military officer faintly overlaid with a Derbyshire accent. This man, who I saw ever more clearly, was taller than Henry, his uniform coat was slung over his shoulder, his beard was unkempt and his dark hair uncombed. Max.

'Next minute you'll be telling me you're here on a pleasure cruise with your entire ménage and that my esteemed stepmother is adorning some yacht in the harbour.'

I swung my legs over the bed, stood up shakily, shook out my skirts and clutched the edges of my blouse together. Fortunately at that moment Nora also stirred so to hide my embarrassment I held a cup of water to her lips.

'What is wrong with her?' asked Max.

'I don't know. I haven't been told. It may be cholera.'

'Cholera? If Nora's suffering from cholera I'm a Cossack. I've seen cholera, Miss Mariella and trust me, cholera does not sleep peacefully in its bed like that.'

'Perhaps we should go outside. I don't want to disturb her.'

'But it's Nora McCormack that I came to see. I got back from Kertch, was collared by the boy Newman and told that he'd been summoned down to the harbour to meet a lady name of Miss Lingwood and my dear old friend Nora. I couldn't believe my ears. Had I not been involved in a bit of a spat I might have come sooner. How is she?'

'I don't know. They sent me a message to say she was dying but she seems to be a little better now. I've been here nearly a whole day and night and nobody pays us any attention. I've done my best.'

'Oh well, that's all right, then. As long as you've done your best.'

He stood back from the doorway to let me pass and I found myself outside the hut at last, where the dawn wind was cold and smelled of the sea. When I glanced round I saw him in the lamplight bend over Nora's bed, stroke her shaved head and stoop down to kiss her cheek. Then he took the missal, the rosary and the little box of earth I'd brought up from the *Royal Albert* and arranged them by the pillow, so she would see them if she woke.

Chapter Eleven

I leaned against the flimsy wall of the hut and wondered what would happen next. Max, as our last encounter in the drawing room at Fosse House had illustrated, could not be relied upon to behave well at the best of times, and I had noticed a crackle of animosity towards me beneath his concern for Nora. Furthermore I was aware that his arrival was the closest I had yet come to Rosa. After all, she had actually been harboured in his camp for some weeks; surely, therefore, he would at least know what had been on her mind.

To my left was the steep slope of the hillside above the harbour, to my right, up a slight incline, the track that ran along the front of the two dozen or so huts constituting the Castle Hospital. The guns were still strangely silent but there was a great deal of bustle on the road as a succession of carts trailed up to the hospital. I was conscious for the first time of being very close to a great many other people, some sick and helpless, others cogs in the machine that was supposed to cure them. The difference between everyone else and me was that I didn't belong here; only my unhappy relationship with Nora gave me any right to be on that hillside at all.

Max emerged from the hut, jerked his head in the direction of the hospital and strode off. I followed, heart in mouth. He was apparently well known to the various groups of men who languished outside the huts because those who were capable sprang to attention, saluted him and stared at me with weary-eyed interest. I didn't look too closely at the bloody patches on their uniforms, their bandaged heads and hands or the greenish pallor of their skin. Nor did I look about me at what was being unloaded from the carts and I tried not to resolve the noises from within the huts into cries and moans of anguish. A couple of women carrying a laden basket of laundry between them stepped aside, smiling and blushing to let Max past.

We came to a square hut with a crooked chimney from which came the dizzying scent of coffee. Max disappeared inside and emerged a few minutes later with a fistful of bread and two mugs, one for me. He then set such a pace that when I followed coffee slopped over the side and burned my fingers. Nevertheless I managed a couple of frantic gulps which, like Mrs Prior's jam yesterday, had the most sensational effect on my body and spirits.

Max didn't stop until we had got beyond the last hut and were on a stretch of open ground leading up to the ruined fort where Newman had invited me to picnic. There he flung himself down on the dewy grass and put his arm over his eyes.

I wondered what to do. Further up the hill was the broken tower of the Genoese fortress and to my left, far below, lay the sea, serene under the hazy sky with birds dipping from the cliff and only the faintest murmur and rush as waves broke on rocks. Behind me were the muted sounds of the hospital and down to the right the masts in Balaklava harbour were packed as close as a handful of spillikins. The grass underfoot was springy and peppered with perky little blue flowers. I could certainly understand why Newman had suggested this as the perfect spot for an excursion.

I sipped the coffee then crept forward, picked up the bread Max had dropped, tore off a piece and ate.

Perhaps it was the taste of good bread and coffee, the smell of the sea, the sense of having come through an ordeal during which I had not abandoned Nora and she had not died – whatever the cause, I felt a sudden rush of happiness, probably the first since lying in Henry's arms in the Hotel Fina, before he spoke Rosa's name.

I sat down and after a while grew so mesmerised by the glinting water and flashing white birds, the soft heat of the sun on my eyelids, the chock and mumble of human sounds from the distant hospital, that I was startled when I realised Max had slightly raised his arm and was watching me from beneath it.

'I saw a woman in Kertch,' he said, 'who I remember thinking at the time reminded me of you.'

I was surprised that I had been on his mind at all. After a pause, during which he seemed to doze again, I said, 'Why have the guns stopped firing?'

'Oh I wouldn't worry, they'll be off again before too long. Like I said, there was a bit of action yesterday in which the French took the Mamelon, one of the Russians' chief bastions to the east of the city, and we captured the Quarries. Usual pile of casualties on both sides but at least we made a move.'

'That's good, isn't it?'

'Very good. Oh yes, wonderful news. Something for the papers to write home about.'

His tone was so insulting that I stood up and backed away a few paces. The wind caught my hair and lashed it across my face and I tried to tuck the untidy ends back into place. Max leaned on one elbow and squinted up at me. 'What are you doing in the Crimea, Miss Lingwood?'

'Nora and I came to find Rosa.'

'Rosa. Yes. I see.'

'As you know, she's disappeared. We are anxious about her.'

'How touching. So here you are with Balaklava harbour at your feet and the whole British camp as your playground. Where she leads, you follow.'

I was silent.

'You've got the wrong hospital of course. She was up at the General Hospital in Kadikoi. The Castle Hospital was scarcely built back in the spring. They waited until the crisis was over and there were only a handful of casualties a day before setting up a new hospital.'

'Why do you think she didn't stay at the General Hospital?'

'Well, now, let's see. Rules, mostly. Other people telling her what to do. Far too much counting bandages, not enough washing wounds and mopping brows for Rosa's liking.'

'But if she was at the General Hospital why didn't she write to me?'

'Perhaps she did. The post, I'm told, is shocking. Or perhaps she had no words, Miss Lingwood. Sometimes we all run out of words.'

'And then my mother wrote to you, I believe, asking if you had news of her. Perhaps if you'd replied you would have saved us the trouble of coming here.'

'I wasn't aware that saving you trouble was part of my business in the Crimea.'

'As you can imagine, my aunt, indeed our entire family, is sick with worry. I understand from Lieutenant Newman that Rosa was actually staying in your camp. A letter from you would have helped a great deal.' I turned my face away and tried to control my voice. 'But then of course you don't know the other side of the story. Before we came here Nora and I visited my fiancé, Dr Henry Thewell, who is very sick in Italy. He also wanted me to find Rosa. I think that he and she might have tried to elope together.'

He laughed extravagantly. 'Elope. What a perfect word. Is that what your little Clapham mind has told you happened to Rosa? I hardly think so.'

'Since I've been here I've heard rumours that she was last seen going up to meet a man in some cave . . .'

'If you've heard rumours they must be true.'

I tried to remain polite and smooth-voiced. 'You must have some idea what happened to her, Captain Stukeley.'

'She came up to our camp and asked me if she could stay for a while. She was sick of the hospital she said because there were too many restrictions and too much bickering among the women. Though she seemed very happy with us and the men loved her, one day she disappeared.'

'But surely you went looking for her?'

'Of course I did, but I didn't find her. Do you suppose that I'm keeping Rosa hidden away somewhere? What is this, Miss Lingwood? I am here to fight a war, not act as a chaperone to my stepsister.'

'But do you think she was connected to Dr Thewell in some way?'

'Of course she was connected. We're all connected, God help us. Do you know, Miss Lingwood, one of my reasons for joining the army was to get away from my family. And now look at me, more trammelled by family than any other man in the Crimea. Yes, Thewell visited her a couple of times in the camp. And then, yes, when he became a bit strange and took himself off to a cave above Inkerman she heard he was very sick so followed him to try and persuade him to come back. For all I know she never got there. Whatever happened, he reappeared in the camp, she didn't. I rode out to Inkerman but there was no sign of her. Then I visited Thewell, who by that time was up in the General Hospital half dead, spitting blood, in a raging fever. He spoke her name constantly but was either incapable or refusing to say more. For weeks I neglected my men and risked life and limb to go looking for her. I went to towns and villages and markets and asked for her. No Rosa. So there we are, Miss Mariella. I've done my best and I won't stop looking but I don't need you here. You've had a pointless journey, I'm afraid. So pack your bags and off you go.'

'Later.'

'Not later. I have orders to tell you to leave now.'

'Who ordered it?'

'Barnabus.'

'Well, I am not under orders from Barnabus.'

'He tells me that he's received a flurry of telegrams from London. Your father has pulled strings and wants you home. Your name is mud with Barnabus. Apparently he'd secured you a snug little berth and you never showed up.'

'I was looking after Nora.'

'Well, now I'm here to keep an eye on her so there's no need for you to trouble yourself.'

'I will go home in my own time. When Nora is better.'

'I'm sorry to press the point, Miss Lingwood, but you have strayed into a war and here everyone is under the orders of the military. If we say you go home, home you go.'

'I'll go when Nora is well enough to travel. I won't abandon her. And I want to find Rosa.'

'If Nora has Crimean fever it could be weeks before she's well. If she ever recovers. Didn't it occur to you, Miss Lingwood, that you would be risking your lives by coming here? Haven't you been reading the news? Nora's suffered more than enough already. She deserves better than to have her life endangered on the whim of some spoiled girl from Clapham.'

'It wasn't a whim. My fiancé, Henry Thewell, is dying of consumption. He insisted that I come and find Rosa, and Nora was so keen that she made all the arrangements.'

'Whatever the reason, I want you to go home. I'll take care of Nora McCormack.'

I gathered my skirts. 'You'll care for her like you cared for Rosa,

I suppose.' But before I'd taken more than three steps my upper arm was seized, my name was spoken with biting authority and I found myself being marched, or rather half dragged because my feet tangled in my hem, further up the path towards the ruined fort.

The higher we climbed the more the wind took my hair until it was a storm across my face. Max gripped me so tightly that I knew my flesh would bruise. In the shadow of the high wall it was suddenly cold and dank but out of the wind. Though he released me he stood very close, at least a foot taller than me so that I couldn't avoid noticing his bare throat and unshaved face, and that there was not a glint of friendship in his dark eye. 'You are a bloody little fool and you will leave now. I'm not giving you a choice. You're absolutely right that Rosa has disappeared into thin air, is probably dead, and yes I do feel responsible even though I had no idea she was coming out here in the first place and certainly didn't want her underfoot up at the camp. But I'm sure of one thing: you're not going the same way as her. This is no place for you. The Crimea is full of vermin and disease and foul weather, not to mention the rockets and shells which are never choosy about where they fall.'

I chewed the inside of my cheek and tilted my chin so I was looking up past stones stained with lichen and bird lime to the blue sky.

'Take Nora McCormack,' said Max. 'Tough as old boots. Been to hell and back in Ireland already, lost everything and survived, but half an hour in the Crimea and she's at death's door. This is a filthy war. It has already murdered four armies. These soldiers you see out here now aren't the ones who charged into battle at Alma or Balaklava or Inkerman because most of the survivors died of frostbite or scurvy up in the trenches above Sebastopol. Instead we are left with recruits so raw that when someone shouts an order half of them fall over with fright. What arrogant little voice in your head, Miss Lingwood, tells you that you can dip your toe in this war and get out in one piece when tens of thousands of soldiers haven't managed it, nor has Rosa, nor your precious Dr Thewell? And now Nora McCormack is another victim. Even if you don't die, what state do you think you'll be in when you get home? I'm a soldier. I have spent my life doing what I'm told by my senior officers, even when I know that both the officer and the order he gives me are barking mad. I obey because that's what I've been trained to do, and my regiment is my home. But you, you'll take one look at this war and you'll go home so dumbstruck with disbelief you'll never be able to look your parents in the eye again.'

'I know there are risks. I know the choler—'

'I'm not talking about cholera. Cholera is a quick death. There were times last winter when I thought the poor bastards who died of cholera in Varna last summer were the lucky ones. I'm talking about the war, Mariella. Your death here, like everyone else's, will be utterly meaningless. They fling us about like handfuls of sand. Please, go home.' He had changed tack and now stood beside me with his back to the wall, eyes closed, his face a series of slashing vertical lines and hollows. 'Mariella, I beg you, go home.'

'I will, Max. I will go when I'm ready.'

He gripped my chin and turned my face towards him. I tried to jerk away but he wouldn't let me; I clawed at his wrist but each time I came close to breaking free he seized my shoulder or upper arm to draw me back, his mouth inches from my face. 'Do you remember I told you about a woman at Kertch who reminded me of you?'

'I remember.'

'Well, let me tell you a little story. Kertch will be billed as a great victory for the British, just you wait and see. I can imagine the headlines. We sailed up to the town with our flotilla of smart modern ships, and our hand-picked allied forces of Turks, French and British and the place fell with barely a shot fired. We lost only one man in three days as we disabled their guns and burned their munitions' warehouses. Good old allies, got something right for once. Meanwhile I saw the woman I told you about twice. The first time was just after we set foot in the town. She had obviously decided that the only way to deal with the fright of our invasion was to carry on with life as usual, so she had taken her washing down to the sea. She had a young child with her, maybe three or four years old, a boy with brown hair and a high crown to his head. He was tied to her wrist with a long length of striped fabric, same as her skirt, so he wouldn't stray as he paddled in the water. I remember the woman because of her skirt, which had a most unusual orange and green stripe to it and because her hair was the same colour as yours and very long, tied back with a handkerchief.

'Kertch was a beautiful town with white warehouses along the beach, and the streets, as I've said, were very busy. There was an uneasy atmosphere, not hostile, not friendly but watchful. The shops were open and the residents were eager to please because they knew they were in our hands.

'The next morning we marched on to Yenikale which we also took easily. Our job was to disable the Russian supply route through the Sea of Azov. In all we destroyed about two hundred boats and their military supplies, and in addition, mostly because of the actions of the retreating Russians who didn't want their stores to fall into enemy hands, mountains of wheat and flour went up in flames.

'So then a couple of days later I was sent back to Kertch by our commander, Sir George Brown, because he'd heard that some kind of trouble had broken out. He didn't want our soldiers to get too involved because he said it wasn't our job to govern the town, simply to ensure that no more supplies got through to Sebastopol, but he said I was to take a few good men and check that all was well.

'The place was so unrecognisable that at first I thought I'd taken a wrong turn. The shops, the mosques, the church, the synagogue, the warehouses had all been stormed by the allied troops and their contents ransacked. Anything too big or valueless to be carried back to the ships had been dragged onto the streets and smashed. I met an officer from our merchant navy with a bundle of green silk under one arm who boasted that he and his cronies had broken into one of the richest houses of the town, found it empty and penetrated even to the ladies' bedrooms. He'd carried off, of all things, that length of silk and a bundle of hair stashed into a sequinned evening bag, which he thought must have been chopped from the lady's head before she left. He said that fortunately the hair was the very same colour as his sister's, and that she would be glad to have it as her own was rather thin and she wore false fronts. The silk, on the other hand, would make an excellent dress for the lady he hoped to marry.

'I let him go because I'd glimpsed a bit of familiar striped fabric. It was the young woman I'd noticed before on the beach, only this time she was in an alley with her back to a wall, surrounded by three Turkish soldiers. One had wrapped her long hair round and round his fingers so that he could pin her to the wall and hold her upright while he raped her. The skin on her forehead was stretched thin and her eyes were staring, he dragged so hard at her hair. That's when I understood why a lady might choose to have her hair cut when a town got invaded. Lying at the woman's feet, with his neck broken and his head smashed like a little egg, was her boy.

'We beat the men off and I had them marched to their ship where they may or may not have been court-martialled. Then we took the body of the child outside the town and buried him. His mother could barely stand. Afterwards I escorted her back to the beach and insisted that she be put aboard a steamer and taken to Constantinople, for her own safety. She didn't say much but I understood that she was a German Jew, not that it mattered what nationality she was – the Turks, on whose behalf we are supposedly fighting this war, were undiscriminating in what they took and who they hurt. Likewise the French, or the British for that matter. Later I was taken to the museum where I found one of our officers picking through a broken glass case and stuffing his pockets with jewellery from the ancient world. The rest of the statuary, anything that couldn't easily be carried away, had been shattered. Two thousand years of history smashed up due to the fact that the allied commanding officers just don't pay enough attention to detail. I can't blame the men. After all, they aren't taught that war is the lowest common denominator, but those who have been educated should know better. And now you, Mariella, have come tripping here in your little boots on a personal mission to find Rosa, who matters less than a straw in the wind out here, as she quickly discovered. And nor do you, so go home.'

I watched a white cloud drift by, then another. It reminded me of the morning room in Fosse House, the curtains blown in a summer breeze, a puff of muslin for a tucked nightcap. Max folded up suddenly and sat on his haunches, head down. I pushed myself away from the wall and walked past him, back towards the hospital, my skirts blowing far out behind me, Balaklava to my left, the sea to my right.

Orange and green striped fabric, calico probably, thickly gathered at the waist. A week earlier and the woman might have been in Constantinople among those I had passed on the dockside.

When I got back to Nora's hut she was still asleep. I knelt down by her bed and rested my head against her knee. The wooden box was clasped in her hand; I guessed that it must contain another unbearable fistful of history.

Chapter Twelve

Next time the little nurse-sharer came back to the hut I had a list of questions. 'What is your name?' 'How can I boil water?' 'Where may I wash laundry?' 'Could I, for the next couple of days, rest on your bed while you are working in the hospital?'

She stared at me as if I had spoken a foreign language, her lower lip disappeared under the upper due to a pronounced overbite, then slowly, in a thick Lancashire accent, told me that her name was Mrs Whitehead and that I might take a tin kettle to the diet kitchen for boiled water, buy arrowroot from the purveyor and get Nora's sheets boiled in the laundry hut. She said they were desperately busy because of all the wounded who had suddenly arrived, really the first in any numbers since the hospital opened in April. There'd been an amnesty – hence the silent guns – when the allies had been allowed to go and collect their casualties from beneath the Russian bastions and now they were all turning up at the hospital in what she called a *bit of a state*.

By the time Mrs Whitehead returned some hours later the guns had started up again in the distant trenches above Sebastopol. She brought a jug of hot water and a wad of flannel so that we could apply a stupe to Nora's chest to draw out the fever, and showed me how to feed her sips of arrowroot mixed with boiled water to build her up. Mrs Whitehead, whose every movement was calm and measured, told me that she was an experienced nurse grown sick of working with rich patients in stuffy country houses. The Crimea, she said, was something of a change.

When I mentioned Rosa's name she shook her head. 'Rosa Barr? Wasn't she the one who disappeared in the Inkerman cave? I've heard of her, of course, but I never met her. I wish I had. But I was with Miss Nightingale at Skutari and then when she came over last month she brought me to add to the numbers. So I never met Rosa Barr, who was gone by then.'

'You actually worked with Miss Nightingale. What was that like?'

'Well, till then I had been used to deciding my own activities as a nurse so I found it very strange to be commanded by another. But we were one body of women, those of us who did as we were told, and I liked that.'

Next morning I found that my bags and boxes, last seen on board the *Royal Albert*, had been dumped outside the hut. There was no further note from Barnabus and I realised that Max had been right; in the scheme of things Miss Mariella Lingwood's decision to stay in the Crimea against her father's wishes was of no importance.

The first item I unpacked was my writing case so that I could send a businesslike note to Henry telling him that although I was up at the Castle Hospital I had no firm news of Rosa. My dispassionate tone reflected rather the great distance between us and the hurt he had done me than the sympathy due to a mortally sick man, but I couldn't help myself – the act of writing even those few lines was almost unbearable. In a longer letter to my parents I thanked Father for the trouble he had taken, apologised again for the worry I had caused but said that it was impossible to leave the Crimea without having discovered what had happened to Rosa. *You see*, I wrote, *compared to this, everything else seems insignificant. And I am here in part for Henry, whose one thought was Rosa. Please forgive me if I have caused you pain.*

Once these were written and put into the post bag I was so frightened by the coolness of my own words that I rummaged in my trunk, took out poor Aunt Eppie's sewing case and, in the intervals when Nora slept, set to work. My first task was to detach a tier from a muslin petticoat and construct a sunhat with a veil that would serve the double purpose of shading and also hiding my face. Any patient capable of getting out of bed spent his time smoking, drinking and staring at everything that moved, particularly me. Sometimes a man's expression when he glanced at my bosom was so voracious that I envied the nuns their habits and the nurses their repellent uniforms.

Next I removed several yards of stuff from my skirts and

broadened the waistbands so that I could dispense with a corset, and remodelled the sleeves of my blouses to allow my upper arms and wrists freedom of movement. Suddenly I was in demand. Mrs Whitehead said that the wounded men often had perfectly good jackets in need of a little repair and she would look some out, if I wasn't too pushed. Within an hour a mound of clothes had accumulated beside me. At first I was repulsed when I picked up bloodied trousers or coats but I gritted my teeth, soaked away the stains, dried the fabric in the sun and darned the tears. The nuns and nurses brought strange nether garments and gowns damaged by over-wear and strenuous washing. I had never sewn so many plain seams, exercised such ingenuity in recovering fabric from hems, sleeves and gathered skirts, or been so thankful that one of Aunt Eppie's first lessons had been invisible darning.

The Crimean fever washed through Nora in wave after wave. Sometimes she slept like one in a coma, then she'd wake up and thrash about or shake with the chills. When Max came back he found me piling every item of clothing she and I possessed onto the bed. He had brought her a bottle of French wine, and lavender water which he sprinkled on her pillow, and then he sat by the bed stroking her hand. I waited outside the hut with my sewing, somewhat mortified that his touch seemed to soothe her more than mine.

After nearly an hour he emerged and doffed his cap. 'Still here, Miss Lingwood? There's a sailing tomorrow, I believe. The *Hollander*, bound for Gibraltar. I could arrange a berth for you in a trice.'

I went on with my darning but out of the corner of my eye I noted that he had folded his arms and was lolling against a nearby hut, watching me. 'So Clapham meets the Crimea. What an unnerving sight.' Next minute he was striding away to talk to a group of rough-looking women who had appeared from nowhere and were waiting for him at the top of the path.

An hour later, while I was still smarting, a young soldier came to the hut with a parcel containing two soft blankets. 'From the British Hotel, as ordered by Captain Stukeley.'

Chapter Thirteen

My patient's condition began to improve. One morning when I had changed her bed and was tucking the folded edge of the top sheet under the mattress Nora said, 'Now what are you fussing with that for?'

'Nora.' I was so relieved I almost kissed her. 'Are you really awake? Do you know where we are?'

'So. You stayed.'

'I'm sorry you have been ill, Nora.'

'And what news have you of Rosa?'

'Not much, except that she disappeared. She seems to have met up with Dr Thewell and then never come back. Or so Captain Stukeley says. He was here to see you, by the way.'

This news actually made her smile. 'I thought that was a dream. And what had he to say for himself?'

'He's very angry that we came. He says there's no point in us staying because he's already searched for Rosa and not found her.'

She gave a deep sigh. 'You should not be wasting time with me. You should be looking for her.'

Lieutenant Newman was waiting outside the hut with a bundle of mending. 'Captain Stukeley said I wasn't to bother the wives in the camp. He said you were looking about for a bit of extra work and that I should come and keep you company.'

I did not point out the heap of sheets brought to me that morning by Mrs Whitehead, who'd discovered that the rats had got into the linen store and chewed the corners of a neatly folded pile. Instead I took his clothes and threaded my needle. He wouldn't sit down but stood to attention, head on one side, shuffling closer and closer until he was actually hanging over me. 'Something is going on, Miss Lingwood. You'll see. Any moment it will flare up again. A week or so ago I would have said we'd just be hanging about for ever but I was wrong. That same night after you rode up to our camp the French took the Mamelon and us the Quarries so it was a great step. Only a matter of days now and in we go again. The Malakov will be next.'

'How did this jacket get in such a state, Lieutenant Newman?'

'Well, you know. The Quarries was a bad affair. My first bit of fighting under real fire, actually.'

His head sank on his long neck. 'But you survived,' I said, taking his cap, which was twisted in his fingers, and straightening it out for him.

'I survived. That's it. So I did. Not very creditably. We had to run forward under the Russian guns into their rifle pits. They were waiting for us because they knew all our moves before we made them. My men are mostly twice my age but I had to give them orders. What do I know? I stood with my arm up screaming and they rushed past me. I watched them fall and I didn't move. Just couldn't make the old legs work.'

His top teeth bit into his thick lower lip and released it again and again until I said, 'So what happened next?'

'In the end I followed them. But only after the Quarries had been taken. I was staggering about over Russian bodies piled up inside. Once you were in those pits there was no easy way out. Our job was to turn the Russian guns so they were broken or facing back at the enemy. But the Ruskies came at us again. You're inside these pits and you see these columns hurling themselves towards you and your hand's shaking and you can feel the wind on your face as the grapeshot comes at you. I think I just stood there with my bayonet and waited for a Russian to run up against me but in the end they turned tail. I don't know that I fired a shot.'

I worked away, trying to find some word of comfort.

'So next it will be the Malakov,' he said, 'which will be down to the French because we don't have the numbers, but once they've got it, we will rush in and take the Great Redan and then the way to Sebastopol, at least the south side, will be wide open.'

'You make it sound very straightforward. If it's so easy, why haven't the allies gone in before now?'

'Good question. One or two snags, Miss Lingwood.' He crouched down beside me so that his shoulder was pressed against my knee as if he were an over-friendly Labrador rather than an officer, and drew a map in the dusty earth with the end of his riding whip. 'The Great Redan is a bit of a beast, V shape, like this, with the point facing us, just about bristling with guns. And look, there's a hundred yards or so of open ground to cross between our trenches, here, and the Redan. And on the way there's the abattis which is like a thick fence made of brushwood and such, and beyond that a ditch.'

This was familiar territory to me; like when Father used to stand me in front of his tilted drawing board while he brandished his pointer and showed me the latest plan, a street of houses drawn to scale, front and rear elevation, bird's-eye view, and then the bit I liked best, a section through the earth showing layers of London clay, pipes, rock and underground streams.

'Last week,' said Newman, 'I watched the French when they ran at the Mamelon and by God, the ones in front fell like skittles.'

I dared another glance into his wet blue eyes and I knew that if I reached out my hand so much as half an inch his face would drop against my bosom and he would weep like a child. 'Perhaps it won't be you. Perhaps your company won't be asked to go in.'

'It will be us. I'm sure of that. It's bound to be us. They believe in Stukeley, you see. By the way, Captain Stukeley says to tell you that he'll be visiting Mrs McCormack again this evening, if convenient.'

So then of course I had to tidy Nora's bed, wash her face and bring her a clean cap – which was just as well because as it turned out Max had also made a considerable effort. His hair and moustache had been trimmed and his dark eyes restored to their usual brilliance. A gaggle of women followed him, presumably to glimpse his broad shoulders and long legs.

He nodded to me, very formally, 'Miss Lingwood,' then, at the sight of Nora propped up on the pillows his face broke into a delighted grin. 'Well, Nora McCormack, have you come back from the dead to be a nuisance to me at last?'

'I have, Max Stukeley.'

He gave her a smacking kiss on the cheek, pulled up a chair and placed a basket on the bed beside her. Like Little Red Riding Hood, I thought.

'Now then,' said Max, 'I've been talking to Mrs Seacole at the British Hotel about you and this is what she's sent. Chicken broth and rice pudding. Very light on the stomach and just the thing to get you out of this bed double quick. So you eat these up like a good girl.'

'Don't you be calling me a good girl.'

'I'll be calling you what I like. You are a wicked old woman to have come out here and got yourself ill like this. Why did you do it?'

They were so absorbed in each other that they didn't notice me leave the hut.

'Why do you think? I can't have Rosa lost and not go looking for her.'

'Don't you trust me to do my best for her, Nora?'

'I believe you have other business to attend to. Besides, I envied you both. I wanted to see what was going on.'

'Ah, now that's more like it. Now we're getting closer to the truth.' He adopted an absurdly exaggerated version of her accent: 'Well, I'm telling you, Nora McCormack, that you'll discover your County Sligo tales have met their match with the Russian prisoners. If you're a good girl and keep quiet I'll be telling you one of their stories.' He dropped his voice. 'I've heard them speak of a rusalka, the spirit of a drowned girl who haunts the river. At night she'll try and lure us handsome young men into the water with promises of eternal happiness. And then in the day she'll disguise herself as a snake and sleep in a tree.'

'Well, I doubt she'd have any trouble getting the whole of this foolish army to go prancing after her and drowning theirselves.'

'Ah, now then, but these Russians are less unforgiving than your Irish. If a man wishes to come out of the water, he has only to make the sign of the cross and he can return home.'

'And how would an irreligious pagan like you know how to make the sign of the cross? Nonetheless I should like to meet these Russians and learn some new stories.'

'Hurry up and get well then, Nora McCormack, and I'll take you up to the camp.'

'Well, now, Max Stukeley, how would I talk to a Russian when I've none of their language?'

'Well, now, Nora McCormack, it could be that our Russian enemy is not half as ignorant as we like to think, and that some can speak English better than our good selves. But Nora, is there anything I can do for you before I go?'

His voice became so low and tender that I couldn't hear him and to my annoyance I noticed that the sheet in my hands was spotted with blood from a pricked finger because I hadn't been paying sufficient attention to my work.

Chapter Fourteen

Derbyshire, 1844

The weather grew so warm that Rosa and I had to retreat from the box hedge in search of deeper shade. 'We need a secret place in the woods,' she said, 'but I haven't been able to find one.'

Everything in the extensive grounds at Stukeley was managed and manicured, even the woods where the stream had been diverted to form a series of pools and gushing waterfalls amidst plantations of birches and oaks. '*Artful*,' said Rosa, 'but not natural. I know which I'd prefer. I wonder if Max would help us build a shelter of some kind.'

I would rather not have involved Max because he was so prickly and had such a disturbing effect on Rosa. However, now that she had the scheme in her head she and I spent the morning hunting for the ideal spot in the woods, then hung about in the stable yard waiting to pounce on him the minute his lessons were over.

By the end of an hour they had argued about the location of the projected den or *arbour*, as it was now to be called, the best method of construction and who should have use of the sharpest knife. In the end they fixed on a hollow above the stream where two conveniently planted saplings could be tied together to form an arch. A frame was then made of interwoven branches, which would in turn be laced with bracken and leaves to make a canopy. At first I tried to help but being the least useful I had the bluntest tool and when I tried to wrench up a stalk of bracken it cut my hand.

Fortunately, that morning, Aunt Isabella's rosewood side-table had been stained by a splash of water from an overfull vase. 'What I need is one of your lovely little lace mats, Mariella, to cover it up. Your mother says you could make one up for me in a trice.' So

I had a good excuse to sit against a tree trunk with my crochet and watch the others.

'This is going very well,' said Rosa after a while. 'For once you seem to know what you're doing.'

'Plenty of practice,' said Max. 'I've camped out several nights at school. Can't stand being cooped up in a dormitory.'

'Doesn't anyone notice you're not there?'

'People only want you to be where they expect when they actually look for you. The rest of the time you could be anywhere.'

'My father always wanted to know where I was,' said Rosa. 'It was his only rule. And I bet Mariella's never been anywhere forbidden in her life. Do you realise that she is the only one of us three who has a proper family, both a mother and a father – and even a perfect substitute brother called Henry.'

They stopped work for a moment and stared at me. Rosa's face was flushed with the heat and her blue eyes were wistful and affectionate, but Max's scrutiny was much more dispassionate, like the look I'd seen him give a pheasant that came crashing suddenly through the undergrowth.

'Anyway,' he said, thrusting another frond of bracken into the web of branches, 'I need practice at this type of thing. Father says I'm to join the army.'

'The *army*. No, Max. You can't.'

'Actually I don't mind the idea.'

She was a tousled sprite among the bracken. 'You can't join the army. What use will you be if you do that?'

'More than I am here.'

'I'll never see you. You can't abandon me.' For a moment she was intent on ripping a leaf apart. Then she said harshly, 'I took Mariella to see the Fairbrothers.' Slash, slash went his knife, but he said nothing. 'What will happen to them if you don't even try to make things better?'

He didn't answer but scrambled away up the slope to fetch more bracken while I crocheted furiously. Suddenly Rosa threw down her knife and cried: 'Oh what's the point?' and went crashing down to the stream. For a few seconds her pale dress was visible through the trees, then she disappeared from view.

I was about to follow her but Max shouted: 'No, stay here, I'll go.' I heard his footsteps among last year's fallen leaves before the quiet of the woods settled about me.

At first I was relieved that for once I wasn't the one who had to comfort Rosa. It was so hot and their argument had been so fierce and momentous that I was glad of the peace. All afternoon I had been longing to try out the new arbour so I picked up my crochet, crept down into the hollow, tucked myself inside and sat cross-legged under the mesh of bracken. The woods around were filled with birdsong and I had an excellent view over the little dell, the flashing green leaves of new birches and the clear water of the stream bubbling over the pebbles of its artificial bed.

For a while I stitched peacefully and as I had chosen a simple design of connected trebles the work grew rapidly. Besides, I had a secret companion; the one letter that Henry had written since I came here was tucked into my pocket – just a few lines telling me about his studies and asking me not to forget him, but enough to satisfy me. I took it out and read it for perhaps the fiftieth time, then worked on my crochet again.

My hand went still because I had heard a distinct rustling behind the arbour. Perhaps I shouldn't be here on my own. Was it poachers? But all was quiet again.

I made a few more loops . . . another scratching of leaves. There was something behind me in the undergrowth and I couldn't see what it was because of the arbour. If I came out, what monstrous thing might spring at me? And if I didn't move, what would suddenly appear and snatch me away?

I sat absolutely still and the woods were still too, just the fluting call of a bird.

I worked a row of crossed trebles.

More rustling. The hook froze between my finger and thumb. Then I heard a snort above my head and there was Rosa's face contorted with suppressed laughter peering down at me between the leaves, and a few feet away, Max. As soon as I saw them they exploded with laughter and dropped down beside me.

'We've been watching you for ages,' said Rosa.

'Your fingers move so fast when you work that they become a blur,' said Max.

I tried to laugh but instead I cried because I had been so frightened.

'Oh no, oh Mariella, I'm so sorry,' cried Rosa. 'Don't be upset. You were irresistible. You looked so peaceful in there, like a little kernel in a nut.'

'Show me how you do it,' said Max suddenly, sitting right up close so that his knee overlapped mine. 'I want to learn.'

My hands were still shaking and I shrank away because I thought he was teasing me but he seemed deadly serious. 'Please.'

I worked a couple of chain stitches, very slowly, then gave him the hook and yarn. At first he only made knots and twists, but then I put my hands on his and guided them as they wound the yarn and thrust in the hook. His fingers were stained with sap but very deft and soon he was making stitch after stitch. It was very odd to see him so still with his dark head bent over something as unlikely as a bit of crochet and to have his sharp knee poking my ribs. When the hook slipped out and the yarn tangled I had to start him off again.

Meanwhile Rosa crawled against my other side, wrapped her arms round my waist and rested her head on my shoulder, kissing me from time to time on my wet cheek. The woods were entirely benign, full of green and golden light and wonderful, shifting shadows. They were both very gentle until it was time to go back and Rosa took it into her head to stand at the top of the steep bank and race down so that Max could catch her just at the moment when she was about to tumble into the stream. I watched as her hair fanned out and she gathered speed, faster, faster and crashed into him; he staggered back a few paces then set her safely on her feet.

'Now you, Mariella,' he shouted, holding out his arms. 'Come on, you don't have to go very fast.'

'If you like I'll do it with you,' said Rosa.

'I can't. I don't want to. Don't make me,' and to my shame I started to cry again as I looked down at them, Max with his shirt untucked and his eyes unusually kind, Rosa already halfway up the bank in her eagerness to help me.

Chapter Fifteen

The Crimea, 1855

After five days of being unnoticed by the authorities at the hospital my luck ran out and I received a visit from an untidy woman, possibly a soldier's wife, who told me that the superintendent of nurses, Mrs Shaw Stewart, wished to see me in her office.

By now my clothes had developed the same sad creases as everybody else's, my hair hadn't been washed for over a week and my caps were limp. Nevertheless I put on bonnet and gloves before I set off, quaking, for my appointment.

The lady in question was seated at a desk in a hut very like our own except that it was furnished with just one bed, a small table, a couple of chairs and a mountain of papers. When I knocked she kept on writing while I hovered by the door and rehearsed my excuses.

Mrs Shaw Stewart was undoubtedly high born; her black merino gown contrived to be elegant even in the heat, the skin on her broad brow was fine and white, and the slenderness of her hands was a sure sign, as Mrs Hardcastle would have said, of pedigree. I intended to create a common bond by alluding to Lady Mendlesham-Connors but when Mrs Shaw Stewart at last gestured to a chair her first remark blew away any thought of polite conversation. 'Rosa Barr was your cousin, I believe, and Dr Thewell your fiancé. Of course I knew Miss Barr. She and I travelled out together with Miss Stanley. We were first at the hospital at Koulali and then we both came over here in January to work at the General Hospital. Actually, I was very fond of her and admired the spirit with which she undertook all her work.'

I was speechless. Mrs Shaw Stewart continued: 'Nothing can excuse Miss Barr's behaviour. Believe me, Miss Lingwood, we have been given a near impossible job here in Balaklava: the doctors throw obstacles in my path as if we were engaged in a ridiculous game of chess rather than a shared mission to cure the sick; I am constantly having difficulty with the nuns, who try to distribute their wretched tracts to all and sundry; dear Miss Nightingale nearly died here and was thrown upon my care when I hardly had a glass of clean water at my disposal, let alone accommodation for a great lady. The last thing any of us needed was for your Rosa Barr to behave as she did.'

'How did she behave? Mrs Shaw Stewart, I long—'

'Before I came here I was trained in establishments in Germany and London. I know what discipline is. And I have my faith. But these other ladies – so-called, they're not all – come out here driven by some kind of missionary zeal and Miss Nightingale and I are left with a clutch of hysterical women on our hands, and a thousand wounded soldiers, and doctors who won't let us have so much as an egg or a spot of eau de cologne from the stores unless they sign half a dozen documents first. Your Rosa Barr wanted to be the personal saviour of every soldier she came across. And I do mean *every*. She was forever arguing that our own soldiers shouldn't be given priority over Russian prisoners if they were more in need of help. She wouldn't stick to the rules. She couldn't see why a lady's reputation is compromised if she sits up alone all night in a ward full of men. There are *boundaries*, Miss Lingwood, and your cousin would recognise none of them. So what happened to her doesn't surprise me though of course I'm full of sorrow. What it means for me is one less pair of hands and several difficult letters to write when we do finally learn the truth.'

'What do you think . . .'

'I have no time for speculation but, to be frank, in my experience certain girls who place themselves among thousands of men miles from home are bound to get into trouble. Your cousin Rosa put herself beyond anyone's help the moment she went up to live in the camp and work among the men in the trenches. You see, she went out on a limb and lost all sense of what was right. I'm sorry, Miss Lingwood, I know that you are engaged to Dr Henry Thewell. This must be particularly painful for you . . . But a liaison between one of her nurses and a member of the medical profession was what Miss Nightingale feared above all things. We have had to fight so much prejudice among the doctors and now this.'

'Mrs Shaw Stewart, while she was still working for you, how did Rosa seem in—'

'She seemed, as we all seemed, utterly bewildered. First a famine, then a feast. First no beds, or half beds, beds either without mattresses or without legs, then so many beds they're stacked in their hundreds, taking up space. One minute we have nothing to eat except salt beef and stale biscuits, the next we have so much butter and preserved venison and plum pudding that there is a danger the men will grow bilious. Which reminds me. Jam.'

'I . . .'

'Jam. A jar of raspberry jam was found to have been taken from the shelf in Mrs Whitehead's hut where you and your servant are staying.'

'Well, yes I . . .'

'Miss Lingwood, two points. The first: every single item from the "gifts" stores, sent by kind people from England, has to be accounted for or the entire system will collapse about our ears. We have already had to send two women home for pilfering. The second: every open jar constitutes a hazard. You left the jar half open under the bed. Fortunately it was found before the entire hut had become infested with cockroaches.'

'I'm sorry. I—'

'Which brings me to the final matter. I took on Nora McCormack because I remembered Rosa Barr speaking about her very favourably while we were nursing in Skutari together. She had learned many excellent practices from watching this Mrs McCormack at work. However, it was against my better judgement to allow a woman to come here without references, and of course I was punished for my lack of caution because she immediately got sick.'

I knew what was coming, I even considered interrupting again but she held up her hand. 'There is no place for you here, Miss Lingwood. I understand and to an extent applaud your concern for your cousin but you cannot stay. Everyone knows that a major offensive is imminent and in that case the hospital will soon be full of wounded and you will be nothing but a burden on us. I expect you to be gone in a week but in the meantime you can continue with your sewing. Everything in the Crimea falls apart so you will not be short of work.'

'Of course. Thank you. I shall be de—'

'Meanwhile I do not expect you to associate with the Roman Catholic nuns, should you come across them. Mrs Whitehead, however, is sound. Church of England. Father a clergyman. Minor. And keep your distance from the convalescents or walking wounded. A man may be at death's door but his thoughts will always be suspect.'

She picked up her pen, which I took to be a sign of dismissal. 'By the way, Miss Lingwood, you might like to know . . .' She paused significantly while I waited by the door, listening to the distant pounding of guns and the clash of metal utensils in a nearby hut. 'This is the hut in which Miss Nightingale stayed when she was ill. For weeks, in this very place, her life hung in the balance. That was the bed where she rested her head, and on the other side there was a little camp bed on which her devoted nurse, Mrs Roberts, slept, whenever she was able. That is the table with folding legs, as you see, so that it can serve as a tray, at which Miss Nightingale wrote notes and letters, even in her delirium, such is her dedication. Every day a messenger came to the door to receive a report on her health so that he could take it back to the troops. At one point during her illness Lord Raglan himself came to visit her. Even the Queen sent a message. Such is the esteem in which Miss Nightingale's name is held by every soldier, of whatever rank, in the Crimea and by our dear friends at home. This is why, Miss Lingwood, at all times Miss Nightingale's nurses must be above reproach: so many great men and women have staked their reputation on our success.'

Chapter Sixteen

26 May 1855

Dear Mariella,

We received yours this morning from Pescara in Italy, in which you tell us Henry has sent you off to the war, to find Rosa. Father has been out all morning sending telegrams but he is now standing at my elbow, instructing me what to write. He says you are to come home at once. He says this whole affair is like a fable he was told when he was a boy, in which a cheese falls off a cart and rolls down a hill, and the carter is such a fool that in order to find out where the cheese went he sends another one rolling after it, and then another, because each time he loses sight of the cheese when it reaches the bottom. By this I presume he means first Henry then Rosa then you have disappeared in the same way. He says that he is amazed at Henry for sending you to such a dangerous place as the war; it would be bad enough if you were a man, and if you'd been a second son he might have considered letting you go as a soldier, but as it is you should come straight back, no expense spared, and no more will be said about it. He tells me to write that he wants to show you a new street of houses that he has just completed on the other Wandsworth site. There are bay windows on the first and ground floors, and a decorative flourish to the porches he believes you would admire very much. If you are in need of money for the voyage home he will send it at once.

We are all puzzled by the lack of progress in the war. It seems a strange war to me, in which nothing happens. Rosa's friend, a Miss Leigh Smith, has called twice now to enquire after you. She hopes that you might teach at her school, Mariella, and speaks highly of you. She is to come with me to the home one day and speak to the governesses about education, their own and their pupils', which they will appreciate very much as nobody asks their opinion on anything. The weather here in London is so warm that we encourage them to sit in the garden during the afternoon, though the patch of grass is quite small, as you know, and the flowerbeds are plagued with slugs. Before Mrs Hardcastle came home – she is back, Mariella, and I must say very annoyed by your decision not to travel with her, she talks of nothing else – I ordered some cane furniture, but she says I have been very impractical, not to say extravagant because there is nowhere to store it in the winter and the governesses could have perfectly well used dining-room chairs carried out to the garden.

Mariella, I can't help thinking that if you were here you would make cushions for the new cane chairs and the governesses would be very comfortable indeed.

And now the main news of this letter is that your aunt Isabella is to be married. She is engaged to Mr Shackleton, whom you met, and they are to set up house in Dulwich. We are all very surprised by the speed with which the engagement has taken place but Isabella assures me she has grown very attached to him. The Hardcastles (as you may remember, Mr Shackleton and Mr Hardcastle are distantly related) are especially astonished and Mrs Hardcastle says it makes her wonder if she can risk going away again when so much happens the instant her back is turned. Isabella asks me to tell you that if you do see Rosa, please let her know that she is to have a new papa, and that she may make her home with them of course. Nora also will be considered for a position in the new house though Isabella cannot easily forgive her for what she calls gallivanting to the Crimea and has grown very fond of Ruth so may take her, which in my opinion would be no great loss to our household. She also says that if you really do reach the war you should find her stepson Max Stukeley and let him know the news.

Mariella, Papa has now left the room and I feel I must scribble one last private note to you, which he will not see. I can't help saying that your behaviour of late has surprised me so much that I scarcely recognise you as my daughter. I have been very angry with you, Mariella, and so worried I scarcely sleep and I have thought you selfish and undutiful, but lately, I think particularly since Mrs Hardcastle came home, I have come to see things in a different light. Please make sure, incidentally, that you wash your hands regularly with carbolic soap and boil your drinking water. Mrs Hardcastle says these are methods of preventing most illness. But Mariella, I find what I feel is pride and envy.

I wonder, by the way, if you might, on your return, devise a means of sewing a canopy or awning of some kind because at the end of the day the garden at the home is a suntrap. . . .

Chapter Seventeen

The Crimea, 1855

On Saturday 16 June, Newman turned up with yet another badly ripped tunic and a wounded hand following a fall from his horse. 'Idiot thing to do, Miss Lingwood. What a fool. Been riding all my life and now this. M'horse suddenly took against me and before I knew it I was on the ground and dragged half across the parade ground. Went to the Medical Officer but he patched me up double quick. Right as rain. Stiff arm is all but fit for service as usual. My uniform suffered more than I did.'

He looked utterly dejected and I pleaded with him to stay and drink a cup of tea to keep Nora company but he said he was in a desperate rush, too much happening back at the camp, no time even to tether the horse, so instead he hovered about, blood seeping through the bandage on his hand and his lower lip drooping while I examined the damage to his jacket. The horse, presumably the same that had thrown him the day before, stood peacefully by and looked about with mild brown eyes.

The material on the jacket arm was frayed and rubbed up to the elbow and the epaulette had been wrenched half off. 'Wondered if you could manage to do it quite soon, Miss Lingwood. Wore that jacket back in the Quarries. Saw me through. I expect you've noticed the guns never stop firing these days. Must be getting ready for something. Need the old lucky jacket back again just in case.'

'Of course. It will be done by tomorrow. And how would it be, Lieutenant Newman, if you were to take me for a picnic to the fort, as you suggested? If you have time.'

'Absolutely. I should like that. Wonderful idea. Mrs Seacole will provide.' He came very close and murmured confidentially, 'Miss

Lingwood, I was wondering – I've been asking a few of the men about your cousin, Miss Barr. They say there was a man who used to come and knock on the door of her hut. Very persistent. A doctor. Thought I should tell you. I'm so sorry. Must be difficult for you. He was the one she went away with.'

'Thank you, Lieutenant Newman.'

'I'm sorry if this gives you pain.'

'Lieutenant Newman, you have told me nothing new. Don't worry. I'll have this done for you by tomorrow.'

'Tomorrow. That's it. What a fool. Should have let go the reins but he sort of turned on me, the brute. I held on for dear life.' He was crying again and a dribble of saliva darkened the wool of the jacket on my lap. To save his dignity I didn't look up. 'Well, goodbye, then. Miss Lingwood, Miss McCormack.' He stood at the hut door, peering into the gloom.

'That'll be *Mrs* McCormack,' said Nora's voice from within.

'Beg pardon, of course, Mrs McCormack.'

'You take care, then, Lieutenant Newman. God bless you.'

Still he didn't go but hovered about, casting his long shadow while his horse cropped the parched grass and I snipped away at the frayed ends of cloth and thought of Henry knock-knocking on the door of Rosa's hut.

I delayed other work to finish Newman's jacket but I need not have worried because there was no sign of him all the next day. While I waited I sewed a soft inner lining for Mrs Whitehead's cuffs and collars to prevent her skin from being rubbed raw by the coarse fabric of her dress. The bombardment above Sebastopol seemed to have trebled in volume and force so that smoke hung like storm clouds over the hills. By five o'clock Newman still hadn't come.

The rhythm of hospital life continued and a couple of carts came trailing up the track bearing wounded. It seemed that the Russians were still able to return fire after all and were as capable as us at lobbing rockets and cannonballs across the enemy lines. At six o'clock the nuns closeted themselves away for evening mass and I found myself envying their ability to cut off from the nervous tension in the hospital; when the guns went quiet momentarily their steady voices could be heard intoning Latin prayers. Later on, at about eight, Mrs Whitehead told us that it was rumoured there'd be a major offensive the next day and that finally the allies would break through and reach Sebastopol. 'Just think,' she said, 'it's amazing to even consider it, but it could all be over by this time tomorrow.' With her usual efficiency she settled on her bed, face to the wall, and tucked herself away into sleep so as to be fully prepared for whatever excitement or horrors the next day might bring.

Nora and I weren't so lucky. Sharing a narrow bed was torture – we were hot and cramped and tormented by fleas. Far into the night I heard the click of her beads and a whispered litany of *Hail Marys* until when the guns went silent at last she relaxed and her breathing grew steady.

That was my loneliest time when it seemed to me that I clung by my fingernails to the edge of the war, to Russia itself, and that nobody would care if I dropped off altogether. I tried to place everyone in my mind: my parents and Isabella in their beds in Fosse House; Henry, in his dim little room in Narni, yearning for Rosa; Max preparing for the battle in his camp up close to the enemy lines; Rosa. Oh God. From the bottom of my heart I longed to know what had happened to Rosa.

I had discovered that in the allied camp every newcomer was a diversion, every unusual event endlessly discussed so if Rosa was anywhere within a radius of twenty miles she would know that Mariella Lingwood and Nora McCormack had arrived in the Crimea.

So why didn't she come to me? Unless she was too ashamed, or incapable, captured or lost. Or dead.

I dozed at last and woke in the small hours, pre-dawn. When a rat scuffled across my foot I hardly bothered to kick it away; I was merely irritated that its activities made it more difficult for me to hear what was happening outside. Silence, then the crack of a rocket. And another.

I slid off the bed, reached for Nora's boots, tapped them sharply in case anything had nested in them during the night, put them on and let myself out. The hospital huts were quiet although a few windows were lit by flickering lanterns carried from one bed to the next. A cold wind blew off the sea as I crept between the huts up the path towards the fortress. Dawn was breaking over the hills to the east above Balaklava and in the distance came the sharp rack-a-cack of gunfire and shells.

How quickly a place became haunted by disturbing memories. This fortress reminded me of the picnic I should have had yesterday with poor Newman, and of the woman with the striped orange and green skirt whose child Max had buried in Kertch. As the sky silvered the racket from the guns increased and the harbour woke up to another day of urgent activity. Even to my inexperienced ears the quality of firing seemed different to yesterday's incessant bombardment. Instead it was sporadic and vicious, followed suddenly by the boom of cannon from the sea. There could be no doubt that this was the day of battle. I sat on the edge of the path, arms tight round my knees, watching the sky. The dawn was soon pinkish gold and the air full of salt. The gunfire hurt me, it seemed to reverberate in my blood.

Chapter Eighteen

Derbyshire, 1844

Rosa developed a fascination for finding out more about Mother's philanthropic concerns, particularly those connected with hospitals. One afternoon she brought pen and paper up to the bare little room on the top floor that Mother and I used as a schoolroom, and asked if she could make a few notes. She wanted to know how she too might become a member of a hospital Board of Visitors and what exactly would be her responsibilities.

After a while I grew very bored with the conversation and slipped away, partly to see if either of them would notice. As I crossed the staircase hall I saw that the library door was open and sunlight was making rectangular patterns on the red and green rug inside. Of course this was the only room I'd not visited because it was kept locked and Rosa was refused entry, so I crept right up and took a peek.

The library in that sudden blaze of light was both beautiful and intimidating. In places the books seemed to go on and on from floor level to high ceiling, and on top of alternating stacks of oak shelves were gabled nooks in which had been placed marble heads of great men, or so I presumed, I didn't recognise any of them. The symmetry of the rows of books, the careful arrangement of table and chairs in the window, the armchairs on either side of the hearth, the pillars of cupboards and tiny drawers ranked along the far wall were all enchanting to my tidy mind. Unlike the rest of Stukeley, which was filled with Aunt Isabella's taste for anything floral, this room was austere and purposeful. I loved the smell so much that I crept further in, picked a book at random off the shelves, gave it a good sniff, took it to a table and opened it.

Greek. I turned the pages sadly. There was nothing here for me after all.

'You should sit on the other side of the table,' said a voice behind me, 'so you don't cast a shadow on the page.'

I jumped and closed the book hastily. Sir Matthew Stukeley, to whom I'd barely spoken three words in the month since my arrival, stood in the doorway smiling at me. He was an unlikely spouse for my buxom aunt being thin with a protruding lower lip, narrow face and fearsome side whiskers. His voice came from deep in his throat and Rosa said he reminded her, to look at and listen to, of an old nanny goat, an opinion perhaps influenced by the fact that the pair didn't get on, *at all*, as Mother said. For one who worked in such a noisy place as a lead works he moved very quietly and I had found time spent in his aloof company at dinner, even though he never spoke to me, quite an ordeal. That afternoon, however, when I risked a frightened peek into his eyes, I noticed that they were indulgent, even affectionate.

He gave the door a little tug so that it nearly closed, and with his long fingers turned to the title page of the book. Rosa said her stepfather's family was from *nowhere*; our mothers were the daughters of a squire but the Stukeleys had been only lead miners until a couple of generations back. If this was really the case Sir Matthew had peculiarly fine hands, unlike my father's which were calloused and lumpy as a result of accidents with bricks and sledge-hammers.

'Do you read Greek?' asked Sir Matthew.

'No. Sorry.'

'Sorry for what?'

'I shouldn't be here. I'm sorry. The door was open. I just wanted to see. I couldn't help it.'

'You mustn't be afraid of looking at books. You can come any time. Books are for everyone. I've watched you at table. You have wonderful manners. I know you will be very careful. It's one of the great disappointments of my life that neither of my sons has turned out to be a scholar. Do you read Latin?'

'No. Oh no. Rosa can, a bit.'

'Rosa can do everything, *a bit*. She infuriates me with her piecemeal attitude to things. Who is your favourite author? Perhaps I have work by him in here. I do have some novels.'

As I read very little apart from periodicals I couldn't name a single writer. Mother said I was too young for most novels and I daren't mention that Rosa and I were reading *Oliver Twist* in case he asked me questions about chapters we hadn't yet reached.

'Poetry,' he said. 'Do you like poetry?'

'Oh yes, definitely.'

'Well, who is your favourite poet?'

I couldn't think of any poets either except for a name Rosa had mentioned recently. 'Byron. I like Byron.' And then I scolded myself because of course I really did know the work of one poet very well: Henry's favourite, Keats. I could even have recited the song 'Meg Merrilies' from start to finish.

Sir Matthew was laughing and I noticed that he had exceptionally fine teeth. 'Do you indeed? Are you sure your mama knows that? Well, I've got plenty of Byron here. Which one of his poems would you especially like to read?'

I hung my head miserably.

'Well, listen, Mariella, you feel free to read any book you like, so long as you don't take it out of the library. Let me show you where everything is. Poetry is on these shelves here, and I have a small collection of plays which may interest you. Here are reference books, mostly scientific, these are prose essays. Here are the Latin authors, here the Greek. In time I'll get round to labelling all the shelves but for now you'll just have to find your own way.'

I crept about feeling like an impostor because until that moment I'd had no interest in books and he was treating me so respectfully that I was bewildered. Was this really the same Sir Matthew who sat stiffly at the end of the table, answered my mother and Isabella in monosyllables, ignored Rosa, needled Horatio, treated Max with contempt and waved away unwanted dishes with the merest flick of his index finger?

I felt I ought to make at least a little effort in return so I risked a question: 'What do you keep in those cupboards and drawers?'

'Cupboards? Oh yes, of course. Well, I keep precious things in there. Some books are too expensive or rare to be exposed to the light at all. I'll show you one day, maybe, when I've found out how much you really like books. And in the meantime, tell me, what do you think of our Derbyshire?'

'I like the hills,' I said.

He laughed again. 'Just as well. We have a lot of hills. Anything else?'

'I like being with Rosa.'

His smile faded. 'Rosa. Well, I suppose you are first cousins and nearly the same age. So what do the pair of you get up to?'

'Oh. Well. I sew.'

'Yes, I've noticed your sewing.' His eye fell on my neck. 'Did you sew that lovely little collar?'

'Yes. I did.' Then I couldn't resist adding, 'And these cuffs.'

I held out my hands and he smiled kindly. 'They're very pretty. I don't suppose Rosa sews.'

'She's learning fast. And she teaches me other things.'

'What does she teach you?'

'She shows me things. We explore.'

'And have you explored in here with her?'

'Oh no. We know the door is usually locked. And she says she's forbidden the library.'

'I'm afraid I once found her eating a particularly juicy apple over a very rare book. That's why she's not allowed back until she's grown up a little. But you can come any time, provided you keep your visits to yourself. I don't want any petty jealousy. I'd enjoy the company, if I'm at home, and I may even have time to teach you a bit of Latin, which would help you keep up with Rosa. What do you think of that idea?'

He returned the book to the shelf and I assumed that the interview was over. As I crept to the door he called me back. 'Will you come again?'

'Oh yes.'

'Tomorrow at this time, then.'

He was standing with his head bent, drumming his fingers on the table and I felt sorry for him. He must be lonely if he wanted to pass the time by teaching me Latin. But as I raced away to the Italian garden and crawled into the box hedge I worried about what had taken place. How could I keep my promise to Sir Matthew and not tell Rosa, from whom I had no secrets? But she hated Sir Matthew and would be scornful if she knew I'd agreed to be taught by him. In the end I decided that nothing would come of my trip to the library anyway – Sir Matthew was bound to forget about the arrangement by tomorrow and in the meantime my life would be much more peaceful if I kept quiet about it.

Chapter Nineteen

The Crimea, 1855

Late in the morning the wind dropped and the air grew still and hot. A boy came running up from the harbour and shouted that the French had taken the Malakov: it must be right because the tricolour had been seen waving above the parapet. But then a couple of Turks who drove up with a cartload of lemons said that on the contrary, the French had been driven *back* from the Malakov which the Russians had held with no difficulty at all.

My latest task was to sew buttons onto dozens of hospital nightshirts. Nora, who was dressed for the first time, sat beside me outside the hut with her head back, soaking up the sun. Only her lips moved and I hoped she was praying for Max and Newman. Then I saw a messenger galloping up the track so I flung down my sewing and went to the cookhouse for news.

Wounded were coming. For some incomprehensible reason the British had rushed forward and attacked the Redan even though guns to their right were blazing at them from the undefeated Malakov. They had been scythed down by a storm of grapeshot and bullets until the few left standing were driven back to the trenches. At a rough guess the British had lost several hundred men, the French over two thousand.

Hour by hour the news got worse. I persuaded Nora, who was sick with dread and weakness, back to bed and received the next bulletin from Mrs Whitehead, who spoke in a whisper. 'There are three thousand French casualties, they say. The trouble was that one of their generals mistook rocket-fire for the signal to attack, so his men went in too early and the element of surprise was gone.'

'But I thought the Russians were supposed to be almost defenceless by now.'

'Turns out the Russians have been playing games with us. They hid a line of guns behind their bastion, then yesterday pretended they were incapable of returning fire and saved their ammunition. It seems they were well prepared, saw our lanterns and campfires last night and knew we must be about to attack, so they had their guns and reinforcements ready.'

'And the British?'

'Slaughter, Miss Lingwood. Raglan sent us into the Redan anyway, even though the Russian guns were still firing from the Malakov. Our men were mown down on open ground or as they tried to climb the Russian defences. Very few even reached the Redan and now hundreds of wounded and dying are lying under the Russian bastions in the blaze of the afternoon sun, and no one is able to reach them because no armistice has been agreed.'

All afternoon, while carts of wounded rumbled up the hill and Nora slept, I sat at the door of Mrs Whitehead's hot little hut, sewing on buttons. I was trying the old trick of disengagement but it didn't work. The blood fizzed in my veins: I was too hot, too restless, too useless. I even thought of begging Mrs Shaw Stewart to employ me in the wards or tagging onto one of the nurses and asking to be given some menial task, anything to help make things better.

Then I saw a rider come clip-clopping smartly up to the hospital, dismount, speak to one of the orderlies, disappear from view, and reappear unexpectedly on the path above our hut. I now realised that he wore the familiar uniform of the Derbyshires and looked dusty and dishevelled.

'Miss Lingwood? Ma'am. I've been sent up from the General Hospital. Relative of yours there, I believe. Captain Max Stukeley. In a bad way. Wants a word before he goes under the knife, if you could spare him a moment.'

A groan came from inside the hut. I nodded to the officer, told him I would leave at once, went in and picked up my bonnet. Nora was propped on her elbow and her voice was much stronger than at any time in the last week. 'Take water. Clean water for the boy. Don't let them give him dirty stuff. And don't you taste a drop from anyone else either. There's no point you making yourself ill. And take clean dressings for the wounds. Those bandages you were making yesterday. And don't let them cut a limb from him unless they must. They're too slap-happy with the knife. I know. I seen in Ireland that if a wound is kept clean amputation may not be necessary. If he can move the limb it's worth saving; if they take it he's bound to die.'

'I'll do what I can.'

'Don't let him die. I'm telling you. I won't want you back here if he dies. And put these in his hands. Tell him I'm praying for him.'

She clutched my wrist and dropped the green rosary beads into my palm. I refilled the water glass by her bed, threw on a shawl and went to the door. 'Mariella.' I turned, startled to hear her use my first name, but she only nodded and gestured that I should be gone.

As I dashed forward my strongest feeling was at first excitement because Max had summoned *me*. I, Mariella Lingwood, was wanted. Never before had I walked with such a sense of purpose and so regardless of the difficulties that would reach me when I got to my destination. But this euphoria lasted only a few moments before the implications of Max's injury took hold. Then I was transported back to the theatre at Guy's Hospital watching Henry perform an amputation: the sudden gesture with his arms, the gathering silence, the splinter of bone. If the child Tom had not survived, how could Max? I walked faster. I must save him, for Rosa's sake. If he died there'd be just me left.

And I realised that if Max had been hit in the thick of fighting, Newman had probably been in the fray too.

I started to run, little steps that collided with my skirts and made me breathless. In a few minutes I had left the safe eyrie of the hospital and was plunged into the harbour where there was so much traffic that I had to elbow my way through a throng of sailors, and Turkish and Sardinian soldiers. Then I went marching up the road to the General Hospital which was tucked into the side of the hill above the railway, its first huts almost level with the top of the masts that clustered in the harbour below.

I found chaos and although it was only just dark the hospital blazed like a concert hall. Outside the huts men lying on pallets formed a helpless queue. I heard a yelp of pain, and realised that in fact there was a dreadful low dissonance that was the sound of suffering. Nurses and orderlies moved among the sick men with flasks and pails or bundles of lint, and doctors leaned over one body after another, muttering instructions, testing limbs, moving on. When I passed too close to one of the pallets a hand shot out and gripped my ankle. All I could see beneath me was a gaping wound in a man's neck and so much blood on his shirt that at first I thought he was wearing a red jacket. There was no wrenching my ankle free so I crouched down and stared into his maddened eyes but he couldn't speak, just kept his vice-like grip.

I don't know what to do, I don't know what to do, I raged in my head. Someone help me. I don't belong here.

In the end I picked up the man's other hand and let it rest in my own, noting how rough his fingers were and how filthy the nails. I stroked his cold palm and watched a couple of flies zoom lazily down and feed in his throat. Fighting nausea, I forced myself to look into his eyes. His fingers released their grip on my ankle but his sightless gaze never left my face as I whispered fatuous words of comfort. After ten minutes or so his eyes went vacant. One moment he was there, the next, not.

I backed away and trod on the toes of a fat nurse who stared at me in astonishment. 'Who are you? Who sent you?'

'I am looking for Max Stukeley. Captain. Derbyshires.'

She shrugged. 'I don't know him.'

'He was injured. He's waiting for an operation.'

'Over there. Try there.'

Stretcher cases were lined up under an awning outside a hut which was hung with lanterns and full of bustle. The air stank of blood and some sweet, heady smell I later discovered was chloroform and I glimpsed bright lights, screens, trestles and stooping figures. I moved down the row until I found Max who was lying with his arm behind his head, face dead white, eyes burning up into mine.

I dropped to my knees beside him.

'Took your time,' he said. 'Had to have myself put back in the queue.'

'I did my best.'

'Ah yes. Your best.' He beckoned me closer. 'The leg's smashed. Coming off. Wanted to see you before they finally do for me. Just in case. Rosa's things are up at the camp and you must take them. Couldn't have us both disappearing without a trace. Even if I survive this I'll be despatched home double quick, so I won't get up there again.'

'Rosa's things.'

'Can't bear to think they'd be lost. All I have left of her.'

'I'm sure Rosa's not lost for ever, Max. I'm sure she'll come back.'

He laughed drearily and turned away his face.

'What happened to your leg, Max?'

'Two minutes out of the trench. Shell came over. Smashed above the knee when it exploded. Useless. Useless. Could scarcely crawl.'

'It's not your fault that you were hit.'

'Isn't it?' His hand suddenly reached up, clutched me first by the shoulder, then the back of my neck and pulled me down so that his face was inches from my own and his breath was hot on my mouth. 'Do you think I willed it? It's possible. Sometimes my mind detaches itself and thinks, dear Christ, I'd rather be dead than here. I pray to God that's not what I willed because those men who went on marching died for me. I yelled for them to get out of that trench behind me, and in the first minutes I fell. They went on to their deaths.'

'What about Newman?'

'Don't know. Didn't see. He tried to help me but I sent him away.'

'You weren't to know those men would die.'

'I knew that Raglan ordered us in to save his own bloody face. We stood no chance. The man has fixed ideas. Hates the French. Won't let them run away with the idea that the Brits are cowards. We knew it was suicide but we went all the same.'

'Then why did you go, Max, if you knew what would happen?'

'Orders. I obey orders.'

'You never used to.'

A spark flickered in his eye. 'That's it. Never used to.' His hand slackened on my neck and was about to fall.

'Max, drink this.' I raised him up so that his head was against my breast. His hand closed over mine on the flask and he drank thirstily. The weight of his helpless body, the sudden intimacy both moved and shocked me but my voice was calm. 'What else can I do for you? Tell me.'

'Like I say, couldn't bear to think of Rosa's things getting lost. Can't bear to think of her out there somewhere. We argued on the last day. Usual story, parted badly. She was pig-headed, always thought she could be everyone's saviour. When she came to live at Stukeley it was like a burst of sunshine – should have taken more care of her. Not sure there'll be anyone left back at the camp to keep an eye on her things.'

'I'll fetch them, Max.'

'That's it, then. Off you go.'

'Nora said I must stay with you.'

'For God's sake, don't talk to me in that dismal voice. Can't stand it.'

'So there's nothing else you need me to do?'

'Fetch Rosa's things. Leave the Crimea. Go home. I've told you, time after time. Now you've seen for yourself what's happening to us all.'

His head jerked and his eyes burned with pain but I stroked his dry, hot cheek to make him listen to me. 'Henry used to say that some doctors were too eager to amputate. He said if the bone broke cleanly and hadn't cut through flesh, it would mend. Even though he's a great surgeon, he said surgery isn't always the answer. Nora said the same. Don't let them take your leg unless they have to.'

'Not in a position to argue. Would rather live, with or without a leg. Just about. Can't think why. What'll I do with one leg?'

'Any of a hundred things.' At that moment I couldn't think of a career suitable for Max that didn't demand two legs. 'Become a clergyman.'

A splutter of laughter. 'Brilliant. An absolutely first-class Miss Mariella Lingwood solution. That's it, then. Problem solved.'

'Can you move your leg at all?'

'Rather not try. Thanks all the same.'

'Get them to use these dressings – I'll leave them here, tucked under the pillow. And tell them what Henry said. Dr Henry Thewell. Tell them. I'm sure they'll listen if they hear his name.'

He gave my shoulder a weak push. 'Mariella. Go. Now. I want you gone.'

'But I'm to stay with you. Nora said.'

'Leave. You're bothering me to death.'

His eyes closed. I lingered another moment, watched the trembling curve of his eyelid and remembered the boy who had shinned up the pillar of the new porch at Stukeley and tapped on my window, Nora's fondness for him, how he had infuriated and enchanted Rosa in equal measure, and how he had stood beside the woman in the striped skirt at Kertch while her son was buried. I dribbled the rosary into his hand just in case, and then, because I couldn't help myself, kissed his unconscious lips.

Chapter Twenty

When I left the hospital I was so sick and shaken I hardly knew what to do but as Max had told me to collect Rosa's things, off I set in the gathering dark, up to the camps.

The Crimea was a dangerous place and not just because of the shelling. I had learned that no property was safe from criminals and vagrants, even at the hospital where stores were kept firmly locked. Livestock that survived having its legs chewed by rats disappeared overnight and clothes left to dry on exposed washing lines were whipped away. Anyone might be out in the dark ready to strip the clothes from my back or worse. Mrs Seacole's British Hotel was well lit and a crowd of men had gathered outside – for a moment I considered asking to be taken in for the night; the hotel looked so comforting, surely I would be safer inside than out, whatever Lady Mendlesham-Connors might think.

As I moved onwards sporadic fire came from the trenches and spurts of light filled the sky but the night was otherwise quiet and after a while there was little traffic on the road. The vast camp rustled and murmured in its tents and huts while dark figures moved quietly about or stood over the fires. I was challenged once or twice but as soon as I spoke my English name in my lady's voice I was allowed to pass. The Ninety-seventh camp was even further than I remembered, a long trek along worn paths. After a while a wagon lumbered by and I hung on to a metal bar and allowed myself to be dragged forward at a faster pace. The air was full of gunpowder and the stars above Sebastopol were lost in a pall of smoke.

By the time I reached the Derbyshire's camp it was pitch-dark and I was hungry and footsore. A heavy-eyed sentry directed me to a mess tent where a group of officers was at table. At first I was too shy to go in but someone spotted me, I explained who I was and when I mentioned first Max then Rosa the tent fell quiet. One or two of the men had half risen when I appeared – after all I was wearing a narrow skirt and re-modelled blouse that made me look like a soldier's wife – but by the end of my faltering introduction all were on their feet. Though they were polite and eager to please they were worn out and in low spirits. A junior officer was ordered to take a lantern and show me to Max's hut where I could spend the night if I wished.

As we walked between lines of tents he told me that Newman was unaccounted for. It was thought he'd made it to the abattis – the head-high barricade constructed of brushwood, rubbish and torn-down trees – and someone remembered him dashing ahead across the open ground beyond the trench but he'd not been seen since. They believed he had been hit and was lying out on the battlefield, like a good many others in the regiment. Since no armistice had been agreed it would be suicide for anyone to step out under the Russian guns and try to fetch him.

The young officer unlocked Max's hut, hung the lantern from a hook in the roof and told me he would send a man with tea and supper. Like Newman he was probably under twenty and had a drawling accent and immaculate manners, though he was in no mood for further conversation. After he'd gone I dropped down on a narrow bench set against one side of the hut, took a gulp of water from my flask and closed my eyes. Outside there was a burst of firing so intense and close-seeming that had I not been exhausted I would have flung myself under the bed. As it was I remained slumped until there was silence again. Then I roused myself, opened my eyes and found that I was staring across the hut at Rosa.

In all there were three pictures nailed above Max's bed. The first was a near perfect reproduction of the portrait of his mother that Rosa had shown me in his bedroom at Stukeley, except that in this version her two sons had been omitted though the sitter leaned forward and looked into some distant place with the same abstracted, laughing charm that I remembered from the original. Next was an illustration from *Punch*, a cartoon of two miserable soldiers in a blizzard. And then there was a portrait of Rosa, captured in a posture that I knew well, cross-legged on the bed, head in hands, hair falling on either side of her face and deep in a book. It was an accurate, hasty sketch, presumably by Max, who had caught the shape of her bones, the length of her nose, the fine long fingers exactly, and it provided clear testimony that she had been in this hut. Behind her head in the picture hung the same two sketches, Max's mother and the *Punch* cartoon, and even the planks of wood which made up the side of the hut behind the bed had been lightly drawn in, knots and all.

The picture had the most shameful effect on me; of all feelings at such a time I felt a stab of jealousy because Rosa and Max had sat together in this hut while she posed for him, looked up into his face and smiled or sighed impatiently. They'd been closeted away from the war, quite alone.

An orderly brought a tray with tea, soup, bread and a bowl of clean water. After he'd gone I closed the door and ate. Rosa's head remained bent over her book. She was so immediate that I could almost hear her light breathing and feel the warmth of her scalp through her hair. I knew exactly how it felt to comb those long tresses, to lift their weight and slide hair pins among them. While she read I used to plait her hair, whiling away the time until she got just to the end of the page or chapter, forlornly excluded by her ability to lose herself in a story. I was frustrated by all the unreachable things that were going on in her head at that moment.

And what had she been thinking about while this picture was being drawn? Just the book? What else? Had she been thinking of me? Of Max? Of Henry?

Rosa. Rosa, look up. *Speak* to me.

Meanwhile other details of the little hut emerged from the shadows: the few books on the shelves – a military manual, a Bible, a copy of Tennyson's *In Memoriam* and Dickens's *Bleak House* (probably the book Rosa was reading whilst being drawn); a shelf on which were arranged a series of notes and papers, writing equipment, comb, soap, tooth-powder. A couple of chests were stacked in one corner, presumably to store Max's clothes, and tucked under the bed but clearly visible was Rosa's box with her name painted on the side in my own precise block capitals, last seen on the dirty pavement at London Bridge Station.

It was half an hour before I could bring myself to touch that box but at last I lifted it onto the bed, pushed back the latch and opened the lid. The smell was so intense that I was blown back across the hut. It was as if essence of Rosa had been stored there: lemons, the fragrance of her hair and skin.

I knelt by the bed, gathered an armful of clothes and sank my face into them. She was present in the texture of the soft wool against my skin, the undergarments I'd made her, the sleeve linings and collars. Each item was well worn but carefully laundered and folded. I searched for marks left by her on the fabric but could only find her fragrance – citrus, musk, Rosa. My mind's eye flickered again and again: her hair skimming my face when she turned her head suddenly, her bare legs gripped round the branch of a tree, her eyes shining into mine in the flickering green light of the box hedge. Rosa. Rosa in the garden at Fosse House, hands behind her back as she marched ahead of us, Rosa holding me tight in her arms and pressing her face into my neck: 'I love you more than anyone else in the world.'

She was so nearly there in the flesh that I half expected her to come prancing out of the box, but actually most of the contents were of such little value to anyone other than me that I wondered why Max had been so worried about them. Her life seemed to have been pared down to its essence: a few clothes, but not her heaviest skirt, a face flannel, a handful of handkerchiefs (the *RB*s embroidered by me), a few blank sheets of notepaper. We had packed so much more. Pastels and charcoals for drawing, her sewing things, medicines chosen by Nora, arrowroot, laudanum, calomel, valerian, eucalyptus, plaisters, soaps, salts – all were gone. And if I'd expected to find clues of her affair with Henry there were none except that right at the bottom there was a leather-bound notebook and a length of pale green silk that I used to wear as a scarf sometimes in the neck of my evening gown to avoid exposing my naked bosom. And this silk had been folded into a kind of packet to hold a pile of folded papers.

On the front page of the notebook in Rosa's clear print were the words: NOTES ON NURSING. ROSA BARR. AUGUST 1854.

The next page was entitled: *Guy's Hospital. Visit by Miss Barr and Miss Lingwood.*

1. Viewed medical ward (male)
Observed patient with rash on chest. Conversed with nurse.

2. Witnessed Operation – amputation above the knee. Male child. 13.
Surgeon – Henry Thewell.
Anaesthetic – Alcohol.
Noted high level of speed and accuracy.
Surgeon wore frock coat. No apron.
Successful but what living hell will that child be in to the end of his days when he remembers today?

And then a scribbled note in the margin: *Subsequently died. What was the point?*

I turned more pages.

SEPTEMBER 1854, LADY ISABELLA STUKELEY SUFFERS PALPITATIONS
Miss Barr assists with bleeding of same. Four leeches applied. Patient observed to be much calmer by nightfall. (Dr Raymond attended. Miss Barr has no faith in him. Mr Philip Lingwood says that his wife and her friends consider him to be a good doctor because he agrees faithfully with his patients' own diagnosis of their ills.)

JANUARY 1855, KOULALI HOSPITAL
Notes on medication. Haphazard in extreme. For the same condition two different doctors might order powdered rhubarb (10 grams), or tincture of opium (30 drops). Where is the method?

I turned the pages faster, faster. Surely now I would find mention again of Henry's name.

RUSSIAN NURSES
The Russian army employs volunteer nurses who work right up among the troops. And are said to have adopted a method of sorting the mortally ill from those in need of urgent attendance, and those lightly wounded.

Her last note of all was written in very thick script, as if she'd pressed too hard on the pen.

I might as well be the keeper of a LARDER for all the good I do.

I put the notebook aside and held the green silk bundle on my lap. Then I lay back and pressed it to my breast. Finally I unfolded the silk so the papers fell out in a sheaf across the bed. But when I picked the first one up I realised that the handwriting was my own, not Henry's as I'd expected. I unfolded another. Again, a letter from me. In fact all the letters were written by me and were my dutiful accounts of life in London since Rosa went to join Miss Stanley's party in the Crimea. And then there were earlier letters, in ever more childish handwriting, including my first ever note to Rosa, sent long ago on my return from Stukeley.

30 June 1844

Dear Rosa,

Now we are home, and everything is as it was before we left. In fact Mother says it's as if we had never been away, even. Father was very surprised to see us, and annoyed because he had to leave his work early today, to meet us at the station. On the train journey, Mother and I talked a little about the reason why we'd been sent away. We didn't know. I woke up this morning and wondered where I was . . .

One final item had been wrapped in the green silk, an envelope folded over and over to protect its contents: Rosa's sapphire locket containing the little plait of hair, hers and mine, and the greying lock that had been cut from her dead father's head.

The night was surprisingly cold and I had grown used to sleeping next to Nora so in the end I wrapped myself in Max's sheepskin, which enfolded me in stifling animal heat. A similar coat hung, reeking, in Henry's room in Narni. Poor Henry, if he wore it now the weight of it would crush him.

Then I lay on Max's bed and listened to the shifting boards of the hut and the crack of gunfire which, being so close, jolted me wide awake time after time. My hand rested on Rosa's notebook and the locket was clasped round my neck but my senses were so troubled that between waking and sleeping I swam through a river of images. The bed linen, sheepskin and the hut itself smelled disturbingly unlike anything I was used to – Max, presumably, earthy, masculine, a hint of aromatic oil. By now he must have gone under the knife and his amputated leg would be lying in a heap of other butchered limbs. Perhaps pain and shock had already killed him. I rubbed my cheek against the wool of his coat as if I might somehow force the blood to keep on pumping in his shattered body.

Wrenching my thoughts away, I began to puzzle over the simplicity of Rosa's possessions. There had been not a hint of an illicit relationship in her box, in fact no secrets at all. Perhaps Max had found other evidence and destroyed it. But if Rosa had betrayed me, if she had fallen in love with Henry, why had she kept all my letters? The locket was more significant. She had taken off the locket, the most poignant reminder of her past, perhaps as a sign that she had discarded me.

Again my mind strayed, this time to the battlefield and to Newman under the smoky stars. Alive or dead? Poor boy, what had he been thinking about when he ran away from Max into a hail of bullets?

I curled into Max's sheepskin, my right leg aching in sympathy with his as I remembered the swing at Stukeley, the pair of them swooping out over the little ravine, their laughing eyes turned on me. We dare you, Mariella. That easy, confident stride of his, the forcefulness with which he had hauled me up the path to the ruined fortress and held me against the wall.

Chapter Twenty-One

Derbyshire, 1844

A week or so after Max's revelation that he was to join the army Rosa took me on a long walk along the blowy top of the valley, down into a dip, across a little stone bridge above a peaty stream, up the other side and round to the hill opposite Stukeley Hall so that we could gaze across at the house in all its complicated glory, amidst its gardens, walks and plantations. The weather was overcast and perhaps threatened rain but Rosa insisted it was high time I saw more of her stepfather's estate. 'If we go a little further we'll have a view of the lead foundry and that I do want you to see.' I could tell by her relentless grip on my wrist that she had something disturbing in mind.

Even from a distance the foundry, a brick shed with a pitched roof, vibrated with noise. Above us on the hilltop was a high, round chimney, billowing smoke funnelled up through the soil from the furnaces.

'Have you ever been inside the foundry, Rosa?'

'I wanted to but my stepfather said no. Of course.'

'I wonder why. You'd think he'd be proud, as he owns it.'

'He said it would frighten me. He took Mother there once and she was ill for a week afterwards because of the heat. But *she* would be. I would be perfectly all right, even though it's an evil place. I wanted Max to do something about it. My plan was that one day he would manage the lead and Horatio the cotton but Max will have nothing to do with any of it.'

'Is that why you were so angry with him that day we built the arbour?'

'Of course. If he joins the army I'll never see him. And what if he gets killed? But anyway, Max says Sir Matthew will never split his estate and even if he did he wouldn't trust Max with his precious business.'

'So you can't blame Max.'

'I can. He should try and change things. Nobody else will.'

I squinted down at the opaque windows. 'Well, I can understand why he wouldn't like to work there.'

'I want to have a look inside.'

'Even if Sir Matthew gave me a special invitation, *I* wouldn't go. I wouldn't dare. Listen to the noise.'

'Well, that's just as well, because he won't ask you. Why would he?' She sat for a while looking down intently at the foundry, hunched forward like a cat about to spring. 'In fact, why don't we go now?'

'Now? We can't. Oh no. Oh Rosa, it's too late, it's almost teatime.'

'Yes now. Let's go. Come on. Follow me,' and she was on her feet, flying down the hillside to the little nick in the wall wide enough to allow a person through but not a sheep.

'Rosa. Rosa.'

'Hurry up. I don't think Stepfather's there today. He said something about Sheffield so it's a perfect time.'

There was no resisting her; the steep slope pulled me downward and the valley floor lurched ever closer until we were level with the cottages in Stukeley village. 'I'll stay here,' I cried but the thought of waiting in a windswept field surrounded by sheep and stared at by more Fairbrother-type village children was unnerving so we went on down the mud track, alongside a river to the lead works. The air was full of metallic smoke and the scant leaves on the few trees were smutty and parched. A line of carts stood waiting in the yard and we passed heaps of slag twice as high as the building. Half a dozen or so small children were spread across the bottom of one of the mounds, bent double, plucking up handfuls of mud and sifting through it.

'Rosa. Rosa,' I whispered urgently but she took my hand and drew me towards a little door set in a much larger one. The tension in her fingers and the gleam in her eye meant there was no stopping her; in she would go.

The noise this close was already deafening but when she opened the door it was as if we'd stepped into the thumping heart of hell.

Heat and violent movement and the bone-rattling clang of metal seized my body and shook it out of its muscular shell until I was as limp and viscous as a worm. Even Rosa was transfixed as the reflection of flames from the furnace leapt in her face. We saw dark figures move against a fury of metal, a gaping furnace, pipes and chutes, and saw coal plunge in a black shower into the fire with such a noise and stink that I was sure our hair would be singed off our heads and our eyeballs seared wide open for ever. I screamed: 'No, no, we must go,' and dragged her back to the door and out into the Derbyshire afternoon where even the dank air of the valley bottom smelled sweet by comparison.

None of the children seemed to notice as we passed, though Rosa paused for a moment as if tempted to speak to them. Then she marched away along the lane. 'Come on, I haven't shown you everything yet.' The ground was sodden, the mud had been churned up by cartwheels and on our left the river, as it emerged from the lead works, was a sullen brown. And then, after a few more yards, we came within sight of a familiar group of cottages.

'Now do you understand?'

'It's the Fairbrothers' house.'

'And look at the water.'

'It's very dirty.'

'When Stepfather built the lead works he still allowed people to stay in the cottages. It's usually the poorest, who can't work. Most of them get sick, like the Fairbrothers.'

I was afraid that she would make me visit the Fairbrothers but instead she led me up the hill, through a gap in the wall, and back towards Stukeley. 'You see. That's what bought Stukeley. That horror. You couldn't even bear to stay there one minute but children half your age are there twelve hours a day picking through the slag. I hate him. That man.'

We plodded on in silence because I had no idea how to comfort her, especially as it seemed to me that she had brought this latest misery on herself by going to the foundry. First I gripped her skirt, then tried to link my arm through hers but she shook me off. By the time we reached the hilltop we were panting and a drizzle was falling on our dirty faces. I wiped hers clean with my thumbs and at last she relented, held me tight and kissed me. 'Nothing you do hurts anyone. But I wanted you to realise. I hoped that if Max took over the foundry he would manage things better, but he won't. You saw Petey Fairbrother. He'll be dead soon, and all because of me.'

'Of you?'

'Oh yes. I live at Stukeley, don't I? And the money that paid for that monstrous house and those ridiculous gardens was from other people's misery. Sir Matthew says there's no proof that the children are ill because of the lead, he says some children are just born weak. He could move them out of the cottages where the water and air is so bad; or he could clean up the lead works – there are new ways of lining the pipes, Max says; or he could divert the water from the Stukeley gardens so they had a clean supply. There's lots he could do but he won't do a thing without proof. In fact he hates me because I tried to talk to him about it one day. He wouldn't listen and in the end I shouted at him and called him a murderer and that was it. So now you know. How can I live like this? What can I do?'

I stood beside her, head hanging, unable to work out whether what she told me was true, and quite sure that the kind man who gave me Latin lessons couldn't be knowingly responsible for all this.

Rosa stroked my head. 'I'm sorry, Mariella. Don't be angry with me. I was wrong to take you there and frighten you. But you mustn't be afraid. You are not to blame for any of it.'

'Nor are you, Rosa.'

'I *am* to blame. I am because I know about it and I eat at his table and sleep under his roof. And yet I do nothing. Nothing.' She clenched and unclenched her fists and her eyes were brilliant with rage.

'What could you do? What?'

'I don't know. Be clever. Know more. Run away.'

'Where to?'

Suddenly she laughed. 'To you of course. Now I have you. One day, I'll run away to you.'

Chapter Twenty-Two

The Crimea, 1855

The next morning the entire camp was up early and surging towards the trenches – officers, soldiers, stretcher bearers, orderlies, some still in yesterday's soiled uniform, eyes bloodshot, hair dishevelled, some with wounds dressed in bloody bandages. Regimental doctors, soldiers' wives and hangers-on all hurried out of the camp and stood waiting behind the allied defences. I tagged along with the other women, who carried baskets containing water and bread.

One, very tiny and bright-eyed, edged closer to me. 'You're something to do with Rosa Barr.'

There it was, the surge in the blood. 'Yes. I'm her cousin.'

'I thought so. We all say you look like her.'

'Do you know her well, then?'

'Oh yes. She was a good lady. Shared everything.'

'Was. You say, was?'

'Well, she's gone, obviously. She went off with her mad doctor and never came back. Surely you knew. We all thought that's why you're here.'

'Did you see them together?'

'Of course. He was forever up at the camp. Clamouring for her. So in the end she followed him.'

'What do you think happened to her?'

'I don't know.' She stood on tiptoe to whisper in my ear. 'But why would he have come back all wild and speechless, and her not seen again?'

I laughed; I nearly told her that Henry was my fiancé and I knew him to be incapable of harming a fly but the words died on my lips.

As there had still been no armistice hundreds of men had been left all night on the open ground in front of the Russian bastions and now once again the sun was climbing high and hot in the sky. The women said that yesterday some of the men had tried to drag their wounded fellows off the field but had been driven back under a hail of bullets. The mood was ugly, the soldiers foul-mouthed as they cursed the Russians for not allowing the armistice. The trouble was that the Russian wounded had fallen within their own bastions so only the French and English lay out in the sun. Therefore the Russians could afford to take their time.

We came to the brow of the hill where I had stood with Lady Mendlesham-Connors to peer out over Sebastopol. A crowd had collected because from here it was possible to view the city but be relatively safe from stray cannonballs. Lord Raglan was among the group of high-ranking military who were looking out at the Russian bastions, their highly polished buttons and buckles winking in the sun, Raglan himself identifiable because he had only one hand pressed to the small of his back and was surrounded by a cluster of aides with papers and field glasses. Their horses were tethered in the shade of a stone parapet further down the hill. On her own, a little apart and still on horseback, was Lady Mendlesham-Connors herself.

I tried to hide under the brim of my sun bonnet but it was too late, I'd been spotted. Lady Mendelsham pulled her horse's head away from the rest and came trotting over, bellowing my name so that others looked round and the soldiers' wives backed away. Somewhat to my surprise she was touchingly pleased to see me. 'Dear Miss Lingwood. How dreadful. This has been a disaster. My husband is beside himself. He won't speak to me. Raglan has as good as collapsed – they can't get a sensible order out of him. I can't bear to think of our men out there. Look, look.' She swung round so that she could train her field glasses on the bastions, sighed deeply and passed them to me.

Without the glasses all I had seen was the maze of trenches zigzagging across the plain before Sebastopol and the great Russian fortresses smoking under the hot blue sky. Sprinkled in front of them, like confetti, were patches of red, blue and the odd dot of white. Once I'd adjusted the lenses I realised that these colours were soldiers lying heaped together or scattered far apart: blue

French uniforms under the Malakov, red British coats under the Redan. Beside the fallen men were weapons, flags, ladders, wool bags, all the detritus of the war. Overhead vultures wheeled and plunged.

Lady Mendelsham's voice shook. 'They will die of thirst. I've seen it happen before. Their wounds will fester. We could still save some of them, if they'd only let us.'

'There are so many,' I said.

'What did you expect? The men go out in their hundreds. On this occasion it was a massacre. No hand-to-hand fighting, just bullets. I've told my husband it was all wrong but, as I said, he won't speak to me. They're all at their wits' end with Raglan because he won't make up his mind what to do next.'

'What could he do?'

'Get on his horse. Ride out there. Speak to the Russians. Pride and protocol prevents him. Not to mention fear, probably. Pride is what led to his lunatic orders. I do wonder. Well, that's it, I'm going home. I feel I can do no more good out here. Why don't you come with me? We could share a cabin, if need be. What do you think?'

'My maid is ill. My cousin . . .' I turned the glasses again to the scattered colours on the battlefield. Where was Newman?

'Well, the offer's there. You'll do no good here, getting underfoot.' She reached for the glasses and smacked her whip on the horse's rump. 'The pony I lent you, by the way. Took himself home. You might have said you'd got back safely. I was worried.' She pointed towards the cluster of horses and there was the unmistakable, battle-scarred Flight, flicking his tail and nudging up under his much taller neighbour's flank apparently with no other purpose than to annoy him.

The sun baked down and a breeze stirred in hot gusts. The sky was a burning pale yellow and the sea a shimmering rim of gold behind the Russian bastions. Nobody moved. Time dragged. The wounded men must be dying in front of our eyes. Occasionally a soldier threatened to rush out onto the field and grab his friend but was held back by others. From time to time there was a spatter of fire from either side and shells fell among the dead and wounded. Sometimes I wondered what I was waiting for: I needed to go back and see if Max was alive; I should return to Nora. But I couldn't. I stayed put, watching the shadows shorten at midday and then lengthen again, the birds performing hateful dives to feast on broken flesh.

Then at last in the mid-afternoon a murmur went up among the troops and those with field glasses pointed towards the harbour where it was said that British and Russian boats had met to discuss the terms of an armistice. A few minutes later there was a groan of relief as white flags appeared above the Redan and the Malakov and then were marched slowly forward across the open land. In a great wave hundreds of men rose from the trenches, French on one side, British on the other and hurried forward, bearing stretchers and spades.

I stumbled, heat-struck, behind the stretcher bearers, aware that just to my right a swarm of flies buzzed over a corpse. The smell of rotting meat was faint at first, then grew overpowering, rancid, sickening. The men were clinical, rushing from one body to another, and on the rare occasions when they found a flicker of life a shout went up and doctors and stretcher bearers raced to the spot. On and on I went, past the little group of Russians holding the white flag, through a shallow trench littered with bodies, and right up to the abattis which formed a shield in front of the Redan. Ranked along it were Russian officers in full uniform, very tall and well groomed, smoking cigars and gossiping. One of them caught my eye and gave me a lazy wink. Then his expression changed as he nudged his companion and pointed to me. I blushed while two pairs of insolent Russian eyes ran across my mouth, neck, breast, waist and feet. For those few seconds, as I froze under their impertinent gaze, I could have reached out and touched the enemy's great coat. The second officer nodded and made a little grimace so that his lips turned down, then threw a remark behind his shoulder to yet another man.

I rushed past them to reach the English bodies piled up along the barricade where a storm of bullets must have fallen among them. I'd recognised Newman by his bandaged hand. He was caught on the abattis, arms outstretched, back arched as if he'd been attempting an over ambitious gymnastic trick. His back was to me and his uniform was oddly tight as if he'd gained several inches of girth since we last met. When I tiptoed round the side of his body I saw that his face had been blown away and his brains were spattered in a dark, fly-blown sludge on the tangled branches. Only his jaw and ear were left. His second-best jacket was bursting at the seams because his body had swollen in the heat and his unbandaged hand was black. Yet this was definitely Newman: I knew his blond quiff of hair, the shape of his boyishly large ear, the injured hand.

I sat down on a clean patch of grass near by and waited for orderlies to come with a stretcher. The muslin on my bonnet blew back and forth in the hot wind and I covered my nose and mouth in an attempt to stifle the smell. But I forced myself to gaze at Newman's hanging body.

It was relatively quiet close to the Russian bastions; there were only the low voices of the enemy officers, the squabble and screech of vultures, unemotional orders from English doctors, an occasional muttered oath or prayer.

On the way back to the allied trenches I passed a party of a hundred or so men digging a pit into which would be tipped the corpses of the common soldiers. Ahead of me four stretcher bearers carried Newman's body towards the burial ground beside the camp. But I didn't wait to see him laid in the earth, there was no time. When I reached Max's hut I packed the contents of Rosa's box into my carpet bag and set off back towards the General Hospital to find out if Max, at least, was still alive.

PART FIVE

Chapter One

When I arrived back at the General Hospital in the late evening I found that the air of crisis had been replaced by a weary calm, though there was still a line of stretcher cases awaiting surgery. I hardly dared mention Max's name for fear of being told that he was dead but in the end I spoke to an orderly who directed me to a hut where he lay unconscious. For a long time I stared down at his face because I couldn't bear to see what they had done to the rest of his body. Despite his ashen complexion it was a good face, with none of his father's narrowness of feature or softness of chin, though he had inherited the high Stukeley bridge to the nose and hollows under the cheekbones. The thick, waving hair and dark brows were his mother's.

Then I plucked up the courage to look further along the bed. Two feet. Yes, there was no doubt, two feet at the end of two legs, one heavily bandaged.

Shaking with relief, I whispered into his ear in case he could hear me. First I told him I'd been up to the camp and rescued Rosa's things. Then, for want of any other cheerful news, I added that his stepmother was to marry a moth-collector half her size. When I waved away the flies prancing in his nostrils and eyelids he didn't react and they immediately flitted back. I put my hand in his but his fingers didn't move.

This was my first incursion into a ward since my visit to the Barrack Hospital in Skutari. I made a mental note of what I'd write in my next letter to Henry: *amply staffed by orderlies and doctors; smell of carbolic; patients covered in fresh linen and wearing hospital nightshirts; evidence of lavish supplies of medicines and bandages* . . . I did not intend to mention the grey rat crouched under one of the beds, the flies sucking at a bloody clod of lint covering a man's forehead, the filthy apron worn by a passing surgeon. Nor would I write about the wagon into which I had seen four corpses being loaded or the sobs of an officer who had lost an arm and an eye in a spray of grapeshot.

A portly doctor came in, squinted along the ward and approached. When he bowed over my hand I noted that his whiskers must have taken half an hour to groom and I wondered why so august an individual should bother with me. He told me that against his better judgement they had spared Captain Stukeley's leg because he'd been so insistent, though even if he survived he wouldn't walk for months, if at all. In the meantime he would probably die of infection, as they'd warned him. It was all very well to try and knit a broken bone but a man's chances of recovery were much higher if there was a good clean amputation and the stump kept moist with champagne until it healed. It turned out that the reason for his deference was that he somehow knew of my connection with Dr Henry Thewell, of whom he spoke perhaps too effusively – brilliant surgeon . . . highest survival rate of patients . . . utterly dedicated . . . shame he got so sick.

'By the way, Miss Lingwood, it might interest you to know that I have a pile of books left here by Dr Thewell. I'll look them out for you.' Then he cast an expert eye over Max's bandaged leg and darted away to be important elsewhere, before I could ask any awkward questions.

I sat a little longer by Max's bed, stupefied by the hot, fly-infested air, the presence of so much mutilation in an enclosed space and the way the men twitched under their sheets when there was a burst of shelling above Sebastopol. The hut was haunted by all the sick men who had passed through it in the foul Crimean winter, and by Henry and Rosa who had, at separate times, worked in these wards. I imagined them pursuing each other from bed to bed, he in his stained frock coat, she neat and lithe despite her bulky dress, united in their frantic belief that given enough strength of will and the right conditions, everything could be changed for the better.

Max never stirred, though when I held my palm half an inch from his lips I felt a faint warmth which proved he was alive. Nora's beads had been pushed half under his pillow and before I left I wound them back round his fingers.

Chapter Two

Narni.
20 June 1855

Dearest Mariella,

You will probably be as surprised to receive a letter from me, the sick man of Narni, as I am to be writing to you, Mariella Lingwood, in Balaklava, of all places. Your letters astonish me. There you are, actually in Balaklava harbour, a place that haunts me, waking and sleeping. Though I have read and reread them both many times I am thwarted by the usual Mariella restraint. She writes of the Crimean Peninsula as she might write of Clapham Common. My dear girl, I simply cannot imagine you there. When I think of you in your wonderful gowns, neat, precise, shy, I cannot see you at Balaklava where everything is the opposite of you. How did it come about? You were here, I remember, though I was so feverish at times I scarcely knew the difference between dream and reality but Lyall assures me that it was indeed you, my little Mariella, with your maid, that we went for a picnic among the ruins and that you then rushed off to the war to look for your cousin Rosa. Still I would not have believed it had I not received those letters, marked Balaklava.

As I say, I have been very ill but now I feel so well I wonder what I am doing here, languishing in the heat of Italy when I could be in the Crimea, or at home, perhaps of some use in the hospital. Lyall is with me still and very hopeful of my complete recovery before long, though he thinks it unlikely that I'll be joining you at the war. He assures me there's not much wrong with my chest now. Only general weakness in all muscles, and especially my stomach, which I'm sure will improve with time. I remember your visit to me in Narni with some anxiety. Your father has written to me in considerable irritation about your sudden decision to go to Russia. He blames me. Dear Mariella, if I said anything to disturb you, please forgive me. Lyall tells me that sometimes in my delirium I rave like a madman.

When I saw your handwriting I was suddenly overwhelmed by a flood of memories. The strongest? The turret room in the Elms: your grey eyes full of trust and affection and hope. And now the memory tortures me. I should have taken you in my arms and claimed you but you were my Mariella, my innocent sister-cousin and I felt that to touch you would be to shatter you. But now I regret that moment, as I regret so many. How lovely to feel an English wind and see rain falling on an English lawn. I would give all I possess to stroke your cool English cheek and hold your undemanding hand in mine.

By the way, I am wondering if you have yet managed to meet up with Miss Rosa Barr. When I saw her she was living in one of the camps, I believe, among the men. If you are with her, please send my regards. Remember me also to the doctors in the General Hospital, if you go there, particularly Radley and Holloway.

The heat is trying here. My room is airless and I am still not strong enough to walk far. A carriage ride shakes up my wretched bones. I spend a great deal of time at the window and know the habits of everyone in the street. In the afternoon they bring out their rickety chairs and sit in the shade. They watch me and I watch them. I find it hard to imagine the Crimea in sunshine. I hope the wounded are decently dressed in hospital clothing. In January the men lay in the leaky hospital bell tents covered by their filthy uniform coats because we had nothing else to give them. Rosa told me that there were flannel nightshirts and waistcoats in the stores which hadn't been issued because we doctors were unaware of their existence so hadn't put in a requisition. I wish to God I had known before.

Lyall is determined to stay with me here, though I certainly no longer need a doctor. He says that to be in the presence of so many antiquities more than makes up for the lack of excitement I provide. He can't walk five paces in Narni, he says, without falling over a Roman step or raising his eyes to a Roman arch. Perhaps we will both be back in England by autumn.

But really, what I should love to do most of all is return to the

Crimea. I cannot bear to think that everyone is there without me. I feel so powerless. And perhaps your cousin Rosa is still lost. Have you any news of her, my dear?

Mariella, I hardly know how to sign off this letter.

God bless you,

Henry Thewell

Chapter Three

The Crimea, 1855

When Nora sent me back to the General Hospital two days later I found Max in much the same condition as before, whereas the patient in the next bed, who'd been shot during the same assault, was sitting up with the remains of his arm swathed in a bloody bandage and supported by a stump pillow, cracking jokes about emulating that most famous amputee of all, Lord Raglan, who had lost his right arm at Waterloo but lived to command an army in the next war. If only I hadn't intervened Max might be on the mend too. As it was the infection in his ruined leg was probably poisoning him, inch by inch.

I leaned over and hissed into his ear: 'Get better. Now. Please, Max. Don't die . . .' and then started back as he opened his eyes.

'Hoped you'd gone home,' he said. 'How's Nora?'

'Nora is improving all the time.'

'Glad to hear it.' He dozed while I stood at a distance, a little flower of joy opening inside me because he was better. After a few minutes he woke up again. 'Still here.'

'As you see.'

'I suppose I have you to thank that I have two legs. You and your Dr Thewell.'

'I only said—'

'Odd thing, I try to get rid of you, but back you come. Bloody persistent. Well, let me thank you properly, Miss Lingwood.' I gave him my hand but instead of shaking it he kissed it on the underside of the wrist near the palm. His black, morphine-stung eyes never left my face and I felt my pulse beat against his lips.

'You must recover,' I said. 'The doctor assures me that amputation was the only possible way of saving you. If you don't get well, I'll be to blame.'

'Right, then. Can't have that. Will live.' He seemed to be fading into sleep but as I withdrew my hand he said, 'Besides, there's Rosa.'

After that Nora's fever returned, there was a fresh bout of cholera in the camps and the nurses were too busy to keep an eye on her. When I was at last able to visit Max again I found that his bed was now occupied by a lieutenant with a bandaged shoulder.

Although the poor sick man was sleeping I gave his hand a shake and hissed: 'What are you doing here? Where is Captain Stukeley?'

He couldn't speak. In a frenzy I ran the length of the ward and found an orderly. 'What happened to Captain Stukeley?'

'Captain Stukeley?'

He was so stupid and slow I didn't wait to ask again. A nurse in a pepper-and-salt gown was walking between the huts. 'Captain Stukeley. Please, do you know what happened to him?'

She shook her head and walked on. I raced from hut to hut and at last found the elegantly bearded doctor I had seen on my first visit. 'Please, sir, what happened to Captain Stukeley? Did he . . .?'

'Somewhat recovered. So much so we sent him to Skutari, and I'm hoping thence he may go to our new hospital at Renkioi, and so on home. He didn't want to go, kicked up the devil of a fuss but he's far better away from here with that leg. Less chance of infection. And he'll be no more use to the war, in any event. By the way, I have Dr Thewell's books for you, if you'd like them.'

While he made his ponderous way along the row of huts I paced up and down in an effort to regain a little composure. Had Max thought that I failed to visit him again because I didn't care whether he lived or died? He'd left no message, even for Nora. How typical of him to be so ungrateful and perverse.

The doctor returned a few minutes later with a large and weighty parcel, loosely wrapped in brown paper and string. 'Some important medical volumes here,' he said. 'I'm sure Dr Thewell will be missing them.'

The afternoon was very hot and the parcel awkward to carry but I struggled down as far as Balaklava harbour where I sat on a crate near the water. Half a dozen or so ponies were tethered close by in a little compound, and a heap of baskets due for transportation up to the trenches was being unloaded from a cart by an Armenian peddler. After a few minutes, as a ship began her slow withdrawal from her tight-packed mooring, I realised that I had attracted quite a little crowd of spectators so I got up and walked on towards the Castle Hospital. The parcel of books remained on the crate where I had left it and I turned a deaf ear to the voices shouting after me in a variety of tongues.

Chapter Four

Lord Raglan died, some said of a broken heart because of his role in the calamitous assault on the Redan, others that he'd been struck with cholera, though Nora said he'd lingered too long for that to be true. His coffin was carried on a 9-pounder gun, escorted by the Grenadier guard of honour who would accompany him from the British headquarters to Kazatch Bay, near the French-occupied harbour of Kamiesch, from where it would be taken by steamer to England.

So Lord Raglan, at least, was going home. Nora was well enough to get up and watch the gun carriage begin its journey past a mile-long line of troops, fifty men and three officers from each regiment, and behind them dense crowds of silent British and allied soldiers. 'This is the best bit of organisation we're like to see for a long time,' she said. 'These men may well weep. Word among the nurses in the hospital is that Raglan was the best the British military could provide, so heaven help us.'

We all waited for something else significant to happen but nothing did. The allied generals seemed to be licking their wounds after the ignominious defeat of 18 June and despite their besieged state the Russians were as defiant as ever: their bastions were all but impregnable and the Russian spirit, as demonstrated by the cheerful, well-groomed officers who had paraded by the barricades while we collected our wounded, was undaunted. Raglan's replacement, Major-General Simpson was widely known to have pleaded not to be given the promotion; it was said that those in government opposed to his appointment thought him a raving lunatic and that he and the French commander, Pelissier, had no respect for each other at all. So there was stalemate.

After another fortnight Nora was sometimes strong enough to perform light nursing duties such as feeding the weakest invalids beef tea or sago pudding and applying poultices to their skin. In another week she was able to clean and dress wounds. Since her recovery meant that I had now lost even the most spurious excuse for my presence at the hospital I lived in daily expectation of being sent away, but instead Mrs Shaw Stuart handed me the keys to the linen store and put me in charge of the heaps of sheets, pillow-cases, towels, bandages, aprons and nightshirts that were daily required at the hospital. In addition I was expected to give needle-work lessons to soldiers' wives who wished to make a living on their return to England. We began unambitiously with buttonholes and as a reward for diligence graduated to lazy daisy so that after a few days my pupils had black and white flowers sprawled along the battered hems of their petticoats.

Meanwhile the now familiar mantra boomed in my head. Find Rosa. Find Rosa. Each time I'd reached the same dead end: Henry banging on the door of her hut, and the Inkerman cave from which he came back alone. If I could only go there to see for myself and understand the lie of the land, but more than ever I was pinned to the hospital, and since Newman's death and Max's banishment I had no escort.

In desperation I consulted the list Nora and I had made on our first morning in Balaklava: *Item Three. Go among the troops.* In fact this was much easier than I'd ever imagined. We didn't need to go among the troops, the troops came to us in their dozens, driven up to the hospital by heatstroke, wounds received under fire from the Russian bastions, dysentery, typhus or cholera. We talked to everyone about Rosa – my sewing women, orderlies, tradesmen, peddlers, patients, visitors. Always the same story: 'Wasn't she the one who went up to the cave and never came back?'

Late one afternoon Mrs Whitehead appeared in the doorway of the linen store and beckoned me outside. Though I was now reduced to wearing the least number of clothes possible while still remaining decent, I was soaked in perspiration while Mrs Whitehead's face was beetroot red because she still had to wear the heavy gown and sash that marked her out as one of Miss Nightingale's nurses. We stood in the shade, covered our faces with muslin scarves and fanned ourselves vigorously because, as if the rats were not plague enough, the hospital, like everywhere else in the camps, was under attack from swarms of flies.

She said, 'I think you should come up to my ward. I have a patient there who claims to have seen your cousin Rosa.'

When I threw back my veil a couple of flies the size of collar studs smacked onto my lips. 'Did he say when?'

'A week ago.'

'Did he say where?'

'He's been on picket duty up by the Tchernaya line. You should come.'

'Wait while I find Nora.'

The patient, O'Byrne, was a gaunt Irishman whose feet dangled several inches beyond the end of his hospital bed. When I asked in a whisper what sickness had laid him low Nora shrugged and said, 'Later, Mariella.'

Though the windows of the hut had been covered in nets, and doors at either end were open to encourage a draught, poor O'Byrne was still the victim of a concerted attack by flies which zoomed down in droves onto his swollen hands and cracked lips. Nevertheless when he saw me he smiled appreciatively, revealing just two rotten teeth. 'Well, now, miss, aren't I the lucky one to be receiving such a lovely-looking visitor as you.'

'I was wondering if you would repeat to Miss Lingwood and Mrs McCormack the story you told me earlier,' said Mrs Whitehead.

'Mrs McCormack, is it? Now what part of Ireland might you be from?'

'Sligo.'

'Is that right?' His eyes were misty. 'And which of your family was lost?'

'None that I'll be talking about with you,' was her reply. 'Now what's this you've been saying about Miss Rosa Barr?'

He was not one to be hurried in front of a captive audience. 'Of course we'd all heard of this girl who'd gone missing up by Inkerman. Your cousin now, miss, was it?' The tip of his tongue came out to moisten his lips and six fat black spots landed on his mouth. 'We'd been given a description of her: tall and slender, with a head of golden hair. And we'd heard that she'd had a lovers' meeting up in some cave and never come back.' His eyes flickered over my face. 'So, anyway, it's a warm night and I'm mighty bored waiting to see what might be hurled at us next from them Russian bastions, so I takes myself for a stroll beyond the French pickets by the Tchernaya. It's cool up there, looking over the river, with the sun going down.' Pause while he closed his eyes and passed his hand across his face. Then he stared up to the ceiling, as if a vision had suddenly appeared. 'Far below me, I see her, by the water. A girl in a blue dress. She is just standing there, in her bare feet, with the water rushing over the hem of her skirts, and her hair lifting in the wind that's blowing. She's so still, and it's such an odd sight after so many weeks of being in the camps among the men, that I say nothing and do nothing, but after a while I look about me, to see who else might be noticing her. It's not safe down by the water, you could be picked off any moment by one of them Russian sharpshooters up on the hills. And then I thinks to myself: Well, I do believe it's her, the girl that's gone missing. I shall make my way down there and see what I can do for her. I notices that she holds her hands behind her and is walking back and forth just there in the shallows of the river, and I can't see her face.'

I disliked the man's maudlin blue eyes as he glanced up at me slyly from time to time to make sure that I was drinking in every word, but my hands were shaking. When he was silent I found myself both applauding his art and furious that I had fallen into his trap.

'So I begins to wind my way down to the river, though it's dangerous, with the French pickets watching me on one side, the Ruskies on the other. And just for a minute or so the woman is out of sight, as I take a bit of a tumble on a difficult piece of terrain. And when the river again comes into view, she is gone.'

He closed his eyes, as if in a reverie. Only a fool would have anticipated any other kind of ending but I was limp with dashed hopes.

'So I suppose you went looking along the river and couldn't find her,' said Nora.

'Exactly so. Up and down I went. I even called her name, since we all knew it. *Rosa. Rosa.* But there was no sign. In the end it grew dark and I felt my life to be in danger, so I came away.'

'It could have been anyone,' I said. 'A Russian woman from Sebastopol.'

'It could that. But I swear it was the English girl. There was something about her, the way she moved, her hair falling across her back and face, the ragged nature of her gown, that made me sure it was her.'

'And that's it, is it?' said Nora.

'That's it.'

I gave him a coin and thanked him. It was a great relief to leave the stifling hut and emerge into the warm, salty air where Nora and I parted from Mrs Whitehead and walked past the last of the hospital huts. She was still quite weak and slow, and when we reached the fortress we sat with our backs to the broken wall facing the sea, our legs stretched out before us and our skirts tucked up to cool our calves and ankles.

'He's the sort to give the Irish a bad name,' said Nora.

'What was the matter with him?'

'I suspect he's been over-friendly with the women up at Kamiesh, Miss Lingwood, and the association hasn't agreed with his constitution.'

'And what about his story?'

'Well, now, I'd say it was stuff and nonsense. Can you see Rosa all airy-fairy down by some river? What he didn't mention was the amount of liquor he'd taken before he went on his late evening stroll.'

'Yet there were some details that sounded like her. The fact that she was by the river ... the blue dress ... Perhaps I should go up there, just in case.'

'You'll do no such thing. You're to wait until I'm a little stronger and I'll come with you, if you must go.'

We were silent for a while as the indigo sea sighed and shrank back and a slight, cool breeze got up. 'While you were ill, Nora, I wished I had asked you more about Rosa. Sometimes I think you must know her far better than I do, having lived with her all those years.'

'Well, now, is it too late?'

'What was Rosa like, when you knew her at Stukeley?'

'Probably as she had always been. I have found that with her, over the years, she never changes. She is insatiable to know what is going on in people's lives, and how she might be a part of them. We used to talk a great deal about the opportunities that might one day open up for her. She always said that you, Mariella

Lingwood, her truest friend, were far away in London, but one day she would get back to you and make a life.'

'I cannot surely have been her only friend.'

'She had no time for most of the other young ladies who came to call. I fear she did not put herself out much for them. And of course try as she might she could never make friends among the village girls, it was too unequal.'

'She had Max.'

'Ah, but he was seldom there. By the time I arrived at Stukeley he was nearly ready to take up his commission in the army. He used to come home in bursts, and he and she would go galloping off together away from the valley or spend whole nights in front of the fire talking and talking and then he'd be gone, leaving her more desolate than ever.'

'What did they talk about?'

'Well, how would I know? Her usual obsessions I would imagine. You. London. The future. What work she might do. But he was not a reliable companion. He was a wild boy, what with his drinking friends and his love affairs.' I caught her sideways glance at me.

'I thought Rosa was the one Max loved.'

'So she was. He always came back to Rosa. But that didn't stop him casting his eye about. And he nearly died that time in Australia, you know. One of his fellows did perish, of thirst. Some lunatic idea of setting off to find a source of water in the western desert. At any rate, that little experience seemed to satisfy his wanderlust for a while and he came back to Stukeley more often.'

'He certainly thinks a great deal of you, Nora. He was very angry with me because we had come to the Crimea and you had fallen ill.'

'Well, so he should think a deal of me. The welcome Rosa and I gave him each time he came home. Our own private parties we used to have, when nobody was about late at night in the kitchens. Those were the best times.'

'And were you happy at Stukeley?'

'As I have said, I developed a fondness for those two. And Lady Isabella became very dependent on me, which is something, I suppose. But I had no liking for Sir Matthew Stukeley, or his other son, and generally I loathed the house – I could not get used to its extravagance.'

'So how was it you came to be there in the first place?'

'I needed work. My great-grandmother had been from a family of Derbyshire lead miners, but then she was sweet-talked by a roving Irishman name of McCormack who carried her across to Sligo. We'd heard nothing of the old family over the years but when the ship docked in Liverpool it seemed to me that Derbyshire was the one place in England where I might find a little kindness among people of my own. So I went on and on walking and asking directions until at last I found someone who'd heard of these relatives of mine, name of Fairbrother, and that's how I came at last to Stukeley.'

Fairbrother. When I closed my eyes the Crimean sunset played across my lids and the warm stone at my back was soothingly immutable. What was it Henry had said about the invisible soup of the dead? Now it seemed to me I was jostled so close by the absent, both living and dead, that they almost suffocated me.

'I found no comfort among the Fairbrothers, that's for sure. One poor widow and two living children, one of those half dead.'

'Only two children.'

'It was clear that I could not stay with them in my penniless state, so I ups to the great house and I says who I am and where I'm from and whom I'm connected with and at that moment it is Rosa who comes to the kitchen and sees me there with my head in my hand. I remember the scent of her to this day when she touched my arm though I had the dirt of a hundred roads on me. She asked what I could do and I said that I was best at nursing the sick and she said, "Well, then, you might be just the person we are looking for." Then she made me tea and sat beside me while I drank and those blue eyes of hers never for one instant left my face.'

For several minutes longer we stayed side by side under the fortress. The sea rolling against the cliff and the quiet bustle down at the hospital were less vivid to me than the kitchen at Stukeley Hall, where every utensil was large and new, the servants ranged about in their starched uniforms, hostile or suspicious, while Rosa, with her unerring nose for an opportunity, seized a pot holder, grasped the kettle, asked a dozen questions and broke as many unwritten rules.

But then Nora put her heavy hand on my shoulder to lever herself up and told me it was time to go back, the men would be clamouring for their suppers.

Chapter Five

Derbyshire, 1844

Sir Matthew Stukeley was kinder to me than he was to anyone else in the house and I loved him for it. Our lessons were irregular and depended on whether or not I could slip away, for instance while Rosa and her mother were engaged in the mutual endurance test that was Rosa's occasional piano practice.

I liked going to the library. It gave me feelings close to those I had during that first walk in the rain with Henry up the garden at Fosse House under a shared umbrella: a quiver of excitement, a sense of being singled out, of having pushed myself beyond my usual boundaries. And I was soothed by the beautifully waxed wood of the library table, the slanting light that fell through the long windows, the view of green sloping lawns beyond the glass.

I treated the Latin language like an embroidery pattern to be filled in a stitch at a time. And as I ploughed through the translations and made a neat list of new words in a little notebook provided by Sir Matthew I appreciated the tranquillity of the room, his touching dedication to our work, the sense of order as the unknown part of the Latin poem shrank and the English translation grew. I liked the fragrance of cigar that hung about him, hiding the faintest whiff of the lead works. I associated him with the enchanted library, with spotless cuffs, with the sense that though he was as old as my father he was not my father, so was therefore both interesting and reassuring at the same time.

He sat at one end of the table with me on his right hand. I liked the way his clean-nailed index finger ran along the words. I liked the neatness of the open book set at a precise angle on the wide, empty table. I liked the fact that in the library at least there was no danger of intrusion from anyone else, and that all I had to do was sit still and listen. His voice had a slight Derbyshire intonation and his sentences were well formed and clipped, almost as if I could hear the full stops.

He and I were extremely polite to each other. When Rosa wasn't looking I had made him a pen-wiper embroidered with his initials and he spread it out appreciatively and said he would make a point of always using it. 'It is a miracle to me that you have made so much of two letters, M and S, and formed them into a monogram. Tell me again, what is the name of this stitch?'

'Satin stitch.'

'Well, I hardly like to think how long it must have taken those busy little fingers of yours.'

'Barely an hour, really.'

My hand rested on the table and he turned it over to study the fingertips. 'As I thought. Poor little fingers, covered with pricks from the needle.'

'I wear a thimble but I'm careless sometimes.' Nobody had ever given my hands this amount of attention, not even Rosa, and now I thought about it my pink-tipped fingers did look very capable and dainty.

He asked how I had spent the day so I gave him an edited version which made no mention of our sorties into the village, to Rosa's secret places or to her wilder games with Max. He was interested in my father's work and the houses he was contracted to build along the new railway lines, and he questioned me closely about Henry, whom he used to call my *adoptive brother*.

'He is a fortunate boy,' he said, 'to have been taken under the wing of your parents. And to have found such an affectionate little sister.'

'Oh, I'm not his sister. I'm more a friend than a sister.'

'And what is the difference, Mariella, in the way a friend might behave, as opposed to a sister?'

That was a difficult question. 'A friend is *chosen*. Of course I don't have a sister or a brother but I should think I would feel the same way about them all the time. Whereas my friendship with Henry grows and grows. I never know how it will end.'

'And am I a friend now, Mariella?'

I peeked into his eyes and my heart gave a little leap to think this important man might wish to be my friend. His smile was teasing and it occurred to me that I might be able to please him even more. 'I'm not sure.'

'What would I have to do to prove myself your friend?'

'I couldn't say.' I gave another little sideways peep. 'I should have to think about it.'

He laughed aloud and pressed my hand. 'Mariella, you asked me if you could see what is kept in those little drawers over there. Well, I'll show you if you like.'

'Yes, please. If you don't mind.'

'Come over here, then. Sit in this low chair.' He opened the top drawer, removed a folded linen cloth and spread it across my knees, very tenderly, in the way that his footman might have tucked a napkin over my lap at dinner. The side of his head came quite close to my face and I noticed how the hair above his ears grew so thinly that I could see where each strand emerged from his scalp. 'These things are very precious so it's important that we look after them.'

He then removed a drawer from the cabinet and placed it on my lap. I gave a little gasp because though I had been expecting specimens of some kind, butterflies or moths, I was not at all prepared for *beetles*. But there they were, perhaps a dozen, pinned neatly onto the stretched cloth at the bottom of the drawer, each one with precisely arranged legs and a beady body.

He was laughing at me again. 'Forgive me. I couldn't help it. I wanted to see your reaction and you didn't disappoint me. I was sure you wouldn't scream, like most girls. But be brave now and study them carefully. Aren't they beautiful?' He perched on the arm of my chair and pointed out a rotund little specimen. 'These are all water beetles, and this one is known as a whirlygig. Oh, but just a minute, we don't want your hair getting mixed up with the exhibits. Allow me.' He scooped back my hair until it was all behind my shoulders and held loosely at the back of my neck. 'If you look very closely you'll see that the upper part of his eye is designed to see above water, the lower part, beneath, and that's because the poor little chap is destined to spend his entire life spinning about actually on the surface.'

Was it an accident, was Sir Matthew even aware, that his index finger was very softly stroking the back of my neck under my hair? The sensation was at once thrilling and disturbing. But after a moment he took the drawer from me. 'Come and look over here. Take your pick and we'll examine another.' I put aside the napkin and went closer. As he opened the drawers one by one he laid his hand on my shoulder, giving it a little squeeze each time I exclaimed over a row of spiders, caterpillars and even frogs. A strange smell rose from the cabinet, both clean and dirty at the same time. I discovered that my shoulder got an extra warm squeeze when I leaned over and paid attention to a particularly colourful or strange specimen.

After a few minutes of this I grew flustered by the way that the routine of our lessons had changed so abruptly and I said I ought to go and find Rosa. At once he became much more formal. 'Of course. Of course.' As usual we shook hands solemnly before I left, and I thanked him. But as I reached the door he held me back and beckoned me into the middle of the room, where I stood with my hand on a chair-back, waiting.

'Do you remember today's poem?' He repeated in a low, slow voice: '*My lady says to me that there is none / with whom she'd rather spend the days than I* . . . When I read that line, Mariella, I thought of you and me, and how little time we have together, and what fun we have.'

As usual I felt strange when I left the library. The fact that I still kept the lessons a secret from Rosa bothered me and I was a little frightened by the way Sir Matthew had spoken that bit of poetry in a throaty voice with his eyes very fond as he looked at me. So I resolved that I wouldn't go back again, and that I would tell Rosa about the lessons straight away.

Then I thought: But if I do, she'll be angry with me so I'll just drop the lessons, and she won't find out. But then Sir Matthew would be offended and I badly wanted him to like me. And anyway, it had been gratifying to make him laugh and it would be interesting to try and do it again. And next time, or the time after, would be the one when I finally plucked up the courage and asked him to do me a very big favour.

Chapter Six

The Crimea, 1855

The latest batch of Russian deserters brought news that their generals were planning an attack on the River Tchernaya, south-east of Inkerman near the Traktir bridge, and that the entire Russian army was on battle alert. Reports from French spies and gleanings from Russian newspapers bore out this information so that night after night the allied army was up in the small hours in preparation for a Russian offensive which we assumed would be their final attempt to rout us from our entrenched positions above Sebastopol.

No attack came, though the camp remained restless and battle-ready. The regimental hospitals emptied themselves of convalescents in case of front-line casualties and Nora reported that anyone who could be spared from the cholera wards was kept busy making beds for the anticipated influx of wounded. I had to audit my entire store and prepare a mountain of fresh linen, and supplies of lint and plaster were requisitioned for the coming onslaught. My sewing classes ground to a halt for want of pupils who drifted back to the camps and waited there for something to happen.

On the night of the fifteenth we heard that there had been a massive movement of Russian troops from their positions on the hills to the east of the River Tchernaya and our beds were shaken by shellfire from the trenches above Sebastopol. But then, in the small hours, there was a sudden volley of guns from the hills north of Balaklava and Mrs Whitehead's face, bedecked by a startlingly white nightcap – a gift from me – rose from the pillow. 'That'll be the Rooshans (Russians),' she said. 'It's begoon (begun).'

We got up and dressed hurriedly though I had no idea what for. The French and Sardinians, who were positioned on the Fedoukine

Heights opposite the Russian encampment above the Tchernaya, would bear the brunt of an attack so on the face of it we had no particular function in the coming battle, but then, as Nora said, it wasn't human nature to sit still in one place while history was going on near by. And in the end it was Rosa, of course, who made up my mind. O'Byrne's story might well have been the fanciful ramblings of a syphilitic Irishman, but his sighting of a girl in a blue gown by the Tchernaya was the last word we'd had of her.

Nora and I had a long trek up past the General Hospital at Kadikoi, behind the British and Sardinian camps and into the hills. An entire army of camp followers was on the move, the wealthier on horseback, the rest – wives, tradesmen, members of the ordnance teams and navvies – on foot. Every face was turned to the incessant pummelling of the guns, some exhilarated, others full of dread but the sense of common purpose raised the spirits, the lassitude of the last weeks was all gone, something was happening and we were part of it. When Nora stumbled I reached out my hand and then thrust my arm through hers. Once or twice I asked if she was strong enough to continue and she responded curtly: 'I have faced a worse march than this in my time.'

'Have you, Nora? Was that in Ireland?'

Her silence was forbidding.

'I suppose there are some things that we never forget,' I said.

'Nor should.'

'I have never forgotten Stukeley, though I was hardly there six weeks. Everything about it remains powerfully in my mind. Perhaps because we left so suddenly. Sir Matthew took against us, you see.'

'Well, that would be like him, he was often a harsh, unpredictable man.'

'I always felt for Rosa, that she had to nurse him at the end, when they disliked each other so much.'

'Do you know, Mariella, I sometimes think it was a deliberate choice on his part, to make her suffer by choosing her to be the only one he would tolerate in the sickroom.'

'How terrible. Why would he do that?'

'He was forever trying to punish her for refusing to be the type of stepdaughter I presume he would have wanted. She was a fool to herself for agreeing to nurse him but then you know Rosa. If someone was needy she never could resist them, no matter who they were or how they'd treated her in the past. And he had few other friends at the end. Indeed, I could put it even more strongly than that. There are some who are convinced that his fall from the horse, in a crowded lane, was by no means an accident.'

'You don't mean that he was pushed?'

'Oh nothing so obvious. Perhaps he fell and wasn't helped up in time to avoid those trampling hooves. Perhaps there was a little jostling round his horse. Either way, none of the witnesses could give a clear account of what had happened.'

The cannon-fire was so close that the ground juddered and set little stones rolling on the track and the sky ahead was dark with smoke. 'And your relation, Mrs Fairbrother, what did she think of Sir Matthew?'

'If the poor soul thought anything at all it was the same as everyone else. She feared him and she disliked him in equal measure I'd say. But then he could be charming as well as curt. He had his dark little ways – the villagers learned to keep a particular eye on their young daughters when he was about – but he could also make a grand gesture. I believe that it was my connection with the family that persuaded him to employ me so I'm grateful for that, although he couldn't stand the sight of me and would never so much as let me change the sheets on his bed when he was sick.'

'What happened to the Fairbrothers in the end?'

'Well, now, that was something I never quite got to the bottom of. Before Max would take up his commission in the army he did an odd sort of deal with his father; that he would forgo any entitlement to the estate if the wretched cottages down by the river were demolished and the families found a home elsewhere, but until that happened he would not go near his regiment. So my poor cousins the Fairbrothers lived in a brand-new place in the village, and though they hadn't the wits to thrive, at least they had some comfort. None of the family is living now.'

A number of officers' wives overtook us on horseback, followed by the redoubtable Mrs Seacole who rode alone, her face framed by a flapping sun bonnet and her mule laden with panniers. Our conversation was at an end because as we drew nearer the battlefield the din of musket-fire and artillery was bone-shaking even though we learned from returning ambulance wagons that the fighting was already in its dying gasps, and that the Russians were on the brink of a crushing defeat.

We gathered on a hilltop behind a throng of British onlookers, just above reserve squadrons of English and French cavalry in perfect formation though their horses were wild-eyed and straining forward. To our left French and Sardinian troops were lined up waiting for the signal to attack and others were streaming down the hillside. In the valley there was chaos under clouds of smoke, a churning mass of bodies, the clash of bayonets, and the pounding of cannonballs fired from the great guns positioned above.

Though the River Tchernaya was narrow and shallow it flowed between steep little banks upon which the soldiers floundered. Along the hillside to our right ran an aqueduct raised several feet above the ground to carry water from a reservoir in the hills to Sebastopol harbour. Bodies were piled up along its perpendicular sides, felled by enemy gunfire as they attempted to cross. Within ten minutes of our arrival, wave upon wave of Russians had fallen as the French and Sardinians chased them across the river and up the hillsides.

I had already learned that in a war everything looks better from a distance. This scene, a riot of blues, browns and reds, was from the same ideal of battle that had made my heart thump for joy at the sight of the march past of troops before Buckingham Palace. From my lofty height even the clambering of Russian soldiers on the sides of the aqueduct resembled the antics of children in a party game. The allies had waited for the Russians to reach halfway up the valley sides before chasing them back under blistering fire, leaving heaps of brown-coated bodies as if the retreating army was a carelessly packed bale shedding straw. At one point I saw a line of half a dozen Russians bowled over by a single cannonball.

After an hour the remains of the Russian army had retreated to their encampment on the heights and a quiet fell over the battle-field, punctuated from time to time by the odd burst of fire. I half expected everyone to get up, shake themselves down and walk away, but no, the fallen men stayed fallen and gradually, from all sides, a stream of soldiers, officers, doctors and orderlies moved doggedly forward and started work among the dead and wounded.

I followed Nora across parched, tussocky grass. The field was still smoking and from time to time a crack of rifle-fire was followed by a howl of pain. A nearby French orderly cursed the retreating Russians who were known to shoot indiscriminately both at wounded enemy soldiers and the fatigue parties who went out to carry them from the field, but the threat meant nothing to me. I was too absorbed by the thousands of dead men, their atrocious wounds, the river banks draped with bodies, the stained waters of the Tchernaya and my own inadequacy as we began our search for the living. Some had fallen as if frozen in time with their arms flung out and their expressions fixed in surprise or excitement, others had curled up to die, hands over their faces. While some had stomachs, legs, arms even heads missing altogether, others appeared untouched. They were all so fleshy, so recently scythed down, so way beyond my experience in their sudden shift from life to death that I felt as light and helpless as a feather in the wind.

When a living man called out to me I knelt to give him a sip of water. His head was too heavy to support in my hand so I rested it on my lap and it was only then that I realised from the colour of his bloody uniform that he was Russian. His foreignness repulsed me, the coarseness of his features and skin, his black cropped hair, beaky nose, scabby beard, the fact that though his head was pillowed by my thigh, he and I had no single thing in common, not even a word. But then he raised his hand and took a loose lock of my hair between his finger and thumb. His skin was ingrained with dirt and the thumbnail discoloured by a bruise, yet he held the strand softly and rubbed it to and fro, as if to polish it. Then he looked up, gave me a misty smile and tried to speak.

'What?' I whispered. 'How can I help you?'

His lips again formed a word and I put my face nearer his.

'What are you saying?'

A French ambulance party was approaching; they were upon us, had plucked him up by his knees and armpits so that he gave a howl of pain, dropped him onto a stretcher and carried him away down to the river where he would lie among other enemy wounded.

I stayed where they had left me and wrapped the same lock of hair round my finger. I swear that the word he had spoken was *Rosa.*

Nora was a few feet away kneeling over a French soldier as she raised his arm, supported it against her bosom and applied a neat bandage to a gaping wound in his wrist. Despite his lack of understanding she was chatting away to him and I could well imagine the mix of encouragement and instruction as she fixed him with her stern eye. Then she stood up and summoned a stretcher bearer, pressed her hand to the small of her back and braced her shoulders for the next casualty.

We learned later that more than eight thousand Russians fell during that battle, nearly two thousand French and a hundred or so Sardinians. Many considered that the allies should have pursued the Russians while they were in retreat and thereby gained a more conclusive victory but as it was we all returned to the camp.

The next day I braved Mrs Shaw Stewart's office and asked if I might be allowed to work in the hospital. She was at her desk, writing what looked like an immense report and she stared at me in disbelief. 'Have you any experience as a nurse? Then what you ask is absurd. I have enough to do responding to memos from Dr Hall about the ones who are already there without yet another untrained lady drifting about causing havoc. You would have no idea how to behave.'

'I only ask to act as a kind of orderly or—'

'If I'd thought that all this time your intention had been to worm your way into the hospital I'd never have let you stay.

'But I was at the battlefield yesterday . . .'

'Who gave you permission?'

'I didn't ask permission. I didn't think—'

'Exactly so. You are not a nurse, Miss Lingwood. You have no idea of the discipline required. Our reputation as nurses in these military hospitals is sufficiently fragile that we cannot risk any more scandal. There is no question of your working on the wards and I wonder you should ask.'

Chapter Seven

Stukeley Hall (of all places),
Derbyshire
20 July 1855

Dear Mariella,

Well, I was very glad to receive your letter and hear that Nora is improving and you are able to be useful. Not everyone would be in those circumstances. Father is a little more reconciled than he was, all the more because we are getting invited to some very grand places on account of you and the war.

Ruth has been told to send you all the embroidery silks and needles you asked for.

We have received another letter from Henry, who says he is well, though I must say his handwriting is not all it should be. Nor does the content, dwelling as it does almost exclusively on Rosa's disappearance, suggest an altogether healthy mind. I would be more concerned for you, Mariella, had it not been for the coolness of your last letter, particularly in relation to Henry. Your father and I have discussed this matter at length and decided, as a first step, that I should write to Dr Lyall, asking him to give us a candid account of Henry's health. We are very sad – it would not be an exaggeration to say that you and Henry are constantly on my mind – that it seems so many years of study, not to say all your hopes, should have come to this sorry end. But that is war and I trust you are bearing up.

So it seems that the next wedding after all is not to be yours but Isabella's. The Dulwich house upon which she and Mr Shackleton have taken out a lease is small but Father has looked it over and says the plumbing is modern and the roof sound.

Isabella has plans to hold what she calls Crimean *drawing rooms. Amongst our friends nobody talks of anything else but Rosa's disappearance and the fact that you have followed her. We have heard rumours from returning officers that Rosa may have attempted to plow her own furrow (I use Mrs Hardcastle's expression) which Isabella says would not be unlike Rosa. She surprises me sometimes by her fortitude in this respect. Everyone is relieved that Miss Nightingale seems to have come through the crisis in her health and she is always mentioned in our prayers, after the Queen.*

We have heard news of an allied defeat and we cannot understand this as all the word from the Illustrated London News *and* The Times *has been that the allied forces are much the stronger and the Russians are on their knees in the city of Sebastopol. Your father, as you well know, is a great supporter of Palmerston but even he has begun to doubt.*

Meanwhile here we have a hot summer and last week there were two deaths at the home due to the heat, I cannot help thinking, one heart failure, the other some stomach disorder, possibly typhus, though I hate to write that word and hope it was some other malady. The doctor was undecided.

You will be wondering what I am doing here in Derbyshire. The fact is Horatio Stukeley is also to be married in September and he wrote that if Isabella wishes to claim any of her remaining possessions from the house then now is the time because it is all to be remodelled inside. Isabella was of course eager to recover her few sticks of furniture, as she termed them, to help furnish the Dulwich house, though when we went up to the attics at Stukeley it seemed to me that she had retained some very good furniture from our father's house in Bakewell that I remember from childhood and can't think how I wasn't offered them at the time. Of course I am the younger sister and as I recall after his funeral we went home and walked through the old rooms and she said take anything, dearest, but my tears were falling so fast I could hardly see. At any rate there is a very pretty writing desk with a stand on top for ink and pens, and a sewing cabinet with three little drawers which I used to arrange for Mother, setting all the cotton reels in order of colour and tidying the needle book, which I think you would have loved, but Isabella says both these are cherished items of her own and ideal for the new house. She never sews, as you know, and there was some tension between us when I said you ought to have the sewing cabinet which has lain dusty all these years in the attic at Stukeley.

The woman (girl) Horatio is to wed is called Georgiana Stokes Lacey (actually I believe that we must call her 'the Honourable') and her family owns a great deal of land and property including an iron foundry and cutlery factory in Sheffield. The family is therefore prospering at present, from the war, I gather. She is only a younger daughter, with thin hair and a round face but nonetheless.

Horatio Stukeley is taller than I remember, already quite bald like his father and with very large hands. I never found him easy to talk to. Incidentally here at Stukeley the younger brother Max's portrait is hung prominently above the stairs, and a letter from his general praising his courage under fire at Inkerman is displayed underneath. Apparently there was hope of further promotion but that has been dashed by news of an injury. We have no details but Isabella assures me Max is not the type to die; they have all worried about him needlessly before. Georgiana alludes often to the prospect of his return. Her fascination with his brother might give me cause for concern, were I Horatio. The fact that Max is now injured seems to make him even more interesting to Georgiana. I am sorry that he is hurt – I was very taken with him when he called at Fosse House last year, and for your sake I wish he was still in the Crimea. I used to reassure myself that at least there was someone approaching a family member out there who might watch over you.

We have been given bedrooms on the second floor as so much of the first is to be rearranged for the Hon. Georgiana, though no work has begun as yet. Isabella is sorry not to have her old bedroom but my memories of Stukeley are not so joyful that I would care to be accommodated in the same chamber as when we last were here.

I've noticed that since her engagement to Mr Shackleton, who is very deferential to her wishes, Isabella has become more critical of Sir Matthew. Certainly when we visited here that summer I wondered at her choice. I never liked Stukeley as you doubtless realised. I've never known time to hang so heavily on my hands, though I was pleased that a friendship had sprung up between you and Rosa. I missed you, sometimes, as I remember, because I was never sure where you might be.

I shall be glad to leave. The house is in a state of great upheaval. The Hon. G. enlisted our help in clearing the library, which she wishes to make into a sitting room because she says it commands the best view of the lawns. But tonight, before dinner, Horatio came in and found us emptying the shelves and said he did not remember giving permission for any such thing to happen. We were all very uncomfortable because he went inside and shut the door behind him and was even heard to lock it. During dinner he and Georgiana didn't speak to each other at all. An unpromising start, one way and another. I pity them both.

But then at home Mrs Hardcastle and I are scarcely on speaking terms either and she now attends a different church, though I'm told by Mr Shackleton that she finds the service very high. I'm afraid she has not forgiven Isabella for marrying Mr Shackleton. He, after all, is worth four thousand a year while Isabella has next to nothing. I miss Mrs Hardcastle and without her sponsorship the second governesses' home cannot go ahead. Your father is less generous than he used to be. He is sad without you, Mariella, even though your trip to the Crimea has been good for his business in terms of connections. So the house is very quiet and soon even Isabella will be gone. I do not think the governesses require all my time and I am going to cast about for a new cause. Rosa's acquaintance, Barbara Leigh Smith, came with me as promised to the home and it was wonderful how invigorated we all felt looking ahead to a time when girls might one day have a full and varied curriculum to follow in their schools. Some of the poor governesses became quite animated when they remembered their old pupils. Although Isabella will never stay in the room with Miss Leigh Smith due to what she calls the shadow cast by her doubtful birth, Barbara and I get along very well. This has been an unusually hot summer, as I said. The garden is parched. When we are back at Fosse House we shall begin work on Isabella's trousseau, though it will be a sad business without your help. She is to wear gardenias in her hat.

We hear that hot weather has brought the cholera back to the camps. I rely on Nora to ensure you only drink clean water. It is very late, but too close to sleep. There is nearly a full moon and I can see down into the Italian garden where you and Rosa used to play.

If I were to write that I missed you, you should not take it as a matter of reproach,

Maria Lingwood (your mother)

Chapter Eight

The Crimea, 1855

The Crimean climate was a strange beast, sometimes British in its habits, with tranquil blue skies and puffs of white cloud followed by days of drizzle or gusty wind. But this was an illusion that had caught the allied armies out time after time; the winter nights were colder, storms more violent, winds stronger and the summer sun fiercer than anyone expected. And the weather was more fickle; a hot morning could turn into a frosty evening, a placid dawn be blasted away by hurricane.

Crimean winds brought salt from the sea, dust from the worn plain above Sebastopol, grass seed, bad smells, cholera (according to some) and, above all, rumour. Sometimes it seemed that I never actually heard news spoken but that it blew into my head on a gust of hot air. We knew, for instance, that the war was actually being fought on three fronts, of which we were just one. In the Baltic the allies had successfully bombarded Sveaborg in the Gulf of Finland, thereby threatening the security of St Petersburg. Near the border of Eastern Turkey, on the other hand, the town of Kars, which had a British garrison was under siege by the Russians. So the prevailing state, as in the trenches above Sebastopol, was stalemate.

We knew that the famous French chef, Alexis Soyer, was reforming our regimental kitchens so that a regular soldier was no longer issued with a slab of raw meat each morning and expected to find the means to dress and cook it by dinner. We knew that the French General Pelissier and our new General Simpson still rarely spoke to each other if they could avoid it. We heard that Miss Florence Nightingale was well on the road to recovery and might return to the Crimea soon in order to resume her aborted inspection of our hospitals, a prospect regarded as a dubious blessing by many of the nurses and most of the doctors. And I knew that Captain Max Stukeley, having spent six weeks at Renkioi in Turkey in a new, pre-fabricated hospital designed by Brunel, and therefore the last word in hygiene and comfort, had refused point-blank to be invalided home and was back in the Crimea.

I expected him to visit Nora at some stage, of course. It may be that I even dressed my hair more carefully in case I should bump into him. Otherwise I refused to allow myself one moment's speculation about the state of Captain Stukeley's injured leg or the likelihood of his paying us a call. Instead each afternoon I sat with my posse of women in the shade of the laundry store and taught them the intricacies of tucking and pleating, and the correct method of inserting a sleeve into an armhole.

But one day, as we were engaged in the delicate task of turning a cuff, I became aware that every gaze had brightened and was now directed above my head, and that I was being watched.

A voice behind me said, 'Miss Lingwood, as I live and breathe.'

I pulled my thread so violently that the fabric puckered but I would not look round. 'Captain Stukeley.'

'I wonder, Miss Lingwood, if you might spare me a moment of your valuable time.'

I was furious with myself for being so unnerved that I could hardly keep my voice steady or my head from jolting round, so I spent several minutes demonstrating how invisible hemming should be used to fasten the edge of the cuff to the inside of a sleeve and that no stitch should be more than a tenth of an inch in length. Then I ran my needle through the fabric and stood up, only to find that Max was deep in conversation with a besotted little woman who, despite her lack of skill, was agreeing to make him a bespoke dress shirt for an officers' dinner next week.

We walked a few paces up the track that ran along the front of the hospital in full view of dozens of inquisitive spectators. Max was shockingly pale with bloodshot eyes, long side whiskers, slashing furrows in his brow and cheeks, and scarcely any flexibility in his right leg. All in all, apart from the fact that he was upright, he looked little better than when I had last seen him in a hospital bed.

'Everyone thought you would be sent home,' I said.

'Did they now? I'd hardly let them pack me off for the sake of a sore knee. Too much unfinished business. And it's just as well I insisted on coming back or I'd have missed the inspirational sight of Miss Mariella's sewing school for wives and widows.'

'I'm sure there are more interesting things going on in the Crimean Peninsula.'

'Very few. You'd be surprised.' When I glanced at him from under the muslin shade of my hat I was relieved to note that despite the fact he had aged ten years there was still a caustic glint in his eye. 'But Miss Lingwood, I believe I am much in your debt. Had it not been for you my right leg would now be rotted away in a pit.'

'Hardly my doing.'

'As I remember you were quite forceful in recommending that I insist on an alternative to amputation.'

'Nora gave me the idea and I only mentioned that Dr Thewell . . .'

'Thewell. That's it. We have him to thank.'

His tone was so sour that I changed the subject: 'You mentioned unfinished business.'

'Just a little. One piece of unfinished business: the war. Second: check on the health of my dear old friend Nora McCormack, but as I have already found her in command of half a dozen orderlies I believe she must be nearly recovered. Third task: find Rosa.'

Nowhere, I noticed, had the well-being of Mariella Lingwood registered on his list. 'We have been managing without you – we have asked for Rosa constantly.'

'Nora said there'd been a sighting of a woman near the River Tchernaya.'

'By a drunken Irishman. But we were at the Tchernaya after the battle and of course there was not a sign of Rosa. Although I swear a wounded Russian soldier spoke her name to me.'

'There is a connection – the River Tchernaya runs due north-west through the village of Inkerman and into the sea – but I can't help thinking your first instincts were right and your Irishman was simply carried away by his own fairytales.' There was a new air of brutality under Max's mockery, and my pleasure and relief at seeing him were fading rapidly. 'I've decided to go back to the cave above Inkerman where Rosa was last seen.'

'Isn't it very close to the Russian lines? She cannot be—'

'Miss Lingwood, would you care to stroll with me up to the fortress?' He held out his arm and quirked an eyebrow. The gesture, which was accompanied by an abrupt change of tone, was too emphatic to be refused and though I wouldn't take his arm for fear of what Mrs Shaw Stewart might think, I did walk a pace or two ahead of him until we were out of earshot of the last hut.

'Mariella, while I was in the hospital I met a soldier who had spent many months recovering from a neck wound, and who grew very excited when I happened to talk about Rosa. He told me that he had been treated for various ills by your Dr Thewell, and had such faith in him that he was even prepared to make the trek to Inkerman, though he never reached the cave. Instead he met Thewell on a hillside, frostbitten, half-dressed and raving about a woman called Rosa. My friend took Thewell back to the hospital where I later visited him. By then, as I told you before, he was beyond saying anything intelligible.'

'So you've learned nothing new . . .'

'Soon after Rosa disappeared I went to the cave and there was no sign that she had been there. I glanced inside, looked around and walked further up the hill, trying to imagine where she might have gone. That's all. During these last weeks at the hospital I have cursed myself for not being more thorough.'

'But what would you hope to find now? You surely don't think Rosa is still camped out there.'

'I don't know what to think.' He was the coldest I had ever known him, made even more remote by his impeccable uniform and the pallor of his skin. 'But there are things I knew of him, things he said, which make me very fearful of what might have happened.'

I stared at him for a moment, then said, 'I'll come with you,' though my voice was so uncertain he had to dip his head to hear me.

'You will not.'

'I don't know what you're implying happened to Rosa. I don't understand you. But I would like to go to that cave, if only because Henry and Rosa were both there.'

'I have no intention of taking you.'

'Then why did you tell me you were going?'

'To warn you, to prepare you for the worst.'

'I shall come. You can't stop me.'

'It's too dangerous. You would be no use to me whatever.'

'Then you shouldn't have said anything.' My sewing class had gathered in the distance to witness our argument and I lowered my voice. 'You cannot expect me to wait here while you go off on your own, in the state you're in.'

'And how long do you suppose you'll be allowed to stay at this hospital if it becomes known that you have spent a day riding about the Crimea with me?'

'Nobody need find out. And anyway, I hardly care.'

'Well. Well. If Miss Lingwood wants to come, who am I to refuse? And yet I remember seeing you ride at Stukeley and it was a pitiful sight. Still, I suppose if I don't agree to escort you there's no telling what you might do.' He raised his cap in exasperation and limped back to our audience who clustered around him as he made his laborious way along the path.

That evening I received a note saying that I should meet Captain Stukeley the following morning at six o'clock by the gates of the British Hotel and that I was to dress appropriately. I had braced myself for Nora to be scathing about the planned trip but to my astonishment both my hut-sharers approved of my decision. 'There's something about you,' said Nora, 'that seems to have given you a charmed life in this war. Perhaps you will protect Max from harm.'

'I'd have gone,' said Mrs Whitehead, in a surprising burst of flirtatiousness, 'but then I don't know a woman in the Crimea who wouldn't want to go riding with Captain Stukeley, no matter how many legs he'd lost.'

The three of us then spent half an hour considering what I should wear. In the end Mrs Whitehead lent me a sadly faded blouse and scarf that we thought would allow me to pass as a peasant woman or camp follower. 'And you must droop more at the shoulders if you wish to be truly inconspicuous.'

Nora insisted I wear a visible crucifix round my neck. 'If you get taken by a Russian they'll treat you more kindly if they think you have the faith. They'll respect a Roman Catholic. And you're to leave that locket and the engagement ring behind, just in case. They'll only lead to temptation.'

'I don't plan to be taken by a Russian.'

'You cannot be sure of anything. Max is not so nimble at present as he used to be. You keep your eye on him and don't let him get overtired. And don't go burdening him with one of your headaches. Make sure you drink plenty.'

I twisted the ring from my finger and handed it over with the locket, though it left a little dent in the skin which I kneaded self-consciously with my other hand.

Chapter Nine

Despite these preparations the expedition began badly because the only sign of Max at the British Hotel was the two great horses tethered inside the gates. When he finally emerged it turned out that he had been eating a substantial breakfast provided by Mrs Seacole, and had expected me to come to the door. So by the time we set out at six-thirty we were already at odds because each of us claimed to have been kept waiting by the other.

He had borrowed for me a black horse with a starred forehead whose owner had been killed in the assault on the Redan. The size of the beast intimidated me but his name was Solomon and he appeared to be a far more stable character than Flight, though just as battle-worn. Even though his gummy eyes were plagued by flies – despite a shade plaited out of frayed rope – he merely swished his tail and swung his head gently from side to side. Max, meanwhile, had kitted himself out in Armenian trousers bought at the market in Kamiesh and a long shirt borrowed from an orderly which he wore as a tunic belted in at the waist. Round his head he'd wrapped a long white scarf, like a Turk, and the overall effect was of a frail brigand. He was followed out of the British Hotel by Mrs Seacole herself, who beamed at me as she stuffed a saddlebag with flasks and food. As we left she gave my horse's rump such a whack of encouragement that he danced on the spot.

We hardly spoke at all during the first few miles. My last experience on horseback in company with Lady Mendlesham-Connors had ended so disastrously that all my concentration was required to ensure that I stayed in the saddle and even when I did risk a few words I was instantly crushed. Having witnessed the difficulty with which Max mounted his horse, I said, 'It cannot be safe for you to be in the Crimea with such a wound. What good will you be on the battlefield?'

'More use than the average general, Miss Lingwood. More use than a fit man, I'd say. Better to throw damaged goods into the fray than waste our few remaining able-bodied men.'

My next attempt was equally unsuccessful. 'Did you hear me tell you in the hospital that your stepmother is to marry again?'

'I have no interest in the antics of that woman.'

'And I understand that Horatio is also engaged to be married. Do you know his bride?'

'One of the Stokes Lacey girls. He chose the richest family in the county. Money but no heart. They deserve each other.'

I gave up. Gloomy and stiff-legged, Max bore no resemblance at all to the reckless officer who had defied Henry by galloping pell-mell across the Crimean plain in a steeplechase. Despite an increasing sense of isolation I kept my head up as we travelled through the vast encampment of tents and huts where the men were engaged in time-wasting activities such as rifle cleaning or slow marching. To my unpractised eyes all seemed much as usual but from time to time Max glanced about to check he was not overheard and exchanged a surreptitious word with a fellow officer. When we reached the French camp he roused himself to hurl good-natured insults across a camp fire but refused offers of coffee. I was introduced as 'ma cousine, une vivandiere . . .' which did nothing to quell lascivious winks and smiles.

The further we rode, the more miserable I felt. I had been so busy last night preparing for the practicalities of this ride that its object had not fully dawned on me. Now I suspected that Max so dreaded what he might find in the cave that he couldn't bear even to articulate his fears. If he truly believed that the outcome of our journey would be an appalling confirmation and an end to hope, no wonder he was hunched into himself, always alert but never animated, paying me such little attention that at times I wondered whether he'd notice if I turned tail and rode back to Nora. In the end I grew too frightened to think coherently. Though I tried to convince myself that it was impossible to imagine Henry doing Rosa – or anyone else – deliberate harm, when I thought of his behaviour in Narni the only certainty seemed to be that I didn't know what he was capable of at all.

When we came under the Sapoun Hills the landscape changed to craggier countryside where outlying allied pickets stood in their shirtsleeves under makeshift awnings. The Turkish outposts were characterised by rolled-up prayer mats and a reek of tobacco from the distinctive narrow cigars smoked by the soldiers. Now that I no longer doubted my ability to stay on Solomon's broad back I had become alert to the danger of Russian sharpshooters. Shells and rocket-fire hammered from the bastions and having lived for over two months at the edge of a tented community of thousands of men it was very strange to be riding into near-uninhabited territory. Gradually the road became emptier and the babble of voices, though not the crack of shellfire, died away altogether. We passed into a once fertile valley where ruined cottages stood amidst desolate gardens, every last item of furniture stripped away and the vegetable plots a mass of weeds. In places the track was littered with the detritus of passing armies, a broken boot, a bent cartwheel, the carcass of a mule picked bare.

Then the hills became wilder still, scattered with rocks and scraggy brushwood, divided by roughly quarried ravines where the silence was broken by crows screeching overhead and the spasmodic rattle of artillery. At a place where the path divided Max dismounted, took a flask from his saddlebag and propped himself on a ruined wall. The exertion of the ride had made his face ashen although he remained tense and vigilant.

He unscrewed the top, watched as I swallowed warm, metallic water and then drank from the same flask. 'There's not much point in going further.' His voice was dull and his eyes empty of any spark. 'If we carried on we'd eventually reach the road to Sebastopol. High up this other path is where your Thewell lived like a hermit in the weeks before he was sent home. It's just a cave in the side of a hill – and dangerous: we'd be easy targets.'

'Please don't talk about him like that, *your* Thewell.'

'I beg your pardon, Miss Lingwood.'

'He is not *my* Thewell. It is cruel of you to refer to him as such, as I think you must realise.'

I tried to look calmly upwards as if the prospect of being picked off by a Russian gunman was a hazard I ran into so frequently that it meant nothing to me any more. The cave, little more than a black fingernail in the rock, was far up on the hillside above an apparently precipitous drop.

'But how did he survive?' I whispered.

'His patients, those who made it this far, brought him food and fuel in return for advice but it can't have been comfortable. I remember that in the winter the wind from the sea funnels like a dervish through these valleys.'

'Why would he choose to come here, of all places?'

'He may have had a particularly strong feeling for Inkerman. I think we all have, those of us who fought here.'

'He never mentioned Inkerman in his letters.'

'Well, he wouldn't. Most of us prefer to draw a veil. But look around you.' He pointed to a fragment of white in the grass near my foot. Stone? No. Bone, or bones. A finger picked bare. And now I looked closer I saw that it was attached to a hand that had pressed up through the soil as if its owner had tried to scratch his way out. And then I noticed a couple of rusty buttons in the grass and a shred of cloth, a bullet, a bit of metal, another bone. The more I looked, the more I realised that the ground was littered with the half-buried debris of battle.

'However carefully you tread here, you walk on dead men's faces,' said Max.

I listened to a breeze rattle through dry grasses, a dribble of falling scree. In the Tchernaya the soldiers had fanned out over acres of open land and hurtled into the valley, leaping over their fallen comrades. Here they would have been bundled together, no racing for dear life from the pursuing enemy.

'Inkerman was fought in a fog and nobody knew where the next attack would come from. It was said that not even the Russian general had a map of the terrain though the enemy, in a rare fit of competence, crept up on us in the dark and some men never had time to wake up before they found themselves in hand-to-hand combat with a Cossack. We were mad with fear and confusion.'

'We couldn't line ourselves up in formation, didn't have a strategy. Shocking mistakes were made.'

'I caught sight of your Thewell once or twice during that battle of Inkerman, though at the time I didn't know who he was. Doctors don't tend to put themselves in the firing line but he never hung back, I'll give him that. Thewell was upon a man the instant he was shot down, staunching the wound and giving him water. It's a miracle he survived.'

'And later, when I knew him better, he told me about wounded soldiers he came across who'd have survived perfectly well except that retreating Russians had gone by and stabbed them in the face or stomach as they lay pleading for water. Those needless and fatal Russian bayonet wounds obsessed him. The trouble with your—with Thewell was that he thought of war as a kind of sport that unfortunately resulted in casualties, like rugby. It's acceptable for a man to have his neck broken in a scrum but not for the opposing team to trample on him afterwards.'

'You speak of him scathingly, as if he were an amateur.'

'We all behave like amateurs. We fight this war as if every move we make is disconnected from the next. After Inkerman a kind of horror filled the camps. We realised that there was no taking Sebastopol that side of winter because we had allowed the Russians far too long to fortify their positions. And we couldn't go home because there was too much pride at stake and too many men had been lost for no gain. The weather turned bitterly cold and a week or so later the hurricane blew away our tents and sank our supply ships. The men's clothes got wet and couldn't be dried out. After Inkerman Thewell never really settled to work at the hospital because all he could think about was the men dying of cold in the trenches. Which is how he came to be working in the front line, and met Rosa.'

'He felt responsible for what was happening. He thought he could trust the military. He didn't understand.'

'Then he shouldn't have got involved.'

'Well, I shall certainly go up to the cave. Just to be where they were. You can wait here if you like.'

He staggered to his feet and we led the horses along a path that ran behind the ruins of a little church, then zigzagged steeply up the side of the hill. At the church we paused and peered into the gloom; a few broken tiles on the floor, the remains of a wall painting, elliptical-eyed saints with round haloes and stiff robes, but otherwise a ruin denuded of anything that could be ripped away, with pockmarks in the walls, stains on the stone floor and a torn scrap of canvas blown into a corner.

Max stood in the doorway supported by his right arm. 'I like this chapel, don't you Miss Lingwood? It makes me feel just a little bit more stable, even though I know some poor bastards will have crawled here to die during the battle. But I laugh to think of all those ladies back home worshipping in our churches the same God as the people of Sebastopol. Whose prayers will He answer do you think, given that He'll obviously have to choose to keep one lot happy over the other?'

I didn't respond for fear of his rage and mockery. As it was I had to step hastily back to let him by and even then his arm brushed mine as he lurched suddenly on his wounded leg. After that I let him get well ahead before I followed him. His hostility was relentless and when he touched me so casually I ached because of his indifference.

Although the sky was now full of cloud it was very hot on the path, and despite Nora's warning, a pinprick of headache had begun in my forehead. My only comfort was in Solomon who kept so close that his nose nudged my upper arm and whose ambling gait suggested that this little stroll was nothing to him after the rigours of battle. Eventually, after another sharp twist, we reached a small plateau backed by the cave and fronted by a low wall of rock. Above our heads the sun was a pale disc behind a thick layer of yellowish haze but the heat was intense.

Henry's cave was head high and quite wide, but ran back only a dozen or so feet into the rock. I stood at the entrance and put my hand on warm stone. I expected to be moved at reaching a place of such significance but I felt nothing. Max led the horses inside where the heat was marginally less oppressive, the air reeked of damp minerals and animal droppings and the ground was stained by fire. As a dwelling place the cave's only redeeming features were that the rock wall provided some concealment, and there was a sweeping view to a bridge over the Tchernaya, the ruined village of Inkerman, and on the other side of the valley another rocky hillside. The river broadened as it meandered to right and left, and disappeared behind the spur of a hill on its way to the sea. There was no one in sight except, in the far distance, a squat figure herding a dozen or so goats and when there was a pause in the barrage of artillery fire I heard a faint jangle of bells.

I scraped my toe through the embers in the cave floor and scanned the walls for clues that Henry and Rosa had been here but found only a bit of rubbish, charred tins and a broken bottle. At the back of the cave the floor met the roof unevenly, leaving a narrow slit. Cautiously I inserted my hand. Nothing. I again searched my heart for a flutter of excitement or anguish because here I was, in the very spot where Henry had spent his last weeks in the Crimea but I only felt numb. He seemed so far from me now that I could scarcely summon an image of him except for a fleeting glimpse of his damp hair and the fumbling of his hot hand in the little room at Narni.

Max pointed to the scrubby hillside opposite. 'On the far side of that hill is Sebastopol. A road runs beside the river and along the estuary. The French are encamped over there but the Russians will be watching all the time. When he came here Thewell certainly brought himself to the extreme edge of the war.'

'So what is it you are looking for, Max? You think Rosa died here, don't you?'

'I think Thewell was beyond reason.'

'He was a doctor.'

'He was mad.'

'You're very cruel. He was ill.'

The bleakness of his eyes and the rigidity of his wounded body were formidable. 'Mariella, are you so blind that you can't see what was going on? Didn't you realise, all that time in London he was utterly obsessed by her? Once he'd met up with her here he wouldn't leave her alone. He came up to the camp night after night, hammered on her door and shouted her name. She told him that she didn't love him but he wouldn't listen. In the end I dragged him away to my hut where he sat on my bed and wept like a child. He said that Rosa was passionately in love with him, that she had pursued him from the moment he met her in your drawing room, and driven him insane with her persistence ever since. Wherever he went in London there she was: in his hospital, his new house, some public lecture he gave. He even came to the Crimea in the hope of forgetting her, but still she followed him.'

'Perhaps that was secretly why she wanted to come.'

'You sound like Thewell. Nothing would convince him that he was the last person in the world Rosa could love. There he was, huddled in his great coat, his fists clenched on his knees and his face contorted with tears, repeating over and over again: She loves me, she loves me.'

'Why are you so sure she didn't love him?' Each time the word *love* passed between us its resonance struck me afresh, like a strike on the breast.

He shook his head and studied my face with such intense concentration that I began to shiver. 'My God, do you really have to ask? Have you never realised that there was only one person in the world who she loved with her whole heart? My poor Mariella, how simple your life would have been without the inconvenience of Rosa. I presume you'd be Mrs Thewell by now, fussing over the sugar tongs.'

'Is that all you think I'm capable of?'

The hardness broke in his eyes and he gave a brief, rueful smile. 'Anyway, in the end Thewell did leave the camp. We hoped he'd gone back to the hospital but he came here instead. Rosa was beside herself with guilt. It was all her fault, she said. She'd misled Henry and broken your heart in the process. We argued fiercely. She said she had to follow him and make him come back. I said that if she went to the cave, she'd give his sick mind more proof that she loved him. But I was called away one night and by the time I came back it was too late. She'd gone.'

'And then?'

'He was a soul in torment, Mariella, out of control.'

'But he wouldn't have hurt her.'

'Who knows?'

'No. No. I won't believe it.'

'Mariella, Rosa never came back.'

'No. She's not dead. There have been too many hints of her. She was seen at the Tchernaya ... There were Russians who seemed to recognise my face ...'

'It will be easier once we know.'

I listened to his uneven footfall as he left me and climbed the path above the cave. Then I tried to imagine Henry driven to such an extreme by love – hammering on the rough wood of Rosa's hut, his lone voice howling for her in the sleeping camp, so unlike that composed surgeon who had raised his arms and imposed silence on a crowded operating theatre or the gentleman who had kissed my mouth with such precision. I remembered how we had stood at the window together and watched the rabbits while he proposed and how after he'd gone I'd sat alone in the unchanged morning room. And for one outrageous moment I envied him: to have felt so much; to have existed in the grip of such a passion.

And Rosa? I could well imagine her headlong flight from the camp, her determination to set things straight. But what had been her feelings when she arrived here and found him crouched over the fire, the incredulity in his eye when he saw her through the flames, the flash of hope?

The cave was very quiet and the stale air laden with heat. From the valley below came the screech of crows and then a low rumble of cannon-fire. The horses chomped at their hay and eyed me without interest. I crept to the mouth of the cave where a light breeze stirred as if the valley had drawn breath but could hold it no longer, a seed-head twirled onto the hem of my skirt and yellow clouds were pillowed on the hills opposite.

Why had I doubted her? I saw her swinging out above the ravine at Stukeley, pounding along the path to the Fairbrothers' cottage and kneeling beside the dying boy. In one of his last, scribbled notes to her Henry had written: *I am terrified by your utter faithfulness*. He had known what he was up against, all right. How cramped she must have felt by his obsession, how trapped and tormented by guilt.

Rosa, where are you now?

No answer.

When I listened for her voice in my head, it was gone.

All this time, on the journey to the cave, I had been expecting a sign, something significant, the shade of Rosa, perhaps. After all, she had drawn me thus far, shimmering through the hospitals, leaving her name on a dozen tongues, haunting my memory with her insatiable need to show me even the most hidden part of her life. And now? Silence. When I tried to imagine her in this apology for a secret place, I couldn't see her here at all. Instead, I was faced at last with her complete absence.

Chapter Ten

Derbyshire, 1844

From the very start of my seventh lesson I was so nervous that my heart beat too fast and my armpits were damp. I would ask him this time, I would. I had it all planned. I had even practised my speech. He was so loving and patient that he couldn't possibly refuse. It wasn't much of a favour, after all, just a matter of doing what was obviously right. And afterwards I imagined that everything at Stukeley would be perfect, Rosa would be amazed by what I'd achieved, and when I went back to London she would have a happy life without me because she and her stepfather would be friends.

When Sir Matthew opened the library door he ushered me in with a playful bow, closed it softly and held back my chair. Then, as usual, he tested me on what I'd already learned. If my answer was right he patted my arm, when it was wrong he groaned and sank his head in his hand which normally made me giggle, though on this occasion my laughter was forced.

As I wrote down the next answer I broke my nib. Whereas Father would have been annoyed, Sir Matthew only smiled. 'Not to worry, Mariella, there are plenty more where that came from. And it gives me a chance to use my favourite present.' He produced a box containing a dozen or so steel nibs, invited me to choose one, fitted it, cleaned his fingers with my pen-wiper, dipped the pen in the ink and handed it to me. We both watched the shiny blue trail left by my meticulous copperplate.

'Look how often I have used my pen-wiper. It seems a shame, on the one hand, to make it inky, on the other every stain reminds me of the thoughtful little head that dreamed up such a wonderful present.'

When should I ask him? Now, when our heads were bent together over the page, or later, when I sat in the armchair for him to arrange another drawer of specimens on my lap and hold back my hair? Or perhaps that wouldn't happen today. Perhaps if I didn't hurry up the clock would strike and it would be time to leave.

He leaned back. 'My Mariella is not showing much aptitude today. Is something troubling you, my dear?' His eyes were so kind I wanted to cry. 'Never mind the poems today. Take the book away with you, if you like. But come here. Come.' His grip was very firm as he pulled me to my feet and led me to the far side of the library where the specimen drawers and cupboards were. I had learned to give his fingers a shy squeeze, which was always returned and seemed to please him, so I kept my hand in his and allowed a tear to fall from my cheek onto my lips.

He stooped down, gazed into my face, then held my head against his tobacco-steeped waistcoat and said softly, 'What is this? I can't have my lovely little girl weeping. Ah, now, let's sit you up here and have a look at you.' He picked me up and sat me on top of a set of drawers so that my eyes were level with his and my knees were pressed to his chest. Then he held both my hands and stroked my knuckles with his thumbs. 'Now, what is it?'

'I'm very unhappy because of something I've seen.'

'Aha, and what is that?' He kissed my cheeks, first one then the other, and laid his forehead against mine so that our noses touched and I smelled his cigar breath. 'Tell me.' I let my head fall forward so that we were even closer, like when Rosa and I lay face to face in bed.

'In the valley . . .'

Part of me was very comfortable that he stroked my back and pulled me towards him so that my knees went either side of him, under his arms. It was like when Henry used to pick me up and twirl me round in the garden, or when Father carried me to bed. But Sir Matthew's body was different, his smell was wrong and I didn't know him quite well enough to be this near. I must speak, quickly. 'Please, I just wondered . . . There's a family by the river. One of the children is very ill. Their name is Fairbrother. I think if they had a different home . . .'

With one hand he held my head against his chest, with the

other he fondled the back of my neck. 'Fairbrother?'

'I don't expect you quite realise that the little boy is dying. I don't think you can know about it or I feel sure you'd do something.'

'You are a funny little girl. I thought you were told not to go near the Fairbrothers.'

'Oh everyone knows about them.'

'Everyone?'

'Mother is always very interested in helping the poor in London,' I said hastily.

'Is she indeed?' To my relief, he wasn't annoyed at all. In fact he seemed to love me all the more because he kissed the backs of my hands and gently hooked my hair behind my ears. 'You see, the trouble is, Mariella, life is not as easy as you think. I have to take a hundred difficult decisions every day and each one pleases some people and hurts others. What if I moved one family? What about the many others who live in the same valley? I would be ruined if I had to build new houses for all those people. And if I lost all my money, then I couldn't pay anyone and none of the workers would have a job, so their children would go hungry and what a lot of misery that would cause.'

'But the river is so dirty.'

For the first time I saw a flicker of impatience in his eye. 'Well, never mind, let's forget about the dirty old river. Which drawer shall we look in today?' He put his hands on my waist as if to lift me down. His thumbs came uncomfortably high, just under my chest but I put my arms round his neck, thinking that I mustn't let this opportunity go, I'd never find the courage again. 'But if there was clean water at least,' I said. 'Then all the families could benefit.'

He rubbed his thumbs up and down my ribs. 'You have been thinking about it carefully, haven't you?'

'Father could help. Father knows all about pipes and drains.'

'Does he indeed? Well, if I ever need any advice I'll ask him.'

'So please. Will you do something?' I pleaded.

'Mariella, that's enough now. One of the reasons I like this library is that I don't need to think about my work here. So no more talk about cottages.'

I sighed, then played my final card; I pushed his hands away and slid backwards as if I didn't want any more to do with him. He was silent a moment, but when he spoke his voice was completely different. 'Oh so the little girl is peevish that she can't have her own way.'

'It's not that. But I can't be happy knowing Petey Fairbrother is so ill. It doesn't seem right.'

'That's the way it is, Mariella, I'm afraid. You'll have to learn to live with the knowledge that not everyone can be happy all the time.'

'But you could make us happy. Just by making sure they had clean water. If you were to have a channel dug from the woods—'

'What do you mean, us?'

'Me, and the Fairbrothers and—'

'Where does all this talk of channelling clean water come from?' All the warmth had drained from his eyes and I suddenly saw him much more clearly in his smart frock coat and cravat as Sir Matthew Stukeley, who sat at the end of the dinner table cutting his food into small, regular pieces and not talking to anyone. 'Ah, now I understand. This is Rosa, isn't it? You and she worked it out together. Is that it?'

'No. No.'

'She told you what to say to me. I suppose that's why you keep coming here, to do Rosa's dirty little jobs for her.'

'No, it's not like that.' I started to cry properly because nobody had ever talked to me so coldly in my life.

'Did she take you down to those cottages again? Did she? But I ordered you not to go near them.'

I was weeping helplessly, battered by his terrible rage. 'Sir Matthew, I promise you Rosa doesn't know I'm here, she knows nothing about it, she told me not to tell you about going to the Fairbrothers but I don't think you can understand how much she wants to help . . .'

He stalked off to a row of shelves and took a great interest in the back of one of the books. 'No. Not now. That's an end to it. Off you go. I'm in no mood for this.'

I slid off the chest of drawers and stood weeping in the middle of the library. Then I crept closer and tried to entwine my fingers in his but he twitched away. 'The truth is, Mariella, I don't believe you. I expect you've told her all about our lessons. My God, it would be typical of Rosa to try and use you for her own ends. I'm going to have to punish her.'

'No, no, Rosa doesn't know I'm here.'

'Why did you disobey me? You knew you shouldn't go to the cottages. That instruction was quite clear to both of you.'

'We were only trying to help. Please, don't be cross. Please. I only want you to be friends. I want to make things right so that she will see what a kind man you are.'

'Stop this crying. I don't blame you. But Rosa should know better. I've told her before. She will not keep in her place. When I first met her I thought she had the face of an angel. Instead I find that she is disobedient and wayward, and that makes me regret marrying the mother. Do you understand – she is spoiling everything? No, she must be punished. I've a good mind to beat her.' He looked at me speculatively. 'Yes. I have a whip I used to keep for Max. Perhaps I should use it on Rosa.'

'No. No please don't. Please, don't punish her, punish me.'

He marched across to one of the cupboards, took a key from his pocket and removed a varnished stick with a loop of leather at one end which he smacked across his palm and ankle, as if to try it out. I followed the lick of leather and cringed.

'So you want me to punish you instead of Rosa.'

'Yes . . . I don't mind . . .'

'Come here, then.' He took hold of my arm and studied me as if deciding which part of my body to hit. With the end of the whip he mapped me out – my shoulder, upper arm, and hip. He even raised the hem of my skirt to look at my quivering knees. For a moment I sobbed helplessly, supported only by his grip, then he threw the whip aside and spoke softly again. 'Mariella, I have no intention of punishing you. You've done nothing wrong, except to do as Rosa told you, though I'm sad that Rosa's opinion seems to matter more to you than mine. There, stop this crying.'

'Promise you won't tell Rosa what I said. Promise you won't punish her.'

He led me over to the armchair, stroked my head, kissed my hand then very gently pulled me into his lap. 'Now, hush. I can't have you spoiling your pretty face with tears.' I raised my face and he wiped my eyes with his scented handkerchief, crossed his leg, which brought me even tighter against him, and gave me another hug. Then he took my chin in his hand and studied my face, first my eyes, then my mouth, gave a little laugh deep in his throat and kissed me on the lips.

It was just a little kiss, the merest pressure of his mouth on mine and something very odd, a flick of his tongue between my lips, but it made me so nervous that I pushed myself away from him and stood up. Then I didn't know what to do and I certainly didn't want his anger to come back so I curtseyed and for good measure seized and pressed his hand. After that I picked up the book of poetry and hurried over to the door thinking: Thank goodness, it's over and he's forgiven me. He won't tell Rosa.

I looked back one more time and he was sprawled in the chair with his legs apart and his hands clasped together under his chin, watching me with his usual, moist-eyed affection. Then I let myself out, slipped into the hall and ran hard into Max.

The new shock made my teeth knock together and my knees vibrate against my petticoat. But Max was relentless and before I knew it had dragged me into the cubbyhole under the stairs.

Chapter Eleven

The Crimea, 1855

I stumbled to the mouth of the cave, cupped my hands round my mouth and funnelled my cry across the valley. 'Rosa.' At first my voice was so weak that it was huffed away in the hot breeze but I shouted again: 'Rosa.'

I went on and on calling her name until my voice broke and the cannonade above Sebastopol had become a mocking echo. 'Rosa. Come back. Rosa.' By now her name was a grinding sob scraped across my throat.

My shoulder was roughly shaken and a hand covered my mouth. 'For God's sake, Mariella.' Though I dragged my head from side to side and tore at Max's wrist he held me firmly and ordered me to be quiet.

At last I went limp but as soon as his grip slackened I turned on him. 'No wonder you hate me.'

'What are you talking about?'

'After your father sent us away from Stukeley that time, what happened?'

'Nothing happened.'

'I don't believe you. He told me he was going to punish Rosa.'

He put his finger on my lips, as if I were a child. 'Mariella, have you forgotten the war? Ssssh. Quiet.'

'I told your father about Rosa's visits to the Fairbrothers. He will have made her suffer because of me.'

'Mariella, does everything always have to begin and end with you?'

'This does. Nora said he even made Rosa nurse him as a kind of punishment. What else did he do to her? Tell me.'

'At least come inside, out of sight. Good God, I've scarcely heard you raise your voice above a murmur and you choose to have a fit of hysterics here.' He took me firmly by the hand and led me into the gloom. 'If you must know, you were just another irritation, a further nail in the coffin of their relationship, nothing more. Father couldn't abide Rosa so he found ways of tormenting her. Our swing was cut down on the grounds that it was dangerous, the box hedge torn up to create a different vista, she was forbidden to go more than half a mile from the house on her own.'

'And did she keep to his rules?'

'Of course not. She was an expert at defying him. Even when he used his own sick body to confine her she turned the tables on him by regarding him as part of her training to become a nurse. The more degraded he became, the stronger she grew.'

'But she must have found out about my lessons with him. Why didn't she ever reproach me in her letters or when she came to London?'

'Because she loved you too much.'

'No. No. How can I bear it? And now she's gone. Oh God, I wish she would come back.' I tore at my skirt and scarf as if I might somehow purge my body, hating the child who had sat so pertly on Sir Matthew's armchair with a starched napkin arranged on her lap, too full of her own sense of power to see the danger. And this last year, those coy moments with Henry; to have been so self-obsessed and regardless of what was happening before my very eyes. Fool, fool.

I fumbled ineffectually with Solomon's harness, my one idea to get away from the deadly emptiness of the cave. Max stood with folded arms, watching. 'Mariella, you were only a child. You weren't to blame. Compared to Rosa you were easy prey. We all should have kept a closer eye on you.'

'What do you mean, compared to Rosa?'

'Why do you think my rich father married your penniless aunt? Rosa was the lure, as I later realised. He probably thought once he'd got her to Stukeley she would become his little playmate – she told me he'd cornered her in the Italian garden but that she repulsed him with a few well-chosen words. So it's no surprise he tried to embroil you in a secret relationship.'

'She trusted me. I went behind her back. And now she's sacrificed herself for me.'

Max rested his elbow on Solomon's patient neck and studied me. With his other hand he wiped a bit of grime from my chin. 'You delighted her. You were quite literally the light of her life. She never stopped talking about you, her London cousin. Whenever I let her, if I slipped my guard for a moment, she wanted to discuss you: your hair, your eyes, your clothes, your voice, your talent with the needle.'

'I wasn't worth it.' But I no longer struggled with Solomon's reins. Everything was changing. The cave was empty of Rosa and Henry but Max was there, leaning against the horse, quite different to the stony-eyed man who had left me an hour before. The noise of the guns was muffled by stone and in the unaccustomed quiet I was absorbed by the same dark gaze that had burned into mine when he crept at dead of night into the Stukeley bedroom.

'You didn't find Rosa, then,' I said at last.

'You were right, she's not here. I searched the hillside for some sign, recently turned earth perhaps. But the whole of Inkerman is a graveyard. I felt absurd.'

Even the horses were still, and the guns' percussive accompaniment had ceased to matter. Max ran the back of his finger up my cheek and my headache swam against my temple. 'I have often thought how much I should like to see you smile again, like you did when you found me in the hospital – that's it, such a slow, tentative smile.' His thumb ran across my lips and I buckled against the horse. My wits were tagging behind my senses and when I put my hand on his chest to keep him at a distance my fingertips pulsed.

'I thought you loved Rosa,' I said.

'Of course I love Rosa. She's my mad girl, my sister. But you have a wholly different effect on me, you and your frothy petticoats and sideways peek from under your bonnet.'

'Well, I had no—' His moustache brushed my lips and my bones were liquid. Just for a beat the old Mariella hesitated but there was no stepping back, I wanted him too much. So I put my hands behind his head, closed my eyes and gave him my half-open mouth. Max kissed with the vehemence he applied to every other aspect of his life, my body was pulled up hard against his long, lean frame and the tepid kisses I'd once exchanged with Henry turned to dust.

When we looked at each other again we were shaken and shy. The strangeness of having kissed Max Stukeley, the vulnerability of his eyelids and the softness of his mouth hurt me. My body was new and needy, clothed in its borrowed blouse and narrow skirt. I held his face between my hands, caressed his jaw and cheekbone and drank in the taste of him.

As he kissed my ear he whispered, 'We should go. Already it's almost too late. We'll never reach the camp before dark.'

'No. No. Max.'

'Miss Lingwood, your reputation will be in tatters.'

'What does that matter compared to this?'

His lips pressed my palm and the underside of my wrist so tenderly that I folded myself against him and slid my fingers under his sleeve so I could touch his naked arm. I loved the textures of him, the shock of flesh on flesh, the softness of his neck and roughness of his cheek. In the end he held me under his arm and with the other hand fumbled to unpack a striped blanket and throw it on the floor of the cave. In the half-light I lay with my head pillowed on his shoulder and knotted my legs over his uninjured knee. That little dent in the hillside was both my home and a place where I was utterly different, exorcising the memory of the Narni bedroom as I breathed the scent of Max's flesh, threaded my fingers through his black hair and leaned over to kiss his mouth until he clasped my head and pulled me into a blacker, wilder space where my only sensations were of the smoothness of his warm skin and the need to be touched and held.

'Why did you change?' I whispered. 'You've done nothing but try to send me away. I thought you hated me.'

'So I do, every inch, especially here, this soft, secret place behind your ear. But when I heard your cry just now I thought you'd been captured by the Russians and I said to myself: What a fool you are, Max Stukeley, to be scrambling about looking for the lost Rosa, and putting at risk Mariella.'

He kissed my eyelids and I disappeared further and further from my usual self, my lips closed on his tongue, my body adjusted itself to accommodate his weight and my hand learned the curves of his shoulder and throat. Mrs Whitehead's blouse separated itself from the waistband of my skirt and he stroked my back, his kisses feathers against my ear. 'Actually you didn't stand a chance. I had it all planned in that bloody hospital at Renkioi. Fourth piece of unfinished business: make love to the obstinate little minx, Mariella Lingwood.' His fingers performed a slow dance on my flesh and when they closed on my breast my back arched. He kissed my collarbone and my breast through the thin material of the blouse and I lay against his fragile bones, listening to his heart.

As the sun set the sky cleared, a segment of moon rose above the hill opposite and a couple of bats flitted out of a crevice in the rock and scooped into the darkness. We clung together while the sky flickered with rocket-fire and the ground shook. As night advanced and the heat of the day sank into the rock, I tightened my hold. To love Max was to walk a tightrope above an abyss. All around us, under their thin covering of earth, the hundreds of dead men sighed and stirred.

'I still can hardly believe you survived,' I said. 'It terrifies me to think I might never have seen you again, or been able to lie with you like this. Why are we alive and not the others? What gives us the right?'

He stroked my hair and gave me a slow, sad kiss. 'Mariella, we have no right. In a war, it is a matter of half an inch either way that makes the difference between life and death.'

'How can you bear to fight, knowing that?'

'Death is part of the process, one outcome among many. Some days I shake with fear, others I am euphoric at the thought of another battle. It makes no difference either way. The war goes on, we fight, we live or we die. We have no choice.'

'But if it's a bad war, if there's no point...'

'You sound just like Rosa. But I told her, it's a matter of trust. I expect my men to obey me without question and I do the same. That's the rule, right down the line.'

'And what did Rosa say to that?'

'Rosa said she could never have been a soldier. After all, she didn't last in the hospitals for more than a few weeks because she couldn't keep to the rules.'

'Mrs Shaw Stewart's view was that by working among the men in the trenches Rosa had gone out on a limb.'

'That's exactly it. That is Rosa.'

'So then she came here, to Henry.'

'And after that, where next? How much further could she go?'

It grew colder, and the night filled with kisses rolled so fast towards morning that I felt the floor of the cave wheel under a smudge of stars. In the small hours, shivering and stiff, we got up, harnessed the horses, led them outside and paused for a moment to look back. We had left nothing behind us but a stony space. And below us was the valley, the hills on either side still bathed in mist and the river emerging like a strip of mercury as it flowed first to the right, then round the edge of the hillside out of sight.

Rosa had stood here, holding her hands to the warmth of Henry's fire, cornered by his frantic demand to be loved. And in that moment, filled with my own new love, I saw through her relentless eyes the possibilities of that ribbon of water with the road running alongside on its way to Sebastopol.

'Max.'

He held my arm and followed my gaze. 'No. Not even Rosa would be that rash.'

'She wouldn't have seen it as rash.'

'Sebastopol?'

'She hated the war. She longed to make a difference. To work with the Russians would have been an obvious choice.'

'She would never have got past their pickets.'

'Knowing Rosa she just gave her name and walked on.'

'Why did Henry let her go?'

'Perhaps he was sleeping. Perhaps she told him where his duty lay and made him go back to the camp.'

We stood side by side and watched the river coil away under a fuzz of mist. Then I followed Max down the path, past the little church and into the valley. At the bottom there was a parting of the ways; one track led between boulders and scrubland to the road beside the river, the other to the camp.

He and I had no choice. We turned our backs on the river and rode towards the allied camp. I kept my eyes on Max whose high-stepping horse walked confidently ahead, and on the sky swimming with pale light, and tried not to be startled by every cracking twig, every rattle of artillery from the trenches, or to think that in two hours, an hour, half an hour, I would be parted from him.

Soon we were riding into more and more company. This time the pickets were alert and nervy and we were challenged again and again. The camp was wide awake but furtive with scurrying forms moving from tent to tent, campfires quenched, the rattle of arms.

By the time we reached the Castle Hospital it was almost broad daylight. Max dismounted and we kept out of sight between the horses as he kissed me, his eyes soft with love. 'Walk away,' he said. 'I'll watch you.' He was so new to me; the miracle of our night together was still within reach. And I remembered all too clearly another goodbye: Newman's tears darkening the cloth of his jacket, his body splayed on the abattis.

At last I let Max go. When I looked back he was still there. All I could see of his face was the gleam of his pale brow.

Neither Nora nor Mrs Whitehead was in the hut and I stood in the familiar, creaking darkness straining to hear hoof-beats as Max rode back down the hill. Then I thought again of Rosa, and how she must have left Henry while he was sleeping, or said a firm and final goodbye, picked up her skirts, and hurried down the rocky path to the valley below.

Chapter Twelve

Early the next day, on the morning of 5 September, the final bombardment of Sebastopol began with a vehement burst of fire that rattled the hut, shook the boxes on the shelves and had even the rats scuttling for shelter. Usually such a violent bombardment was soon followed by a pause but this time it went on and on as if some fatal ague had broken loose on the earth. After a few minutes a pall of smoke rose in the blue sky and even though we were several miles away our jaws clenched with the racket.

But I couldn't any longer see myself as separate from the city; allies on the outside, enemy within. What must it be like to inhabit a quiet suburban house, say a Russian version of Fosse House with airy rooms, tasteful furnishings, a lifetime's belongings, and then have it shattered like an egg shell? I thought of the morning room with my mother's writing desk and my sewing table neatly set out for a new day's work. Those bits of furniture were as constant as the earth itself, immutably there. But to stand among the rubble, to creep from one broken building to the next, to be sure of nothing except that the next second the city would suffer another strike. Is that really what Rosa had chosen?

Meanwhile I discovered that a note had been pushed under the door summoning me to the presence of Mrs Shaw Stewart.

I washed my face, brushed the dust from my hair, changed my skirt and blouse and put on a clean cap and apron even though it grieved me to set aside the clothes I had worn to Inkerman. Then I marched down to the hut in which Miss Nightingale had once languished. I couldn't help noticing that my progress attracted more attention than usual from passing orderlies and walking wounded so I knew that I had certainly been found out – my expedition to Inkerman with Captain Max Stukeley, not to mention my delayed return to the hospital, were known to all.

This time Mrs Shaw Stewart stood up and placed one hand on her desk when I appeared in the doorway. She wore a black bonnet tied with recently pressed ribbons, her skirts must have been supported by half a dozen petticoats and she wore no apron. I assumed that this was the garb she wore for dispensing bad news.

'Miss Lingwood, I sent for you yesterday but you were not to be found.'

I sighed, anticipating explanations, pleading, a packing of bags and a search for accommodation in Balaklava.

Her voice was normally soft and refined but that morning she had to raise it above the clamour of the guns. 'If you choose not to disclose your whereabouts I shall not press you. In some sense it is no business of mine as you are not one of my nurses, though common courtesy, after all I've done for you, might have suggested that you owed me an explanation.' Long pause while I studied my dirty thumbnail. 'The reason I wanted to see you was that recently you requested to be allowed to work on the wards. Unfortunately since then no less than three of our women have been stricken with cholera. Had you been among us yesterday you'd have known that Mrs Whitehead, who has been a stalwart in the cholera wards, has herself become a victim. If you are still willing you may undertake to help with the nursing of her. It is hardly ideal but of course my nurses must be attended by women, and as we have been notified that hundreds of wounded could arrive at any moment, I have no one experienced to spare. You will take directions from Mrs McCormack, and the usual rules governing all nurses will apply to you, though as yet I am not prepared to give you a formal contract.'

Her grey eyes were disdainful. There was no doubt that she too had a very good idea of where I had been the previous day, and with whom. In fact it occurred to me that allowing me to work on the cholera ward was perhaps a form of chastisement.

'Of course,' I said. 'Yes. Of course. Gladly.'

'You understand the dangers, I'm sure. I should like you to write to your family that this decision was entirely voluntary and instigated by you. And obviously it is for a probationary period only. After that we shall see.'

She sat down at her desk and took up her pen. Thus dismissed I backed away but then, driven by some reckless urge to redeem

Rosa in her eyes, I said, 'Mrs Shaw Stewart, about my cousin, Rosa Barr. I believe that she has gone to Sebastopol.'

She was too well bred to show surprise other than by a lift of an eyebrow. 'Sebastopol. Whatever for?'

'To nurse. After all, that was all she ever wanted to be allowed to do.'

'What proof do you have?'

'No proof, except what I know of Rosa.'

'As if we don't have enough sick men of our own. How could she think of going over to the enemy?'

'It would make no difference to Rosa whose sick men they were.'

She smiled faintly. 'Well, Miss Lingwood, if she is really in Sebastopol, I think we must keep her in our prayers more than ever.'

The cholera wards were set apart from the rest and at that time, just before the final assault on the Redan, the hospital was sufficiently empty to allow the small number of women patients to be kept in a separate hut to the men. When first I opened the door and crept inside I was nearly blown back by the stifling atmosphere. Windows and doors were shut to exclude the flies, camphor was burning to clear the air but nothing could conceal the stench of sickness.

My first patient, Mrs Whitehead, who had been so girlishly excited about my trip to Inkerman only two evenings ago, had worn herself out working with the cholera victims and been found lying in a heap on the way to the latrines, her normally spotless gown soiled and her complexion the telltale livid grey that marked the first phase of cholera. By the time I arrived at her bedside she was vomiting back every mouthful of rice water that was dribbled between her lips and a doctor had prescribed the usual medicines: calomel to make her expel the toxins, opium to bind her stools, water and saline to ensure that a supply of fluid was retained in the blood. On this treatment she had begun to fail.

Nora took me aside and muttered, 'We owe it to this woman to save her. I have been down to the British Hotel and taken advice from Mrs Seacole who has seen more cholera cases on her travels than most of these doctors have treated head colds. This is what you will do. Leave all those wretched medicines to one side, especially the opium which will take the fight out of her, and give her nothing but lime juice squeezed into the rice water. You must dose her every five minutes. Do not move from her side. When she begins to get the cramps call me.'

After she'd gone I sat hunched over my patient as if only by keeping my eyes on her could I be sure that her life wouldn't slip away. Sometimes I found myself retreating to the cave above Inkerman, sometimes I followed Rosa into the valley and along the river to Sebastopol, sometimes Nora came, held Mrs Whitehead's hand, prayed over her and crossed herself, but mostly I was left alone with my patient while the distant guns roared along the allied front.

By now I understood exactly the source of every burst of fire, and that when there was a brief interlude it was only because the guns had to cool and the men to rest. An orderly, sent to wash the floors, told me that there was so much smoke over Sebastopol that it was hard to tell what was going on inside the city, although someone had reported that the great buildings were being reduced to rubble and that during a lull in the firing the bastions swarmed with enemy soldiers trying to repair the damage before the bombardment began again.

When the cramps came Nora helped lift Mrs Whitehead up and we rubbed and rubbed her back and arms with eucalyptus oil to keep the blood circulating and stop them turning blue. I remembered Henry telling me that the chief cause of death in cholera patients is a thickening of the blood as vital serum is drawn to the intestines in order to remedy the infection there, hence a chilling and cramping in the extremities. To escape the agony Mrs Whitehead tried to curl herself in a ball and hurl herself onto the floor but we pressed poultices to her neck and chest and fed liquids into her resistant mouth.

'So,' said Nora, as we laid our patient on her stomach and began the process of oiling her feet and hands again, working her calf muscles and kneading heat into her cold, sweating flesh. 'You say Rosa has gone to Sebastopol.'

'It's what I think. I don't know.'

'Well, it's true that girl could never keep her nose out of anything, especially if it didn't concern her.'

'But if I'm right how will she survive this bombardment?'

'I shall pray for her. And if needs be, if things get too bad, you and I shall just have to go in there and pluck her out.' Our eyes met for a moment and she raised an eyebrow – a challenge or a promise – then we bundled Mrs Whitehead up in blankets and put hot bricks at her feet.

When the chaplain wound his cautious way along the ward I muttered, 'But she's not dying yet.'

He shook his bald head, in far too much of a hurry to argue. 'Nevertheless I shall anoint her so the job is done, in case.' Stooping over the lamp he read from *The Book of Common Prayer*, a page he must have known by heart: 'We humbly commend, the soul of this, thy servant, our dear bro— sister, into thy hands, as into the hands of a faithful Creator . . .'

I didn't join in his prayer because it seemed to me that he was sealing her fate. I had already seen quite enough of men being returned to dust so I resorted to the only cure I knew by stitching Mrs Whitehead back together in my head. Hadn't I spent all my life disguising the human form with my frills and lace, my crochet, appliqué and embroidery? I had cut yard upon yard of fabric and shaped it with gathers, darts and seams until I had turned myself into a walking gown with head and hands. And now here was the cholera unravelling Mrs Whitehead faster than I could bind her up again, shearing the hair from her head, stripping her naked, shedding flesh from her bones, intelligence from her eyes, the smile from her lips.

Chapter Thirteen

For three days, as the bombardment of Sebastopol went on and on, I left the cholera ward only to eat and sleep. When I emerged into the light I squinted like a kitten and sucked in the clean air. But even had I been a free agent there would have been no walking up to Cathcart Hill to find out what was going on. Apparently the allied commanders had at least learned one thing from the June defeat: a cluster of spectators on the hills not only drew enemy fire but their attention to the fact that significant moves were afoot. There were whispers that renewed attacks were planned on the Redan and the Malakov for 8 September, and that once the bastions had been taken the allies would march onwards into Sebastopol.

I heard nothing from Max, though I so longed to see him that every time a door opened, I heard a male voice or saw a red tunic I was convinced it would be him.

'Well, now, why on earth would a captain in the British army be sending messages to you at a time like this?' demanded Nora. 'Whatever it was that went on between you that day you have come back soft in the head, I see. Just you be careful with that Max Stukeley.'

'I don't want to be careful. I've always been careful.'

'Well, then I think the pair of you deserve each other, is all I'm saying. In fact I would go so far as to say I envy you, Mariella Lingwood, but I only hope that your heart does not get broken in the process.'

During the night of 7 September the weather changed so suddenly that I woke up in the small hours rigid with cold and had to pile on layer upon layer of clothing. In the end I gave up trying to sleep, wrapped myself in my thickest shawl, braced myself against an icy wind and went to the ward where I found an orderly attempting to light the stove for the first time since spring. Yet, despite the cold, Mrs Whitehead's condition had improved, her lips were no longer purple and her breathing was steady.

It was not until I had hugged my patient, rushed away to fetch a bowl of broth and have a requisition signed for extra blankets that I noticed another great change: silence. No guns. There could be no further doubt that the renewed assaults on the Malakov and the Great Redan were about to begin.

All that morning we worked distractedly and spoke in whispers as we waited for news. The first account came from the orderly who brought the breakfast bread and coffee and told us that during the small hours British and French troops had piled forward into the trenches. 'Of course they had to start going down way back in the early hours because the passageways are so narrow they'll only take two abreast. And they say the men could scarcely walk for the size of their packs – two days' worth of rations. The idea is that they will race up the sides of them bastions and then on, right through to Sebastopol.'

I was sure that Max would have gone forward with his men; I imagined him confined to the trench, the discomfort of his injured leg, the beetly damp of the earth walls, the whispered orders, the exchange of banter. Last time he had survived less than three minutes before having his leg half blown off. This time he would be so slow. What chance did he have?

The next news came from Mrs Whitehead's doctor, who had been up at headquarters the previous day and was smugly in possession of every last detail of the plan of attack. He told us that the French sappers had dug their trenches so close to the Malakov that troops would be able to step out under its very walls and spring a great surprise on the Russians. Then, as soon as the tricolour was flying over the Malakov, the British were to break out of their trenches and charge the Redan.

Just before noon we gathered on the windy path outside the huts and heard the volley of fire signalling the French attack. Ten minutes later we saw four rockets shoot across the murky sky, said to be a sign that the British should begin their assault on the Redan.

I went back to work; I fed Mrs Whitehead arrowroot flavoured with lemon juice, I changed her sheets and bathed her face, and still there was no more news.

Then word was passed from ward to ward that a messenger had come galloping up to warn us of the imminent arrival of ambulance wagons. Though the Malakov had been taken by the French the British had again failed in their assault on the Redan. Just as before, when the troops emerged from the trenches they had been picked off in their hundreds by the waiting Russians. At six o'clock the number of casualties was confirmed: ten thousand allied soldiers, thirteen thousand Russians.

By midnight the hospital was awash with so many wounded men that even I was allowed to work among them provided I stayed close to Nora and did as I was told. I pressed tourniquets onto wounds pumping blood, I dripped water into gasping mouths, I held up bleeding limbs to be dressed. It seemed to me that I must be soaked to the neck in blood and every time I knelt by a stretcher and looked into another suffering face my heart missed a beat in case it might be Max.

If a door was opened the wind bit our skin and tore at the flames in the oil lamps but we hardly noticed. Nor did we lift our heads when a series of explosions blasted into the night and brought terror into the dull eyes of our patients. And at four o'clock in the morning, when the earth shook with yet another great blow, I hardly gave it a thought as I fell into my bed, even though I did not believe, given all I had seen and all that I may have lost, that I would ever sleep again.

Chapter Fourteen

I woke a couple of hours later to silence; outside my hut, the hospital was shrouded in an autumnal mist. When I reached the ward I saw that Mrs Shaw Stewart was stooped over Mrs Whitehead's bed and I hesitated, fearing a relapse, but my patient was fully conscious and though feverish was able to drink a little tea. Mrs Shaw Stewart, who had probably not been to bed in twenty-four hours, took one look at me, told me I was in no state to be on the ward and sent me to the laundry store to audit our depleted stocks.

I unlocked the door, watched a rat scuttle into a distant corner and then began counting sheets. My teeth were rattling as I went through pile after pile, checking and rechecking as the numbers slipped from my head. If Max had been in the forefront of that attack on the Redan he could not have survived – with his wounded leg he would have been a slow-moving target for even a novice. I remembered his long, warm limbs, the firmness of his hands, the heat in his eyes when he kissed me. And I remembered the wreck of Newman's body pinioned to the abattis.

Gradually I became aware that the path outside was clustered with men looking at the sky above Sebastopol and when I went among them I heard the astonishing news that during the night the Russians had fired their own bastions, including the undefeated Redan, and evacuated every single living soul – about ten thousand civilians and soldiers – across a floating bridge extending from the south of the harbour to the north. Then, once the last man was safely over, they had burned the bridge behind them.

The men spoke to each other in low-voiced disbelief: our generals, for all our massive superiority of firepower, and even though, with full control over the bastions, they could easily have driven the entire enemy army into the sea, had allowed the besieged Russians to escape and done nothing to stop it. So there were the Russians snugly entrenched in the north side of town. Meanwhile the south of Sebastopol, emptied of all its inhabitants, was ours.

Some men were smiling at the news, others cursed the generals for allowing the bastard Ruskies to escape, others were too exhausted to react at all. I went back to Mrs Whitehead and bathed her hands and neck.

What had happened to Rosa?

All that day Nora and I asked everyone who'd listen whether they'd seen Max, but there was no word of him. She gave me a pair of tweezers and showed me how to pluck squirming maggots from a festering gash in a man's shoulder. I removed the bandage from a bleeding stump and swabbed the wound. For half an hour I sat beside a boy who had no visible mark on him but whose fingertips gradually turned black and who died racked by homesickness. As the freezing wind gusted through the huts and blew the flies into oblivion we stoked the inadequate stoves and piled more blankets round our shivering patients.

At midday I scribbled a note to Max Stukeley of the Ninety-seventh Derbyshires, and gave it to one of the drivers.

There was no end to the trail of ambulance wagons and as the day went on the condition of the injured men whom they brought grew worse. They had been plucked out of the trenches and from the deserted bastions, some so horribly burned by gunpowder that there was not an inch of skin that hadn't been blasted away. One man, Laidlaw, had lost half his spine from a shell wound but was in an elated state, convinced that he'd been floored by a slight blow to the head. When I gave him a sip of lemonade he smiled at me fondly.

'Miss Lingwood, ain't it?'

'Yes, however did you know?'

'Seen you up at the camp. Rosa's cousin, they said.'

'You're with the Derbyshires?'

'That's it.'

I managed to utter the name: 'Captain Stukeley?'

'Couldn't say what happened to him, ma'am. I seen him up on

the Redan waving his arm and hollering us to follow. But not all of us could. The Russian fire . . .'

'And then what?'

'Next thing I know I'm lying in a ditch under a dead man.'

I was called away to another patient. When I went back to look for him Laidlaw was being carted out to be lain among the dead.

At three in the morning we were sent to bed but I sat in the hut with my hands clenched and my head full of the wounds I had tended. Laidlaw haunted me more than any other with his ragged smile, the way he had sailed into death all unknowing. When Nora came in half an hour later she said not a word but held out her hand. She was holding a scrap of paper, the note I had sent up to the Derbyshires' camp. On the back was scrawled the word: *Sebastopol.*

'What does it mean?' I asked.

'Well, for heaven's sake, girl, it means that she's there, just like you said, and he's gone after her.' She tied on her bonnet, tore a blanket off her bed, folded it in half and flung it round her shoulders.

'Nora?'

'If Max has gone to Sebastopol then we must follow. He will need us.'

We packed our baskets with lint and bread and water, hunched our shoulders against the bitter dawn wind and set off down the path into Balaklava, which was the quietest I'd ever seen it, as if the ships themselves were sunk in a torpor, then on up past the General Hospital where hundreds of lamps were burning, and into the camp.

Although it was only days since I had last ridden this way with Max, everything had changed. In the waking camp men emerged from their huts with an air of slack despondence and beat their sides against the cold. Fires were coaxed into life, pots clattered but the men were grey-faced and uninterested. As we walked on we seemed to gather a train of men after us, all heading for Sebastopol. More and more men overtook us until we came to the deserted trenches and looked over the plateau towards the smoking bastions.

We were confronted with bands of swirling grey: the strip of sea, the pall of smoke over the city, penetrated occasionally by fire, the blank sky. Nora and I locked our arms together and stepped out beyond the British defences. The trek across land pocked with shellfire, in the teeth of a blistering wind, felt insanely reckless: it was like being on a shore where the tide has suddenly pulled itself incomprehensibly far out but may at any moment come rushing back to engulf us. Towards us came wagons laden with the dead and a dejected group of Russian prisoners, escorted by a party of jaunty Frenchmen.

Now it was all too clear why the British had sustained such a crushing defeat under the Redan. Our trenches ended some eighty yards from its towering sides and our men must have been mown down, a few at a time, as they clambered into the open. And the Redan was preposterously steep sided. How had anyone hoped to scale it under the Russian guns? How had Max, with his injured leg? The stench of corruption was powerful and the sides of the Redan were littered with scaling ladders and other pathetic remnants of the British assault – broken guns, caps, boots, knapsacks.

The feeling grew on me, as we scrambled up the side of the Russian bastion, that I had somehow got myself into the wrong side of a looking glass and it was as if we visitors to that reflected world were intruding on intensely private territory. Although most of the dead and all of the wounded had been removed from the inside of the bastion, the stink of decay was appalling. The inner defences, a warren of earth and stone works, had been reduced to heaps of broken guns, charred gabions spewing broken rocks, bits of clothing, boots and hats, and a few scraps of individual men's lives, a torn slip of paper, a crust of black bread, a kettle and a red handkerchief. On the far side, set deep under the Redan, the door to a bomb-proof shelter swung open and a soldier emerged grinning because he'd found a cage containing a little yellow bird.

As we left the bastion we came up against the first evidence of authority – a British cavalryman on a lofty black horse. 'Apologies, ladies. Strict orders. No one is to pass this way.'

'We had a message from Captain Max Stukeley, who we believe is inside the city.'

'Unlikely, ma' am.'

His horse was turned sideways to block the track and he gazed straight ahead to quell any further argument. Back we went into the bastion and found another track leading down to the city. But here too our way was blocked by a cavalryman. By now we were accompanied by a furious posse of soldiers. 'The French have gone in, the Turks have gone in. They'll take everything. What about us?'

The officer remained impassive while the men retreated and stood at a distance. Nora, however, swore under her breath, took hold of my arm, dragged me behind the horse and marched me on down the track, with the cavalry officer shouting after us and the band of soldiers yelling encouragement.

The track led past the pitiful remains of a domed church and into a deep ravine running down to the outer suburb of Sebastopol. Along this same scarred track hundreds of Russians must have marched each night at the start of their watch, heads full of the hours ahead, of the boredom and sudden shocks, the prospect of injury or death. Now the only Russians left were the dead. The street was paved with broken shells and shot that crunched underfoot and this sound was oddly clean and comforting compared to the sight of broken houses, the corpse of a man crawled into a doorway, another neatly propped against a wall, a dead horse lying on its side with its torn belly swarming with flies.

'Where do we go?' I cried to Nora. 'How will we ever find them?'

It seemed like a violation to witness the city in this state, as if she had once been a gracious woman dressed in fine clothes but was now sprawled naked. The houses were reduced to doorways and window openings, the churches tumbledown and charred, no single building intact as the wind gusted along alleys and sent grit and rubbish skittering against piles of rubble. The deeper we got into the city, the more the streets teemed with French and Turkish soldiers laden with plunder stuffed under their arms or bundled on their backs: petticoats, bits of crockery, icons, garden tools, pictures, chairs, even bedheads. For a mad moment I caught an atmosphere of festival.

Beyond the stench of smoke and carnage there was a sudden whiff of brine and I realised that we must be almost at the sea. The road became deserted; no one was frantically searching from house to house, no more allied soldiers with their armfuls of booty.

In fact a pall of silence had fallen and a few men were clustered round the door of a vast building that looked, from its ruined grandeur, as if it might once have been a civic hall.

A British officer was on the steps and held up his hand. 'It's the hospital,' he said. 'You don't want to be in there.'

'We are looking for Captain Max Stukeley,' said Nora. 'Have you seen him?'

We didn't wait for a reply. Inside were the remains of a grand lobby, the fragment of a balustrade, the shattered head of a plaster cherub. The few from the allied camp who had dared enter had covered their mouths and noses and peered about with outraged eyes: Mrs Seacole was there, a reporter with a notebook, a couple of officers, an English doctor. Nora and I paused a moment, then stepped in among them.

Chapter Fifteen

Derbyshire, 1844

Rosa showed me her last secret on a hot, hot day when the lanes were coated with dust, even the flies were too crushed by the heat to raise themselves from the hedgerows and the molten sky sank on the hills like a plump cushion.

She and I were listless and cross with each other because she had suggested a swim but when we reached the pool in the woods I refused to go in. The water looked cool and clean but you could never be sure and when I dabbled my fingertips a water boatman skimmed away across the surface. 'You can swim while I watch,' I said.

'It's no fun by myself. I do things on my own all the time when you're not here. We could race each other across if you came in with me.'

'I can barely swim. I only ever try when we go to the seaside.'

'Well, paddle, then.'

'Max will go with you.'

'I want to do things with you to make the most of you while you're here.'

In the end we wandered off along the path through the birch wood and out onto the hillside.

'Where are we going, then?' I said, when we had panted right to the top and could see down into the narrow valley on the other side.

Rosa had twisted her hair into a knot to allow the air to circulate more freely on her neck and her cheeks were unusually pink. She was looking dead ahead and her expression, both obstinate and nervous, frightened me.

'Where are we going?' I said again.

'You'll see.'

'I'm very hot.'

'It'll be cool where we're going. And anyway, it's not much further.'

But it seemed a very long way to me. The lane wove between dry stone walls to the valley bottom and then into a little copse with a stream rushing over stones. When I looked back I could see we had come far, far down and that it would be a steep climb home. The lane wound on for about another half-mile until we came to a little hamlet of stone cottages and on the left a much larger house, set well back behind high walls and locked gates, which of course proved no deterrent to Rosa.

'Come on,' she said marching down to the end of the left-hand wall, and the next second had thrust her way through a gap between it and the adjoining hedge. As usual I had no choice but to follow, and there we were, looking onto the house from an oblique angle at the side of the garden.

'Do you know the person who lives here?' I asked.

'Yes.'

'Are we going to call on them?'

'We might.'

The house was very tidily built with six windows on the first floor and four below arranged two each side of a white front door under a little porch with three steps leading up to it; an unremarkable house set in what must once have been a well-stocked garden but was now a mass of poppy heads, delphinium and willow herb gone to seed.

All the windows were firmly shuttered. 'They're out,' I said.

'Bound to be.'

She was very unlike her usual self, neither marching brazenly up to the front door nor making one of her forays into this private place by dashing down the garden. She just stood.

'If you think there might be someone about, could we ask for a glass of water?' I said. 'I'm very thirsty.'

'There won't be anyone. Can't you tell? The house is locked up.'

'We could try.'

She now set off past a little stable block to a straggly lawn overgrown with dandelions, an ancient swing dangling from the branch of an apple tree, a slope down to the river.

'Where are you going?' I cried.

She didn't answer, but stood stock-still, looking up at the house.

Chapter Sixteen

The Crimea, 1855

The hospital was stone cold because its windows had been broken during the bombardment. In the last few days of siege more and more mortally wounded men must have been dragged down here and left to die on pallets, trestles and stretchers until every available inch of space was filled. They were lined up in their dozens, abandoned during the desperate escape across the floating bridge: the long dead, the recently dead and the just alive, steeped in excrement and blood, some crawled up against pillars or walls in an attempt to separate themselves from the rest, some so long dead that they were in the same state as Newman's corpse before the Redan. Others still twitched and groaned, their mouths gaped open by the pressure of their swollen tongues.

At one end of the room there was a flight of steps leading downwards. We covered the lower part of our faces with our shawls and wove our way across the floor, which was sticky with blood. More bodies had been piled on the stairs and below was an even darker space lit by a pair of guttering candles.

In one corner a British officer sat on the floor with his legs stretched out and his back to the wall. His black, tortured gaze met mine across a waste of corpses. In his arms he held the body of a woman and in his hand, clenched against her shoulder, a crumpled envelope. She was wearing a stained apron over a torn blue dress and her head had fallen back on its slender neck. Her face was upturned, her mouth half open, her eyes wide, and her fair hair was hanging down like a flag across his red tunic.

Chapter Seventeen

Sebastopol
6 September 1855

My dear love, my Mariella,

This I think really will surprise you – first to be hearing from your cousin Rosa at all, then when you see where I am.

Early evening, in a cellar, actually, my current bedchamber, and it could do with a touch of the Mariellas, being somewhat lacking in all the comforts at which you are such an expert. I have been sent by one of the nurses to try and sleep – not even I dare argue with her, she being half as tall as me, twice as wide, very fierce. I sit at the bottom of a flight of steps, holding my paper up to the light. We are covered in smoke at present and light of any kind is at a premium.

If I send this, Mariella, it will be out of weakness and I'm sorry. I promised you I'd write often, didn't I, and your letters of course arrived faithfully each week. But I found myself faced with a somewhat stark choice: silence or lies.

I had made a vow to myself, saying: I won't haunt her, I won't pester her, I'll leave her to imagine that I simply crumbled away like all the other Crimean dead. But I can't bear you to be grieving and angry with me for disappearing without a word. So here's my word. This war is hell, start to finish. And now I have been just a little too bold for my own good and put myself beyond reach. There is a way out, we've watched a bridge being built to the north of the town, but I can't cross it because I am pulled back again and again for another glimpse of the British camp. I need to see the lights from the campfires and the occasional flash of a scarlet uniform. I like to imagine that even though I don't want him to, there is a chance that Max, the enterprising and valiant, will find me, and bring me back.

I have come to the end of the world, and it is a bitter end. Despite what I have written above, I discovered that I couldn't stand my own kind any longer. The British fumbled carelessly into this war, never mind the consequences, and go on killing and killing because that's the habit they're in. So here am I, living the consequences. We've run out of everything: doctors, bandages, medicines, but still the wounded are hauled from the bastions and the shelled buildings and we can't send them away or do anything for them. Cholera rages. I don't have clean water. All I am is a hand to hold while a man dies.

I have this idea in my head of my wretched stepbrother Horatio inspecting his lead works and sifting through a crate-load of ammunition with his damp fingers. Then he writes in black ink: SEBASTOPOL, *charges an extortionate price and sends it across the sea. I sit under the splintering sky and think I am Rosa, I am nothing, except a soft bit of flesh on which one of Horatio's bullets will fall.*

You came to the railway station and waved me goodbye, dressed in your best bonnet and bravest smile. But I saw your face dissolve, like one of my watercolours, and as the train drew out of the station I knew I was loved. I mattered then.

But whatever you do, don't be sad or sorry that I haven't come back. Remember that this is what I chose.

Are you married? Are you snug behind the polished oak of your new front door? Has Henry made you happy, Mariella?

I saw him on the battlefield, perhaps he told you. He was far from being himself. I wish I knew that you are happy. To Henry you are a constant. I know this because I have been guilty of the same thought. But do you want to be a constant? I have watched you when you're roused – in the carriage when we drove back after our visit to the hospital, the look in your eye when you turned on me – and I am frightened and excited by what might happen next. Max called it the power of the needle. She awes me, he said, because I do not know, nor does she, what she is capable of were she to put all that energy elsewhere. You ensnared us both you know; we sat in his hut at night under the clamour of shelling and tried to conjure you up.

I think I will send this letter after all. I think I must. I know an officer who could take it over the water and see it safely despatched to London. I thought I could bear to disappear but I find I can't. It's too late, Mariella. I reach out my hand, I listen for your voice and I can't find you.

So I allow myself the comfort of knowing that your deft fingers will unseal the envelope and draw out this page, that you will sit with your feet pressed together and your back straight, but leaning very slightly forward, as you do when you are concentrating, the light falling on your carefully parted hair, and when you've finished reading you will fold the letter in your lap and pick up your sewing again.

But for a while longer I will exist, I think, in each of your immaculate stitches,

Rosa

Chapter Eighteen

Derbyshire, 1844

The back of the square old house had French windows overlooking a stone terrace. Rosa went right up and pressed her face to the glass. 'Shutters again,' she said. 'I told you. They're not here.' Then she banged on the window.

'What are you doing? We should go. Someone will come.' I tried to pull her away but she hammered on the glass until I thought it would break. Finally she gave up, raced down to the river, kicked off her boots, unrolled her stockings, threw them to one side and waded in.

'Rosa, what are you doing? Mind you don't cut your feet. Why are we here? Surely this is private . . .'

When she was halfway across she turned back, her skirts scooped up in her hands and her white face full of pain. 'My house. This was my house. Father's room where he used to read was that one at the end.'

I turned to look back at the blinkered windows and dusty paintwork.

'When he died the house was inherited by some nephew so Mother and I had to leave even though he only comes north once a year to shoot and he isn't pleased to see me then, I can tell you. At other times I can't get back inside however often I come. I have to do it all in my head. I open the front door and stand in the hall, I smell the floor polish, I see his hat on the stand and his stick against the wall and I bang open the door of his study but I can't get any further. I can't see him because he isn't there.'

We stared at each other. Her grief was intolerable because by now I knew her so well that her pain had become my pain. She turned away and began kicking up a storm of spray until she was a blur of flying hair and water droplets.

For a while I chewed my lip and wondered what to do. Then I went over to her boots and placed them neatly side by side, shook out her stockings which were still warm from her legs, and rolled them up. Finally I took off my own shoes and stockings and dabbled a toe in the river. My feet were pricked by sharp stones and the water was surprisingly cold.

She laughed as she plunged towards me and seized my hand. Then she pulled me deeper and deeper and clutched me tightly to her chest while the water rushed past, dragging the hems of our dresses. Our wet cheeks collided and our hands were gripped together as she led me in a wild dance until all I could see were sparks of water, the swirling sky and her delighted, hungry eyes.

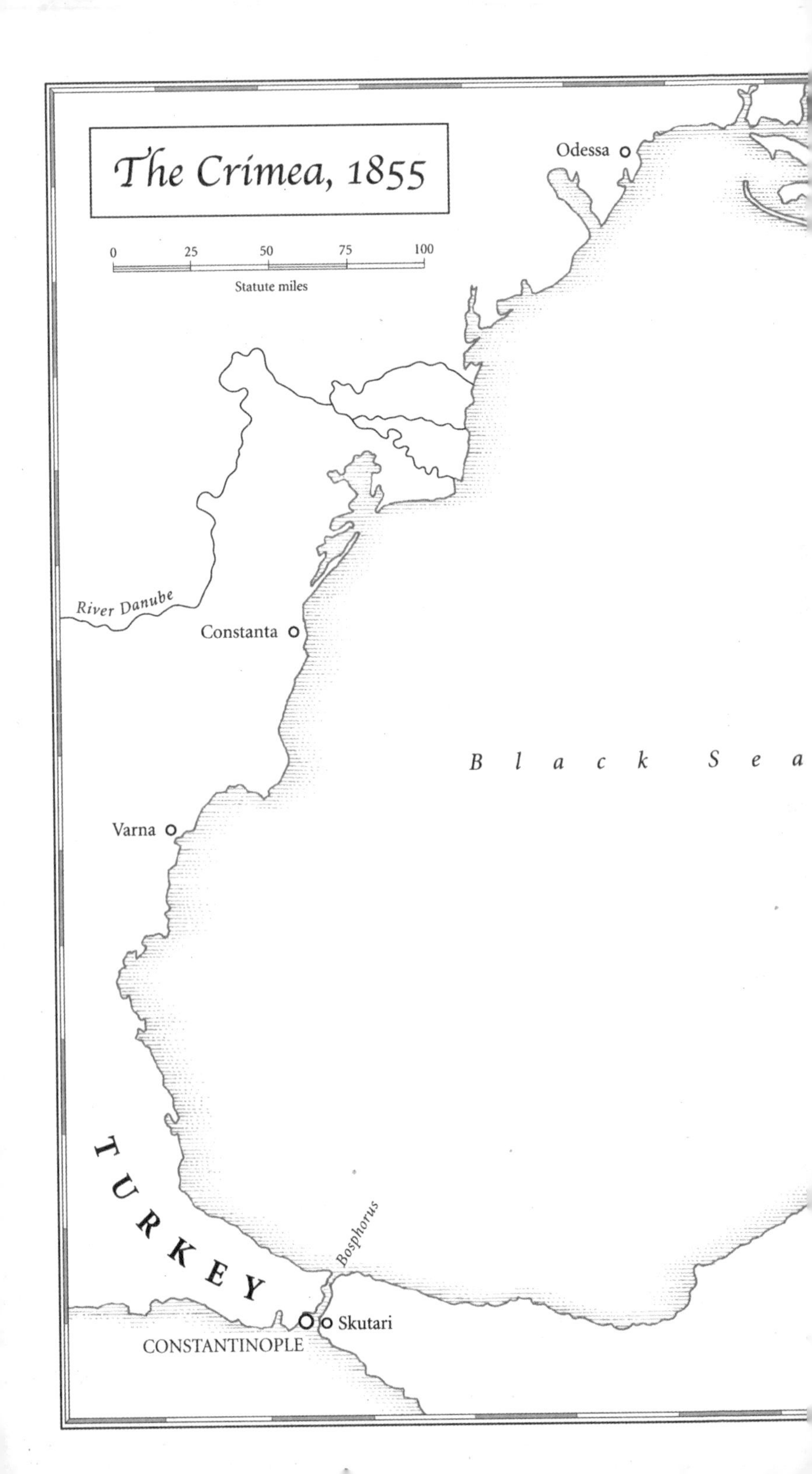
The Crimea, 1855
0
25
50
75
100
Statute miles
Odessa
River Danube
Constanta
Black Sea
Varna
TURKEY
Bosphorus
Skutari
CONSTANTINOPLE